PUTIN'S GAMBIT

FORGE BOOKS
BY LOU DOBBS AND JAMES O. BORN

Border War

PUTIN'S GAMBIT

LOU DOBBS
JAMES O. BORN

A TOM DOHERTY ASSOCIATES BOOK

NEW YORK

PUTIN'S GAMBIT

Copyright © 2017 by Lou Dobbs and James O. Born

All rights reserved.

A Forge Book
Published by Tom Doherty Associates
175 Fifth Avenue
New York, NY 10010

www.tor-forge.com

Forge® is a registered trademark of Macmillan Publishing Group, LLC.

The Library of Congress Cataloging-in-Publication Data is available upon request.

ISBN 978-0-7653-7652-7 (hardcover)
ISBN 978-1-4668-5140-5 (ebook)

Our books may be purchased in bulk for promotional, educational, or business use. Please contact your local bookseller or the Macmillan Corporate and Premium Sales Department at 1-800-221-7945, extension 5442, or by email at MacmillanSpecialMarkets@macmillan.com.

First Edition: June 2017

Printed in the United States of America

0 9 8 7 6 5 4 3 2 1

Putin's Gambit *is dedicated to all the men and women of the U.S. military who serve the nation and protect us all.*

ACKNOWLEDGMENTS

All the military officers and NATO personnel who quietly helped with this book.

Tony Martindale for his excellent military insights and phenomenal photography skills.

PUTIN'S
GAMBIT

1

Major Ronald Jackson had spent months on deployment in both Iraq and Afghanistan, as well as a brief peacekeeping stint in Kuwait after an invasion of Islamic State fighters. It was that time in combat and the fact that he was one of the few officers from his original unit still in the Marine Corps that made him feel like he had earned his right to a cushy embassy detail here in Germany. In point of fact, which was the only thing the marines dealt in, he was responsible for several diplomatic buildings, from the missions in Frankfurt and Bonn to the U.S. embassy here in Berlin.

He'd dropped in on the new lieutenant in charge of the security and the twenty-six marines at 0 dark thirty. At thirty-one, Major Jackson no longer partied all night and found rising before the sun and driving from the base outside Stuttgart a simple task. He smiled as he recalled how much he hated a CO who did shit like that to him when he was new to a post. Security for the embassy building off Pariser Platz looked pretty sharp, and the marines were alert.

He took his time walking alone after he'd gotten the lieutenant out

11

from under foot. It was a brilliant, sunny day with the temperature in the midfifties. He liked wearing his overcoat because it hid the shrapnel scar on his right arm he'd received his last tour in Afghanistan. A lucky grenade pitch by a dark-haired youth had left him in the hospital for three weeks. Now he noticed the cooler weather in his elbow. He'd always thought that kind of thing was just bullshit the old vets talked about. Old war wounds really did change with the weather.

Major Jackson wondered what his best friends from the unit were doing now. One of them, Derek Walsh, worked on Wall Street but didn't seem all that happy when they talked. Another, Mike Rosenberg, was settling into his new job with the CIA. He'd been the G-2 in their unit and done an exceptional job. The fourth member of their clique was still, like Jackson, in the Corps. Bill Shepherd was in a combat brigade at the same base as Jackson in Böblingen near Stuttgart.

Their relationship was like being in a family with four brothers who were all competitive. They each made the others better. He liked it. They were the four horsemen, and each had skills that complemented the others'.

A young corporal snapped to attention near the front gate. Jackson returned a salute as he glanced over his shoulder to ensure there was a rifleman on the roof as required when the threat alert was raised like this. Someone had picked up some extra chatter, and the goddamned Islamic State was beheading people all over the place now. YouTube had videos from as far away as Perth and Chicago showing the masked executioners at work. The videos had all gone viral, with the media replaying them endlessly.

Major Jackson wished the cowards would face real military men head-on. No marine worth his salt would consider terrorists anything but cowards. It didn't matter what loudmouth TV hosts said about their abilities. No one could stand against a well-trained marine unit. He wished the marines would be unleashed on them one day soon. That would end this shit quickly. Those limp dicks in Washington never *acted*, they only *reacted*, and the assholes from the so-called Islamic State had them reacting all over the place. It felt like the United States had stripped NATO of soldiers in an effort to refocus on the Middle East.

The rapid deployment force they'd been setting up to respond if the Baltics or other NATO members were attacked by Russia was a year behind schedule. Jackson wondered if the current administration was just pushing it off until a new administration took office. That would be the easiest thing to do, but maybe not the smartest. He had hoped the Russian annexation of Crimea would've woken people up to the real threats in the world.

He stood and took in the activity on the street in front of him. Typical tourist and light vehicle traffic moved casually down the street, reminding him of his hometown of Sacramento. The Germans had proven to be a friendly people who seemed to appreciate the U.S. military presence, at least where Major Jackson had been.

He noticed a Mercedes step van ease toward the main gate, the driver obviously listening to someone sitting behind him. The major wasn't one for profiling—he'd seen it by the California Highway Patrol back home and been a victim of it—but the young man with dark hair driving the van caught his attention. He turned and stepped toward the gate, calling out to the corporal on duty and the PFC sitting inside the monitoring booth directly behind the gate.

Then it happened. Just like he'd seen in training. He'd even witnessed it live once in Afghanistan. The driver popped out of the van with an AK-47 in his hand. Major Jackson did not hesitate. He sprang forward as the corporal brought up his M-4 carbine. The major was reaching under his coat to grip his M-9 pistol.

The passenger door opened, and men started pouring out as if they were a SWAT team.

Major Jackson screamed at the corporal, "Fire that weapon, marine," as he brought his pistol's sights on target. He noted that the first man had a small machine pistol that looked like a TEC-9, and another carried a German assault rifle. They also moved like men who knew their objective and had trained for it.

Major Jackson heard a shot and saw the corporal stumble back and collapse onto the ground, his neck spurting bright red blood. He squeezed off two quick shots and dropped the man who had fired the assault rifle.

He acquired the next target and fired twice more. The man flopped onto the wide sidewalk.

Now the four remaining men rushed the gate. Gunfire came from the booth as the PFC joined the fight.

A huge flash came from the rear of the van, and the major immediately recognized it as a rocket-propelled grenade. He'd seen enough of them in the mountains of Afghanistan. He dove away from the security booth and rolled toward a heavy potted plant designed to keep a vehicle from coming through the gate toward the building.

He felt the bone-rattling explosion an instant before the rubble of the booth filled the air around him. Shards of glass struck his exposed leg. He ignored the pain and popped up over the metal reinforced planter and fired at the man closest to the gate. The short man had slapped a plastic explosive on the lock. The explosive detonated early, causing the man to disintegrate into a red mist as the gate was blown off its tracks, allowing the last three terrorists inside the compound.

Major Jackson rolled and took aim, killing another attacker and then scanning the area to see if the PFC from the booth was dead. The bloody uniform twenty feet away indicated that he was.

The rifleman on the roof was now firing, but without much effect.

Another group of three men piled out of the back of the van and charged the gate. It was lost, but Major Jackson knew it was his job to hold as long as possible. He reloaded with his extra magazine of 9 mm because he had lost count of his shots.

He raised the pistol from a prone position and managed to hit the two men inside the gate, then turned his attention to the next group.

The rooftop rifleman dropped one man. The second man stumbled, and the major put three rounds into him on the ground. The last man standing, a big guy in his forties with thick hair and a graying beard, rushed the major, firing his own pistol.

They ended up on the ground together, the man so close the major could smell sardines on his breath. The rifleman kept up fire, and dirt spouted near Major Jackson's head.

The large, smelly man was badly wounded and had dropped his pistol.

Major Jackson wanted him alive so someone could figure out what this was all about and who was responsible.

The man reached into his pocket and in a heartbeat retrieved some kind of remote detonator.

Major Jackson froze and looked the man in the eye.

The man spoke in accented English. "You put up good fight. It won't matter. This is just the start." He mashed the button.

Major Ronald Jackson, graduate of the University of California, nine-year veteran of the marines, son to a city planner and a speech pathologist, felt the heat as he heard the blast and knew that the entire step van held some kind of high explosive and was their plan B.

After the initial flash, everything went dark.

Vladimir Putin was just finishing his breakfast in his office inside the palace at Novo-Ogaryovo. The fresh produce he ate most mornings came from the personal farmland estate of the patriarch.

He didn't like to rush his breakfast, but he knew people were waiting to meet with him. He conducted most of his business at the palace about twenty-four kilometers west of Moscow. It was quiet and comfortable here, and Putin felt this was where he belonged. It was quite different from his childhood apartment he had shared with two other families and rats in St. Petersburg, which was known at the time as Leningrad. This was the kind of living that he had grown accustomed to and why he had made sure that no matter what happened, he would be one of the wealthiest men in the world.

He was already a little on edge for having missed his usual morning swim. His judo practice was still scheduled for the afternoon, but this meeting was important, more important than anything they had planned in quite some time. After finishing his second quail egg, a delicacy he had come to enjoy, he stood from the table and checked himself in a mirror. Even in simple slacks and shirt with no tie, he liked what he saw.

Putin stepped through the door into his private office, then used an intercom to have the secretary send in his guests. An older, obese man with virtually no hair on his head waddled in, followed by a man whose build was very similar to Putin's own. He greeted them warmly. They were old friends—two of a handful of men he trusted implicitly.

He motioned the large man, Andre Maysak, who was in his mid-seventies, to a wide, comfortable chair, which Putin himself usually occupied. "Sit here, Andre. We have much to talk about."

The older man, who was a member of the Politburo and a dominating force in the Foreign Ministry, straightened his tailored Joseph Abboud suit and plopped down with great effort.

Putin would need Andre if the General Assembly rebelled, and, if necessary, to suppress any dissent. Among other things, Andre knew where all the bodies were buried.

The man about Putin's age, Yuri Simplov, was a deputy director of the SVR, the foreign intelligence service for the Russian Federation and successor agency to the KGB. Because of his background in intelligence, Putin had come to rely on the SVR to handle a number of problems whether it had legal authority or not. If Andre knew where all the bodies were buried, Simplov knew how to blame Putin's enemies for those brutal crimes.

Simplov always dressed in simple, off-the-rack suits, mostly so no one would suspect that he had amassed a fortune through his association with Putin and his sensitive position in the government service. They had worked together since their days in the KGB and had always had a private rivalry to see who was tougher. If one man ate nails, the other ate nails with rust on them. In this case, it was just who could sit more awkwardly in a hard chair.

Andre looked between the two men and said, "Somehow I don't think I'm about to hear good news."

Putin gave him a rare smile and said, "On the contrary, my friend, this is nothing but good news. It's also something I hope you know nothing about. Operational security has been extraordinarily strict, and I thought we would start to brief key members of the Politburo."

"I'm fascinated and worried at the same time," Andre said.

Putin said, "First, I have to give credit to Yuri for finding ways to accomplish the impossible without having a financial trail that leads back to Russia in any way."

Andre folded his arms, looking at the arrogant younger man who rarely bothered to greet others when they met in the halls of power. He said, "And what are the impossible feats our SVR friend has managed to accomplish?"

Putin said, "It's really two things that are connected. First, he has a way to steal two hundred million dollars from a U.S. bank without anyone suspecting us. And we will use that money to fund a new ally that will help distract the U.S. while we plan our first major military operation in decades."

"And who is this new ally?"

"A group of jihadists associated with ISIS."

That got Andre's attention. He leaned forward and said, "How do we become allies with someone we are constantly at war with? They hate us."

"But they hate the West more," Putin said. "We do not rub our affluence in their face. We do not produce movies that ridicule them. We didn't invade Iraq, and we do not bankroll Israel."

"But how did you even approach them?" Andre asked.

"They approached us," Putin said. "They wanted us to teach them how to hack into a computer system of the world's biggest banks."

Andre cut his eyes from one man to the other and finally said, "And what would be the target of this new military operation?"

Putin couldn't hide his smile, and he finally said, "Estonia."

2

Putin kept his eyes on his old friend from the Politburo, trying to get a feel for what the man was thinking. That was the key to everything accomplished in Russia: knowing what people were thinking.

Finally Andre said, "Excuse me, but my head is spinning slightly. Do you really think an ISIS affiliate will do as we direct?"

He and Yuri Simplov had debated the question for months. Different intelligence people had game-planned all of the possible scenarios. Some were, of course, failures, but the upside far outweighed the downside. Putin said, "That's the beauty of it, Andre. We don't have to direct them at all. Once they start their attacks, they promised to focus them in Europe and the U.S. for a solid week. We have no say in their targets or what operatives are used, and we just let it run its course. Even if it's only a few days, I believe it will leave the Americans reeling. It will be like a virus. Once the operation has used up all of its power, it will simply disappear."

Simplov jumped in. "We will let our two great enemies, the West and the radical Muslims, fight it out and deplete their own forces."

"No one will know how to respond," Putin said. "Look at France after

18

the Paris attacks. Their law enforcement was busy for months, but they still only caught a dozen terrorists total. Magnify that by five separate attacks, ten, fifty. The attacks will be physical, psychological, and cyber. No one will know how to respond. As a bonus, the jihadists will not be bothering Russia. At least for a while."

Putin waited while Andre absorbed all this. The older man was cautious, but he was also intelligent and experienced. Only a fool would ignore his advice. He understood the Americans, and especially the American diplomats, better than just about anyone.

"It could work," Andre said. "At least temporarily. But once you start any sort of incursion into Estonia, NATO will respond. Estonia is a member of NATO, and they will have no option but to respond to a military attack."

Now Putin said, "Will it? Would you? Is Estonia worth it?"

"I'm telling you NATO will have to respond."

Putin stood and waved his finger like a professor addressing his class. "I think that's where you're wrong, Andre. They have to *act*. That's different than *responding*. They could act by pushing resolutions through the UN. Maybe they even launch a few airstrikes. But if the past is our guide, NATO will follow the U.S. lead, and the U.S. has not taken action against us in years."

"And the European Union," Andre said, "cannot survive without our natural gas."

Putin clapped his hands together and said, "Exactly my point. Now is the time to act. If we wait, we could end up with another Texan in the White House, or worse, a Floridian. Who knows what the next president will do, but I doubt we'll ever be as lucky as we are right now."

Putin liked the grin that was spreading across Andre's face as he seemed to consider all the possible outcomes.

Derek Walsh sucked in a breath so he had an easier time sliding behind the computer monitor. He took a quick look around to make sure no one had noticed, but it was already too late. From three cubicles down he heard, "Hey, Derek, I thought once you were a marine you always stayed in shape." He knew the jibe came from Cheryl Kravitz, the team leader of his group that specialized in currency transactions for Thomas Brothers Financial. Since the crash, Thomas Brothers had shot up to become one of the leading financial houses along with Morgan Stanley and Chase. The growth had been stunning even in the two years Walsh had been working there. Too bad it didn't show in his pay. The company had hired him as part of a "hire a vet" campaign, but it was only lip service. He was still just a financial grunt.

He looked down at his belly and knew that he'd let his fitness slide since his discharge. But it wasn't exactly like he was doing push-ups every day in the service, either. He'd been a captain in charge of logistics and finances, with his only real combat experience coming when he forced his way onto a Black Hawk for patrol in the Korengal Valley during the war in Afghanistan and a couple of attacks on the base. He counted the nine shots he got off in a brief firefight as combat experience, but he'd trade it now to lose thirty pounds.

Walsh just smiled and nodded at Cheryl. Slender and standing almost six feet tall in her heels, she rarely missed anything that went on in the office.

He'd thought about his overall physical shape more in the last three weeks since he'd attended the funeral of his friend and fellow marine Ron Jackson. The major had died in a terror attack in Berlin, of all places. But there had been more attacks on U.S. interests by jihadists, mainly from the Islamic State—or, as the marines called the movement, Daesh, which could be confused with an Arabic word for stepping on something and was considered by some as a slight. New York had seen two attacks: a bomb in the subway that killed a Dutch tourist and shut down the green line for two days, and a modified anthrax attack in the air-conditioning system of a sporting goods store. There were still three people in the hospital over that.

Walsh had seen his other two close friends in Arlington at the funeral. Bill Shepherd was tall and lanky and still in the Corps. Mike Rosenberg was working at the CIA but looked like he'd pass any fitness test for any branch of the service. It made Walsh resent his nickname, "Tubby," for the first time since he'd earned it.

The fact that he had rented a tiny SoHo apartment and didn't have far to walk most nights proved he made too little money and spent too little energy. It was a tiny hovel that he sublet from sublettors who had it under rent control. He didn't even have his name on any official documents for the apartment and got all his mail at the office.

He missed his old team from the 2nd Marines. They were like brothers, and he had lost one to a conflict most Americans only knew from the nightly news. His new employment had teams as well, but they were nothing like a Marine unit. Thomas Brothers team members were a different breed. He was considered fit and tough on these teams. It was embarrassing. A twenty-three-year-old Princeton grad had yelled at him the other day.

Each of the six members of this team was involved in staggering transactions every day, but it never got to Cheryl. She stuck to a schedule of getting up at 5:00 A.M. and checking the exchanges, going to the gym, then staying in the office until after sunset every day except Friday. Then she did the unthinkable and sometimes left the office by six o'clock, whether it was summer or winter, sunny or gray.

All this occurred under the benevolent and watchful eye of Ted Marshall, the supervisor for his section and ultimate leader of three full teams. That made him similar to a major in the marines, but Ted worked hard to be liked. He was the guy who asked about your family. Cheryl was the one who told you that you didn't have time to see them.

At his desk, Walsh inserted his plastic-encased USB security plug into a secure terminal on the side of the lightning-fast computer. The plug was slightly larger than a USB thumb drive and had three lights on the side that flashed when it completed different tasks. It was safer than just a password and allowed the company to see exactly who was involved in the transaction. He still needed to enter an eight-digit password, and if he lost the security plug, virtually no one would have any idea what the damn thing was; besides, it could only work on a Thomas Brothers network. He always needed it on overseas transfers but not on routine work within their own trading house. Sometimes he'd have to use the plug three times in a week, or he could go three weeks without using it. Such was the life of a scrub at Thomas Brothers Financial. Lots of paperwork and trading within the company for clients he never got to meet.

Today he was just checking an account, not making any trades or transactions. He glanced at his watch and realized it was approaching six o'clock, or after midnight in Sarajevo, where he was checking on $4 million in Canadian currency that was in escrow. Some poor schlub like him was working overnight to prepare the final transaction in Europe. He felt for the guy. He needed this to be done quickly because his girlfriend, Alena, expected to meet him before six thirty. There were a lot of things Walsh was willing to do, but disappointing his girlfriend of two years was not one of them. He had known her two years, anyway, and felt confident he could call her his girlfriend of eleven months. If he could only work up the nerve, he'd present her with the engagement ring he'd bought nearly three weeks earlier and had stashed in the top drawer of his desk. He'd used the last of his savings from the marines and now worried about paying his day-to-day bills. For now he was content to make Alena happy by being on time and buying her a nice sushi dinner. He was still a little sheepish from his experience in Germany when he was the paymaster at Camp Panzer Kaserne. His mixup with a local girl who stole his company credit cards and charged a fortune could've gotten him a few years in Leavenworth. She claimed Walsh was part of the scheme. Thank God for good JAG lawyers and a judge who recognized the truth. It was just a petty crime, but it had scarred him, or at least greatly embarrassed him.

As soon as he had checked the escrow, he scurried to his own cubicle and made sure nothing had come up in the last twenty minutes while he was away from his desk. This was the tricky part: sliding out of the office without anyone noticing. It was never good to be the first one done for the day. No one ever noticed if you arrived at seven o'clock every morning, but everyone picked up on someone creeping out of the office first. This was high finance. Medical emergencies were put on hold to transfer money. Children's activities were the stuff of legend, and anniversaries past the third year were virtually unheard of.

He checked his watch—6:17. He felt a brief surge of panic and pictured Alena being hit on by some lawyer, or worse, some photographer who wanted her to be a model in his creepy midtown studio. He shuddered at the thought. The Columbia international affairs grad student from Greece was too sweet to recognize a come-on like that. Life in Larissa or Athens was a little simpler than in New York.

Just as he glanced in the tiny mirror on his desk to flatten out the cowlick in his short brown hair and make sure he didn't have any food crusted around his mouth, Ted Marshall stopped at his desk and said, "You're moving a lot of transactions lately, Derek. Glad we took advantage of that program to grab guys like you coming out of the service. I always pictured marines climbing up hills and shooting little Asian dudes. It never occurred to me the Corps needed financial managers, too. Keep up the good work."

Walsh just gave him a quick nod and mumbled, "Thanks, Ted." It'd taken him a while to get away from adding a "sir" or "ma'am" to virtually every remark. He'd called Ted "Mr. Marshall" for the first week he was here until the portly manager told him to knock it off. He tried to keep his manners intact no matter how difficult it was in this odd social maze of money wonks, computer nerds, and financial sharks. Each of them needed the others to survive, but no one wanted to mix with the others.

He screwed up the courage to casually stand and slowly walk toward the men's room. No one seemed to notice as they each focused on their own work and the room buzzed with a certain energy he'd never felt anywhere else. Once he was past the men's room, it was an easy few steps to the stairwell. He went down two floors by foot, then imagined the bloom of perspiration building under his arms and slipped off at the twenty-ninth floor just in time to catch an express elevator to the lobby. God was with him.

He couldn't help but look at his watch as the elevator door opened in the lobby and saw that he somehow had to make it seven blocks in about four minutes to be on time. He carried a simple zippered notebook instead of a briefcase, and his security plug was secure at the bottom of his inside coat pocket. The marines had taught him the importance of habit and keeping your uniform, no matter what it happened to be, clean and neat at all times.

He slipped out the glass door to cut across the courtyard and onto Nassau Street. He still wasn't certain which would be faster, a cab or an all-out sprint. At the bottom of the stairs two figures stepped in front of him and blocked his way. Walsh mumbled, "Excuse me," and started to spin to his left, but one of the men held out his arm to stop him.

All it took was one good breath to know exactly who these two were. They were part of the new Stand Up to Wall Street movement. Some of his coworkers called them the "aggravate movement," since they were a little more on the aggressive side than the Occupy people from a few years earlier.

One of the men, in his midtwenties and a little shorter than Walsh's six feet one, said, "What's the hurry, big guy? You need to rush home to your Park Avenue penthouse?"

The other man, a few years older, got right in his face and said, "How do you sleep at night doing the things you do?"

Walsh ignored them and tried to step past. One of the men grabbed him by the arm, and Walsh realized this was about to turn ugly.

Major Anton Severov used his Zeiss-Jena knock-off Russian binoculars to scan the low rise of the hills surrounding the town of Kingisepp, about eight miles from the border of Estonia and the city of Narva. His units were slowly maneuvering into place, with the main objective of not being noticed. For the past year they had been conducting war games in the area in and around Estonia, Latvia, and Belarus. It didn't take a genius to figure out what the Kremlin had planned, but so far no one seemed to really care. Severov had been a tanker his entire career, but he fought against the stereotype of the slow-witted brute. Sure, the MiG pilots and the intelligence people had time to dress in the most stylish of uniforms and were the envy of every man at a party, but in every war the Soviet Union and then Russia had been involved in, it was tankers who really led the way. His command vehicle was a T-90 tank with a 125 mm smooth-bore main gun. Aside from a brief skirmish in Georgia, he hadn't had the chance to see what the tank could do. Afghanistan was long over by the time he joined the service. Now it was the Americans' problem.

There was renewed optimism as Vladimir Putin had proven to the world Russia was not a dying superpower. Ukraine had found that out the hard way. Now they were poised to make a bold move into Estonia. A NATO partner. That might not have been the exact orders, but Severov was no idiot. He spoke English almost as well as Russian and subscribed online to *The New York Times*. He'd visited the U.S. three separate times, all of them on official passports back when relations between the two countries were much warmer. He knew their soldiers were tough and well trained, but he also knew there weren't enough of them in Eastern Europe. There had barely been enough in the 1980s under Ronald Reagan, but now, being preoccupied in the Middle East trying to act as a police-man, the U.S. had virtually forgotten about commitments to the countries of Europe.

The plans for a rapid deployment force had foundered, and the best the U.S. could do was base a dozen F-16s in Estonia, as a warning not to cross the border, and park a few outdated tanks on bases scattered across the country. Severov doubted that would be enough to influence Russian policy. The Russian hierarchy had calculated that no one would go to war over Estonia. Just like Crimea. There would be an outcry and a few use-less sanctions, but the U.S. president did not have the spine to stand up to Vladimir Putin and everyone knew it. Especially Putin.

A smile spread across Severov's face as he saw that all the tanks had settled in under trees and spread camouflage netting so that satellites would have a difficult time picking up the movement. He wasn't even worried about flights overhead. No one from NATO had bothered to fly a jet through Estonia or Latvia in the past three weeks. They were still bitching about Ukraine.

He knew the orders would come soon. He'd been told to settle down and keep his men fed, rested, and engaged. If that wasn't a precursor to war, nothing was.

Walsh felt the man's hand on his bicep and resisted the urge to turn toward him; instead he locked his arm to his body and turned away quickly, tossing the man into his partner. Now they turned on him with fire in their eyes. These didn't seem like the peaceful Stand Up to Wall Street people he'd gotten used to seeing urinating in the flowerpots and dozing under the trees and in the green spaces. He didn't want to crouch and give away his intentions, as he kept his eyes on both men, who were now separating slowly, making it difficult for him to face both of them at once.

He felt a third hand on his right shoulder. This one was gentle and barely startled him. Then the soft voice acted like a tranquilizer as he heard his girlfriend, Alena, say, "Let these men go. They're just confused."

That seemed to catch the younger man's attention. He looked at her and said, "Why are we confused?"

"Because you don't even know what you're protesting. Everyone is against unlawful financial transactions, but none of you are qualified to know who's an honest banker and who is not. None of you even have jobs." Her light accent added flair to the comment.

The other man leveled his gaze at her and said, "How do you know we don't have jobs?"

Now Walsh ended the conversation and stepped toward the man, saying, "Because you guys hang out here all day." He let the frustration bleed into his voice. Even if it was a reasonable cause, who could take it seriously? These guys weren't even homeless. They just chose to not work and live off their parents.

Walsh allowed Alena to turn him as she said, "I knew you'd be running late, so I thought I'd surprise you. But I desperately have to use your restroom, and they won't let me in the building without you." She carried an overcoat draped over the wide portfolio she always had nearby.

He couldn't help glancing over his shoulder at the two men one last time as he heard a rally at the far end of the plaza begin. Walsh used the security keypad to get back into the building. He made sure no one but Alena was watching when he punched in his password of 73673734—which spelled *Semper Fi* on a phone—and walked Alena to the ladies' room. Alena charmed the guard at the security desk into letting her leave her portfolio and coat behind the desk until they were done with dinner. The flustered guard only asked if she would be back by ten, when his shift ended. She threw him a glittering smile and flipped her blond hair as she nodded yes. They were both happy with the transaction.

Alena turned to Walsh as they neared the restroom and surprised him with a full hug and kiss on the lips. Then she whispered in his ear, "You're so cute."

A smile spread across his face as he decided she was the prettiest girl who had ever whispered in his ear.

Joseph Katazin, born Joseph Ladov, had spent most of his adult life in the United States, the majority of that in Brooklyn or Queens. His father had been a mathematician at the Nizhny Novgorod State Technical University, and his mother a music teacher from Kiev. All Joseph had ever wanted to do was be a soldier. Just like little boys all over the world. It had been difficult to go against his father's wishes, but he was accepted into the M. V. Frunze Military Academy and, at the tender age of twenty-one, virtually tumbled out of school and into combat in Afghanistan. That was a treacherous stretch of three years, fighting insurgents who were heavily backed by the United States. That fact didn't hit home until the Hind helicopter he was riding in was struck by an American-made Stinger and went down in the Eshpi Valley in the Southern Hindu Kush. He'd survived on his wits and an AK-47 with four magazines of ammo. The crash had injured his back and given him a gash from his hairline to his chin on the left side of his face, which now, at fifty-one, had faded to a thin white line that crossed his lips and gave them a slight indentation. He noticed it every time he smiled, and that made him remember why he hated the United States so much.

The time was drawing near for him to feel some level of satisfaction.

After the service, when he returned home from Afghanistan, his father let him in on a family secret: His mathematics degree had helped him work with the KGB on cracking codes. As a result of his work, he knew several high-ranking KGB officials who took the young Joseph under their wing. They appreciated his service, and a scar on his face tended to remind people that the KGB wasn't a group of accountants or technical people trying to eavesdrop on telephone conversations. Occasionally they did serious work and needed serious people.

Ladov's ability to speak English at his mother's insistence, starting at a very early age, as well as his ability to play the piano, also due to his mother's iron will, made the Russian spy agency realize he could be used for a number of things other than terrorizing prisoners to get information. Eventually he traveled to the United States using the name Joseph Katazin and never used the name Ladov again. For more than a year he attempted gainful employment as a pianist, but even the KGB gave up on that and instead helped him establish the European Trading Company, a somewhat successful import and export business.

Eventually Katazin married a plump but pretty girl who had just graduated from Stony Brook, a Long Island branch of the State University of New York system. As an elementary school teacher, she was an excellent cover. Over the years, however, Katazin had to admit he had developed feelings for her, and now, sixteen years later, with a twelve-year-old daughter, he was quite comfortable in his life and essentially happy.

His wife, of course, had no idea about his background or main occupation. He told her a dog had bitten him when he was a child and left a scar on his face. The bullet hole in his leg was explained as a hunting accident and the reason he shied away from guns now. She was occasionally loving and attentive and more frequently a suspicious shrew. That was partially his fault—he enjoyed the occasional tryst and had been careless in some of his liaisons. His wife had accepted the fact that her husband worked extraordinary hours; after all, he had provided her with a very comfortable house in an upscale area of Brooklyn.

On this evening he was sitting on a bench in the Wall Street district waiting to see confirmation that the start of Russia's biggest operation in years had been successful. He was looking at the rear of the building that housed Thomas Brothers Financial and could barely contain his smile when he saw the beautiful young blonde walking out of the building arm in arm with the tall young man in a suit, one side of his shirt untucked from his pants. Katazin knew the man was a former marine, and although he had apparently gained a little weight, he looked like he could handle himself in a fight.

On one hand, Katazin felt guilty ruining a fellow soldier's life. On the other hand, this was the enemy and a necessary casualty on the new Russia's march toward glory. There was a saying that soldiers were the same the world over and shared a certain brotherhood. This one was just in the wrong place at the wrong time, and Katazin was too good at his job to let the opportunity pass.

3

Derek Walsh had enjoyed the short walk from the sushi restaurant back to his office with Alena on his arm. He loved just spending time with her. She had earned his trust by little things, like not questioning his travel when he visited his mom in Philly, or his buddies from the marines. And although he was keenly aware that she was a prize that a low-earning former marine probably didn't deserve, she had never given him reason to question her fidelity. Little by little she had become an important part of his life, a trusted confidant he could share his insecurities about his job with and never worry about her blabbing his secrets.

The stroll was far superior to the minuscule meal he'd just eaten and paid a fortune for. There was something about his time in the marines and living on a captain's salary that made him flinch at paying more than seventy dollars for a couple of pieces of bait slapped on top of rice. It didn't matter that he now made a little more money; no one was paying for his living quarters or food, and he lived in Manhattan. These dates were killing him. The three sixteen-ounce Ichiban beers he'd thrown down helped ease his annoyance at not taking in enough calories.

As they approached the building his cell phone rang, and he looked at his girlfriend as a matter of manners to see if she minded him answering the call.

Alena smiled and nodded as she pointed to the front door, saying she was going to retrieve her coat and portfolio. He nodded back and was hustling toward the security pad to enter his code when he saw the guard rushing to the door to let her in. So much for security if you had blond hair and a great smile.

As soon as Walsh had the receiver to his ear, he heard the clear and unmistakable voice of his former classmate from the Naval Academy, Michael Rosenberg.

"Tubby! I didn't wake you up, did I?"

Walsh couldn't hide his smile at hearing the nickname he'd earned in Germany. It was true that after his stint in Afghanistan, the German food and beer seemed to slap on weight. "Hey, Mike. I'm still at the office."

"I know that's got to be bullshit. You probably just finished eating dinner at some fancy restaurant in the area."

"And that's why you managed to land such a good government job." Walsh was happy his friend had been recruited by the CIA. It fit perfectly with his assignment as G-2 in their unit in Afghanistan and Germany. As an intelligence officer with the marines, Rosenberg could mix in virtually any circle and had an analytical mind that could rival the best computer Apple could spit out. Walsh patted his belly and realized it was in stark contrast to the wiry Rosenberg, who would use a ten-mile run as a warm-up. "So what's up?"

Rosenberg said, "Just thinking about Ron and the funeral. Then Bill Shepherd called. He's training with some of the local NATO defense forces in case Russia acts up again."

"What would a small marine unit do against tanks?"

"Fight, baby, fight. What else? Besides, they've already trained with a bunch of local soldiers. They would lead an interesting force if it came to that."

"Is there intel Russia will move?"

"There are always rumors that Putin has something up his sleeve.

They're in bad shape economically, and that makes them dangerous. But there's no specific intel right now. Shep is just being a good marine officer and getting prepared. I also think he's trying to keep his mind occupied."

"Were you able to talk to Bill for a while? He was closer to Ron. He still saw him all the time in Germany."

"Just for a few minutes. He says it's not the same with us gone. The G-4 who took your place is useless. Doesn't keep their supplies up to date and is hard to talk to about issues. Not what you want in a unit like that."

Walsh appreciated the vote of confidence. Ron Jackson, Bill Shepherd, and Mike Rosenberg had stood by him during the entire ordeal over the finances of the company. After a moment of silence Walsh said, "Anything going on at work you can talk about?"

"Only in person. You know this is my personal phone. I don't trust anyone anymore."

"That's just you adjusting to the natural paranoia of a government employee." He saw Alena leaving the building and waving to the security guard inside and said to his friend, "Mike, I gotta go. I'm on a date."

"Are you still dating the hot Greek chick?"

"I am." Saying it made him smile from ear to ear.

"Roger that, Tubby. I just called to say hello. Maybe I'll come up this weekend and we can do something crazy."

"I figured a guy with a job like yours wouldn't set foot in a place like Times Square unless he was on duty."

"From everything I can tell, Wall Street is as dangerous as any place in New York."

Alena gave him another hug as he closed the phone. He didn't bother to explain who was calling because she never seemed interested anyway. His heart rate increased as he felt Alena's lovely body next to him, and he wondered if he'd get to see more of it. But that dream ended quickly.

Alena said, "I have an early class tomorrow morning. I think I'll take a cab home."

"I shouldn't let you go by yourself."

She let out a cute giggle, touched him on the nose, and said, "You and your sweet manners. I appreciate it, but I don't know that I could keep you from coming upstairs. And I need to study a little more tonight."

He flagged down a cab and kissed her good night, hoping she'd be free tomorrow.

Fannie Legat's mother had been born in Algeria but raised in France. Her father was a banker, whose parents survived World War II but didn't survive him marrying, as her grandfather said, a *beur*—a "melon," the rudest of French terms for Arabs living in the country. Fannie barely remembered her father, who left them for a plump, blond Norwegian when she was just a little girl. They had languished in the Paris suburb of La Courneuve, about a ten-minute train ride outside the city, known as one of the largest slums for people of all nationalities the government had failed to integrate into the general population. It had been the scene of riots as well as devastating poverty. One of the street poets said, "The sun never shines in La Courneuve."

By the time she was twelve, she was reconnecting with her Islamic roots. Her mother worked so many hours she barely noticed her daughter's transformation, even when she donned a hijab after she reached puberty as a show of propriety. The headdress also concealed her growing anger toward the treatment of Muslims by all of the Western nations.

But someone in the French government had noticed her exceedingly good grades and by Allah's grace she was admitted to EMLYON, a college of economics and finance in the eastern city of Lyon. It was in a class on international trade and economics that the seventeen-year-old Fannie met a twenty-two-year-old immigrant from Egypt named Naadir Al-Latif. He was the first to encourage her to embrace her heritage completely and led her to her new name of Yasmine Akram because he said it meant "most generous." They both laughed at the idea of her gaining an expertise in money and also adopting that name.

It was through a small group of Muslim students that the new

Yasmine Akram started to follow the teachings of what some Western governments would refer to as "radical clerics." Their teachings turned on a light in her soul, and she realized it was her duty to contribute to the struggle Islam faced every day to convert others and dissuade nonbelievers from interfering in its activities.

A boring year of working in the financial district of Paris after graduation led her to jump at the chance to travel to Syria and support their version of the "Arab Spring." But learning about fundamental Islam is not quite the same as living it day in and day out. The other fighters did not want a woman on the front lines, and she was relegated to helping the wounded and working in logistics. Her ability to speak French, German, and English made her invaluable in dealing with the outside contributors to their cause. She was shocked how many French firms willingly did business with anyone who had the money. They supplied arms to the Assad regime while also sending weapons to the rebels. It was one of the greatest capitalist schemes of all time. It made her both proud and ashamed of her home country.

Yasmine herself had other ideas about how she could contribute to the struggle. At five foot seven and athletically built, calling herself Abdul, she was able to reenter the rebel's camp as a man and was given an AK-47 almost without question. She still embraced the first time she had a Syrian soldier in her gun sights: Watching him drop to the ground, lifeless, after a short burst from her assault rifle was a life-changing experience.

Her prowess on the battlefield soon came to the attention of some of the local commanders. One of the sharper young men recognized her for what she was and quietly pulled her off the line, introducing her to an entirely new set of soldiers for Islam. Some people called them the Islamic State or ISIS. Either way, they had big plans for spreading the conflict beyond the borders of Syria and Iraq. It would be a waste to have a young woman like her killed by artillery. With her lighter hair and the ability to speak several languages without accent, she could pass for French or German with very little effort. Besides, funding was becoming a major issue for their cause, and her background in economics made her that much more appealing a recruit. The successes of ISIS had been covered by world media with flair. Recapturing neglected cities from ill-trained Iraqi conscripts had made their efforts look heroic and the organization appear ready to take over the whole country, but the truth was much more complex. The group was constantly evolving, with splinter groups squabbling endlessly about everything from tactics to proper religious etiquette. The Islamic State had become less of a state and more of a movement. This would change with the upcoming operation. Fannie believed they were on the brink of a new era. After they were established, with a country and permanent funding, she could tackle the other issues that affected her, like the group's view on women. "One battle at a time" was her private motto.

All that had led her to the Café Schilling on Charlottenstrasse in Böblingen, Germany, just outside Stuttgart. Now she only used the name Fannie Legat. Her main job while she was in the area was to plan attacks against U.S. military personnel and other targets if she were ordered to. But funding had been an issue for many months now. It seemed the Zionists and the Americans controlled most of the money in the world, at least to hear her superiors tell it. But it was true that attempting a large-scale attack required money. She had several confederates living comfortably in an apartment near the center of Stuttgart who had been running up tabs at local restaurants and other businesses. But the men were true believers and would gladly give their lives to help in the ongoing struggle.

As she sipped some coffee in the middle of the night at an outdoor table next to a palm tree—the café was trying to have a Mediterranean look—she noticed an athletic-looking U.S. Marine major with short brown hair, reading a report while picking at a piece of toast.

Maybe this could be an opportunity while she waited for funding to come through.

4

After Derek Walsh watched Alena drive away in the cab, he intended to stop and have a hamburger and a few more beers, then grab a few hours' sleep in the comfortable queen bed in his tiny apartment and head into the office as late as possible.

Although he admired farmers who were up before dawn working, he had little respect for the financial managers who would come in before the sun rose. He had read an article about how money managers contributed little to society. If everything were to go to hell and you needed a skill in the future, money managers would be out of luck. They didn't build anything, cure anyone, protect anyone, or carry anything. It led to a fairly widespread depression among thoughtful money managers who considered their contribution to society.

It was a mild autumn evening, and surprisingly few people were on the street. He could've easily hailed a cab, but the nine-block walk would do him good. And one of his favorite diners was right on the way.

When he was about two blocks away from the office, he noticed two men at the far end of the block walking toward him. He was always alert, but these two seemed harmless enough. They were white; one of them was middle-aged, the other young and thin. They showed no interest in Walsh. His mind was on Alena anyway. Sometimes she was a ball of fire emotionally, but more often she displayed an aloof, cool demeanor and didn't seem interested in anything intimate. He enjoyed having such a beautiful girlfriend, but if he looked at his life as a whole, he wanted to settle down and start having children. He'd fantasized about telling his son how he fought in the war and then moved on to Wall Street and made a fortune. He intended to do all this from the dock of their spacious home in the Florida Keys. That was his dream, anyway.

The two men were only about twenty feet away from him when Walsh looked up again and assessed them quickly. The older one was perhaps fifty and had a fading scar across the left side of his face. The younger man was barely twenty-five and had the wiry look of a meth user. He was prepared to file them away in his memory as they passed when he noticed the younger man reaching under a loose Knicks hoodie. The movement caught Walsh's eye, and he immediately tensed and turned his body slightly as he'd been trained in the marines. It could be anything, but it looked like the younger man was reaching for a pistol.

It was that little reaction—training that had seeped through all the other bullshit in his head—that allowed Walsh to move quickly when the younger, slim man drew some kind of blued steel automatic from his waistband.

Walsh did not hesitate. The marines frowned on hesitation. He did exactly what he had always been taught. He literally sprang into action.

It was late, or early, depending on how you looked at it, but he couldn't sleep, so Major Bill Shepherd had slipped off base.

He had managed a call to his former comrade Mike Rosenberg at the CIA and, like many other good military officers, used this back channel to get a better view of world affairs. As he had feared, the U.S. was mainly focused on Middle Eastern threats. The bombing in Berlin that had killed his friend Ron Jackson pointed to the rapidly expanding targets of the Islamic State.

Although the Russians were considered a threat, they weren't, at the moment, killing Americans, so the administration devoted little effort to the sleeping bear. Washington was just going along with NATO's actions to discourage aggression, which involved the U.S. forces in Europe. A few F-16s had been moved around, and a rapid deployment force was in the works, but not much else. If the balloon went up, the men of his brigade would be expected to do a lot. He wanted to be prepared.

He quietly studied the status report for his brigade. He couldn't tell anyone he was secretly thrilled at the thought of combat and considered the possibility of moving the team into either Estonia or Belarus as part of a NATO response to any Russian activity. He knew to keep things quiet, and his unit was small enough to operate under the radar. But the army units on the same base were more obvious and some of their commanders realized they might have to act fast. The movement of dozens of tanks attracted attention. Everything was still theoretical, but just the thought of having a chance to knock out a T-90 or any other Russian armor was exciting, and the reality would mean his decision to join the marines would be completely validated.

Shepherd's father and two brothers were in the navy. Although his father was a retired admiral, Shepherd had avoided the Naval Academy, then searched the New York area for an acceptable alternative. Not interested in West Point, he had to travel south to Lexington, Virginia, where he enrolled in the Virginia Military Institute. The college, formed in 1839, was the first state-sponsored military academy and had a proud tradition, most notably featuring "Stonewall" Jackson as an instructor. As far as the marines went, Shepherd considered Lieutenant General Lewis "Chesty" Puller, a highly decorated combat commander with five Navy Crosses, to be the academy's greatest marine graduate.

Shepherd had completed one tour in Iraq and two in Afghanistan, but his father didn't view trading small-arms fire with insurgents as serious military activity. Even so, he was the only one of the three brothers to actually see combat. Military people sought action. No fighter pilot wanted to spend his entire career training. Kids on computers did that. Military personnel prepared for battle, and all of them wanted to make their country proud. They still talked of faith, glory, and honor. Shepherd knew that if the Russians made a move into any of the bordering countries, he'd have plenty of chances to see glory, find honor, and keep his faith. The old saying that there were no atheists in a foxhole was equally true when facing down Russian armor on a highway.

He just wished there were more assets in case the Russians tried something. The lack of leadership from the top of the U.S. government had led to an absolute debacle in the Middle East. Now, not only intelligence assets but more and more military assets were being directed at conflicts that had little hope of being resolved. Maybe if the United States had taken a more active role early on, things would be different, but a stuttering foreign policy and a spineless view of aggression now threatened the security of Western Europe.

Despite what U.S. officials kept saying, the world was a much more dangerous place. Perhaps not as many people were dying at the moment from military conflict, but the potential for a showdown between major powers was growing exponentially.

After talking with Mike Rosenberg, he wondered if his other friend from the unit who had left, Derek Walsh, missed the marines more than he let on. He was a big shot on Wall Street now but still managed to drop Shepherd a line either through e-mail or on Skype at least once a week. Maybe he'd try Walsh early tomorrow afternoon when it was midmorning on the East Coast. He'd seen both Mike and Derek at Ron Jackson's funeral, and they all had been disturbed by his death. It made Shepherd want to focus on the assholes in the Islamic State, but he'd settle for Russians.

Just thinking of "settling" for the Russians reminded Shepherd of a training class he took at Quantico with Rosenberg, Walsh, and Jackson. They were all newly minted second lieutenants and just getting to know each other. Already they were falling into certain roles, with Jackson seeming wiser and more even-tempered than the others even though he was the same age. Rosenberg was already assessing situations and providing them with intelligence like any good G-2. Walsh could figure out their resources and tell them exactly where they could and couldn't go based on their meager money and available transportation. And Shepherd was always the one who listened to everyone else, then acted, or sometimes acted, then listened to everyone else. They were the perfect team, and he missed them terribly.

During this training class, they had gone out for a beer in the little town called Woodbridge in northern Virginia. The place was packed; it was some kind of trivia night, and between the four of them they knew the answers to almost everything that came up. Soon girls were flirting with them, and as was his way, Shepherd was gathering phone numbers as fast as he could. He always found it easy to chat with women, and that made it possible to set up his friends as well. But that night he had chatted with one woman too many, and her remarkably fit and tall boyfriend and his three friends took exception.

None of them were in uniform, but most people in the area could tell a marine officer by the haircut and bearing. That didn't deter these local rednecks in the least. Shepherd wanted to kick everyone's ass, but he "settled" for just the one guy. Even then Shepherd knew he could trust his friends to have his back and never worried about the other men. He could focus all his attention on the loudmouth up in his face. As it turned out, Walsh, Rosenberg, and Jackson handled the other men with little problem. But the big man confronting Shepherd had a wicked right cross and knocked him off his feet almost immediately. That's the way things worked out in bar fights, and he had to accept the sore nose if he was dumb enough to get into a fight in the first place.

Before he knew it, Shepherd's friends were easing him out of the bar with a bloody nose and what turned out to be a really good black eye, but nothing more serious. Those were the three guys he could trust as long as he lived. Or, as it had sadly turned out, as long as they lived. Now he only had Walsh and Rosenberg to depend on, but he was glad he had them.

Shepherd's mind dialed back to the present as he flipped a page to see just how many portable antitank weapons he would be able to scrounge up if the time came. From the corner of his eye he caught an attractive young woman sipping coffee at the edge of the café. She had dark brown, flowing hair and high cheekbones that set off deep green eyes. He couldn't tell her nationality, but she wasn't the typical fair German girl. She had a grace and style that pointed toward France or one of the United Kingdom countries.

Maybe it was time for a break from his work.

Neither of the men confronting Derek Walsh expected him to be so aggressive. And clearly the younger man didn't know how to handle 220 pounds barreling into him. He bounced off Walsh, grazed the wall, and ended up on the sidewalk.

Walsh saw movement out of the corner of his left eye and instinctively raised his left hand to block a blow by the other man. At least *he* appeared to be unarmed. Walsh pivoted and threw his elbow into the man's face, knocking him into the street. As he turned around, the man on the ground had his pistol up. Walsh didn't hesitate to fall on him, holding the arm with the pistol in it. They struggled, and Walsh felt the strain in his respiratory system. His breathing became labored, and his heart pounded in his chest. What the hell did these guys want? He rolled on the ground, tossing the smaller man to one side while still holding the arm with the pistol.

The second man, the older one with a scar, somehow got back in the fight and took the gun from the man Walsh had in his grasp. The older man had the gun almost to Walsh's temple when Walsh was able to raise his left hand violently and knock it away just as the man pulled the trigger.

The shot was deafening. It caused a dog to bark in the distance and made everyone at the scene freeze. The man brought the gun around again, but this time Walsh swept his leg and knocked him to the ground. A car came around the corner, the headlights raking the building and all three of them.

The younger man shouted something in another language. It sounded

Russian. He started to run. Walsh made a fist and struck the older man several times in the side, feeling his ribs crack.

The older man struggled to his feet and managed to kick the gun away from both of them. As he stood, he staggered, then leaned down and scooped up the gun and set off running.

Walsh sat up and leaned against the building panting, watching both men disappear around the corner as the car that had scared them off came to a stop. He heard a woman's voice say, "I just called 911."

Walsh nodded and raised his hand in thanks. But he couldn't help wondering why the men attacked him, and why, after he had the gun in his hand again, the older man chose to run instead of shoot.

In the distance he could hear a siren.

5

After Vladimir Putin had showered and changed into comfortable evening clothes, Yuri Simplov showed up. Putin was in an good mood because he had seen both of his daughters in the afternoon and then was able to spend more than an hour and a half in judo practice. He worked on all forms of martial arts, but judo was his first love and the first martial art that really focused him as a child. He practiced it for hours on end. It was his form of meditation, and he now had two sergeants from the perimeter security patrol who were perfect to practice with. They were built like Putin, athletic but not too bulky, and they were aggressive opponents. They were both approaching their midforties, but Putin could still get the best of them in most circumstances. His early sixties had hit him harder than he expected, and he worked longer than ever to keep his edge and stayed in shape. And throwing around two army sergeants did wonders for his confidence.

Judo also taught Putin how to size up an opponent, in life as well as on the mat. He had been doing that to the Western leaders for years and finally found that he had a decisive advantage over the current crop of politicians. Maybe not all of them, but certainly the ones running the U.S. and France. That was why the timing of this operation was so important. He had to start thinking of his legacy. How would he be remembered? He wanted to lead Russia to the forefront of world affairs once again.

The dinner with his daughters and their respective boyfriends had been light and easy. Both the girls had been adults when he and their mother divorced, and neither seemed to hold it against him. His divorce settlement had been generous enough to ensure that Lyudmila didn't make waves.

The girls had filled him in on all their activities. He couldn't have been more proud of them. For much of their upbringing he was a lower-level functionary, and they lived very modest lives. In their early teens he started to get better positions such as the head of the FSB or the domestic security agency. Then Yeltsin's inner circle took notice of him. When the Russian general prosecutor started an investigation into money laundering by Yeltsin and his associates, Putin fired the man. Sensing they could control Putin, Yeltsin and his men promoted him to prime minister.

The timing was fortuitous. Yeltsin's health had been failing for years, and before long he passed away.

Putin's older daughter, Maria, who had been called Masha since birth, lived in the Netherlands part of the year. His younger daughter, Katerina, or Katya, lived right here in Moscow. Both girls' private lives had been kept out of the media completely. Incredibly, they had managed to attend the University of St. Petersburg under assumed names without anyone ever knowing, even their classmates. They were true daughters of an intelligence agent.

But now he was entering the parlor where Yuri Simplov waited.

Putin found Simplov studying two pieces of art that were technically on loan from a museum in Amsterdam.

The way his friend quickly turned and the look on his face told Putin things were in motion.

A smile spread across Simplov's rugged face as he stepped forward and said, "The trades have been made successfully, and the distraction attacks will now start in full force."

Putin kept his face blank as he said, "And all of our connections are secure?"

"Completely. Our U.S. agent is a bit of an odd duck, but absolutely reliable."

"Odd duck?"

Simplov gave him a smile and said, "He's been stationed in New York for a long time and handled many situations for us. He tends to take things a little personally. That's one of the ways we manage him. He hates to lose. He'll stay on an assignment after he's been told to move on. He'll do anything to finish an assignment totally and completely. That's just the kind of man we need at this time."

Putin nodded his head. That was exactly who they needed. "But if there's a problem he's insulated from us, correct?"

"He's well insulated. He has been in the U.S. for decades, running a small import/export business in New York for most of that time, and hasn't traveled to Russia or any of our satellites. He's married to an American woman and has a daughter."

Putin chuckled. "Does he make any money?" That was the question he always had for any operation that used a business as a cover.

Simplov shrugged and said, "He does okay. We haven't had to send him much money over the years."

Now Putin looked his old friend in the eye and said, "And the Muslims? No one can know anything about our temporary alliance with them. If they shoot down our planes and kill our soldiers in Syria, we must not be seen to be allied with them."

He wanted Simplov to see just how serious he was about this aspect of the operation. This was exactly the sort of op he liked working on as a KGB agent years earlier, but as the president of Russia it was a wild gamble that could cost him everything.

Simplov took a breath as he gathered his thoughts and said, "We have had very limited contact with them. No one knows anything of our actual intentions in Estonia. I have not risked activating any cells there, and we will draw our scouts directly from the military units already on the border. There is a tentative plan to use a Muslim woman from France who has excellent language skills to assist our military scout. I believed there was less chance of someone watching an unknown French woman than one of our agents already in Estonia."

Putin patted him on the shoulder and said, "As long as the French woman can be eliminated if necessary. Good, good. Well done."

"The money transfers have been discovered, and it is my understanding that the U.S. authorities in the form of the FBI are involved in the case. Our man in New York will do everything he can to slow down the investigation."

Simplov said, "I told you that some of our tech people had developed an algorithm that would cause computers on the New York and London stock exchanges to start a sell-off catastrophic enough to trip the built-in circuit breakers. It is a relatively simple algorithm that works on the same principle as the computer program that manages trades. It will cause two major trading houses to sell, which will trigger the other houses' computers to start to sell. It will be a cascading effect, gaining momentum quickly until the trading is stopped."

"And the money transfers?"

"Introducing the algorithm was the challenge. It was introduced at almost exactly the best time, so that now the news should break just as the public learns of the out-of-control stock panic."

Putin understood the world of finance. The sell-off would be temporary; its primary impact would be psychological. The Americans were already nervous about the markets after their long recession. This was precisely the kind of distraction he appreciated.

"Won't the Americans be able to trace the source of the algorithm?" Putin asked.

"It will come back to a Swiss bank," Simplov said, "where I've been assured they will find a dead end, at least in the near term. This entire operation is simply about delaying the discovery of our efforts until after we have control of Estonia."

Putin was pleasantly surprised at how effective the plan had been so far. He embraced his old friend and patted him on the back.

It was a Monday morning, and Derek Walsh was thinking about Alena on his way to work. He'd had real trouble committing to women since his days in Germany. His girlfriend when he was stationed there had done a real number on him. He truly believed she had feelings for him, but all she really needed was access to his company credit cards. After stealing the cards and racking up thousands of dollars in iPads and other electronics, she'd been arrested, and he'd been disgraced. It didn't escape him that she looked quite a bit like Alena. The fall weather and cool breeze only made him think of Germany and his bitter encounter all the more clearly.

Alena had done a lot to help restore his faith in women. Although she had some expensive tastes and he figured she thought he made more money than he really did—no one really understood how many grunts there were in the financial world—she had bought him expensive gifts as well. The Tag Heuer Aquaracer watch on his wrist was one of them. He also had an extra debit card she'd insisted on giving him so he could access her bank account in case of emergency. He'd only used it once, when they were on a date and he was short of cash. But he did notice she had over $4,500 sitting in her checking account. At least she wasn't after his money. That meant something to him after being burned.

He'd be late getting to work but had played it off to the bosses as a breakfast meeting. In truth, the meeting was just a cup of coffee with a local Deutsche Bank analyst, and they discussed the sad state of the New York Jets—something Walsh had learned New Yorkers did a lot of over the years and had gotten very good at.

When he came up this way toward Wall Street, Walsh always gave the same three homeless people a five-dollar bill each. They were all veterans and down on their luck. Two had been in the navy, and one was an old Ranger who had served in Vietnam. Walsh sat with him one evening and listened to his stories of combat just before the withdrawal of U.S. forces. These poor guys had been virtually forgotten and almost completely ignored since the start of the First Gulf War. But they had done what was asked of them in a much more difficult time with no public support.

He stopped for a few moments to talk with the Vietnam vet, who, ironically, was named Charlie. The man once told Walsh his last name was Williams and on another occasion told him it was Wilson. Walsh knew not to pry but just do what he could to make the man's life a little easier. Charlie occasionally stayed at a shelter near Walsh's tiny apartment in SoHo and would walk with him all the way to work on nice days.

Charlie gave him a jack-o'-lantern grin with three teeth missing as Walsh approached. The older man said, "I haven't seen you in a few days, Captain. Everything all right?"

Walsh smiled back and nodded. "Been busy at work."

"Good for you. I like to see any former military man succeed. Even if he was a marine."

As Charlie walked along with him, Walsh stopped at a bakery with a window onto the sidewalk and bought the man two doughnuts and coffee. He knew how Charlie took his coffee and didn't say anything, just handed him the food.

The older man accepted it with a smile. After a minute of walking and throwing down the doughnuts like pieces of candy, Charlie said, "The cops find out anything more about the two thugs that tried to rob you?"

"They told me it was just a robbery and that I should feel lucky I wasn't hurt."

"Typical cops, just explain things away without trying to solve anything."

Walsh normally would have defended the police, but in this case Charlie was right. It just didn't feel like a robbery to him. It was more calculated. He couldn't put his finger on it, but he had been much more alert in the past week.

As he reached the courtyard that led to the entrance to his building, Walsh stopped and stared at the animated crowd of Stand Up to Wall Street people. Two dozen cops were trying to keep them from destroying a cruiser they'd flipped onto its side and move them off the property.

Walsh looked at Charlie and said, "I haven't seen these guys this active since they started protesting."

Charlie said, "It's not just them, there's problems all over the city. I don't catch much news, but someone said there had been more terror attacks and people are getting scared."

Just then Walsh's phone let off an alert tone he had set for breaking news on the financial markets. He fished the phone out of his pocket and swiped the screen. The markets had been open less than thirty minutes and were already down hundreds of points. Computer trading had been stopped, and the London Stock Exchange had halted trading altogether.

What the hell was going on?

Joseph Katazin sat in the home office of his comfortable Brooklyn residence. The converted bedroom held three TVs mounted in different corners, a pressboard computer desk, and two black leather rolling chairs. On a separate oak desk, paperwork related to his business was piled in a seemingly random order.

The room had little natural light because files and invoices sat on the windowsill and took up more than half the window space. Even though it was fall, the sun was shining. That was good: It would give these Americans a false sense of security. Nothing bad ever happened in sunshine.

Katazin was still amazed he was allowed to take such a big part in an extensive operation from outside Moscow. On the other hand, if something went wrong, he had no illusions. He would be the scapegoat, and no one in the Russian government would acknowledge that he ever had anything to do with them. And if he somehow escaped American custody, his own government would stop at nothing to eliminate him. There was nothing more terrifying to a government than a loose cannon who knew too much. This was not Hollywood. There were no tales of forgiveness and redemption. Only success or failure.

He'd really done very little so far. A few financial transactions, that was it. The only thing that really made him uneasy was the alliance his government had made, however temporary, with extremists who cared little about Russia's interests. Katazin wondered if they even realized these Islamic extremists would turn on them in a heartbeat. But he worked with the resources that had been provided, and so far they had done everything they said they would.

Yesterday, Katazin had been able to leak the story of Thomas Brothers Financial sending money to an account accessed by terrorists. In addition, if anyone cared to look into it, Thomas Brothers would be missing hundreds of millions of dollars. The story hadn't broken to the general public, but there were already rumors burning across the Internet.

He had a lot to keep track of. Some would say too much, but after years of relative inactivity, enjoying the good life as an American, he was ready for some excitement. His meeting in Battery Park in forty minutes would give him a better idea of how things were really going and whether his superiors were happy with him.

There was a barely audible knock on his closed office door. He turned and rolled across the hard wooden floor in his black leather chair to unlock the door, letting it open a few inches. He saw the pale face of his twelve-year-old daughter, home from school with strep throat.

She croaked, "Papa, can I watch TV?"

He motioned the girl into his office, and she automatically climbed up on his lap. He rocked her gently and said, "Yes, but don't tell your mother. She doesn't approve of TV when you're home from school."

She gave him a weak smile as he felt her forehead. She was still warm but getting better. She scurried out of the office, and he heard her pounding down the stairs. Her mother wouldn't be home for another few hours, so he was safe from her murderous stare for overruling one of her strictest edicts. But his daughter's smile made the risk worth taking.

Someone once told him they would rather have the flu in America than be healthy in most Eastern European countries. That was probably accurate. Most Americans never appreciated how good they had it. They would scoff at the thought of waiting in line for groceries or a new pair of jeans.

Now they were about to get an idea of how the rest of the world lived.

Major Anton Severov sat in the billowing tent hidden by tall trees on the border with Estonia and stared at his commander. The temperature had dropped in the last two days, and he felt a chill, but at the moment he wasn't sure what the cause was. He took a step back and absently plopped onto a wooden bench. It was just after sunset. He wondered why this assignment couldn't wait until tomorrow. All Severov could do was stare at the plump colonel with jowls that wiggled as he turned his head. The man was a stereotype of a Russian held by Westerners. He had a bottle of Dovgan vodka sitting on his camp desk, and he continued eating pork chops as if they were cookies on a stick, smacking his lips as he tore the meat from the bone.

Severov said, "Sir, I don't understand. I'm a tanker, not Spetsnaz. I have a company to administer. I have been lining up my tanks for days and making sure they have plenty to eat and are well covered from satellite surveillance."

The jolly colonel said, "Listen, Anton, you need to see this for what it is. You being asked to do this is an honor. It actually makes sense for a change. There's little enough of that in the army."

"But a scout? In civilian clothes? Isn't that something intelligence should do? What good is the GRU?"

The colonel's eyes shifted in both directions, and he lowered his voice. "Don't talk like that, Anton. The fact is you were told to do this and you're going to do a good job."

"If I'm not in uniform, I could be shot as a spy."

"That's the beauty of the European Union. No one knows where you came from or where you're supposed to be. A German will think you're a Pole, a Pole will think you're Ukrainian. And besides, you're going to have someone with you that's supposed to speak several languages."

Severov still wasn't convinced and stared off into space as he tried to find a new angle on this assignment. All he had ever done was arrange tanks in attack formation and fire the main gun. His dream was to meet NATO soldiers on an open battlefield, not creep around towns and villages dressed like a tourist.

The colonel said, "Relax, Anton, you could have fun. You eat some good food, meet pretty girls. You'll be traveling with someone as soon as you cross the border. I'm told your contact will be with you for several days. Just scout out what routes are acceptable to the tanks and supply train and look for possible resistance. You're the perfect choice. An intelligence officer won't know where a T-90 can go or if a building would house enough soldiers."

Severov said, "I could walk all of Estonia in a few days. Why so long?"

"You think too small, my boy. This trip could take you into Poland or perhaps even Germany. With the price of oil plunging like it is, no telling what we might need to do to survive. This is what drove the breakup of our great Soviet Union. We had nothing to sell but our oil. At least now we have leaders that are looking to the future and figuring out how to avoid another disaster."

Severov just stared at him. Then he mumbled in a low voice, "We might go into Germany?"

"I'm telling you we're on the verge of history."

"Has anybody in command read history? The last time we tangled with the Germans it almost didn't work out well. If it weren't for the Americans, we'd be speaking German right now."

The colonel put on his paternal act again and chuckled. "Anton, you're a good soldier. Do your duty. You're a good-looking, single young man. Have some fun for a change. I'll have Lieutenant Poola take over your company. He's quite a competent but humorless new officer."

"Poola! The Georgian? He's a Muslim."

"We have almost seventeen million Muslims as citizens. They do their duty just like everyone else."

Severov didn't want to look like a sullen schoolchild, so he sat up straight and tried not to sulk. He didn't like it, but he'd do it. It wasn't as if he had a choice.

Walsh had given Charlie a little more cash and sent him the other direction, away from the growing chaos. The last thing he wanted was his elderly friend getting caught up in a riot. He jogged for the entrance to his building and made it past several of the shouting protesters. The keypad on the courtyard entrance was disabled, and one of the security guards had to unlock the huge glass doors to let him into the lobby. The young Hispanic man, whose name was Hector, gave him an odd look. Walsh gave his usual greeting and passed the man and another guard on his way to the elevator.

He couldn't help checking his phone again as the elevator doors shut. Now the Dow was down almost eight hundred points. That was scary.

On the thirty-first floor, he turned down the wide hallway into the office that held his cubicle. He was barely looking ahead as he kept scrolling through the information on his phone. Once he was in the office he looked up and felt like every eye in the office was fixed on him. Maybe they didn't realize he was *supposed* to be late today. The brightly lit office was augmented by the tall glass windows with the sun streaming through. Now a few of the other workers had turned to look out the windows at the protesters. Another police car had been flipped over, and six cops were backing up in the face of aggressive protesters armed with boards and pieces of a crushed police cruiser. A helicopter buzzed low overhead.

His boss, Ted Marshall, looked grave. The portly Northwestern grad was not his usually jovial self.

Walsh stopped and said, "What's going on, Ted?"

Ted gave him a funny look and said, "Have you been living on the moon the last twelve hours?"

"No, but I don't live here."

Ted, always trying to be the diplomat, said, "Cheryl will handle this. You need to talk to her."

"Handle what?" He was about to ask exactly what was going on when Cheryl, dressed as usual in an immaculate pantsuit, motioned him over toward her office. She was a pretty woman in her early forties, but her no-nonsense approach and brusque manner made her seem much older. She was the perfect enforcer for Ted.

The blinds on Cheryl's office were pulled down. As he stepped through the door he saw a tall, attractive black woman about his age standing with an older, plump white guy fighting a losing battle against a receding hairline. The woman watched Walsh with sharp eyes like a hawk about to dive on an injured bird. The man seemed tired and possibly bored. All Walsh could think of was that they were auditors of some type. Great.

Cheryl shut the door behind him and wasted no time saying, "Derek, these folks are from the FBI."

He offered a hand. The man ignored him, but the woman took it and said, "Tonya Stratford."

"Nice to meet you."

"Take a seat."

He hesitated, wondering if he should ask some questions first.

The FBI agent added in a calm voice, "Now."

The command reminded him of the marines. He just followed orders.

6

Derek Walsh leaned forward in the awkward rolling chair he had plopped into ten minutes earlier. He was still in his supervisor's office, which Cheryl kept immaculate. There were books on marketing and management lining the top row of the shelf behind her wide modern desk. A copy of Jack Welch's *Winning* lay on her desk like a Bible. This was the first time he had thought Cheryl might have delusions of grandeur, thinking that she could move from supervisor at a financial house to head of a major corporation through her management skills, which mainly came down to her making fun of people until they did their job.

Now all of his attention turned to Tonya Stratford. Her dark complexion framed very sharp brown eyes that felt like lasers. He realized she was studying him as much as he was studying her. The woman knew finance, and he could tell she was not used to people evading her questions.

Walsh didn't want to seem like an idiot. He recognized he was sitting silently with his mouth open. Finally he was able to say, "You think I did what?" He didn't have to fake any outrage. It was all boiling up. He was still scared, but now he was pissed off as well.

Stratford's partner, whose name was Frank Martin, sat like a pudgy, middle-aged pet, watching everything unfold but not appearing to understand what was being said.

Tonya Stratford repeated her first statement. "According to your company's records, six nights ago at 7:50 P.M. Eastern Standard Time several transfers were made on your ID from your computer. I'm asking if you have any explanation for why you made the trades at almost eight o'clock at night."

Walsh tried to keep his voice from cracking. "For how much?"

"The total is a little more than a hundred and eighty million."

Walsh raised a hand and started to wave it in front of him. "I've never made a trade that big. I'd remember. There must be a mistake." The panic started to creep up from his stomach into his chest. How often did someone tell these guys they were having a heart attack?

Tonya Stratford just gave him a look.

Then Walsh started thinking clearly. He snapped his fingers and said, "That was last Tuesday night, right? I wasn't even here. I was on a date. I left at quarter after six."

The FBI agent casually looked over to Walsh's supervisor.

She just raised her hands and said, "I can't swear to that. They all slip out every chance they get. No one wants to be noticed leaving. Probably worse than government work. Am I right?"

Tonya Stratford's look shut her up, too. Then she focused on Walsh again. "According to the logs from your security key, which was in your computer at the time, someone using your password and your computer made the four transfers. A hundred million went to an account in Switzerland, and the rest went to accounts in Asia and one in the Cayman Islands, all owned by the Swiss bank. All the money has been withdrawn. You are now a target of an FBI investigation. Is there anything you don't understand about that, Mr. Walsh?"

Walsh stammered, "What would be the charges?"

"For starters, wire fraud. There's a grand theft in there somewhere, and we'll see what else we might be looking at. I'm not charging you at this minute. It's an investigation. What I'm doing is giving you a fair chance to help yourself."

Cheryl said, "Derek, I think you should probably keep quiet. You need an attorney."

Tonya Stratford calmly turned her head and said to Cheryl, "You need to leave."

"Derek needs representation."

"Are you an attorney?"

"No."

"Then get out." She added a "Now" in a flat tone.

For some reason, Walsh felt the overwhelming need to speak to either Mike Rosenberg or Bill Shepherd. He felt like his friends would know what to say and make him feel better. If they had gotten him through the marines, they could certainly handle a couple of FBI types. But he didn't have his friends. Walsh was alone with the two FBI agents. He knew they could hear his stomach rumble as he considered vomiting. He just didn't think it would help.

Michael Rosenberg sat in the media room watching ten TVs at the same time. This section at the CIA headquarters in Langley monitored news reports and sifted them into usable intelligence. Their duty overlapped with the National Security Agency, but they rarely shared information. Watching the news was a good tactic and resource. Why not let guys like Anderson Cooper or Shepard Smith do the work for you? Each of the big networks had correspondents and news crews all across the world. The problem was that CNN tended to focus on the most video-friendly of issues and ignore any with real substance.

Two TVs in the corner, 55-inch Samsung high-definition units, played the political talk shows from MSNBC and some of the Fox panel shows.

The analyst who tracked these shows did it to get a pulse of what the American people were worried about. Or at least what some of the commentators thought the American people should be worried about.

Rosenberg liked watching the shows when he had a chance and hearing everyone's view. His time in the military had taught him the importance of seeing the big picture. He didn't understand how the different networks decided to hire people. But today it didn't matter because he was only watching a New York channel and CNN as they covered a rising tide of violence and unrest that had started in the financial district of Wall Street and spread across the entire city.

At first it appeared to be just the Stand Up to Wall Street group. An FBI report had indicated that this new group was largely leftovers from Occupy Wall Street. Neither seemed to have a cohesive message or any respected spokesman. As far as Rosenberg could tell they just wanted a reason not to work or pay their own way. He had seen them up close when he visited his friend "Tubby" Walsh in New York. They were a surly group who didn't seem interested in civil interaction. They were clearly the ones who'd started this by trashing a couple of police cars and then spread general mayhem with rocks and bottles.

About an hour ago someone had dropped a hand grenade at the entrance to one of the subway stations and killed eleven people. A few minutes after that, on the other side of the city, gunmen fired fourteen shots into a bus, killing an elderly woman and wounding two children. Somehow it didn't feel all that random to Rosenberg.

He was afraid this all fell in with the new tactic of lone assailant terrorists. They all seemed to be vaguely connected to the group ISIS; at least that's how the media portrayed it. There had been three beheadings in the last two weeks. One in Chicago, one in Kansas City, and the last a schoolteacher in Denver.

In Los Angeles, a ritual severing of the hands of four men accused of being thieves had caused a huge reaction from the Latino population. The men all survived and told the tale of a Muslim shopkeeper who had branded them shoplifters. The next thing they knew, a van with three masked men had scooped them up, and a few minutes later they were left to bleed on the sidewalk.

The final piece of the puzzle, as far as Rosenberg was concerned, was the attacks on tourist attractions across the country. The Liberty Bell, the Atlanta Aquarium, and the Lincoln Memorial had all seen violence in the past week. It made him think of a couple of attacks his unit had suffered in Afghanistan. At least his friends were there to help. Now, even though he still worked for the U.S. government, Rosenberg felt all alone as he watched the world disintegrate.

Rosenberg recognized it was one thing to study trends in terrorism, or even watch it on newscasts, and it was another to experience it first-hand. He had seen the results in a couple of the cities in Iraq and Afghanistan, but the closest he ever came was in their forward operating base outside the village of Landigal in Afghanistan. The marines would venture out to strike at insurgents deep in the heart of the Korengal Valley and pull back to the base for resupply. The longer they were there, the more they worked with the local population. His unit even provided protection to the UN medical personnel who vaccinated everyone in the vicinity.

But one evening, in the middle of the base, during a lull in the fighting that had lasted more than two months, when no one was expecting it, trouble had started. Rosenberg was just coming out of the small mess tent with Bill Shepherd at his side and Ron Jackson telling them the story about his football prowess in college. No one bothered to remind Ron that he had told the story before, always with a different, more spectacular ending.

The first sound of gunfire was so close it shocked them all into statues. As always, it was Jackson's measured response that got them moving. He immediately pushed the others to the side and started to look for a weapon.

Shepherd was ready to act that moment and pulled the sidearm he had in a flap holster on his right hip.

Rosenberg, as always, assessed the situation. There were two very young Afghans who had gotten hold of M-4 rifles. The fact that they weren't using AK-47s meant that they had already been inside the compound and were probably trusted by someone. Rosenberg knew these attacks from supposed allies had happened at other bases, but it was still startling to be in the middle of one.

He saw his friend Derek Walsh coming from the side of the supply depot he was responsible for. He was running toward the sound of gunfire and had an M-4 in his hands. Rosenberg considered shouting a warning that he was about to run up on the two shooters, but just then a third man, dressed as a traditional Afghan, wearing a giant backpack, started running toward the command post from the other side of the supply tent. A suicide bomber would cause havoc.

Then Rosenberg was shocked when he saw the man run past Walsh just as they both reached the front of the supply tent. Walsh reached up without hesitation and grabbed hold of the pack. The rail-thin Afghan's momentum and Walsh's sheer size jerked the pack from the man's back and sent Walsh tumbling to the ground.

Return fire from someone near the front of the command post cut all three intruders down instantly.

Walsh sat on the ground holding the pack in one hand and the M-4 raised up looking for more targets in the other. It was the most heroic thing Rosenberg had ever seen anyone do. And he was glad the man who did it was his friend.

At the CIA, on the TV farthest from him, Rosenberg could see that the violence was having a serious effect on the stock market. It had drifted lower over the past week and now, just after eleven o'clock in the morning, it was in absolute freefall. The word "crash" came to his mind.

He wondered how his friend Derek Walsh was handling it.

Major Bill Shepherd was watching the international news as he pulled out a few reports and got a handle on who was on leave and who was at the base. The marine detachment there was used for several tasks. Mainly the Special Forces unit trained with the smaller NATO countries like

Estonia and Hungary. They taught the local soldiers how to use certain portable weapons and gauged what kind of use they would be in a real conflict. Aside from Germany, France, and England, no one would be a great help in a large-scale conflict, but on a limited basis, the smaller countries had some decent fighters.

Even with Russian military exercises occurring near Estonia, no order to go on alert had come down. He agreed that keeping troops on alert caused stress and reduced their battle readiness if it went on too long, but this was a cost analysis. It was too expensive to keep them on alert. It went all the way back to leadership in the U.S., which was lacking by any standard. Shepherd read as much history as anyone on the planet. He recognized that a military was meant to scare, as well as fight. Russia had been held in check for decades by the idea of what the U.S. and NATO might do. Now, after the debacle in Crimea, it was obvious that NATO was simply a hollow threat. Their big move was to station twelve F-16s in Estonia, along with some older armor. That was it. With no hint of repercussions, there was no telling how far Russia might go.

Shepherd had stepped back but had not stood down. It was a slight and technical distinction. He was giving his companies two days off on a rotating basis. The time also allowed him to decompress, recognizing that a leader must rest and take care of himself if he's going to act properly on the battlefield. He'd called the woman he met last week, Fannie. He thought he could work her into his dating rotation. His quick check on the Internet showed she had worked in finance and was from France. There weren't any new posts from businesses in the past two years, so he figured she had a steady job and had not switched around at all. Maybe that meant he could finally go out with a woman who might pay for dinner. She answered her cell phone last night but was on a business trip somewhere in Switzerland. So far he'd only had one quick dinner with her, but she seemed like a winner. Beautiful, charming, and smart. Just the thought of her pretty face put him in a good mood.

A news story on CNN caught his attention, and he glanced up at the TV set in the corner of his office. Everyone seemed to be disturbed about a new financial issue back in the States. One of the big houses was accused of sending hundreds of millions of dollars to bank accounts used by terrorists. That's all they needed: another financial crisis and terrorists with money to spend on operations. The name of the company, Thomas Brothers Financial, rang a bell. He thought that was where Derek Walsh was working. Maybe if he had time later on today he'd call Walsh and Mike Rosenberg. It was one way to keep his mind off the loss of his friend Ron Jackson.

Fannie Legat had not slept in two days. Once the money had come in from New York, she had disbursed it quickly. The U.S. government was able to freeze accounts far too swiftly. The other members of her network needed money to carry out operations and to survive. It was nice to show them how thoroughly she could deliver. She wanted to teach some of these fundamentalists that women were just as valuable as men in most situations. She followed the teachings of Mohammed as closely as her comrades and realized women had played a strong role in the Prophet's life, as well as in the advancement of Islam ever since.

She had spent almost two days making all of the transfers out of the account. It was a long and complicated assignment, and she had to prioritize where the money went.

The backwoods group Boko Haram received over $800,000. They did little to help Islam and were no threat to most governments, but they tended to grab headlines and keep the world's attention focused away from more productive groups who were preparing for major attacks. The path to a new world order. An Islamic order. What the African group lacked in education they made up for in creativity. Kidnapping schoolgirls and threatening religious orders always got the attention of the Western press, no matter how much it actually affected world politics. They had also publicly pledged their loyalty to the Islamic State.

More than $20 million had gone right back into New York City, where it would be disbursed among a number of cells. Most of these were one- or two-man operations, who were directed to start causing as much havoc as possible, building to a crescendo over the next three days. Fannie vaguely recognized that they were trying to harness the power of the mobs that had been protesting financial institutions in New York.

She had sent nearly $40 million to a number of different accounts to pay greedy bankers and European officials who turned a blind eye to her activities. She thought it was ironic that their effort to keep a distance from the transactions would ultimately be their downfall.

Now all the money was moved and she had proven her value. No one questioned the wisdom of having a woman in such an important role anymore. She wanted to take another step up the ladder and prayed that Allah would forgive her ambition. Looking at the Swiss bank building out her hotel window and knowing what would happen as soon as she got the signal made her smile in anticipation.

7

Putin had listened to all of Simplov's news, so now he shared his own interpretation of what was about to happen.

Putin said, "We are deploying our forces at the northern end of the border so that we can conceal them more easily from satellite detection. The force is relatively small and will move quickly once we cross the Narva River. I want it made clear that we are entering Estonia at the request of some of their leaders and will liberate the ethnic Russians who live there.

"This will be as fast an operation as we've ever conducted. That's what I am counting on. What we need to happen is that NATO makes the decision to save its resources and not risk a larger conflict over Estonia. Everything that I have picked up from my dealings with the Germans and the French is that they are not confident in American leadership. That leads me to believe we can do this quick strike, install the right man as president, and once again have a reliable satellite on our Western border."

"And if your assessment is wrong?"

Putin scowled at him briefly. This was one of the few men who could challenge him. But he did appreciate Simplov's grasp of the situation.

"If I am wrong," Putin said, "which I doubt, the force is small enough that we will simply turn it and recross the border. At that point we'll come up with a story about rescuing a specific family who was being mistreated by the Estonians. Something like that. There will be some loss of face, but we could overcome it."

Putin stepped to the window and looked out over the lighted fields outside the parlor located on the eastern side of the palace. "Look at how the U.S. and NATO responded to our adventure in Crimea. They did nothing to stop us. If Ukraine weren't a political and economic nightmare, we could roll in there as well."

"But who would want Ukraine?" Yuri asked.

"Exactly," Putin said. "So this is a test, a probe. We cannot lock ourselves into a course of action that can't be changed. Still, once this has started, we must be committed."

"We better be," Yuri said, "if we are to take on NATO."

"Which did nothing to prevent us from annexing Crimea," Simplov said, "and they will do nothing now."

Putin was aroused by the possibility of going to war.

Derek Walsh appreciated how suddenly Tonya Stratford had escorted him out of the Thomas Brothers building. It was professional and efficient, and she had not handcuffed him in front of his coworkers. It appealed to his marine's sensibilities, but it still meant he was in trouble. Real trouble.

He'd thought about calling an attorney but decided he could still explain this whole thing and save himself a tremendous expense. He was already short of cash, and having a lawyer suck down what little he had didn't appeal to him. Once they were someplace secure they would let him explain what happened and look at his evidence to support his claim.

As soon as they walked through the main entrance and saw the crowds fighting with police, Agent Stratford wasted no time turning Walsh around and handcuffing him behind his back. That was what she'd told him all along would happen. She was businesslike and polite but not particularly friendly. That was still a huge step up from her partner, who seemed more interested in being a bully.

They were able to reach an unmarked Ford Crown Victoria and speed a few blocks to the building holding the NYPD Seventh Precinct offices. The two-story redbrick building faced Pitt Street and had the boxy, efficient style that the precinct serving Wall Street demanded. The agents wasted no time hustling him through the rear door, where they obviously had an understanding with the uniformed sergeant who was waiting. Even the short distance from the vehicle to the door gave Walsh time to hear the shouts of protesters in front of the building. A bottle flew over the wall in the parking lot, and the sturdy-looking, middle-aged sergeant snarled at them to get inside quickly.

A few minutes later they were in a private interview room, and Walsh found himself still handcuffed and sitting in a stiff plastic chair. The room was stark and bare except for three of those chairs and a small table. Tonya Stratford had left with a small envelope of his belongings, and her partner just sat silently, staring at him. Walsh had no interest in engaging the man in conversation. But it was still unnerving. In the car, on the way over to the police station, Walsh had tried to explain that it couldn't have been him making the transactions. He'd stayed calm and reasonable, but every one of his statements was met with more accusing questions, and he had a clear sense that he was the only suspect. He wasn't certain whether they were looking at the simple theft or some kind of treason for dealing with people outside the United States, specifically the terrorists they had mentioned having access to the account. This was crazy, and the FBI had to realize it soon.

Walsh again considered calling an attorney. Things had already gone further than he thought they would. The male FBI agent, Frank Martin, didn't want to listen, but Walsh had the sense that Agent Stratford was open to reason.

His brief stint in combat hadn't been this upsetting. At least there he was with his friends. Now he was isolated. He couldn't even talk to one of his Thomas Brothers associates like Ted Marshall. He'd know what to do, or maybe not. For all Walsh knew, Ted assumed he had stolen the money and never wanted to see him again. He did appreciate that Cheryl had tried to help him at the end until she was ejected from her own office.

It was past noon when Tonya Stratford slipped back into the interview room. He was waiting for some more sharp questions about derivatives and how he initiated transfers. It was abundantly clear that she knew the finance world and probably had been employed by one of the big houses at one time.

Now she sat next to the small table and pulled out a pad. She asked him a series of seemingly innocuous questions about his usual workdays and duties.

Finally Walsh had to look at her and say, "Were you in banking?"

She glanced up from her pad and folded her hands across the table. "The FBI recruits across all disciplines." She cut her eyes across to the semiconscious agent who was supposed to be helping her, Frank.

Walsh said, "Where'd they get him? A loan-sharking operation?"

Suddenly Frank was completely awake and said in a gravelly voice with a thick Bronx accent, "Don't you worry about me, smart guy. You need to come clean and let us help you, because you're a hair's width away from a lifetime in Leavenworth. You're a former military man, you should understand that."

Tonya directed Walsh's attention back to her as she reached into the envelope and carefully pulled out the security plug in the clear plastic sleeve by its nylon lanyard. "Tell me about this?"

He cocked his head because he knew she knew already. "I told you before, it's the security plug required to make any serious trades. I don't always use it. In fact, I try to carry it in my pocket most of the time."

"And this was in your computer the day you made the trades?"

"I keep telling you I didn't make any trades. I think I used it to check an escrow account in Europe on a deal we are facilitating, but no trades or transfers."

"Sorry, the day the trades were made this plug would've had to be in your computer. Is that correct?"

He was tired, and it was catching up to him. He just nodded. An idea popped into his head. "I activated one of the extra security protocols. It would've made the computer's camera take a photo during the trade and store it on the plug." This could solve the whole puzzle. He really didn't need an attorney.

The agents exchanged skeptical looks.

Then Walsh said, "If you stick that plug back in my computer, you'll be able to bring up photographs of whoever used the computer when the trades were made. I set up the protocols myself."

Agent Stratford stood from the chair, looked at Walsh for a moment, then stepped out of the room, with the plug dangling from its lanyard in her right hand.

Suddenly he had a sinking feeling that he was screwed and they weren't going to listen to him with or without an attorney.

Joseph Katazin wasted no time once he was on the East River Esplanade. It was a convenient meeting place for his contact, not far from the United Nations. There was a concern about surveillance from U.S. intelligence services, but during an operation like this, where communication could be crucial, they had set up a regular schedule so that Katazin could meet the contact as necessary. Otherwise the contact would just read the newspaper and have a cup of coffee looking out over the East River.

As usual, Katazin sat on the bench next to him and made no direct eye contact. There was no one close by. There rarely was in the morning. Today Katazin just wanted to make sure all was as it appeared to be on the operation and to express his concerns once more.

His contact was an older man whose cover was working as a translator at the UN. Katazin didn't know exactly what the man's real job was, but he was certainly connected and could get things done.

The pudgy older man, dressed comfortably in a cardigan sweater, spoke in flawless Russian. "You have done well my friend. Everyone is impressed."

Katazin had a hard time hiding his grin because this was not news to him. "I didn't realize how destructive the protesters could be. I've seen things get out of hand on the news before in Baltimore or St. Louis, but this was a new experience. They tied up every police officer in the city. It worked beyond my wildest dreams."

"Then what brings you to talk to me this morning?"

"I guess just general anxiety."

The man chuckled. "Joseph, all you have to worry about is what happens here in Manhattan. You had the trades made as instructed. The money moved perfectly and has funded a number of activities. You've had the protesters deliver as promised, and aside from not eliminating the Thomas Brothers employee, everything has been perfect."

"My source close to the situation said Derek Walsh is in FBI custody. He knows nothing that can compromise us. As long as he is in custody, I'm not worried. I would prefer that he was dead and the authorities thought it was a suicide, but this will work."

His contact nodded his head as he looked out over the East River. "Of the entire operation, I think the financial aspect has been most underappreciated. The cascading effect of having the markets crash and the news of the transfer of money to a terrorist account has been remarkable. The crash is mainly due to an algorithm we had introduced to the New York and London stock exchanges. It cost a fortune to have the hacker create the algorithm and then insert it into the systems so computer trading started selling at an exponential rate, but it was worth every penny."

Katazin said, "I'm not entirely happy with our partners in this endeavor."

"The Islamic extremists concern you? They concern everyone. But the Americans and Europeans seem to focus on them more than anyone. By promoting these lone wolf attacks we are essentially playing on Western fears. It costs us nothing and completely diverts the West's attention from our military ambitions in the East. Once we feel the protests and the terror attacks have wreaked enough havoc in the West, our military will cross the Narva River into Estonia, and no one will lift a finger. By the time anyone realizes we have occupied another country, it will be far too late to take action."

"So you're not concerned that the Muslims could turn on us?"

"Of course the Muslims will turn on us. But probably not for a while. At least this way we get some use out of them before they turn their wrath on us. Keep doing what you're doing, and I will be available if anything serious occurs."

Katazin just nodded as he stood up from the bench and casually headed to the walkway that led up toward the FDR.

Mike Rosenberg continued to watch the news in amazement as the violence across the country seemed to grow by the minute. It was early evening in Europe, and they were having issues as well. The New York Stock Exchange had stopped computer trading, and the word "crash" was being spewed by every financial nerd the networks could round up.

He really wanted to call Derek Walsh to see if he could get an inside scoop, but he recognized Thomas Brothers had so many employees, his friend probably didn't even know who was involved. He could picture Walsh saying, "I don't know shit." Rosenberg would reply, "As usual." Just the idea of the conversation made him laugh out loud. He missed his friends. Especially Ron Jackson.

After a few minutes, he decided he'd call Bill Shepherd. Maybe he could shed some light on what was going on.

8

Derek Walsh was hungry but didn't want to admit it to either of the FBI agents in the small interview room. Frank Martin had barely spoken since they sat down, and Tonya Stratford had come and gone from the room four times and was now working on some notes she had scribbled down on her legal pad. There was a light knock on the door, and a young woman opened it tentatively. She stepped over to Tonya and whispered something in her ear as she handed her a plastic bag. Walsh could see that it was an evidence bag containing his security plug.

Tonya looked up and said, "You can't remember using this plug since last week?"

"I did not use it. I can specifically remember *not* using it. You can check my computer log, and it will show you all the transactions I've made. The last thing I did with it was check an escrow account."

"You do realize we're not some local sheriff's office. We seized your computer and have been searching the entire network at Thomas Brothers. To say they are unhappy with you would be a monumental understatement."

"But I didn't do anything wrong."

"Regardless, the stock market has reacted to the news of the loss, and markets around the world are plunging. It looks like you're responsible for the biggest single loss in the history of finance. At least that's something you can hang your hat on."

Walsh tried to fathom that. Something was going on that was bigger than a few trades. He could feel it. The idea of a conspiracy came into his head. He looked at the two FBI agents. Were they a part of it? Told to make an arrest no matter what? He started considering his options.

They had uncuffed him earlier when Martin had no interest in helping him go to the bathroom. No one had bothered to secure his hands again, so now he let his head drop into them.

Tonya said, "So where do you usually carry the plug?"

He lifted his hands, incensed that it felt like she was listening to the story for the first time. "Usually in a coat pocket, but occasionally I hang it around my neck like a necklace."

"But you don't remember handling the plug? Taking it out of its sleeve?"

"I don't think so."

"Do you use gloves when you handle the plug?"

"Of course not." Then he thought to ask, "Why?"

"Because a cursory check found no fingerprints of any kind on the plug. It looked like someone had wiped it clean. Even if it'd been in your coat pocket, in its plastic sleeve, there would be fragments of a print somewhere on the plug."

Walsh wasn't sure if that helped him or hurt him.

Agent Stratford's partner spoke up. "This is bullshit. All a smoke screen. He made the trades, and he thinks we're stupid enough to believe anything he shows us. We can see photos from that plug all day long, but they don't mean squat. This son of a bitch can make it look like he wasn't involved, but he had to be. That's all we need for now. We need an arrest first, then we can figure out what was done. Let's just book this asshole and be on our way."

Agent Stratford eyed her partner but didn't say anything.

Walsh could see she agreed, at least partly, with her partner. Now he needed to ask for an attorney. It was past the point of what it cost or if it made him look guilty. He was about to be railroaded. The only problem was that a lawyer wouldn't stop that. It sounded like Walsh was going to jail no matter what happened. He was starting to get the sense that this was a well-orchestrated plot. He didn't want to use the word, "conspiracy," but it seemed to fit.

There was a surge of noise outside, and he heard glass shattering. The door burst open, and a young uniformed patrolman shouted, "Everyone to the other end of the building. We can no longer maintain security here."

Walsh offered no resistance. He followed Agent Stratford out the door and down the crowded hallway, with Agent Martin directly behind him. In the rear of the building he could hear shouting and more glass breaking. In the distance, outside the building, he heard the clear sound of gunfire.

Did people really think this was his fault? He needed to do something. Anything.

Fannie Legat had used some of the money she was moving around to rent a hotel room four blocks from the Swiss Credit and Finance building on Bundesstrasse in Bern, Switzerland. The ornate building with carved columns and decorative windows had stood for more than 120 years as a testament to the Swiss commitment to banking. It was a major player in international finance, just like Thomas Brothers in New York. This particular office was open twenty-four hours a day to stand as a link between the major financial markets from Tokyo to New York. This was one of the hubs of the financial world, rivaling Credit Suisse.

The room was clean and adequate but certainly not luxurious. The small cell phone that sat on the table before her had a number entered and was merely waiting for someone to send it. That signal would travel to a somewhat complex explosive device, or more accurately *devices*, located throughout the first and second floors of the building. It had cost $2.3 million to bribe the contractor to hire four Brothers of Islam for a major remodeling job. One, a graduate of Cambridge, with a degree in engineering, had carefully placed sizable chunks of C-4 in the support columns across the entire building. They were also wrapped around key energy components of the building, and the engineer had assured Fannie that the resulting explosion would not only be spectacular but would bring the entire building down upon itself.

This was vital for several reasons. First, an algorithm had been introduced into a number of the major financial markets via a computer within that building. She felt the algorithm was the main contribution of their new allies. It caused financial institutions to think the market was crashing and pushed them to sell immediately. Second, the man she had paid to do that was still in the building, and third, the bank stood for everything she was against. It only dealt with the wealthy, ignored the plight of the poor, and worst of all was hypocritical to its core.

She watched silently as the rising moon reflected off the top-floor windows. Her hand slid across the table and slowly picked up the cell phone. Compared to what she had done the last few days, this was easy. She flipped open the phone and looked up at the building again.

Fannie paused and picked up a pair of high-powered Zeiss binoculars. She focused on the front of the building along the sidewalk and saw a young woman pushing a stroller with a small child dressed in a green all-weather jacket walking alongside.

This was no time for sentiment, but she hesitated just the same.

Still in the Seventh Precinct, Walsh followed Stratford along the busy corridor, and when they paused in a small waiting room with a dozen metal chairs, one of the cops looked at her and said, "Is this the asshole who caused all this?" The statement and the emotion behind it made Walsh realize how much shit he was in. This was not a game, and he was not about to talk anyone out of arresting him. He was the only suspect, and there wasn't anyone who could help him if he was locked up. He needed to get out and somehow get that plug into a computer hooked into the Thomas Brothers network.

The crowd pushed harder and forced them into the main lobby, where he could catch glimpses through the front door of the chaos erupting outside. Then the doors seemed to explode, and a metal garbage can tumbled into the lobby, making more noise than a politician filibustering a bill.

The clamor startled the two FBI agents, who instinctively put themselves between the front door and Walsh. He appreciated the sentiment, even if it only meant they didn't want him to make a run for it.

A burly young man with blond dreadlocks forced his way through the front door holding up a garbage can lid. A cop at the front door tried to pull the lid away from him, and while they were struggling, a second cop swung an ASP collapsible baton and struck the young man in the leg. As soon as he went to the ground, two more men forced their way in. All of them had the dingy look of Stand Up to Wall Street protesters. Now there were more pouring through the door, and the cops were starting to back up. Gunshots echoed from outside, and for the first time Walsh was starting to worry about their personal safety.

The FBI agents slowly edged back and pushed him into the corner of the lobby. His view was obstructed, but it sounded like more and more protesters were floating through the front door. Then he noticed the plastic evidence bag sticking out of the side pocket of Tonya Stratford's jacket.

This might be an opportunity.

Fannie Legat watched the front of the bank building. There were more people than she'd expected at this time in the evening, but the only one she really cared about was the woman with the two small children. Then she considered the area around the bank and realized there was a pastry shop on one side and a park near the other side. This was just a night owl who was giving her kids a chance to play before bed. Maybe burn up some energy.

She couldn't allow children in front of the bank to affect her judgment. It was her job to act and act right now. She gave little thought to the thirty or forty people working inside the building. She had already written them off as casualties of war. Some of them might be innocent, at least of crimes against Muslims. But certainly some of them would deserve to perish in the fire and rubble that the bank building was about to become. It would also make any subsequent investigation into the computer hacking and the transfer of money that much more difficult. In addition, it would be just one more thing for the Western media to focus on.

She chewed on her lower lip, a habit she had developed in primary school. Her mother said it would ruin her beautiful smile and used to make her suck a lemon when she did it. But Fannie still reverted to the old habit when stress started to rise in her.

The woman seemed to be lingering at the front of the building for no particular reason. A man walked by, and she chatted with him briefly. Fannie couldn't wait any longer. She let the binoculars drop slightly and focused on the face of the child next to the woman. She was too far away to make out much detail but saw that it was a girl with blond hair that danced in the wind.

She set down the binoculars with her right hand and picked up the phone with her left. She started her countdown. Three . . . Two . . . Before she could consciously think of the word "One," the woman started to stroll farther down the street, and Fannie took a deep breath to clear her mind. Within twenty seconds the woman was on her way past the bank building and toward the park. There were several others who had now entered her view, but none of them were children. She could see a heavyset woman with a blue coat and more than one man in a business suit. This was it. She pressed the SEND button and leveled the binoculars at the gaudy building.

At the sign of the first flash she knew this would set back investigators looking into her transactions for weeks.

Derek Walsh looked in each direction and realized no one was paying any attention to him. Everyone was focused on the danger at the front of the room. The sound of gunfire from outside only intensified people's attention, and several of the uniformed officers pulled their service weapons.

He lifted his right hand slowly and edged it toward the plastic evidence bag sticking out of Tonya Stratford's jacket pocket. He had no idea what he was going to do with it if he even reached it, but someone had to take control of the security plug. He couldn't fathom a conspiracy that reached inside the FBI, but they weren't there to help him, either. The idea of fleeing the scene to reconsider his options had a certain appeal that grew every minute he was in the police station. But before he did anything he had to get hold of the plug.

Just as he was about to put his fingers on it, the FBI agent moved to her left and dropped her left arm.

Walsh had to snatch back his hand. He stood up straight and took a breath just as Agent Stratford turned around to look at him. She was just making sure he wasn't doing anything stupid. For the moment he provided her with the illusion that he was not.

Then he took another shot at the evidence bag. This time his fingers closed on it, and he started to pull back slowly at first, then a little faster.

She shifted to one side, and he pulled the bag completely out of her pocket, but then it slipped from his grasp, bounced off the FBI agent's leg, and ended up on the ground. There was no way he could reach it without drawing attention to himself.

Walsh tried to ease the clear plastic bag closer to him with his foot. Now there was a surge forward as the protesters were pushed back out of the lobby. He followed Stratford and Martin while casually leaning forward and scooping up the evidence bag. He jammed it into his left front pocket, then shifted slightly so he was off to the left of the FBI agents. Then an opportunity hit him square in the face. One he couldn't ignore. It fueled his idea to flee.

Just as several protesters forced their way back inside, Walsh turned and walked into the hallway they had come from. It was not as crowded as before, and, dressed in a clean white shirt and acting official, he looked like he belonged there. He walked with his head held high and nodded hello to a couple of the cops who were coming from the rear of the building. The biggest vibe he got was that the cops thought he was some kind of coward running away from the action. Walsh could live with that.

In less than thirty seconds he was walking out the rear door and navigating through the lot where cops were battling more protesters. He acted like he was about to enter one of the brawls but simply slipped around the cop wrestling with an irate female protester with braided hair and a long, patterned dress.

He never knew stepping onto the sidewalk in New York could feel so liberating. He broke into a slight jog, but no one noticed because half the people on the street were running from something.

Now he had to run to the truth.

9

Derek Walsh slowed his pace about fifteen blocks from the Seventh Precinct building. His head was spinning. What had he done? He had acted. That's what he had done. Taken action like the former marine he was. It felt good. He liked standing up to a bully even if it was the U.S. government. Or at least a couple of FBI agents. He had acted on instinct, and now he couldn't have regrets. He had to play this hand out.

Walsh walked along Grand Street into Chinatown and kept going until he came to a stop on Mulberry Street, feeling like he just needed to catch his breath and clear his head. The goddamned FBI had his wallet and cell phone. All he had was a plastic bag holding his security plug from Thomas Brothers Financial. The streets were much more orderly here. No one was protesting, and there was no open violence. His run along Grand Street had showed him the chaos in the financial district. He had intended to use this to his advantage, but there was no way he was heading back right now. Walsh needed a plan, which had to include cash and a change of clothes. He might have blended in along Wall

Street, but here he was as out of place as an Oakland Raiders fan at a Super Bowl.

He had to think and consider his position. The marines had spent a lot of money to train him to react under stress, and it frustrated him that none of that seemed to do him any good at the moment. The only person he could think of to call was Mike Rosenberg at the CIA, but he doubted his friend could help, and he was certain it wouldn't look good for a fugitive to be calling a CIA employee.

A police cruiser came down Mulberry with its lights on but no siren. For a moment Walsh was worried they were searching for him; then he realized they were moving much too quickly and were just more reinforcements going down to the financial district.

Walsh had no idea how any of this had happened or who made the trades on his computer. He didn't think there was any way someone could get past the security plug issue. If someone had stolen his plug and returned it to him, no matter how far-fetched that seemed, then he had to get back on the Thomas Brothers computer network and access his security plug to see the photographs of whoever made the trade.

There was only one place he could go and only one person he could trust. He intended to slip back into his apartment on the Lower East Side and get some money and clothes. Then he would go to Alena's apartment closer to the Columbia campus and explain everything to her. He had to be careful because her phone number was in his phone and there was no telling how far the FBI would dig.

He stood up and started to walk casually along Mulberry Street. Soon enough he'd see his chance to blend in with the crowd, but this was not the place.

Bill Shepherd looked at the gates of the base and decided to call up a platoon of marines to augment the army personnel already dealing with growing crowds of protesters. The occasional rocks and bottles sailed through the air, breaking harmlessly on the asphalt in front of the soldiers. There were German police directly in front of the crowd trying to keep them back, but it wasn't clear who they were trying to protect.

Shepherd had grown more and more concerned as the day went on and he listened to reports on the news. CNN was known for exaggeration, but it looked bad. He had called his new lady friend, Fannie, twice to make sure she was okay as she traveled. It concerned him that he only got a voice message. It was a sign of how interested he was in her that he kept the small German phone in his pocket. He'd purchased it mainly for calling his friends Mike Rosenberg and Derek Walsh. There was something in him, a rebellious spirit, that made him want to keep some of his life private from the Marine Corps. Like his girlfriends. He never talked with them about his work. He'd learned a lesson from what had happened to poor trusting Derek when the cute German girl stole his company credit card. Shepherd missed his friends. Now he felt like he was alone in the Corps.

Just like in combat, he had no real clue what the generals were planning and what the global picture was, but here at his own base, with a threat in front of him, Shepherd knew what was expected of him and how to lead men.

It was hard to imagine that a week ago he was training for a Russian attack and trying to keep his men from being bored. Now a couple of bad financial transactions and terror attacks had caused even more problems than tanks rolling across the Fulda Gap.

He saw some movement in the crowd, and then a light rose up in the twilight sky. It was a Molotov cocktail, and that caused some concern among the men standing before the base. They tracked it as it rose in the air in a small arc, then shattered on the ground, spreading flames in front of them.

Part of the crowd was energized by the act of violence, but Shepherd noticed that several of the protesters didn't want anything to do with it and started to file away from the base.

His marines came jogging up behind him with their weapons at port arms. He held them behind the the army MPs for now, but there was no way anyone was getting on a U.S. military base without feeling some major heat.

Fannie Legat did not stay long to admire her handiwork in Bern. She'd lingered for only a little more than an hour after emergency vehicles converged on the collapsed ruin of the bank, just to make sure none of her intended targets emerged alive from the devastation. No one did, and three rescue workers were killed when one of the remaining arches tumbled over. That was a small matter but would play well on TV. The story had already reached the international markets, and many commentators wanted to tie it to the violence that was growing in New York and London. That was fine with her.

There was no time to rest. First she had to drive to the airport, where she was catching a private plane to Estonia. She was supposed to meet her superior in Tartu late that night to update him. Then she would begin her new assignment, which would start in Estonia and last several days. As usual, she had been given no details other than that her language ability was needed and she'd be helping another person. She was assured it was all part of the same operation and she would see her reward soon.

Joseph Katazin felt invigorated by the meeting with his contact, who clearly had a better overall view of the operation than he did. But now the time had come for him to take an active role. The fact that he had just gotten a call from one of his contacts down at the Seventh Precinct saying Derek Walsh had escaped from custody turned the situation from tense to nerve-racking. There were just too many moving parts of this operation for him to keep clear in his head. Even though his job was to focus on the financial aspect and elements in New York, he still was talking to contacts in Europe to coordinate the timing of events. It went against virtually all of the protocols they had used over the years for secrecy, but someone had decided this operation was important enough to throw caution to the wind.

The phone he was using had been provided by someone from Toronto and had international calling. He had talked to another contact with the country code of Germany to explain when the money was coming in and follow up on a few other details. It was a woman, and she had an odd accent. He knew this operation had made extremely strange bedfellows, but he could've sworn she had a Middle Eastern tinge as well as some French in her English. He knew Muslims were involved in parts of this operation, but the whole idea made him uneasy.

He recognized that the price of oil, which continued to drop, was a real concern to the Arab countries as well as Russia. Russia had no recognized industrial capacity and made nothing that the Koreans or Japanese couldn't make better and cheaper. Who wanted a radio that might or might not have been put together correctly by a pissed-off former Red Army corporal who was working in a factory outside Moscow? Russia needed money from oil and needed it badly. Katazin suspected that was the main reason this entire operation had been given the green light. If they waited too much longer, the Russian economy would be in shambles, and they wouldn't have the power to strike out at other nations. This was the old way of doing things. The Russian way of doing things. Grab up some land, divide the spoils, and look to the next place that could be scooped into the Russian sphere of influence. It also gave a warning to the West that the Russian Empire was not dead.

This operation probably meant nothing in the overall scheme of things. A few hundred million dollars moved here or there and some attacks that would kill perhaps a hundred people at most. But it was all a simple distraction. Everything that happened, including the riots and the events unfolding in Europe, was meant to distract the president of the United States, like throwing a ball for a puppy to chase. While he was looking at these issues, thinking they were important, the real intent of Russia would be out of sight and out of mind. It wouldn't be until tanks were rolling through European capitals that the president would react and the U.S. take any action at all. At that point, at least to Katazin, it seemed unlikely they would be able to act militarily. And everyone had seen the effects of sanctions. Iran still went forward with its nuclear plants, and North Korea flaunted any sanctions leveled against them. Even the Gulf Wars were the result of failed sanctions. People liked to talk about the alternatives to war, but the fact was that sovereign nations rarely responded to anything but the threat of brute force. All that was necessary was to stoke the flames of patriotism and make sure the public was behind the government's efforts to use military force. The Russians had been looking for anything to be proud of, and an operation like this would bring out their patriotic spirit.

Patriotism was an odd thing. Just thinking about Russia rising above the other nations of Europe made him proud. He couldn't explain why. He didn't think his life would be any better once his country was a superpower. But he knew he was willing to risk everything, even his American family, to make it happen.

Katazin figured the FBI would be looking for Walsh's apartment. It would be hard to find because he had no lease. Katazin had chosen his patsy well. Generally the FBI was good at finding people, and all he needed was to make sure Walsh was in custody. Or dead. He knew things the FBI didn't know about Derek Walsh, and those were the places he was checking on now. His beat-up BMW sedan wouldn't look out of place in any neighborhood in Manhattan. It was nice enough to belong to a rich man who might have had an accident or two, but it was also dinged up enough to fit a hipster trying to act cool and maybe driving it "ironically."

The Beretta 9 mm he carried in his waistband was the only thing that would get him in real trouble with the New York cops if someone happened to pat him down. But he was a burly white man in Manhattan. No one was going to bother him as he walked down the street or drove his car.

He had waited to call in reinforcements in case he couldn't find Walsh right away. He knew how to use manpower correctly and realized that if Walsh remained missing for any length of time it would be important to have fresh men ready to pursue him.

And this was just one of the things he was worried about.

Fannie Legat stared out the window of the rattling 1999 Yugo cab as it pulled away from the dilapidated airport at Tartu, Estonia. It reminded her of an old World War II film. It almost felt like she was looking at it in black-and-white. Part of it had to do with fatigue, despite the sound sleep she'd grabbed on the plane. A light drizzle and low-hanging clouds did nothing to dispel the grim atmosphere. Twin-engine prop planes littered the tarmac, and the two jets, one from Air France and one from Lufthansa, looked out of place.

The cab driver didn't speak to her when she handed him the slip of paper with the address on it. He dropped her at a café with virtually no one sitting inside. It was the middle of the night, and she wondered how any businesses that served food could be open. She had never met her superior and knew him only as "Sam." She was surprised to meet a good-looking man in his early thirties whose accent gave him away as being raised in London. He wore a business suit with wire-rimmed glasses and could pass for Italian or Spanish unless he was forced to show ID that would surely have a name more consistent with a Middle Easterner.

He greeted her warmly, although she noticed he didn't offer a hand and or touch her in any way. He apparently had little knowledge of exactly what she had done in Bern. But she was gratified to hear him praise her and say that others in their organization had spoken very highly of her. She kept waiting to hear the common phrase "You have done well for a woman." But it never came.

Sam ordered water and a salad with chicken as they chatted in the corner of a big room where no one could possibly hear anything they said. The high wooden ceiling held dozens of fans, and the paneled walls absorbed sound like a sponge. It was simple and ingenious.

Sam said, "Before I get into everything we need to discuss, I'm waiting for one more person."

That surprised her. Usually people in their group met one-on-one. The idea of having self-contained cells and people not knowing other members was vital to the success of their jihad. But these were unusual circumstances. And she recognized they were working with other people and other groups on an operation that had to be gigantic.

She decided not to say anything or voice her concerns about meeting anyone else. Then she saw who it was. Amir Kahmole stepped in the front door and immediately started marching toward their table. She knew Amir from Syria, and he was one of the main reasons she was happy to be out of there. The arrogant fundamentalist viewed women as more of a nuisance than anything else. She was surprised that someone as educated as Sam would be associated with Amir. She was also surprised he cleaned up so nicely and didn't look like a ragged rebel. In casual Western clothes with a cute blue rain slicker, he could've been a student at one of the local universities.

Born in Lebanon but of Iranian decent, Amir wanted a more aggressive stance against the idea of Western corruption and had joined their group. He was an exception to most jihadists. Iran's official policy was to limit ISIS and related groups and support Syria. Amir still held his father's country dear and wouldn't shut up about the Grand Ayatollah, but he was firmly committed to the Islamic State's stance and tactics against the U.S. He was a Shiite who could function with Sunnis. At least on anything that would hurt the West.

He wanted them all dead and was working hard at achieving his goal. That was a classic Iranian move: Be on both sides of a conflict so you win no matter what.

Amir sat down without greeting and looked directly at Sam. "Are we going to speak in front of her?" That was as close to a greeting as Fannie was going to get. She held her tongue but felt like poking Amir through the eye with the steak knife that sat to her right.

Sam calmly said, "In this particular operation you will both be working on the same assignment. I wanted to explain the whole thing one time and for both of you to understand how important it is." He waited while they nodded acknowledgment. Amir still hadn't turned and looked at Fannie. A vein popped in his neck.

After an awkward moment of silence, Amir said, "Will we have to work side by side? Because I would find that inappropriate. She is only a woman and unwed. I shouldn't really have to sit with her now."

Fannie again resisted the impulse to stab him with her knife. Instead she waited to hear Sam's response.

In his cultured English accent, Sam said, "We must work with other groups in this struggle. You will both escort one of our partners. You need only work together in Estonia and possibly further west when we'll need your language ability, Fannie, and your engineering experience, Amir. But you will both be on most of the trip together." He was very calm when he said, "And if you question my judgment again, Amir, you will find yourself in a retraining camp under the supervision of a very strict teacher. Is that understood?"

Amir nodded but added, "It is my duty to explain my concerns before an operation. I feel as if this woman has been given far too much credit and risen too high in the organization, but I understand the need to succeed against the United States and will work with anyone in the world against the Great Satan."

Sam smiled as he looked from Fannie to Amir. "Good, because the man you are meeting is a Russian army officer."

Fannie was shocked, but obviously not as shocked as Amir. The first thing that popped into her head was to call back the American major who had called her. She might find a use for him sooner than she'd thought. It was funny how things worked out so well.

10

Derek Walsh found himself almost stumbling by the time he'd reached Vestry Street in the neighborhood known as SoHo, which started south of Houston Street. He still felt out of place in a sweat stained white shirt, and he had taken several long breaks on his trek from Chinatown and Mulberry Street. He stepped inside a small grocery store and bought a Dr Pepper with the loose change in his pocket. He was using the break to catch his breath and to clear his head. He hadn't seemed to do either successfully.

Several police cars passed him at different times, but all of them were racing along the street with their lights on. A couple of them used their sirens as well, and the drivers focused straight ahead. They looked like more reinforcements headed to a battle.

As he walked along Vestry, he heard an explosion from the direction of Wall Street. It was in the distance, but it was still clear, as was the smell of acrid smoke, which drifted along on a light breeze. He had seen brief reports of what was happening to New York when he ducked into stores and noticed a TV on in the corner, and it was almost impossible to believe. London was suffering worse violence than this, and there had been several terrorist attacks across Western Europe.

Walsh tried to block all of that out of his head and focus on the issues he was facing. How did someone make the trades without his knowledge? How could he get back inside Thomas Brothers and bring up photographs on his security plug? But mainly, for the moment, he just wanted to cover a couple more blocks and get into his apartment to grab some different clothes and the little bit of cash he had on hand. He was pretty confident that the FBI hadn't figured out he had the tiny apartment yet.

He remembered something his friend Mike Rosenberg had said about the FBI being overrated. His lean CIA friend had looked into several law enforcement jobs and had friends with every agency. He said the agents at the Drug Enforcement Administration were the sharpest of all the federal agents. The DEA guys tended to look low key and weren't noticeable in public. They were just as driven and high achieving as the FBI, but they understood what the real world was like. Rosenberg felt the FBI was too stiff and worried about image. He said the FBI had a certain "type." Walsh thought that if Tonya Stratford was the FBI "type," then he was in deep shit. She had proven to be knowledgeable and smart and had a look that could cut through him like a laser. Her partner might not have been as smart, but he seemed to have a certain ruthless quality that would help in looking for someone like Walsh.

Walsh approached his apartment cautiously and stopped on the corner when he noticed a blue Dodge parked across the street from his three-story building. He could just make out a young man with very dark hair sitting in the driver's seat, smoking a cigarette. He was clearly looking across at the apartment building and then scanning the street.

Walsh backed away and considered his options. Just as he was about to turn, someone bumped into him from behind, saying in a loud voice, "Hello there, Derek."

Once they had left their meeting with Sam, Amir had not spoken to Fannie. At least not in words. His look and attitude made it clear that if he had the chance she wasn't going to hold her position much longer. All they had to do was escort some Russian from Estonia down to somewhere south and west.

She hadn't told them about her possible intelligence coup. She had flirted with the handsome army major named Bill Shepherd and even had a lovely dinner with him. She made it clear that once she was done traveling they would spend time together. She knew how most Western men thought, and he definitely believed she meant they would spend time in bed together. But the sight of him sickened her, and all she could think about was getting him to spill his secrets, either in the privacy of the bedroom or under great duress. Either way, he'd be able to tell them things they couldn't get anywhere else.

She hadn't bothered to return his calls, but he left two messages and sounded sincerely worried about her safety as violence bloomed across the continent. Now that she knew her assignment as a guide with a Russian, she was certain she knew what was planned, and she could take advantage of her encounter with the American. If the Russians were such a big part of this operation, the Americans would be, too. She took a moment to call him back and leave a quick message on his cell phone saying she missed him and hoped to see him soon, but she was absolutely safe. She hoped that was true. It was odd that while she fought against one of the most powerful nations on earth, her greatest fear was being murdered by one of her comrades.

Fannie couldn't sleep and decided to explore Tartu, the second-largest city in the country, but more of a quaint town by Western standards. It had none of the traffic of Berlin or Stuttgart and none of the elegance of Paris, but it didn't have tourists or smog, either. It was almost as if it hadn't ever left the old Soviet Union's influence. Beat-up Voleex hatchbacks and Yugos sputtered along the narrow streets, and heavy people with no regard for fashion shuffled along the broken sidewalks.

Fannie had to admit it felt a little bit like a slap in the face to go from planning large financial transactions to acting as an escort for some

Russian army officer. The only consolation was that Amir had to feel even worse about it. His father had fought against the Russians in Afghanistan as a foreign fighter, and Amir had no use for either of the world's major powers.

An alliance with Russia made sense even if it did go against the group's long-term goals. For years Russia had been a target of jihadists. There was no great love for the former empire. But the group's progress against the U.S. had been slow. An occasional success would be met with a massive military response. It could be devastating.

The other issue was developing leaders. Once someone established himself as an inspirational leader or tactical genius, the U.S. had an uncanny ability to find him and strike, either through a drone or the feared U.S. Navy SEALs.

This new alliance with Russia, no matter how distasteful, would draw U.S. resources away from the Middle East and ultimately help their cause. That was all that mattered to Fannie.

She also realized the importance of Estonia to a country like Russia. Not only did they share a border, but Estonia was technologically advanced, at least as far as Internet infrastructure and computers. Far more so than Russia. Anyone with common sense recognized the next phase of global conflict would include serious cyberattacks. Already it was viewed as the only recourse for countries like North Korea. They couldn't hit the U.S. with missiles yet, so they harassed major U.S. corporations with sophisticated cyberattacks and disrupted credit and banking by stealing credit card numbers from retailers.

Estonia could be the piece of the puzzle Russia needed. Fannie didn't care what Russia did, as long as its first act was to hurt the United States. That would start the Islamic revolution she was praying for in Europe. If the U.S. couldn't help, Europe was as defenseless as a baby.

Derek Walsh was startled by hearing his name and feeling someone bump into him. He almost darted back onto his own street but remembered the young man in the Dodge waiting for him. He turned quickly and released a breath of relief when he realized it was his friend Charlie, the Vietnam vet.

Charlie said, "What are you doing home in the middle of the day? You didn't get fired, did you?"

Walsh regained his senses, blinked hard, and said, "No, no, nothing like that." He paused for a moment, staring at Charlie and recognizing one of his old shirts. It looked good on the older man. He had trimmed his gray beard and smelled like he had taken a shower recently. Walsh thought for a moment and said, "Charlie, can you help me out?"

"Anything for a fellow vet. What do you need?"

"I'd like to get into my apartment, but there's someone watching it. It's a young guy in the Dodge across the street."

Charlie took a moment to do some recon like the former Ranger he was. He stepped back from around the corner and said, "Have you checked all sides of the building?"

Walsh shook his head. He liked that Charlie asked no questions. He was just ready to help.

Charlie said, "Give me a few minutes. I'll meet you in the corner grocery store. They don't mind me coming in there, and they won't notice you."

Walsh followed the instructions and hustled down the street to the store owned by a young Korean couple. He used it sometimes to buy fresh fruit and milk. They greeted him like always, with a pleasant smile. He felt awkward lingering as long as he did, but no one seemed to notice, and finally, after nearly ten minutes, Charlie stepped into the store and greeted the young couple by name. Then he stepped directly back to Walsh and wasted no time. "There's no one in back of your apartment. The guy in the front is definitely watching your building. He must not expect you to be sneaky. But I guess with no way to get in the back, he'd only watch your front door. Just follow my lead and we'll get you in there, no problem."

Major Bill Shepherd had seen protests before. Many of the marine officers in Europe had commanded embassy security details and seen how
people could get stirred up about events halfway across the world. Even
if they weren't targeting the United States, he had studied crowds of
protesters in front of other embassies. He had once seen a protest in front
of the Israeli embassy in London that taught him how ugly these things
could get. It was the typical, uninformed protest against so-called Israeli
violence against Palestinians, which was actually self-defense. The London
police had allowed a number of people to hide their faces, not just in traditional Muslim headgear but with ski masks and Guy Fawkes masks as
well. Walsh had seen how that emboldened people, and soon there were
a number of bottles of urine and red paint slung over the wall at the Israeli soldiers guarding the embassy. When the London police tried to
stop this, the crowd turned on them and other bystanders. Before it was
over, two little girls had been seriously injured by the protesters, and the
London police had been forced to use tear gas to disperse the crowd.

Here in Germany it was a more complex situation. It was clear to the
protesters, as well as the soldiers guarding the front of the base, that no
one was going to get on the property. Any idiot could see that the soldiers with their rifles and ballistic shields could withstand just about anything the protesters threw at them. The responsibility really fell at the feet
of the German police, and there were not nearly enough on the fringes of
the crowd to control them if things got ugly. That would mean U.S. military personnel would have to take action, and that was the sort of thing
that drew media attention.

Shepherd didn't want to undercut the army commander, but his marines had had more experience with this at the embassy. It didn't take
much to convince the young army captain to let the marines step to the
front of the defenders. Shepherd was right there with them, scanning the
crowd. It was a mix of people, but most of them appeared to be under
thirty. The crowd was close to two hundred and growing as cars came
down the main road. He was shocked so many people would be out in the
middle of the night. But the news covering the financial meltdown in
Europe and the U.S., as well as pointing the finger toward one specific

U.S. firm, Thomas Brothers Financial, had stirred the public up, and young people with nothing to do could easily enough find trouble.

Most of his marines were behind shields, and everyone had a helmet on. A bottle sailed out of the crowd and shattered harmlessly twenty feet in front of them. Shepherd looked to each side of the crowd to see if the police would react in any way. They looked nervous and ready to flee rather than prepared to keep the peace.

A blond man shouting in English with a German accent edged away from the crowd and closer to Shepherd. "We're not going to let the U.S. ruin our economy. We're not going to let the U.S. continue to occupy our country," he yelled. "You must go. You must go." The last part was chanted and immediately picked up by the rest of the protesters. A crushingly loud "You must go" pounded in Shepherd's ears.

Shepherd looked along the line and could see that his marines were getting anxious and itching to point their rifles. He said in an even voice, "Stay calm, they're just blowing off some steam."

He could tell there was more behind this protest. He just didn't want his marines to make it worse. They stayed in line right at the gate. The crowd surged forward, and the blond guy who was leading the chant came face-to-face with Shepherd.

The younger man smirked and said, "America is done. You will see your world burn."

11

Walsh had found it comforting to talk with the homeless vet. It made him feel like he was doing something proactive. He had to look at Charlie with a sideways glance. This was all beyond him. He had never been involved in any sort of cloak-and-dagger activity. He had always been a financial guy, even in the marines. And now a homeless Vietnam vet was telling him how he would distract the man watching in front of Walsh's apartment, giving Walsh time to slip into the building. All it required was Walsh sneaking behind the first building on the block and coming up between that building and his own. Then, when Charlie distracted the man in the car, Walsh could slide into his apartment unnoticed.

He had a hundred questions. First and foremost, how would Charlie distract him? Then how would he get back out without being seen? What would happen if he was caught? Was the man dangerous? Did he look like a cop? Instead, he just stared at Charlie and mumbled, "Okay."

Walsh had to scale a short, decorative fence to get behind the building on the corner. He felt obvious and vulnerable walking through someone else's backyard, but no one seemed to notice him or look out a window.

There was a gate at the other side, one he had seen from his own building. He walked through it and found himself in the shadows between the two buildings, looking almost directly at the Dodge parked on the side of the road. The sounds of the earlier riots seem to drift lightly on the breeze, but he could hear everything on the street, including Charlie as he slowly approached the car.

Walsh's heart rate started to climb, and for the first time he realized he was also worried about Charlie's safety. What if this guy did something to the old man? Walsh would have to take action. He hoped he was prepared.

He crept up to the corner of the building and now could see and hear Charlie as he approached the man in the car and had his full attention. Walsh was afraid the man would notice him as he stepped onto the sidewalk and made a few quick steps to the stairs leading up to his building.

He heard Charlie say, "Hello, sir. I was wondering if you had some spare change." Charlie approached him as if he had some disability, hunched over and dragging his right leg behind him.

The man mumbled something hostile back toward Charlie.

The old vet said, "That's no way to talk to a senior citizen." And then, with startling speed, Charlie lurched toward the man, striking him across the chin and slamming his head hard into the dash of the Dodge Charger. He pulled the man back upright, and his head lulled to the right of the seat. Charlie turned and gave Walsh a thumbs-up.

Stunned by what he had witnessed, Walsh darted around the corner and rushed up the stairs.

Joseph Katazin was a little concerned. He'd lost track of Walsh. While the man was in custody he wasn't worried about it, but now he'd escaped from the Seventh Precinct, and the New York cops couldn't care less. They had plenty of problems on their hands with the chaos that Katazin had helped spread.

His contacts were associated with the Seventh Precinct, not the FBI.

He knew the federal agents would be looking for Walsh, but even they would be more concerned about the lone wolf terror attacks that were occurring across the country. He could imagine a supervisor yelling at the agent who wanted to look for Walsh when the world was falling down around them. The FBI really wasn't any different than any other police agency around the world. Once you understood how they operated they weren't that hard to outsmart.

Katazin had used his own small army of associates to spread out and look for Walsh. None of them knew exactly what was going on, and that was the point. He didn't trust any of them to keep their mouths shut if they were arrested for some reason. They were simply thugs used by the Russian mafia and available for hire whenever Katazin needed them. There really weren't that many places he thought Walsh would go, but he had people waiting at all of them while he headed to the most obvious.

Walsh was starting to annoy him. Katazin would enjoy questioning him roughly and then dumping him in the East River. By the time anyone linked him to all the other things that were going on, the world would have a very different look.

Walsh had been so nervous he could barely fit the key into the lock of his loose wooden door. Finally he managed to open the door silently and stood in the doorway, peering into the room. His eyes scanned from one corner to the other even though he had no idea what he was looking for. He just didn't need another surprise. If there was someone out front, there might be someone inside. He had to risk it. He stepped in quickly, ready to leap back out if necessary. It wasn't. The room was quiet and empty of other humans.

The apartment was a joke except for the comfortable bed. It was essentially a bedroom that had been cut into two rooms, plus a tiny bathroom and a kitchen that consisted of a dorm refrigerator and toaster oven. In other cities it would be considered a slum. The small closet, which was just a recess in the wall, held four blue suits. The main thing distinguishing them was the manufacturer, and all of them were knock-offs. What was wrong with him? Was he color-blind? Or had he just fallen into the corporate stereotype of wearing a blue suit with a different tie every day?

For no apparent reason he changed from the blue pants he was wearing into a different set of blue pants. He changed shirts as well, but decided not to grab a coat. He felt more casual having an untucked white shirt hanging over his dark blue pants.

Walsh caught a quick glimpse of himself in the mirror as he passed the open bathroom door. He thought for the first time about having cops looking for him. He was an escaped fugitive even if he was never officially charged. He thought about how Mike Rosenberg had once told him that few people actually looked at faces during the day, and that was how people on most-wanted lists remained free for so long. Just the same, Walsh decided he could change his look a little.

He took a minute to step up to the mirror, grab his electric grooming razor, and quickly shave the top of his head. After a remarkably short time he had given himself a classic male-pattern bald spot, with the sides trimmed back a little as well. He used a twin-bladed razor to finish up.

When he had finished he looked fifteen years older.

On his way out, he looked through one of the three drawers on the cabinet in the kitchen and found his envelope with six hundred dollars in cash, his current life savings. He also grabbed Alena's extra debit card and a pair of low-power "cheater" reading glasses he had found he needed more and more frequently. Once he put them on, in combination with his homemade bald spot, he looked completely different.

He didn't want to linger, even though he'd have liked to turn on the TV and see what was happening in the financial district. It was late afternoon, and there were still police sirens wailing in the distance.

He locked the apartment on the way out and paused before he stepped out onto the stairs. He looked through the glass in the doors and saw Charlie still standing casually by the Dodge. He came out the door, saw the driver slumped over in the front seat, and rushed over to the homeless army vet.

As Walsh approached, Charlie looked up. Then he grinned and said, "Nice look. Very smart."

Walsh looked at the unconscious man and said, "Charlie, what the hell? I thought you were going to *distract* him."

"He is distracted. His concussion has distracted him."

"I sure hope he was watching my apartment and not waiting for his girlfriend."

"I'm pretty sure he was watching your apartment."

"How do you know?"

Charlie held up a photograph of Walsh. It looked like it had been taken in the last few weeks when he was leaving his office. It was from a distance, but it was still clearly him.

Walsh said, "Do you have anything else?"

Charlie handed him a 9 mm Beretta, a cell phone, and a wallet. "I kept the cash in his wallet. I figured I earned that. The rest might be information you need."

Walsh didn't argue. He took the gun and shoved it in his belt, then pulled the shirt over it. He looked at the wallet for a moment and saw the guy's name: Serge Blattkoff. He looked up at Charlie. "A Russian."

"I never trusted those bastards."

Mike Rosenberg had gone all the way out to his car in the headquarters parking lot and tried calling his friend Derek Walsh, but he got no answer on the cell phone. Then he read a brief that said Derek was a suspect in the money transfer that started much of the chaos going on right now. His unit was designed to get a big picture of what was going on in the world. That gave him access to a lot of files and a lot of information, but he wasn't an expert on any of it. He was pretty good at tracking down the source of money and the original source of some communications. But his forte was gaining a view of the big picture. He decided it wouldn't help him or Walsh if he let it slip that they were friends. Right now no one was paying much attention to the banker in New York who was being questioned by the FBI. Then he read another brief that came over the computer. It was saying Walsh had escaped from custody and was loose somewhere in New York. With the growing violence and several terror attacks around Manhattan, very few people cared about a banker who managed to escape from the FBI.

Rosenberg was worried, and he hoped no one would make a connection between his phone and Walsh's. God knew there were enough calls between them. Until someone said something, he intended to look into it more closely and see what he could find out. There was no way Derek Walsh was ever involved in something illegal; something stupid, maybe, especially if it involved a woman, but illegal, never.

The first thing he did was find an analyst to talk to about the money transfer that had gone from Thomas Brothers Financial to a bank in Switzerland. He wanted to know who had access to that account and see what he could find out from there.

There was no way he'd let a friend like Derek Walsh swing on the gallows for something he never did.

Walsh couldn't believe the change in Charlie. He no longer acted like a harmless, burned-out homeless guy but had reverted to his military background and taken charge. He seemed to have no remorse for the way he handled the Russian. In fact, it was Charlie who led Walsh away from the unconscious man without a second thought.

Walsh said, "I need to get all this straightened out. I need to get a lawyer."

Charlie snapped his head toward him as they walked along Hudson Street. "You can't be serious? After the shit you told me has gone down today, you think anyone is going to give you a chance in court? The whole system is fixed anyway. Trust me, I've been through it enough times. What you need is the basics: food, rest, and resupply."

This was something Walsh understood: basic military strategy.

Walsh said, "My girlfriend lives near the Columbia campus. I need to get over to her."

"Uptown? The West Side? No way. Too far. Too many cops."

They walked in silence for a few moments. Then Charlie said, "What's your girlfriend's name?"

"Alena."

"She Mexican?"

"No, it's short for Magdalena. She's from Greece."

"That don't sound like a Greek name."

"Her mom was from Sweden. She named her, and that's where she gets her fair skin and blond hair."

"Where is her dad from?"

"Greece. She doesn't talk about him much. Her folks are divorced."

Charlie mumbled, "Too many foreigners in your life. We need to find shelter close by." After looking both ways and making sure they were still safe, Charlie said, "Can you trust her?"

"Of course. We've been dating for almost a year, and I knew her a year before that."

"The cops can make people do crazy shit."

Walsh didn't know why he felt he had to defend Alena, but he dug in his pocket and pulled out her debit card. "She gave me this, and she has more money than me."

Charlie nodded, seemingly satisfied. "People don't fool with their money. If she gave you access to her account, she's okay."

Walsh would have loved to spend the night in Alena's arms, but Charlie was right; he couldn't risk traveling across town. He'd wait till tomorrow and slip by to see her. Right now Charlie was making sense.

"Any ideas where we might stay for the night?"

Charlie gave him a sly grin and said, "We keep walking until Hudson meets Bleecker Street and there's a small shelter for homeless people. You gotta get there early to get a bed, but the woman who runs the place is great. No one has to sign in or say who they are. The only rule is you don't cause any trouble. And believe me, if someone causes trouble, other people staying there take care of it. She'll give us a hot meal, and you can zonk out for a few hours. In the morning you'll have a better idea of what you need to do."

It was hard for Walsh to argue with common sense and military doctrine. He wondered how Charlie had become homeless if he had such a good head on his shoulders. The training men and women received in the military tended to shine through in the darkest hours.

12

Derek Walsh awoke to sunlight in his eyes. He was one of six men in a small room at the homeless shelter. Charlie lay in the single bed next to him, snoring soundly. The previous day seemed like a bad dream. Damn. It was all too real.

The meal of a turkey sandwich and hot soup the night before had made him reevaluate how tough his life really was. Until yesterday, he thought he had a shitty low-level job that he didn't care much for. Maybe he was like so many other Americans and didn't realize how good his life really was. He worked hard and put in long hours, but he was able to buy his own food and live in his own apartment, no matter how small it was. He even had a beautiful girlfriend, and if everything else failed, he'd be able to find another job. He had never even considered how men like Charlie, shattered by their experiences in Vietnam, had abandoned their old lives and ended up on the street, a simple meal of turkey sandwich and soup a luxury they only enjoyed on a rare occasion.

Now Walsh took a few moments to evaluate what was going on. His head was much clearer than it had been the day before, and he could focus without the shock of an FBI agent interrogating him.

He had a good understanding of security systems and computers and had spent his early days at Thomas Brothers Financial working with some of the hotshot IT guys. One of them, a graduate of MIT, explained to him exactly how the system worked. There was absolutely no way to make an international trade without the use of the security plug and a password. The IT nerd had even showed Walsh how to activate the special security protocol on his personal security plug that would take a picture of anyone using it for a trade. Walsh didn't even know why he turned on the feature, but it was cool knowing something few others at the company did. There was only one way to access the security plug and retrieve the photos, and that was by going back to Thomas Brothers and getting on the network. That had to be his goal.

From a military perspective he had food, was rested, and, thanks to Charlie, had the Russian thug's 9 mm safely tucked in his waistband. He was ready to go into action.

Fannie Legat had managed a few more hours of sleep before she picked up her Skoda hatchback and drove to the town of Sillamae to meet her Russian contact. Her plan had been to leave Amir in Tartu instead of unleashing him on some dim-witted, unsuspecting Russian army officer. But the taciturn little Iranian had insisted they were on the assignment together. He had not spoken a word when they drove up from Tartu and had barely spoken since. He found a reason to wander off for a few minutes, giving Fannie some time alone with the Russian major.

Now, near lunchtime, she was already impressed by the young officer. She had been worried she wouldn't be able to deal with him, considering her feelings about anyone from Russia or the United States, but she had been very professional when she met Anton Severov.

His goofy manner and the way he said, "Just call me Anton," put her at ease. They had eaten a quick meal at the odd little diner and adjusted to each other's accents in English. She felt she had a greater command of the language, but her French accent threw off the Russian's ear. She was a little worried about what would happen when he met Amir. Her surly associate seemed to resent the fact that they were working with a Russian, and she was sure that once he saw the Russian was taller and better-looking, Amir would fly off the handle.

She wasn't used to a man showing her so much deference and displaying such manners. He pulled her chair out for her and waited to sit down until she was comfortable. They had a simple meal of the Estonian version of a hamburger, which meant it was a thin, tasteless meat patty between two slices of white bread. The way the Russian major gulped down the sandwich, she wondered when he had last eaten.

He looked across the table and said, "How were you chosen for an assignment like this?"

"Because I speak German."

"I'm sorry, I've just never done anything like this before. I am a simple soldier and used to the battlefield, not dressing like a grocer and wandering through the streets of foreign cities."

She flashed him a smile. He deserved it. "It will be all right. They told me to just show you around, and we have someone else to help us. He might not seem too friendly, but after a while you learn that you want to kill him."

They both chuckled.

"Did they tell you anything about why I was here?"

"I'm not an idiot. I can guess."

"And it doesn't bother you?"

"Let's just say that for now the enemy of my enemy is my friend."

The major smiled and said, "I would like to be your friend, Fannie."

Derek Walsh stumbled along the streets of New York in a long-sleeved white oxford shirt, purposely untucked to fit in with everyone else. The other reason he let his shirt hang past his belt was to cover the Beretta

9 mm Charlie had taken off the Russian who was watching his apartment. That's what was really swirling in his head right now: What the hell did the Russians want with him? The guys who robbed him were Russian, too. The FBI he could deal with. The entire accusation was a mistake, he might even have his day in court, but Russians waiting outside his apartment with guns was a major development that caused his stomach to flutter.

It was about 7:45 A.M., and Walsh had put some distance between himself and the homeless shelter. He didn't want to get Charlie involved in his mess, and he didn't want to risk anyone telling the FBI where he'd stayed. It was best to head out into the streets. He had told Charlie he would go to Alena's apartment, but he didn't think he could get there before eight, and she left for class about then. Protesters were already roaming around in groups, and the cops looked exhausted. It made him wonder what sort of disarray the office was in and if the violence had spilled into the building at all. Things were relatively quiet on this side of town, and he wanted to see a newscast to understand what had happened. It also might give him an idea of how busy the police were going to be today and if they would have time to look for him.

He realized how hungry he was and slipped into a deli for a quick meal. The deli was crammed with rush-hour workers, but he saw an empty table with the TV just above it. He stood and stared at the TV set for a few moments as a story started to unfold about the events of the day before. Thomas Brothers was mentioned by name as being under investigation for funding terror groups. He held his breath, hoping he wasn't identified specifically. He was mesmerized by the video of the Stand Up to Wall Street group going absolutely berserk along the financial district. Police cars and cabs were turned over and trashed. Later in the day people started throwing Molotov cocktails, and a fire spread through one of the parks north of the financial district.

These so-called protesters were nothing like the old Occupy Wall Street people. By comparison the Occupy people were a pleasant distraction. Their message was never clear. Everyone is against greed and abuse on Wall Street. They could have just as easily been against child molesters. Who is going to argue with that stance? But ultimately the Occupy movement left a bad taste in everyone's mouth—or at least a bad smell in the cities where they protested. The parks where they camped were ecological disasters and needed to have the soil scraped off and replaced. The businesses near the protests were crippled when paying customers stopped frequenting them. The Occupy spokespeople rarely made sense or focused on issues that could be addressed. But they never caused widespread violence.

This time it was entirely different. Four people had been killed in separate incidents around New York, and in a suspected terror attack in Times Square at about five in the afternoon, a man detonated a crude homemade bomb consisting of a five-gallon can of gasoline wrapped in other explosive material and concealed in a suitcase. The blast incinerated the bomber and severely burned nine tourists, including a little girl from Toronto. But the focus of the unrest was clearly the financial district.

Walsh stared at the TV news, amazed at the scenes of chaos. Had this really been started by an errant trade? It couldn't be. The markets in London and New York had both dropped drastically before computer trading had been halted, and an investigation into potential hacking was under way in both countries. That news only made things worse, with the early market indicators showing another bloodbath on the way today.

He caught another story about terror attacks and the bombing of a bank in Bern, Switzerland, and worried about his friend Bill Shepherd in Germany. Would American military bases be targets?

Then he knew what he had to do. His friends would help him, specifically, Mike Rosenberg at the CIA. He might have some insights as to what happened and how to fix it. Walsh just needed a phone. He recognized he should call Alena to tell her not to worry. He'd have done it yesterday if the day hadn't been a blur. But right now he needed to reach Rosenberg. He tried to recall his friend's personal cell number. He knew the area code was 757, and he remembered a few more digits. He had to try.

He took a step forward, and as he sat at a tiny round table, a woman next to him smiled and said hello. It took a moment to notice her, as he was still staring at the TV set. Finally Walsh nodded back and realized he might be able to get her to lend him a phone for a moment. He reached in his pocket as if looking for something, then said, "Dammit."

The woman turned her head quickly to look at him.

Walsh turned to the woman and said, "Excuse me. I just realized I left my phone at home, and I needed to call the office."

The woman, a little older than Walsh and obviously well-off in her Burberry jacket and Oscar de la Renta glasses, smiled and didn't hesitate to retrieve an iPhone from her purse. "Be my guest."

He knew he couldn't get up to have a private conversation. It would make this woman nervous, and she might chase him as if he had stolen it. Instead, he dialed the number he thought would work. His heart raced as he heard the first ring, then the next. At five rings he was about to hang up when he heard his friend's voice. It was a blunt and direct "Who's this?"

"Mike, it's Derek."

"Tubby! Jesus Christ, what the hell is happening? You were just on the news here."

Walsh glanced up at the TV and saw his driver's license photo on the screen and heard the words "Wanted for questioning." He stole a peek at the woman next to him to make certain she wasn't seeing it. She was engrossed in a glossy magazine. His right hand moved up to his shaved head, and he remembered that thanks to the bald spot and glasses, he looked fifteen years older than that photo.

Walsh remained very casual as the woman at the next table turned a page in her magazine. "Hello, Mike, I lost my phone but wanted to talk when you had a chance. Is there a good time?"

"Are you insane?" His normally calm voice betrayed the stress he was under. "They're blaming you for the apocalypse."

"It's literally just a big mistake, and I think I can prove it. I could use some help." He kept his voice calm and words bland so as not to alert the woman sitting next to him.

The long pause and silence that followed unnerved him. Finally Rosenberg said, "Let me see if I can find anything on it. Get a cheap throwaway phone and call me later. Only call this number. And wait until after five. I don't want to be on government property when you call."

Walsh heard the stress in his friend's voice and simply replied, "Roger that."

The line went dead, and Walsh was left wondering if he'd made a mistake. Mike had sworn an oath to the country. That might include turning in a friend.

He needed a safe haven, and the only place he could think of was Alena's apartment. He needed to feel her arms wrapped around him for a few minutes and to hear her soothing voice. At least she'd believe him.

Anton Severov sat in the backseat of the shabby little car Fannie was driving. He realized quickly he didn't want her associate, Amir, to be sitting behind him at any point. With a fair command of English, the Iranian student made it clear that he had little use for Russia, either. But since they could help each other, Amir would put up with Severov and his mission. He didn't get to be a major in the Red Army by ignoring threats that were right in front him. Severov kept Amir to the side and in front of him.

Fannie, on the other hand, had proven to be charming and had an excellent command of English. That was their only common language, and he enjoyed hearing her Gaelic lilt. She concentrated as she handled the beat-up Skoda Fabia hatchback that had seen better days. It had that curious chug that many of the Eastern European cars possessed. It was still a step up from most Russian vehicles, but nowhere near the luxurious Japanese or American cars that cost a fortune anywhere east of the Rhine.

Despite the distraction of a beautiful escort, Severov managed to make notes and take some photographs as they turned south toward Tartu on the Tartu Maantee. He made notes of the width of the road and buildings that might hinder the travel of their heavy tanks and supply vehicles. In several of the small villages along the beautiful Lake Peipus with its dark water and narrow beaches, the roads had patches of cobblestones, which had been there since the Middle Ages. The citizens wouldn't be happy with the effects of tank tracks across their decorative streets.

After a while Fannie turned to him and said, "Have you traveled in the West much?"

"I've been to Germany and France a number of times and spent an entire year working at our embassy in London. That is where I was able to really polish my English. I had several trips to America as a military liaison, but most of my time in the army has been further east." He stopped short of saying he had been in Georgia and Turkmenistan, where he had fought in Muslim rebellions.

"How did you find the United States? I've never been there."

"Much of it lives up to everything we hear. It is a land of plenty, and there is ungodly waste. But I found the people to be pleasant and open, and the cuisine to be stolen from virtually every other country." He was starting to chuckle at his little joke when he saw the look on Fannie's face.

"They have stolen everything from others. Stolen Arab oil, Native American land, English determination, and some of the best and brightest people from every country. That is why we can work together now. It's time someone taught them a lesson."

Severov stared at the young woman and realized why it was so hard to defeat the Muslims in some of the Russian republics. This was not someone he wanted as an enemy. But he was still a little uneasy working with these two.

Joseph Katazin was quite pleased with himself. He wished his father were still alive to see how well he'd done. At this moment, in this place, no one was doing more for the well-being of Russia than he was. He swelled with pride as he thought about the plan he had developed with others and was now responsible for by himself. At least, he was responsible for large parts of the operation.

It was still early in the morning, but he didn't want his wife and daughter disturbing him. He'd driven down to his office near the docks where he could see the new so-called Freedom Tower. These Americans and their ability to forget struggle and tragedy amazed him. A month after the attack on the World Trade Center, everything was back to normal in the sprawling country of plenty.

His business consisted of a loading dock, generally stacked with product to be shipped out as part of his import/export business, and a set of five offices. His was the nicest, with two wide windows, carpet, and several nice touches of decoration his wife had insisted on. The business had been in the same location for thirteen years. He never had to worry about making rent; if he fell behind on the import/export business he just asked for a supplement from his superiors, although it was rare he needed extra money.

The business employed five people legitimately, a secretary, a bookkeeper, and the men who worked on the loading dock. He had two additional employees, or at least men the company paid, but they rarely showed their face around the office. These two men thought he was part of the Russian mob and occasionally did things for him in his capacity of working for the Russian government. All they could tell the cops if they were captured was that they worked for a surly mob member who ran an import/export business. Let them prove that in court.

The man he had sent to watch Derek Walsh's apartment, Serge Blattkoff, had proven to be unreliable. He had allowed the former marine to get the drop on him and take his weapon. Serge had a black eye and a broken nose to prove it. This wasn't Hollywood. Katazin wouldn't have the man killed. But he certainly wouldn't trust him with more important missions on his own. However, he recognized that Serge's embarrassment and anger over this incident would be useful, and the young thug would stop at nothing to get back at Walsh.

He had underestimated Derek Walsh, and now the man was a thorn in his side who must be plucked out. He was clearly not in custody. One of the sources said that he fled from FBI custody when rioters got out of control. It was a smart move, and frankly not one Katazin would have expected from the chunky Wall Street banker. He wouldn't make the same mistake again.

Aside from Walsh's disappearance, the operation seemed to be advancing well. It rested on several key elements. The first one was to use Walsh as the dupe to transfer monies from legitimate accounts to accounts in Switzerland where they could be immediately withdrawn. He was relying on a contact with one of the Islamic extremist groups to complete that task. She seemed to have done a pretty good job so far. A news report early this morning documented a "terror attack" on a major bank in Bern, Switzerland. Katazin realized that was the same bank he used to make the transfer, and the bombing was clearly covering someone's tracks. He liked that.

The same associate had paid a fortune to a bank employee to somehow hack both the London and New York stock exchanges with a Russian-made computer algorithm that greatly affected the computer-generated trading. The algorithm exaggerated the appearance of the big funds' selling positions. That caused everyone to *actually* sell in an effort to beat a tumbling market. That resulted in the massive sell-off and fueled the panic in the general public. The master work of programming had been done at Steklov Mathematical Institute and refined at the Kiev Computer Algebra School. Katazin understood some of it from his father's work in mathematics. He knew that only the brightest had developed it and that it had cost a fortune to introduce into the computer systems.

Katazin had watched the news all day yesterday and was quite pleased with the results of his and his associates' efforts to ramp up the chaos. Much of it took on a life of its own with some of the snotty and uninformed European youth protesting any and all American businesses and military installations. It made him chuckle.

The next phase of the operation was ongoing and involved over a hundred individual, lone wolf terror attacks across Western Europe and the United States. Some of these attacks had been attributed to the growing civil unrest and were not even covered by the network news.

All of this activity was just a prelude to what the Kremlin actually wanted to accomplish. Their goal was to swallow up another republic. An important one. Their eyes were set firmly on Estonia, the most advanced and most wired country in Eastern Europe. The Estonian infrastructure would provide Russia with a means of communicating and transferring money unlike anything they had had in the past. It would be a new world, with more land and a base from which the military could move into Latvia and eventually Belarus.

He marveled at how the Americans couldn't understand why Russia continued to make threatening noises when the U.S. did virtually nothing to stop its successful annexation of Crimea and its continued efforts to bring Ukraine back into the fold.

He doubted anyone realized there were still Russian agents planted inside the continental United States. He knew he wasn't alone. There were others he could call on if things got tough. They were too far into the operation to abandon it now.

If he could just find Derek Walsh.

13

Fannie Legat had dreaded the moment her new friend, the Russian major Anton Severov, and her annoying Iranian associate, Amir, finally got a chance to talk at length. The chitchat in the car had been bad enough. It was early in the evening, and they had just sat down at an outdoor restaurant in Tartu. The breeze was comfortable, and the atmosphere of the town was comforting in an old-world and courtly way. It reminded her of some of the older outlying areas of Paris where the tourists hadn't defiled every site and crammed the streets with their wide asses and knock-off fashions. Tartu, Estonia, was not unique in Europe, but for the moment it was perfect.

Severov sat next to her, and Amir across the wide table. The two men could not have been more different physically: Severov tall and athletic, and Amir short and pudgy. Severov had a pleasant smile and was curious about all aspects of the area, not just physical barriers to the Russian military but the history of certain buildings and what the residents were like while not stuck at some job. Amir looked at everyone he saw as a potential enemy and someone he would never have to deal with once he reached paradise. In short, virtually everyone in the world was against him, and he held the same attitudes that had kept Islam down for a century. Fannie even understood how little he thought of her, just because she was a woman. But she had a duty and a job to do.

She had a clear picture of this assignment. It was simple and straightforward. She was to drive the major as far west and south as he wished to go and not ask him too many questions about their pending operation. She was to have him back across the border within a few days or, if they were contacted, be able to race up the narrow highways of Estonia and drop him on a few hours' notice.

The one thing that concerned her about the assignment was why Amir had been included. He added nothing to their operation. He had no intimate knowledge of Estonia itself, he did not drive well, and he stuck out in public. He had some training as an engineer, but the major didn't need that. He knew what his tanks could go through and what they would have to go around. Amir's drawbacks were obvious: There was no way to disguise the fact that he was a Middle Easterner. Even if Iranians occasionally considered themselves to be part of the Far East and wished to distance themselves from the rest of the region, this dark, hairy little cur was no better than anyone else. But it was clear that wasn't what he thought.

Severov finished gazing around in all directions, the way he did any time they stopped in a town, and said to Fannie, "This is a lovely city. Did you know this quaint little country with its ancient buildings is considered the most technologically advanced and wired country in Eastern Europe?"

Fannie smiled and said, "Yes, I did. I'm often reminded by my computer." She was referring to the number of spam e-mails and scams offered to her over the Internet that originated in Estonia, but Severov could've just as easily interpreted it as understanding his military mission.

Amir looked at the tall Russian officer and said, "That's the only way empires like you can expand. Conquer people who have accomplished more and developed technologies you need."

Severov did not appear bothered by the comment. "It's funny to hear a Persian say something like that."

"I am a proud citizen of Iran."

"Why?"

"What you mean, *why*? I was born there. I live there now."

Severov kept a sly smile as he said, "I mean why on earth are you *proud* to be an Iranian? What have they done recently? About the most notable thing they did was kidnap some Americans and hold them for four hundred and forty-four days. I don't see any technological advances coming out of Iran. All I see is crazy little presidents who travel to the UN and spout off about things no one believes."

Fannie had to stifle a grin at the look Amir shot the Russian major.

Derek Walsh stood on the eastern side of the courtyard and watched the crowds on the western side of the Thomas Brothers Financial building as they surged toward the police lines and then backed away in a ridiculous show of useless bravado. The skies had cleared, and it was a comfortable sixty-five degrees. Although he wouldn't want to be a cop standing for hours on end in a heavy Kevlar vest and holding a shield.

This side of the courtyard seemed to be restricted to journalists and spectators. The crowd was noticeably older, and most had the look of professionals. He fit into the crowd with his nice pants and white shirt, and he was now wearing a pair of wide sunglasses. He didn't want to cover his new hairstyle with a hat; people noticed things like a beard or being bald. No one had given him a second look. There was little conversation, and even the cops paid more attention to what was happening across the wide courtyard than to the crowd of more than a hundred spectators. No one noticed him or any of the other spectators standing across the courtyard. The building had been kept open in an effort to show that it was business as usual on Wall Street.

Walsh recognized that very few people would be working in his office today, but the one man he needed to talk to, Ted Marshall, would be there. In fact, he probably had not left. He hadn't risen to his position by being an absentee manager. He would want to personally ensure that the building and operations were secure.

Walsh had stopped at an electronics store run by disgruntled Israelis and bought a prepaid Boost cell phone, giving the guy an extra twenty dollars to not ask any serious questions about his obviously shaky identity. Now he had a phone with a thousand minutes to use, which he hoped would be more than enough to resolve all the issues that were swirling around him.

There were only a few numbers he could recall off the top of his head. He'd been lucky to get Mike Rosenberg's personal cell phone. He also knew Alena's apartment phone number, but not her cell phone number. He had already called her but didn't leave a message, in case someone else came into the apartment. He was adjusting to the fact that he was a fugitive. He could picture his girlfriend already on the campus of Columbia, and she normally didn't get home until after five. He knew she had to be worried about him and wondered how she had tried to contact him. Then he started to consider the possibility that she had tried to find him at his apartment or that the FBI had tracked her down. He'd be careful when he approached her later in the afternoon.

Watching the Thomas Brothers building satisfied several issues. It kept him hiding in plain sight, and he felt like he was accomplishing something by waiting for Ted Marshall to leave the building. He knew his boss would likely come out what was widely considered the rear door even though it opened onto the street. Usually people came through the courtyard, but the protesters made that impossible today.

Walsh was jostled as someone made their way through the crowd. No one on his side of the courtyard was protesting, even though the crowd was fairly large and attracting more spectators as the day wore on. He glanced over his shoulder and realized there were a couple of uniformed cops coming through, and he stepped to his right. It wasn't until the cops had passed him that he noticed Tonya Stratford from the FBI and her sour-looking partner following behind the officers.

Just as she turned her face toward Walsh, he managed to look over his shoulder away from her. He found himself holding his breath waiting for a tap on the shoulder, but nothing happened. When he turned his head back, the two officers and two FBI agents were in the courtyard walking quickly toward the front door. Several bottles were launched from the protesters' side and crashed to the ground near them, making one of the cops jump straight in the air and land cursing at the protesters.

He noticed Agent Stratford look over her shoulder in his direction rather than where the bottle had come from. Maybe it was time to change position.

Joseph Katazin had taken a cab from his business but had to abandon it after about five blocks because of the goddamned protesters. He took some satisfaction in the fact that he was the reason they had poured out onto the street, but he also judged them as spoiled Americans with too much time on their hands. In Russia they would riot over important things like no food or no heating oil when the temperature had dropped below zero Celsius. It was all part of his plan, and he could report with confidence that this part was working to perfection.

The lone wolf terror attacks, at least the ones in the United States that he had some knowledge of, had also sent a chill up the spine of the American government. You could stop conspiracies, but a single, determined man, who believed he was going to paradise if he simply wrapped himself in explosives and walked into a crowded store, was another story. Two of the attacks would be slow in developing because the jihadists had poured a strain of anthrax into the air-conditioning and ventilation systems at Macy's and Grand Central Station. It would be a week before people really started feeling the effects, but the impact would be dramatic. By then no one would care where the Red Army was in Europe. They would be screaming for action about a terror attack on their own soil.

Katazin was happy he didn't have to work with these Middle Eastern nuts after this. They'd served their purpose, and he was glad they weren't currently focusing their rage on Russia, but they were unstable. He had put some thought into what drove them. He could only classify it as an unnatural rage against Western societies. A sociologist he'd spoken with said it was fueled by the disparity of wealth in the region, with the majority of the Islamic world being in desperate poverty while the rich made the 1 percent in the United States seem like paupers. The ruling family of Saudi Arabia, for example, had no concept of cost or money. So much flowed in from oil revenues that they just assumed most people lived like them, choosing to ignore the homeless children and starving families virtually at their doorstep.

The proof of the extravagance of these ruling families throughout the Arab world was shown by outlandishly tall buildings and even completely man-made islands in the shape of palm trees. Billions of dollars were spent merely to satisfy the whim of a few wealthy families.

Another theory went that the Islamic world was pissed off that they were so far behind the rest of the world. One fact that had been pointed out was that the small country of South Korea had more intellectual patents filed in the last ten years than the one billion Muslims around the world. That spoke volumes about their interest in educating the masses and spreading the wealth.

Whatever the reason, and for however long, Katazin had harnessed that rage and was using it to great effect.

The streets of New York were in chaos as he made his way west, toward his best chance to find the wayward Derek Walsh. He was going to get Walsh out of the way, and he hoped he could make it look like suicide. That would delay the investigation into the transfer of money long enough for everyone to fade back into their quiet lives, knowing they had done their patriotic duty.

Katazin was thrilled at the prospect of getting his reward. Whether it was a promotion or recall back to Russia to a hero's welcome, he was ready.

Mike Rosenberg sat in his organized office inside the headquarters of the Central Intelligence Agency in Langley, Virginia. It was more than just an office. He could close the door and be completely sealed off from the rest of the world to work in private. Any information that left his office could be monitored. But his job was to *gather* as much information as possible from public sources, which included the Internet, and work with other analysts to decide what that information meant and how reliable it was.

He was proud of the history of the agency. Few people recognized how significant their work had been since World War II, when they grew out of a little-known agency called the Office of Strategic Services. There were connections to the history of the marines as well, and he realized people around the office respected his former position in the Corps. An intelligence officer in a combat-ready unit was vital. Although it was popular to say that "military intelligence" was an oxymoron, Rosenberg had found that most intelligence officers worked with what they had and were able to save American military lives during combat with the information they provided.

That was his goal today. He wanted to save a former military man, his friend Derek Walsh. Luckily he could justify anything he was about to do by saying he was trying to get a better handle on the growing violence and fear in both the United States and Western Europe. That was all anyone was trying to do at the moment. The riots got worse in the evening in Europe and tended to die out in the United States.

He had spoken to his other friend from the marines, Bill Shepherd, and learned that the military base where he was stationed had seen heavy protest during the night and felt the wrath of a group of Germans that grew to over three thousand. Shepherd said it wasn't that bad, but Rosenberg could tell by his friend's voice that it had unnerved him and he was ready to go out on the line again tonight.

The first thing Rosenberg started to look at was the transfers from Thomas Brothers Financial. He had talked to one of the analysts connected to the FBI who had the information, and it didn't take long to determine that the accounts the money went to in Europe were all connected. Now that he was looking at information outside the United States, things could get complicated, but that was why he liked his job.

14

Major Bill Shepherd sat in his office, staring out through the single window into the dark German sky. It was after nine o'clock, but he wasn't sure how much after. He'd stayed at the front line of the defense of the base until the protesters finally broke up about four in the morning. It was nothing like combat, but it was still tense and kept them on edge.

The stories Shepherd had seen on the news reminded him of an attack on the marine base he and his friends were stationed at in Afghanistan. It was near some shithole village in the Korengal Valley, and he was just coming out of the mess hall with Ron Jackson and Mike Rosenberg. They didn't have their M-4 rifles, but Shepherd never went anywhere without a pistol. Things had been quiet around the base for more than a month, and the air force had been pounding the insurgents all across the valley. It was a much-needed respite from some of the combat they had seen earlier.

Just as they were coming out of the mess he heard gunfire and saw two Afghan men running forward, firing randomly with U.S. Marine rifles. Before he could do much more than reach for a pistol, Ron Jackson shoved Shepherd and Rosenberg to cover. It was a good move, and one that might have saved their lives. Normally in these situations he turned to Rosenberg, who could always give him a good understanding of the situation, but in this case they all had the same information. Someone believed these men were their allies and had given them too much access to the base.

Just as a man wearing a backpack came running up shouting something in Pashto, a marine sprang from the side of the supply tent and yanked the pack right off his back. It was unbelievable. Shepherd just stared in amazement, and the movement had stunned the three intruders as well. A moment later gunfire from marines knocked down all three attackers.

It took a few seconds longer for Shepherd to realize the marine who had just saved the base from a major terror attack was his friend Derek Walsh.

Now Shepherd took another swig of coffee at his desk. The few hours of sleep he'd grabbed in the morning were not enough to recharge his batteries. Because he had taken the initiative and put his marines out front the night before, he'd been called in for a security meeting, and now, after doing such a good job, his marines were expected to be at the front gate and supported by the army personnel.

So far it had been quiet, but he received reports of buses headed their way, and there were already about fifty people chanting catchy slogans like "America, land of the greedy" or "Leave our land." His orders were the same: Treat everyone with respect and use the utmost restraint possible to avoid any incident. That meant taking rocks and bottles against their shields and helmets, even allowing the protesters to shove them if they got as far as the gate. They had requested more German police officers, but this was not the only site of large-scale protests. The German financial markets had started to tumble like the ones in London and New York. People were scared and taking to the streets.

To complicate matters, there had been several sporadic terror attacks at the site of the protests. A suicide bomber had killed thirteen in Berlin and wounded dozens more. The attack in the country's largest city made him think about his friend Ronald Jackson, who had died defending the embassy there.

Throughout the stressful night and day, and into the night again, he'd kept thinking about his friends spread out across the globe. Now it was midafternoon in the U.S., and Mike Rosenberg was probably comfortable in his office in Langley. Derek Walsh was probably busy as hell with the markets going wild. Shepherd had talked with his father briefly before coming out to the gate, and the retired navy man assured him that everyone was safe and told Shepherd to worry about himself. That's what he intended to do, but first he called a couple of women he knew in Germany to make sure they were well. After short conversations, he couldn't resist making another call while he had a few minutes. He dialed the number, and his latest conquest, Fannie Legat, picked up after two rings.

It only took a moment for her to recognize who it was, and then she hesitated. Shepherd asked her, "Where are you?"

There was another hesitation, and he heard voices in the background. It sounded like she was in a restaurant. "I'm still traveling. I probably won't be back in Stuttgart for another few days. How are you? Are you safe?"

He could hear the chanting starting again outside the base. He didn't want to worry her. "I'm as safe as can be inside the base. I just was hoping you were headed home."

She purred with that pleasant accent and said, "Soon. I'll call you tomorrow when I have a little more time, and we can chat."

He wasn't sure he liked the sound of that. Something told him she was out with another man. It certainly was her prerogative, but somehow it made him feel a little like a patsy. As he said good-bye, he heard a crash at the front of the base and sprang to his feet, scooping up a web belt with a Beretta in a holster. He ran as hard as he could toward the closest Humvee.

Walsh couldn't help but fix his eyes upon the door to the building that Tonya Stratford and her partner, Frank Martin, had walked through about ten minutes earlier. Not much had changed in the tone of either crowd.

On the far side of the courtyard, the protesters were taunting police and throwing the occasional bottle. One of them had a strong enough arm to put a crack in the glass at the front of the building with a brick. Walsh was impressed with the power of the throw.

On his side of the courtyard, he noticed a number of reporters among the spectators. A uniformed NYPD police officer with a K-9 made a pass through the middle of the crowd, not even having to ask people to move out of the way. The sight of the muscular German shepherd had the desired effect and made people step back from instinct.

Walsh realized the cop had a purpose and the dog was stopping occasionally to sniff bags, looking for explosives. Although there weren't any obvious protesters, the cops didn't want to take a chance that someone would infiltrate this quiet crowd and detonate a bomb. He'd seen on the news that there had been several attacks like that around the world.

He was relieved to see that the cop paid no attention to him whatsoever. He wasn't carrying a bag and had no heavy coat to conceal anything. If only the cop realized he was carrying a pistol and more than five hundred dollars in cash with no identification, Walsh had no doubt he'd be held for questioning until someone from the FBI figured out who he was.

He looked around the crowd and noticed several younger men in light jackets or windbreakers at the edges of the group. They were hiding the fact that they were looking into the crowd as if they were searching for someone. They were clean-cut, almost military-style, and that's what made them stand out; they weren't dressed in dark suits or shaggy-haired like so many New Yorkers. That made Walsh realize these guys were law enforcement of some kind.

Just then he noticed some movement at the front of the building and saw Tonya Stratford step out of the door with a uniformed police officer and his boss, Ted Marshall. They immediately started walking toward his side of the courtyard, and he understood instantly that she had caught a glimpse of him as she rushed through the crowd earlier. She'd been smart not to spook him and make him run. Now she was doing what they used to call driving the fox to the hounds. She wanted him to see her and try to cut through the crowd right into the hands of the men who were now ready to catch him.

This was not the time to panic. Although it hurt to see the man he needed to talk to being so close, Walsh needed to figure a way out of here. And fast.

As Fannie Legat ended the phone call with Major Shepherd, Amir snapped at her, "Who was that?"

Then she realized both men had heard her flirting over the phone. She gave them a smug smile just to get a reaction. The reaction she got from Amir was exactly what she'd expected. He was stuck somewhere in the eighteenth century, and although he outwardly appeared to detest her, she suspected he had a crush on her.

What surprised Fannie was the reaction of Major Severov. He looked on quietly with a pleasant smile on his face as if none of it was any of his business. She liked that. He had treated her with respect and kept his mission in mind during their short time together. If they weren't eating, they were surveying roads. He was a soldier, not an ideologue like Amir. The hairy little jerk truly believed everything that was spewed at him by his imams, and he truly believed that a woman like Fannie was mainly needed to cook food and pop children out on a regular basis. That attitude had no place in their jihad. She was working to change it, but it was frustrating.

Amir said, "I have no idea why you would keep talking to an American soldier. They are our enemies. One day we might have to fight them in our own lands."

Fannie said, "You mean France?"

"Of course I don't mean France. I mean Iran or maybe one of the Arab lands. They have not hidden their lust for our oil. They cannot keep from exporting their Western goods and attitudes. Everyone is not the same. We wish to live apart from them."

Now it was Severov's turn to tweak the little Iranian dope. "Then why is it that your country insists on butting heads with the United States? You take their people hostage, you export terror, and you make no secret of your desire to become a nuclear power in such an unstable region. You constantly threaten their ally Israel. If you really wanted to be left alone, I would think you would try to live a little more quietly. It seems like every time I turn on the TV some crazy little Iranian is complaining about the Great Satan, the United States."

Amir eyed him silently with a scowl darkening his face. "Russia could just as easily be considered a Great Satan. You are infidels who believe in nothing but your military power. Right now you are look-ing at the innocent people in Estonia and trying to figure out how to get your tanks as far as possible into the country. Please don't be a hypocrite."

"On the contrary. I am a soldier and know my duty. I follow my orders. But I would not walk into this town's marketplace with a bomb strapped to me."

"No, but you have no problem dropping a missile on it or having your tanks roll through the square."

It was starting to get heated, so Fannie decided to intervene. "That's right, Amir. We are here to help him with his assignment. Russia is our ally for now. You don't have to trust the country, you just have to help this man." She took a moment to let that sink in, then answered his ear-lier question. "I am speaking with an American military officer because at some point soon he might be useful in delaying the American forces when they try to stop the Russian attack. If he and his unit are placed on alert, I can pass on that information. There is much more to fighting the Great Satan than spewing the same chants in protests."

Amir flushed red, his dark skin a mask of fury. "Do not talk to me like I am a schoolchild. I know exactly what my mission is and how to accomplish it." He moved his chair closer to her and brought his right hand up as if about to slap her.

Fannie didn't wince. Then, with startling speed, Major Severov reached across the table to grasp Amir's wrist. He jerked once and pulled the little man off the chair onto the cobblestones on the outdoor café's sidewalk where the table was set up. The Russian didn't say a word as he looked down at the confused Iranian.

Fannie liked this handsome major more and more.

Major Bill Shepherd almost rolled the Humvee as he turned the corner and screeched to a stop. The crowd outside the gate had pushed in around a car that had crashed through the barriers and hit the gate, causing a gap people could squeeze through. His marines had done an excellent job of closing in tight around the gap, with several of them holding back with rifles in case there was a problem.

The army personnel made up the secondary defense and ringed the marines. The captain in charge had done an excellent job of keeping a lid on things. Their goal was to keep the protesters from entering the base, not to disperse them. If it came to that, the German police would have to act. The fact that there were only a dozen or so uniformed officers for a crowd of nearly five hundred told Shepherd that they didn't want to be viewed as instigators or oppressors. It was a familiar reaction since some of the riots in the United States several years earlier. The media tended to blame the police presence for the violence, and as a result there was pressure to have fewer police on scene. That led to more disruption to everyone's lives and the endangerment of innocent people who happened to be near some of the riots.

The crowd looked angry, and a few younger men tried to squeeze through the opening in the gate, only to be poked hard with a long baton by one of the marines. At least it wasn't a bayonet like the Russians would've used. No shots had been fired, which was probably the most important thing at this point.

Then Shepherd caught a peek of someone running into the center of the crowd. A moment later there was a blinding flash and a concussion that knocked the marines closest to the gate to the ground. It stunned Shepherd even though he was forty yards away. As he got to his feet, his head cleared, and he realized it had to be a suicide bomber.

There were screams in the crowd, and any organization they had dissolved in an instant. He yelled to the captain to pull the men back from the gate and rescue the wounded marines. Outside, the German police were scurrying around and calling for assistance. There were dozens of people on the ground, and most of them looked beyond help.

Then he heard someone from the crowd shout in English, "The marines threw a grenade." The same voice repeated the phrase in German several times, then again in English, until everyone was saying it.

Shepherd moved forward, wondering if it would help to rebut the lie. But by the time he was near the gate, things were out of control.

He had the sinking feeling this whole string of events wasn't going to end anytime soon.

Derek Walsh realized any one of the young FBI agents would notice him in a moment, and if he waited, Tonya Stratford would be able to point him out. His new look only went so far. She was a professional and had picked him out of the crowd. If he ran, he'd immediately be identified, and he had no doubt these men could run him down. He didn't even want to think about using the pistol in his waistband. He might have been out of his mind with fear over what had happened, but he wasn't stupid. Shooting someone would make him a real criminal, and he couldn't justify that in his own mind.

He looked up quickly to see that Stratford and her little group of people were more than halfway across the courtyard and would reach his crowd of spectators in less than twenty seconds. The men in the back had worked their way up and were now stationed almost behind him.

Walsh glanced around the crowd, sweat starting to build on his forehead and under his arms, his breathing picking up speed as he tried to figure a way out of this. A few feet to his right, a young reporter was scribbling notes on a narrow pad that fit in his hand. Earlier, Walsh had noticed a small clip-on badge that said NEW YORK TIMES. It wasn't clearly displayed, but the short young man with black hair and thick glasses had been standing there as long as Walsh had. There had also been a man with a camera talking to him and taking photographs he pointed out. The young man fit Walsh's needs nicely. He didn't like what he was about to do, but the fact that the man was casually dressed and had shaggy black hair made him the perfect target.

Just as the uniformed policemen who had a K-9 on a leash turned and started to walk back to the crowd, Walsh stole a glance to gauge how much time he had. He let the dog come forward, and just as it was next to the young reporter Walsh screamed out, "That guy has a bomb."

The entire crowd reacted at once. People spread out, a woman fell to the ground and screamed, and the dog, startled by the commotion, turned and faced the dark-haired *New York Times* reporter. As if by magic everyone focused their attention on the slim young man in the middle of the crowd. It was as if the dog had alerted on him, but only Walsh knew exactly what had happened.

Now people were scurrying to get away from the man they thought had a bomb strapped to his body, and the dog handler was trying to understand what had happened. He started to address the man, who was too startled to speak and merely held up his hands as if he had a gun pointed at him. The cop was trying to reason with him when other people started shouting, "Someone stop him."

Walsh looked over to see the young FBI agents consumed by the unfolding drama. He slowly slid backward in the most subtle movement he could muster. In a few seconds he was at the rear of the crowd and no one had noticed him, almost as if he were invisible. Now he turned and started to walk quickly, not running and definitely not drawing attention to himself. As soon as he was around the corner he started to jog. The commotion of the potential bomber was well behind him now, and ahead of him a group of actual protesters was walking along the sidewalk and in the street, trying to scratch parked police cars with whatever they had in their hands. But there were no cops near them. The rowdy main protests had attracted them, and Walsh suspected whatever cops were in the area were now running toward the site of a potential bomber.

He felt guilty for identifying the young man as a bomber, but satisfied at the same time that he'd figured out how to slip away from the crowd. He glanced over his shoulder to make sure no one was following him, and when he turned back he almost collided with a man stepping out of the side exit door.

Walsh's immediate reaction was to say, "Excuse me." It was instinct drilled into him by parents who insisted he be polite, and then the Marine Corps, who insisted even harder that he be polite.

The man said, "No problem, smart guy. Remember me?"

Suddenly Walsh realized it was Tonya Stratford's partner, Frank Martin, from the FBI. He hadn't escaped after all.

15

Derek Walsh kept calm as the FBI agent's grip on his arm tightened. It was the definition of an "iron grip." Frank Martin wasn't pudgy, he was solid, and age hadn't diminished his strength in the least.

Martin said, "You've got a lot to answer for, smart guy. I don't care if you're a veteran or not, you're about to have the most unpleasant experience of your life." He pulled Walsh around, slamming him into the side of the building.

Walsh realized he was about to be searched. He had to think quickly and knew he couldn't take this guy out with a single punch or elbow. Then he saw how close the protesters were and shouted, "This guy is one of the Thomas Brothers stooges. He's trying to keep me quiet. He's trying to keep all of us quiet."

The group of ten protesters, who had been chanting about Thomas Brothers raping the country, turned, almost as one, and stared at Martin holding Walsh against the wall. Two men on the end of the group were tall and clearly in a hostile mood.

The FBI agent looked up to see who Walsh was yelling to. Before he could even say anything, the protesters had surged forward, and one of the tall men shoved the FBI agent hard, knocking him away from Walsh.

The young man was dressed like a lumberjack with a red plaid shirt. The other tall protester, who looked like a derelict in ripped jeans and a dirty T-shirt, stepped forward for his own shove.

Then the whole group swarmed toward Martin.

Walsh didn't wait to see what else happened; he merely turned and started to run across the street and away from danger. He could hear the FBI man saying, "Get back, this is a police matter." That slowed the crowd but still didn't open a corridor for the FBI man to give chase.

As Walsh disappeared around the next corner, he looked over his shoulder and saw Martin pushing through the crowd and getting hopelessly tangled with the protesters.

Walsh ran hard for a few blocks, taking turns blindly. He thought that might make it harder for him to be followed. After ten minutes he found himself near the water in Battery Park. It was alive with small groups of protesters getting ready to march on the city.

He caught his breath and realized it was getting late and he was tired of this bullshit. He was going to lie low, then head over to Alena's to get all of this straightened out. He'd approach carefully and watch for traps, but he figured no one knew enough about his girlfriend to provide any information to the authorities. The guys at work knew her first name and had met her at a happy hour once, months ago. Her place could be a safe harbor.

Major Anton Severov sat at a cramped desk inside his equally cramped room at a bed and breakfast south of Tartu. Fannie had made arrangements and paid for the three rooms, but he had been careful not to let Amir see what room number he was staying in. The little Iranian had a crazy streak that scared Severov. Fannie, on the other hand, seemed to have no business working with a terror group. That also scared him. Until now he had always thought of groups like ISIS or al Qaeda as being nothing but a bunch of nuts you could identify a mile away by their thick beards or their headgear. Now he was viewing them more like their own little country that could use spies and tactics other countries couldn't consider. They were organized, funded, and dangerous.

This operation was a perfect example. He was being escorted, albeit by this bickering couple, and shown the best way for a military operation to take place. When Russian tanks rolled down these streets, they would be doing it faster because they had gotten help from Islamic extremists. He also had a suspicion, although no one told him and he was smart enough not to ask, that the current financial turmoil had somehow been instigated as part of this operation. It didn't take a genius to figure out the rash of lone wolf terror attacks had been coordinated through a terror network.

If he looked at it all in perspective, al Qaeda and ISIS were much more formidable than he would ever have considered. The Islamists he had fought in Georgia were really nothing more than a militia and, aside from inflicting some casualties and blowing up a few buildings, barely slowed the Russian army as it rolled in to restore order. This was something else, and he would have to consider it carefully. He was sure someone in the army had reports that detailed the same concerns, but he would add to his own just to be safe.

The other thing that troubled him was the number of friendly Estonians he had met on his first day of this assignment. It's one thing to look at a military plan and execute it by driving your tank across the countryside; it's another to see the faces of children who might be left homeless when the plan became reality. One older woman in particular reminded him of his mother, who lived with his stepfather and two sisters in a suburb of Moscow. He couldn't imagine someone driving his mother out of her house or threatening his sisters, but that's exactly what was going to happen with these poor people once Russian tanks rolled across the border.

A gentle tap on his door brought him back to reality and made him wish he had a pistol with him. There was no need to protect himself around the Estonians, but his escorts were another story. He slid the tiny wooden chair back and stood up carefully, then waited to the side of the door and listened. A moment later there was another soft tap that echoed in the tiny room.

He said in English, "Yes?"

A woman's voice said, "May I come in?" It was Fannie.

"Are you alone?"

"Of course." She threw in a girlish giggle to convince him.

He wasn't taking any chances and opened the door a crack, ready to throw his weight into anyone other than Fannie. He might not have had a gun, but he was confident he could outfight one of these jihadists if he used the element of surprise.

But the surprise was on him when he opened the door and Fannie slipped into the room wearing a heavy bathrobe and slippers. She flopped onto his bed and gave him a dazzling smile.

Fannie said, "I thought you might be lonely."

Severov was careful to lean back on the desk and not show his desire as he gazed upon the lovely young woman. Since he had heard her phone call with an American marine officer earlier in the evening, he realized how adept she was at manipulating men. He wasn't sure he wanted any part of that. They could end up being on the opposite sides of the conflict at any moment. She even told him the alliance between her group and his country was temporary because, as she put it, "the enemy of my enemy is my friend."

It seemed that Fannie finally realized he was not about to jump onto the bed with her. She stood up and leaned against him. She wrapped her arms around his neck and gave him a long, passionate kiss.

It had been some time since he'd felt a woman like this in his arms. Who cared if she manipulated him? As long as he was aware of what was happening, he'd be safe. And so would his secrets.

Joseph Katazin was waiting in the only place he was certain Derek Walsh would eventually come to. He had eyes all over the city and people reporting back to him every twenty minutes, and so far the only place the former marine had been seen was near his office. Katazin's associate said he thought some cops were chasing him, but Walsh got away. That all made sense to Joseph Katazin. He would probably do the same thing. He would get back to his office to see what intelligence he could gather, but then he would head here. What sane man wouldn't?

Katazin had only brought one man with him: Serge, who still had a black eye and swollen face from the homeless guy punching him outside of Walsh's apartment. He'd decided to use Serge so he could channel his anger as a motivator in case something went wrong.

He had to question Walsh to make sure he hadn't learned anything, then dispose of him as quickly and quietly as possible. It would be to the operation's benefit if Walsh's body was never found. The police would just assume it was a suicide because that was the easiest thing to do. If he'd only been successful that first night and put a bullet in the banker's temple, then left the gun at Walsh's side, it would've looked like the man had killed himself over his guilt for stealing so much money and sending it to Switzerland. Instead Walsh had reported it as a robbery attempt.

Katazin was confident he could correct that mistake in the next few hours.

Derek Walsh had carefully made his way toward the Upper West Side, closer to Columbia University and his girlfriend Alena's apartment. The farther he got from the financial district, the less disruption there was on the street. He had noticed that by the time he reached the theater district, life appeared pretty much normal except that the usual crowds of tourists weren't there. He could understand that no one wanted to risk being out in a major city with all of the lone wolf terror attacks occurring, but it was a little spooky as he cut across Times Square and never had to change his course or pace. About a third of the touristy stores were closed, and many of the people walking across the square were glued to the giant screen broadcasting news.

There had been two attempted suicide bombings in the subway, one by an inept bomber whose remote didn't work. The other was thwarted when someone noticed a suspicious-looking man wearing a long coat and told the cop on the platform. The cop did a masterful job of coming up behind the man and didn't hesitate as he grabbed him and wrestled him to the dirty subway floor. Once the man was handcuffed, the cop discovered a nasty nail bomb wrapped around his midsection.

The mayor had declared that the city wouldn't be intimidated and the subways would still run. It was brash but a gamble. Sooner or later one of the bombers would be successful.

As Walsh continued through Times Square there was not a cop in sight, so he stopped and read the ticker running under a silent newscast showing some sort of demonstration in Europe. As the screen flashed different images, his eyes kept drifting to the one-line feed under the footage. There had now been over fifty terror attacks across Europe and the United States. All the financial markets had stopped trading and were not planning on using computers once they started up again.

Then, as he was staring up at the screen, a photo of his driver's license picture flashed. He was stunned for a moment as he looked up, seeing his face on the giant screen. Now they were getting serious about finding him. He nervously glanced around and realized no one was paying attention to anyone else. His photo quickly disappeared from the screen only to be replaced by film footage of the outside of Thomas Brothers Financial. It showed the increasingly rowdy protesters clashing with the police, who were doing everything they could to keep this from becoming a deadly incident.

Walsh decided not to risk the subway and instead caught an uptown bus to Alena's neighborhood. Looking for a place to hang out until Alena got home, he came across a deli called Doaba off Columbus Avenue. There were no TVs, and the place wasn't crowded, so he quietly ate a sandwich while he waited. Walsh used the Boost phone he had bought at Mike Rosenberg's suggestion to call her cell phone and left a message. He didn't bother to leave a message on her home phone. He knew she was rarely in the apartment before five o'clock, and he'd head there then.

Right now he was happy to be in a comfortable place figuring out what his next move would be.

Mike Rosenberg couldn't remember moving so frantically within the offices of the CIA. There was no way he could get a call from his friend Derek Walsh while he was at work. He locked his cell phone in the car before he came through security, where he was searched thoroughly for anything that might transmit information outside the building. He had a lead as his focus right now, and that was finding out all he could about the bank account where the money from Thomas Brothers was transferred.

It was easy to speak to the analysts helping the FBI, and it didn't take long to confirm that the account was opened in the bank that was blown up in an apparent terror attack in Bern, Switzerland. Immediately Rosenberg recognized this was quite a coincidence. He was sure someone else had figured it out as well, so he kept moving.

The account had been opened by a female using the name Francine Talmont who was listed as white and twenty-seven years of age. That didn't tell him much. Some more digging determined that several FBI agents had been dispatched to interview anyone who might have worked at the bank and wasn't there at the time of the explosion. Sixty-six people were dead and the few survivors appeared to be people working in offices on the top floor. Part of it had remained standing long enough for them to be evacuated.

Rosenberg didn't like the way everything seemed to be going wrong at once. Money was transferred to terrorists, the financial markets were in an absolute freefall, rioting had broken out across Europe and the United States, and there were so many small terror attacks that not all of them were being reported. It felt like too much to happen at once without there being a larger goal.

He was relieved to see that the U.S. military had been put on alert, but that didn't change his unease at the idea of a giant distraction, which he thought all of this was. Since Russia had annexed Crimea and threatened

Ukraine, Rosenberg had been much more careful when he studied world maps, trying to figure out where the next hot point might be.

He still had a lot of work to do, but he didn't want to miss a call from Derek Walsh. He would head out the door sometime after five and hit this all again hard in the morning. By then he'd have more information to act on.

16

Derek Walsh felt out of place on the Upper West Side of Manhattan. There were no protests going on and no real need for a heavy police presence. The population was better dressed, and he felt shabby in his untucked shirt and now-uncombed hair. He'd tried to call Mike Rosenberg on his new throwaway phone, but Mike didn't answer, and he left no message. It was his hope that Mike would see the New York number and realize he should call it back as soon as he was able.

He made the short walk from the deli he'd been sitting in to Alena's apartment building in just a few minutes. Walsh looked at his watch and realized it was almost exactly six o'clock in the evening and she should be home by now. He paused outside the front door of her five-story walk-up and glanced down the street to make sure he hadn't been followed. Was he becoming paranoid? If he was, he'd earned the right. There were very few people on the street and no police officers. It was time to find some respite at the one place he'd feel safe.

There was no doorman even though the building looked like it should have one. As he walked up the four flights of stairs, he did consider the irony of a foreign student living so much better than a would-be Wall Street banker. The place was clean, and her apartment was more than twice the size of Walsh's SoHo flat.

He stepped out of the stairwell onto the new plush carpet in the hallway, then took a moment to straighten his shirt. He wondered how he'd explain the pistol on his belt to Alena. He'd just tell her the truth and let the chips fall. It didn't matter; all he needed now was to see her beautiful face and feel her arms around him. He knew she must be sick with worry over not hearing from him.

He paused again just outside her door, ran his fingers through his short brown hair, and gave the door his special rap, four quick knocks with a slight pause before two more. It was Morse code for "Hi." Alena didn't care much for secret knocks or nicknames. Maybe it was cultural. Walsh hoped to see for himself one day and planned a visit to Greece when he had saved enough money. At this rate it would be years, unless he had to flee because of extradition.

From inside he heard Alena's voice say, "It's open."

Walsh loved her slight accent. He opened the door and felt a wave of relief when he saw her sitting up straight in the antique chair by her wide bay window that looked out onto another building.

Alena stayed seated as she said, "Derek, I was worried I'd never see you again."

As Walsh stepped into the room a male's voice behind him said, "Me, too."

Walsh spun quickly to see a man holding a Beretta pistol, just like his. It took a moment for him to realize it was the same man who tried to rob him. The man with a scar on his face. And he realized for the first time the man had a Russian accent.

Joseph Katazin felt very confident holding the pistol in one hand pointed at the former marine a few feet in front of him. He stepped out from behind the door, and Walsh was smart enough to turn his body so they remained face-to-face. That also gave Walsh a chance to see Serge pop up from behind the tall back of the chair that Walsh's girlfriend was sitting in.

Katazin said, "Recognize him?"

"What do you want?"

Katazin liked the fact that the former marine didn't want to waste any time. "A few answers. Not much more." He paused, then said, "I like what you've done with your hair. Interesting choice, and probably enough to throw off most people."

Walsh let his eyes roam around the room, then focused his attention back on Katazin. "What sort of questions?"

"Who have you talked to? What have you told them? Who is the old guy who hit Serge? You know, the usual." He watched Walsh as the marine turned and looked at Serge, assessing his black eye and bruised face. Walsh's expression gave away the fact that his true concern was for the young lady, and Katazin might be able to use that later.

Walsh stared straight ahead at Katazin and said, "And if I don't feel like answering any of your questions?"

Katazin looked over to Serge and made a motion with his left hand around his neck. He was surprised the dim-witted Serge picked up on exactly what he wanted done. The lean young man with a badly bruised face didn't hesitate to grasp the cord holding the blinds and drape it around Alena's throat.

Before Walsh could say anything else, Katazin jerked his left hand, and Serge followed the order by tightening the cord like a noose around the young woman's throat. She gasped and rose in the seat slightly as Serge pulled the cord tighter across her windpipe. Her face almost immediately went red.

Walsh called out, "No, stop."

Then Katazin heard a phone. It took a second to realize the ringing was coming from Walsh's pocket. But by then the marine was already moving.

———

Mike Rosenberg had done everything he could and still was leaving the building later than he had meant to. One of the things that slowed him down was a presidential address that started at exactly five thirty. The timing of the press conference had told everyone this was important, and the whole building seemed to come to a standstill, every eye glued to the nearest TV set.

Being a former military man and currently employed by the federal government, Rosenberg took the idea of the president being his boss very seriously. He wanted the president to bolster the country and tell the citizens exactly what was happening and the plan to fix it. But once again this president had let him down. He didn't know why he was disappointed; it wasn't the first time. Of course the president urged calm. Every president in history who had access to mass media had urged calm during times of crisis. The most famous was Franklin Roosevelt's "We have nothing to fear but fear itself." This president was not Franklin Roosevelt. He looked more annoyed at the public's reaction than anything else.

Rosenberg and some of the people he worked with wondered if this guy understood threats. Incredibly, his foreign policy had set the country back further than his predecessor's. Cool only got you so far. Now people needed a leader. A true commander in chief, not an empty suit with a few catchphrases.

The security check was quick as he stepped through a scanner. No briefcase meant he avoided the longer scrutiny. As he hustled out to the parking lot, Rosenberg hoped the president's speech had not depressed the rest of the country as much as it had him. Now he really was worried. It didn't matter if everything that happened was a distraction for some kind of Russian military activity; the president clearly had no plan in place to deal with it.

Rosenberg got to his one-year-old Chevy Impala and dug his personal phone out of the console. There was a call from a number with the 212 area code that he didn't recognize. He hesitated before he hit the redial button. This had to be Derek Walsh, but he was nervous about the contact. He knew what agencies like the NSA could do with just a fragment of information. He also wondered if the FBI had linked him to Walsh from their time in the marines together. He didn't want to be considered an accomplice to what could turn out to be one of the most disastrous crimes in history.

Then he pictured his friend, alone, and he knew he couldn't abandon Walsh. Besides, the FBI looked like it was too busy right now with the hunt for a banker who might or might not have sent money to terrorists.

He mashed the button and heard the phone ring.

Fannie Legat slid out of bed in the middle of the night. The tall Russian major snored soundly and never noticed her ease toward the door and back out of the cramped room. He didn't notice her smile, either. It had been a wonderful night. In truth, she wasn't sure why she had approached him at first. She was always thinking of *the Cause* before anything else and viewed him as a potential source of information. She clearly liked him and appreciated his manners, but the American major had similar manners. It was just something about this Russian that melted her will, and she had given herself to him freely in the end. Maybe it was because the Russians, like most Muslims, had very little materially and the U.S. had so much. Did that make it jealousy? Was she envious of the American lifestyle? She shook off the notion.

It was against the established norms of Islam and her own standard of behavior to sleep with a man who was not her husband. It was not like she was a virgin. In fact, before she had seen the true path she had had many liaisons, mostly with other students. But she was a woman, and men paid attention to her. Sometimes it had an effect. She had no regrets about this lapse, but the last thing she wanted was for Amir to find out. She didn't care what the little dope thought of her, but she could not have him reporting back to their superiors that she was free with her favors and sleeping with men.

She hurried down the narrow hallway with her robe wrapped tight. The hotel was saving money by not heating the hallways, and she wanted to avoid anyone who might be out at this ungodly hour.

Just as she reached her room and turned the knob she had purposely left unlocked, the door next to her swung open, and Amir thrust his head out and barked, "Just what do you think you are doing?"

"More than you."

"Harlot."

Fannie answered the only way she knew how, by slapping him hard across the face, then stepping into her room with as much dignity as she could muster. He would be a problem, and she would have to deal with him soon.

Derek Walsh knew that hesitation could kill him, or worse, kill Alena. When the phone in his pocket rang and distracted the man with the gun, he lowered his head and instantly charged forward like a linebacker. He let his full weight slam into the man and heard the pistol clatter onto the hardwood floor and bounce off the wall into the hallway. He turned and reached for his own pistol in one movement. As soon as he had it aimed at the other man's face, the man dropped the cord, and Alena slipped back into the chair, immediately gasping for breath and grabbing her throat with both hands.

His mind was clouded with a thousand details, but he knew he had to grab Alena and get out of there now. He yanked her from the chair and pulled her along as he bolted out the door and turned toward the stairwell. She was keeping up and sounded like her airway was open as they hit the stairway, and he sent her ahead so he could turn and back down slowly with the pistol pointed at the top of the stairs. No one seemed to be following.

Who in the hell were these guys?

17

Putin had made a great effort to make his schedule appear as normal as possible. But he needed to speak with Andre Maysak about the Estonian operation, and everyone involved had agreed that no discussions about it would take place over a telephone.

One of Putin's aides had found a reason for him to visit the administrative offices of the Federal Council in its main building on Bolshaya Dmitrovka Street. The six-story main office building had no architectural significance. It was an ugly, efficient building constructed in the eighties.

Putin's security team had already met with security at the building, which escorted them quickly from a side entrance to the long, sterile hallways. The executive elevator only operated for the highest-level members of the council. Putin and his group took it to the fifth floor, where Andre Maysak's maze of aides and clerical people worked in cubicles that surrounded Andre's office.

Putin walked alone down the Persian rug that led to the two wide oak doors. He pushed open the door to see his old friend come out from his wide desk to greet him.

As soon as they were seated facing each other in matching Karelian birch chairs that were as uncomfortable as they were unsightly, Andre fired questions at Putin like a Western reporter.

Putin held up his hand and said, "Andre, you sound like a nervous old woman. Let me give you a summary. Then you can ask your silly questions." He smiled to put his friend at ease and let him know they were equals in this endeavor.

He jumped right in with the most important information. "Andre, all is well, I assure you. The operation continues without interruption. Most importantly, no one has detected our troops on the Estonian border. We have held different military exercises in the area over the past year and pulled together sixty thousand troops who believe they are part of a new exercise. We picked just the right spot. The troops and three hundred tanks are dispersed over a fairly wide area and not attracting any attention. There's been no movement at all from NATO. Not even the Estonian defense force has noticed our buildup. It's all coming together now, from our choice of a target to our idea of using such a small force."

Andre chuckled and said, "There are few countries that would consider more than sixty thousand troops and three hundred tanks a small force."

"We're lucky to be able to do so. Besides, what's the use of having such a massive military if we never use it?"

"And how will the world look at us for using that massive military on such a tiny, undefended neighbor?"

"Not much differently than they looked at us when we took Crimea. This is a chance to claim a quick, bloodless, decisive victory and show the world that Russia is no longer dormant and cowering from Western military strength."

"And how many civilians will be killed during this 'bloodless' victory?"

Putin did not care for his associate's tone, but he answered anyway. "We hope to avoid casualties. That's the goal. But once the operation begins there is no telling."

Andre shifted uncomfortably in his seat and said, "What about the civilians already killed by the terror attacks in Western Europe and the United States?"

"Those casualties are unfortunate and relatively few, considering the size of the countries involved. They are also necessary. If Russia is to be resurgent, we must be bold. We must act boldly. Besides, the terrorists would have eventually acted on their own to hit the U.S. All we did was convince them to do it at the same time as our operation in Estonia."

"Vladimir, you sound like you're trying to convince yourself. How bad will the terror attacks get?"

Putin considered his answer and everything he had been told by Yuri Simplov. Then he said, "The first wave of attacks is almost over. There will be more, but nothing like we've seen. There are only so many radical jihadists available in the Western countries, and their intelligence services and police services are really quite good at detecting these attacks. But we can't lose sight of our main objective, the military aspect of our operation and the quick takeover of Estonia."

Andre still appeared unconvinced. Putin was frustrated and not used to explaining himself, but he had few enough people to talk to about this operation, and he would need Andre's support later on.

"Do we continue to suffer the EU sanctions and live in fear of toothless resolutions from the United Nations?" Putin asked. "Do we stand idly by while NATO expands and offers invitations to our former republics? This Estonian action will show the world how ineffective NATO really is. It is a chance to assert ourselves and discredit NATO at the same time." Even Putin was surprised at his passion while explaining it to Andre. Maybe more passion than he had realized. He sounded and felt like a patriot.

He grabbed his friend's full attention and leaned forward in the uncomfortable chair. "When this starts, when the army rolls, you, Andre, will need to ensure our support in both the Duma and the Federation Council. The people will back any successful action. Marx had it wrong.

Religion is not the opiate of the people; pride is. National pride is the drug of choice. And our people are crying out for pride.

Even Andre understood this concept.

Derek Walsh walked quickly along the sidewalk, practically dragging Alena by the hand. He'd taken a moment outside her apartment building to say, "Don't ask any questions yet. Let's get a safe distance away." He pulled her east and intended to turn south toward Times Square. His first order of business was to make sure she was safe in a cheap hotel, and the empty tourist district would be the perfect location. Once he knew she was safe, then he could do whatever he had to, which looked more and more like it might be something desperate.

He also needed a few minutes away from her to call his friend Mike Rosenberg back. He would have to tell Rosenberg how he had saved Walsh's life by distracting a man with a gun when the phone rang at just the right moment. That made Walsh consider what had happened. It wasn't just a man with a gun. It was a *Russian* man with a gun. And another Russian tried to strangle Alena.

A few blocks away from her building, Walsh stopped and examined Alena's neck to make sure she wasn't hurt. There was almost no visible trauma, and she didn't seem to have any trouble breathing. But she was still clearly upset and started to ask him questions now that they had paused in their trek.

"Derek, what's going on? Who are those men?" Before he could even answer she added, "We need to call the police." She stopped and stared at him, then said, "What happened to your hair?"

He shook his head and said, "Have you been watching the news at all and seeing what's going on?"

She nodded.

"Everyone is blaming me."

"What? What are you talking about?"

He felt a wave of relief that she had not seen his name or photograph on the news. He gave her a quick overview of what had happened and how he got away from the FBI. It didn't seem to satisfy her in any way.

She just stared at him and said, "I don't understand. Why did you allow someone to make a trade like that on your computer?"

"I didn't *allow* anyone. Someone must have stolen my security plug and used it to make the trade. If that's what happened, I have a security feature on the plug enabled, and it would have taken a photograph of anyone at the computer at the time of the trade. All I have to do is get back to Thomas Brothers Financial and access their computer network. That will allow the plug to bring up the photographs stored on it."

"Have you told the police about the photos?" Alena asked.

"They didn't really listen. I intend to be better prepared the next time we talk. That's why I gotta get back to my office."

"Right now?"

"First we're going to get you to a hotel safely."

She nodded her head and said, "There's a W in Times Square."

"We'll be staying at someplace a little more modest. Maybe the Edison." He ignored the little face she made. This was not one of the times that he was working overtime just to make her happy. He had to preserve his stash of money just in case this thing went on longer than he expected.

After walking for a while and then jumping on a bus, Walsh and Alena found themselves in a nearly deserted Times Square. This would make for easier negotiations with a hotel clerk. It was now dark outside, and the brilliant lights of Times Square seemed eerie shining on an empty street.

They stopped at a McDonald's to grab a quick hamburger. They weren't going anywhere fancy tonight. As they sat in the booth, he decided that Alena had calmed down enough for him to ask, "How did those men find your apartment?"

She didn't stop chewing on the cheeseburger as she shrugged her shoulders. "When I heard the knock on the door, I just assumed it was you. They only got there about ten minutes before you."

That made Walsh consider what linked him to her apartment. The FBI might have interviewed coworkers and learned about Alena, although he hadn't told them much about her and she had never come to an office party. She preferred privacy. Then Walsh remembered another person he had told: Charlie. Had the vet been playing a game or given up information for money? Was that how he was able to get the drop on the younger Russian outside Walsh's apartment? It was unsettling to consider. He turned his attention back to Alena.

Walsh said, "What did they say? Did they tell you anything I might be able to use?"

"They just asked where you were, if I had talked to you, and if I expected you at the apartment." She put down the remnant of her cheeseburger and said, "I think we should go to the police right now."

He shook his head and said, "Please trust me on this. I've got to figure a few more things out. We'll get a room and a good night's sleep, but first I have to make an important phone call."

Joseph Katazin sat up from the floor and immediately grabbed his side. That son of a bitch Walsh was so strong he cracked Katazin's rib when he slammed into him. Katazin had just enough strength left to stop Serge from chasing the couple fleeing from the apartment. Serge already had his CZ model 75 in his hand and murder in his eyes. Although Katazin had questions he needed answered, Serge just wanted to kill. It was a Russian mob point of honor to get revenge for attacks like that. Too bad Serge had no idea that this wasn't mob business and the same rules didn't apply. He'd have to get used to that. Katazin was sure Serge wouldn't say anything to any of his friends, simply out of embarrassment. But with a loud snap of Katazin's voice Serge had frozen in place.

Then the younger man looked back at his employer and said in Russian, "I can catch up to them before they're on the street."

"It's better this way. He might inadvertently lead us somewhere we hadn't thought of. I know you want your revenge, but this won't be the last time we see Mr. Walsh. I can guarantee you that."

Katazin had to be careful to keep in mind that this was only one small part of the overall plan. He needed to spend more time on the other elements. Already the protests and violence had started to subside here in New York. He knew his government needed at least four days of distraction to maximize the benefit to their military. That was the goal.

He wasn't sure what his temporary partners the Muslims had left, but he knew there were still a few surprises. They could disrupt travel easily in the United States, but he suspected there were other attacks he had never even considered.

He stood up and slowly decided he needed to head back to his house to keep his wife happy and quiet and get some much-needed rest. He turned to his young associate and said, "Serge, tomorrow you will have another chance at Mr. Walsh. Unless it is an emergency, I will let you deal with him any way you'd like. Is that fair?"

The Russian with the puffy eye and sore jaw nodded vigorously.

Mike Rosenberg couldn't sit still and fiddled around his small rented house near Interstate 495 just outside Bethesda, Maryland. He was surprised he'd gotten such a good deal on the two-bedroom house north of Washington, D.C., only a short drive from his office in Langley, Virginia. The CIA liked to help their own, and a case officer who was deployed in South America had given him a sweetheart deal for a year. In fact, it was almost as if he were house-sitting. He took the responsibility seriously and kept the place looking like a showroom floor at IKEA.

His long hours at the CIA prevented him from having a dog, but he would often borrow the next-door neighbor's golden retriever and go for long jogs. He also found the dog made it easier to meet women at the local park. Usually he told them he worked for the Department of the Treasury as a quality inspection specialist. No one really wanted to ask questions about a job title like that.

Right now, he had his personal cell phone in his pocket, hoping Derek Walsh would call him back. The 60-inch Sony TV was on CNN as he listened to the news coming in from around the world. He always got the bulk of his news from U.S. stations, then watched the BBC for a different view. He had found the foreign stations were not necessarily more accurate, but it certainly gave him a better idea of how the rest of the world looked at the United States.

Some of the initial protests had petered out in New York, but there were still the ongoing lone wolf terror attacks, not only in New York but across the entire country. Rosenberg had a hypothesis that these attacks had been scheduled to happen around the same time and he believed the first wave of these attacks were spent. The pace and targets indicated that. He was certain more attacks were on the way.

So far the attack that had captured the most attention today was a man who wore an explosive vest and detonated it in the ticket line for Disneyland in Anaheim, California. That struck at the heart of American fears. Dozens of children were injured, but a quirk of engineering, a pillar the man was standing next to, had absorbed and directed much of the blast. It saved dozens of lives; even so, nine people were confirmed dead, and several major theme parks had closed their doors for security reasons. It was that sort of activity that had emboldened terrorists. Everyone liked to use the phrase "If we restrict people's rights, the terrorists win." More accurately it was "If Americans cave in to terrorist demands, the terrorists win." It was a subtle but important distinction.

There was the usual nonstop debate about the president's address, but in this case very few people felt it was a positive message that sent any sort of reassurance out to the American people. Police forces across the United States were trying to figure out what they could do to keep people safe. The plans made so feverishly after the September 2001 attacks had slowly become obsolete. Technology and population shifts and a lack of money to update the plans had left most cities unprepared for attacks like these. Experience was one of the best teachers, and luckily there were still cops and administrators who remembered the lessons from 9/11.

Rosenberg's phone rang, and he grabbed it immediately. He felt a wave of relief mixed with apprehension when he heard his friend's voice. All he could blurt out was, "Jesus Christ, Tubby, what the hell happened?"

"I gotta tell you the truth, Mike, I have almost no more information than when I talked to you earlier. One thing that troubles me is that Russians are involved."

"What do you mean, Russians?"

Rosenberg listened while Walsh laid out everything that had happened to him over the last few hours. It sounded like a spy movie, but he knew his friend wasn't given to exaggeration.

Finally Rosenberg said, "We've got to bring you in where it's safe."

"Bring me in? I'm not a spy. Right now all I am is a goddamned fugitive. I trust you, but I don't trust what the FBI would do. They want to wrap this up, and I'm the only suspect. I can't even give them anyone else as a bargaining chip. Someone thought this out really well."

"If you stay out there too long, you can do something that's a real crime. You can get yourself in more trouble. You've got to find a way to turn yourself in safely. You could come down here and I'll walk you into our headquarters. This is enough of an international issue that we could claim some sort of jurisdiction. You'd get a fair shake."

"I have a plan, Mike. It's gonna take me a day or two to work it out, and if I blow it, then maybe I'll come down to you. I'd ask you to put me and Alena up, but I don't want to screw up your whole career for helping a known fugitive. Besides, what I need to do is here in New York."

"Right now I'm young enough to start a new career. What I am worried about is keeping you alive. Is there anyone you can trust in New York?"

There was a long pause on the phone.

Rosenberg said, "That's what I thought. The two guys you can trust are in Virginia and Germany right now. And my bet is Bill Shepherd has his hands full."

Walsh said, "You believe me when I tell you I didn't do it, right, Mike?"

Rosenberg didn't hesitate. "You don't even have to tell me you didn't do it. I know you. I know you didn't do it." He sensed that Walsh had to pause as relief washed over him.

"Thanks, I needed to hear that. But I also need to figure out who did it."

"I'm working on a few angles from my office. Maybe I'll be able to find something. Call me tomorrow night about this time."

Rosenberg had to sit down after the call. Even when he was deployed in Afghanistan he didn't worry about his friends this much. He started considering different ways to attack the problem. Just like any good marine would.

18

Anton Severov was surprised Fannie could slip out of his room without him knowing it. It just showed how exhausted he was from preparing for this operation and the effect of his vigorous bout of lovemaking with the beautiful French Muslim. He wanted to believe she had some sort of feelings for him, but based on how she described her relationship with an American marine officer, he wasn't about to let any vital information slip. She was giving him an insight into the Muslim mind, and maybe he would understand the Georgian, Chechen, and other Muslim troops under his command a little better. They always seemed distant and defiant, but maybe they really believed they had reasons for that sort of attitude.

He got dressed in the crowded, tiny room and shoved his few pieces of clothing and a notebook into a worn-out duffel bag he'd carried across the border into Estonia. He needed to make a report and would use the special phone he was told was secure, although as with much of the equipment issued in Russia, claims of its effectiveness were almost always exaggerated.

It was still early, barely seven in the morning, and he hoped he'd beaten Fannie and Amir by at least an hour. He needed some quiet time to make more notes and the phone call. First he had to get a little food in him, and the tiny café attached to the hotel offered a good selection of rolls and Danish. The TV behind the counter where a heavyset woman poured him some coffee was set on the BBC and broadcast in English. He wondered if that was because of the expanding tourist trade. The European Union had worked wonders for Eastern Europe, and the conversion to the euro had made travel considerably easier for some of the wealthier residents of Europe. Estonia, with its good Internet infrastructure and ability to reach out to other parts of the continent, had gotten more than its share of eager tourists interested in the history and culture of the former Soviet Union satellite.

The reports on TV showed the rest of the continent in disarray, especially Great Britain and Germany. That was exactly what Severov wanted to see. If those two allies of the United States were seeing such violence, it would make it harder for the military to come to the aid of Estonia. He had seen a few protests on the streets during the drive, but overall the quaint country had been quite peaceful and calm. Sometimes he felt as if he were on a vacation rather than an assignment, and he would have to thank his commander when he returned home. The old man had gotten it exactly right.

Severov was still worried about his tanks and company, but now he would have a clear idea of how to cut across the country most efficiently. His plans now included how to avoid historic areas and not crush beautiful cobblestone streets. He would keep his reasons for making certain detours to himself, but it was his most sincere hope they could accomplish this operation without having to shatter the lives of the pleasant Estonian people he had met.

He finished his coffee and Danish and was about to step outside to make the phone call when Amir entered the empty dining room, marched directly to Severov, and said, "We must discuss something of great importance."

Major Bill Shepherd had grabbed a few hours' sleep before he received a message personally delivered by an army corporal who worked for the base commander. The young man almost looked embarrassed to hand him the note. It simply told Shepherd he needed to be in the main administrative building at 1000 hours to have an "informal discussion" with an ad hoc board of inquiry comprised of military and civilian personnel about the incident the night before involving the terror attack.

Even though he had a little time, the major realized he couldn't fall back asleep, so he shaved and slipped into a clean uniform. He specifically didn't wear a dress uniform or show any of his ribbons on his utility blouse. He wanted to make it clear that it was just another day and he didn't consider this anything more than an annoyance.

Shepherd recognized that if it was serious, the base commander would've given him more information and he'd be entitled to consult with an attorney. He'd have to wait for a judge advocate general to come from Berlin. This sounded like they just wanted a clear report of what had happened.

He watched an army captain supervise the reinforcing of the front gate after the vehicle had been run into it and the suicide bomber had detonated his explosives. It only took five minutes to see that the squared-away young captain knew what he was doing. The terror attack had had the unexpected consequence of dissipating the protest and dispersing the protesters back into Stuttgart. A few lonely and bored-looking German police officers waited on the fringes of the base in case someone came back, and a handful of investigators were picking up whatever forensic evidence of the blast remained.

Major Shepherd walked along the paved road toward the main administrative complex and the large conference room where he was about to face an inquiry by both military and civilian personnel about what had happened when the bomb exploded. There were persistent reports in the media that the marines had thrown grenades into the crowd in an effort to disperse them, and two FBI agents had been sent by the small liaison office in Berlin to make an official report. It was this sort of nonsense that wasted time during critical incidents that frustrated all military officers. But Shepherd was a pro and wasn't going to let these people get under his skin.

He had the casualty figures from the night before and was embarrassed to admit he was relieved no U.S. military personnel were killed. Six soldiers and three marines were wounded, two by the car barreling into the fence and the others by shrapnel from the explosion in the crowd. None of the injuries appeared to be serious, and more men were coming in today to help in the security of the base.

The commanding general himself welcomed Shepherd into the wide conference room that housed the long table. The general, a short, blocky man, looked like he had been born in the army with a crew cut, squared jaw, and arms that could lift a Humvee. He had a bland midwestern accent as he introduced Shepherd to the three other people at the table. One was the base provost, who technically was responsible for the defenses that Shepherd took over. The lieutenant colonel with sandy hair and a craggy face showed no offense at Shepherd stepping into the job; nor had he ever impressed Shepherd as being interested in protecting his turf. The man just wanted the base to be safe and any security matters to be handled efficiently.

A middle-aged woman with dark hair was a representative of the German Ministry of Justice, and he suspected she'd been sent to the panel because she could get there quickly and she had an excellent grasp of English.

The final member, Maria Alonso, was an attractive woman in her early thirties who had sharp, intelligent eyes. She was from the FBI legal attaché in Berlin, acting as liaison with the German police.

After the introductions, Shepherd shifted his lanky frame into the hard wooden chair on the other side of the table and looked across with the feeling that he was being interrogated.

He went through a brief description of the threat they had felt as protesters came closer to the fence and then someone ran a car into it. He made it clear that at no time were hand grenades ever considered as part of defense and that no one issued hand grenades. The first question from the German Ministry of Justice representative supported his concern.

The German woman said in accented English, "But you did have rifles, correct?"

"Yes, ma'am. We are part of the U.S. military. That involves being armed and defending ourselves and our country."

The German woman said, "Which would've meant shooting down innocent German civilians if things had gotten worse."

"Is that a question or comment?"

"A question, Major. We are only here to ask questions."

"I cannot say for sure we would *not* have fired on the crowd if they had broken into the base, but it would have been in self-defense, as a last resort and with only a few designated targets. That has always been our plan. We showed tremendous restraint, and frankly, the German police did nothing to help us. Is that part of your plan, madam? Leave us to fend for ourselves and take the blame if something goes wrong?"

The base commander said in a calm tone, "Let's keep this civil, Major. No one is questioning your leadership." He turned his head and looked down the table at the others and said, "I, for one, think you did an out-standing job. But we have been requested by the German government to look into the matter fully. And look into the matter we will. Is that clearly understood?"

All Shepherd said was, "It is, sir."

He caught a smile sweep over the FBI agent's pretty face. It wasn't condescending. It was mischievous.

Joseph Katazin sat in the older BMW in his own driveway in Brooklyn. He conducted some business directly out of his house, but it was the middle of the night, and he knew this call would test his patience. All the lights were out inside the house, with only the front porch light burning. Occasionally his wife would wait up for him if she really thought he was working at the import/export business. But in the past few years she had realized he had a number of extracurricular activities. She felt certain she knew what they were, but in reality she had no clue. As far as she was concerned he wasn't even a Russian but a Ukrainian. Like most other Americans, she barely knew the difference.

As soon as his phone had rung and he saw the number—because no one on this phone had names attached to the numbers—he knew there was a problem. He answered the phone tersely with a simple "Yes" in English.

The American on the other end of the phone read his tone correctly. He jumped right into it. "I can't guarantee we'll have many protesters tomorrow."

Katazin kept his tone cold and businesslike. "You told me four or five days of protests would be no problem."

"That's before bombs went off around the world and killed a bunch of protesters other places."

"There were no protesters killed in New York."

"There was a scare in the crowd across the Thomas Brothers courtyard today. A cop, or his K-9, picked a guy out of the crowd that they thought had a bomb. It was crazy for a few minutes and scared some of the protesters. Now I hear a lot of them say they're going to take a day off. Maybe more."

Katazin didn't like the sound of this. It was essential for their operation to have four days of protests at a minimum. That would focus people's attention away from potential military action as well as tie up resources. This was one of the easiest parts of the operation, and now it was taking a turn.

Katazin said, "Let's meet sometime in the morning. You keep your people organizing and stirring up new protesters."

"This isn't a money thing. It's a real problem. That is why I called."

"If I'm able to pay you an additional twenty thousand dollars, will we have some loud protests outside Thomas Brothers Financial?"

There was a long hesitation, then, "Probably."

"Then it *is* a money problem."

Major Anton Severov felt it was smarter to take his conversation with the clearly agitated Amir out of the dining room and onto the sidewalk. Once they were safely outside, Severov calmly asked Amir what he wanted to talk about.

The smaller man bowed up, trying to look tough, but his rumpled pullover shirt with its collar partway up and out-of-date blue pants that looked like they belonged to a suit made him more of a caricature. His black hair was slicked back by some ungodly-smelling ointment, but he still had that crazed look in his brown eyes. This wasn't the same Amir who had merely been irritating for the last two days; this was a man who was truly pissed off.

Severov took a half step away from the angry Iranian and said, "What's wrong, Amir?"

"I have been honest in my feelings about Russia, as well as the United States. I think you are both decadent and about to be crushed under the wheels of history. But at this moment I'm sworn to help your cause. I must warn you I will not tolerate you defiling our women."

"Defiling your women? I'm sure I have no idea what you're talking about." He quickly glanced around the sidewalk in front of the hotel's café in case he needed a weapon. There was nothing within reach.

Amir said, "You know exactly what I am talking about. You and Fannie lay together last night, and it is an affront to our beliefs."

"My beliefs, my people's beliefs, include the right of free will and a woman's choice. Don't lecture me about decisions I make about my personal life. And I will tell you right now not to bother Fannie about it, either."

"You think I'm some kind of desert nomad. An idiot you can twist around with silly phrases. I am a graduate of the Lebanese University."

Severov had to keep from bursting out laughing at that. In a mocking tone he said, "Ohh, Lebanese University, I *am* impressed. I've heard it called the Oxford of shitty universities in the Third World." He could tell it took the little Iranian a few seconds to understand the odd American idiom, but when he did, his dark face flushed red and he stormed away from the hotel.

Severov realized it might not have been the smartest thing to do, but it sure felt good. He wondered how much he'd appreciate it when he had to watch his back the rest of the trip.

The hotel Walsh had found was everything he thought it would be: cheap, uncomfortable, smelly, and two blocks from Times Square. The Hanely Hotel was a narrow swath of sixty rooms wedged between an office building and a storage facility. It catered to tourists on a real budget or Europeans who didn't check reviews. The nice thing was that Walsh and Alena seemed to be the only customers, and the clerk understood that an extra twenty bucks meant he wouldn't ask for ID. The kid from the Bronx even said Walsh and Alena didn't look like "wild-assed terrorists," so he didn't think there would be a problem.

They got settled in their room, which held a queen bed with the headboard pushed against the wall and about a foot of space around it on the other three sides. Alena was in no mood for small talk or cuddling once she was done showering in the minuscule bathroom and flopped into the bed wearing only a white towel with a brown stain in the middle.

Now Walsh was thinking tactically, and he liked the corner room that had access to a stairwell directly across from it or the elevators in the middle of the hallway. Looking out the window from the fourth floor, he could see the street below and anyone walking toward the front of the hotel. He had somehow managed to keep the pistol from Alena's sight and hoped he didn't have to explain it. He folded it into his pants and left them on the nightstand as he lay down in bed wearing his undershirt and underwear. Alena was snoring quietly a few minutes after the lights went out.

Walsh tossed and turned as he considered what had happened. He wished he could talk to his three best friends from his time in the marines. Mike Rosenberg was already helping him, and he knew Bill Shepherd probably had his hands full on the base in Germany. He wondered how Ronald Jackson would have viewed the situation. Each of them had strengths and weaknesses, but together they seemed to form the perfect team.

Ronald Jackson had devoted his life to the marines and knew every policy forward and back. He was the bedrock of their friendship. He also had an uncanny ability to locate the best activities during their leaves. A day in a Mediterranean port city and Ron could create enough good times to remember for a lifetime.

Michael Rosenberg was the smartest of the bunch. Perhaps "smart" was not the right word. He was clever, tricky. He had a way of viewing situations and looking at things that no one else would consider. He could piece together fragments of information into a simple report any grunt on the frontline could understand.

Despite his Boy Scout appearance and perpetually shaggy hair, at least for a marine, Bill Shepherd remained calm and unflappable in every possible situation. His demeanor was the same when they were having dinner as it was when they were under fire from an enemy mortar. His clear-headed thinking had saved them a number of times.

That made Walsh take a hard look at himself to figure out what he added to the group. It was clear, perhaps not heroic or sexy but obvious: He was organized. Not in a simple, keeping-things-clean kind of way but from the very basis of his being. He could look at anything and understand how it could be sorted or displayed. No one looked at someone who was good with numbers as heroic, but they always needed him around. He could put together a spreadsheet or expense record and make anyone understand how money was spent. But now, in his current situation, he had to look within himself and discover if he could do more. Maybe this was the kind of test he had expected his whole life. Instead, he had skated from one situation to another without any real hardship.

It looked like those days were over now.

Severov had been unnerved by his conversation with Amir. He needed to talk to someone he could relate to. It was a little early to be calling on the special cell phone he'd been provided. It was supposed to connect him directly to his commanding officer, who had sent him on this crazy mission in the first place. He was surprised to hear a different voice pick up the phone. It took him a minute to recognize the Georgian accent and realize it was the colonel's adjunct, a Muslim officer who had barely given Severov the time of day.

Severov said, "I need to speak to the colonel."

"He's busy. He said you can give me your report and I'll pass it on to him."

"Why would I give a report to you? *He's* my commanding officer. Give the phone to him now or be prepared to explain to him later why he received no report."

He heard grunts and then a long pause before the colonel came on the phone. The colonel was in a typical jolly mood and seemed to have more questions about Severov's trip and how pretty the girls in Estonia were than about the tactical issues he had been sent to study.

The colonel said, "What does it look like, Anton? Will the roads support our convoys?"

"Yes, sir. And I have a good track through Estonia. The rail lines can handle the heavy follow-on equipment and tanks. We won't damage too much infrastructure and will be able to use the country's electronic and Internet capabilities almost immediately. I estimate it will take us two days to reach the far border."

"That is excellent news." There was a pause, and Severov was certain the colonel was thinking something over. Then he said, "How are your guides?"

"They are certainly different from us."

"Of course they are. They're Muslims. Those desert folk aren't used to the twenty-first century." The colonel let loose with a loud cackle.

Suddenly Severov realized how wrong they had all been. Fannie and Amir were true Muslims. True believers all the way. The stereotype of the crazy, headgear-wearing nut was part of their strategy. No one in the Russian hierarchy took them seriously. They would never look at someone like Fannie and think she was a crazed zealot. But he knew she was a killer. They looked just like everyone else, but they were a dangerous bunch. More dangerous than a tank rolling down the middle of the street. At least then everyone knew there was danger. It instilled fear and made people get out of the way. A man with a bomb wrapped around his chest gave no warning.

Severov had realized that Amir's fanatical need to cling to tradition and keep Fannie in what he considered her "place" was a minor manifestation of devotion to a cause, but that didn't mean he was a lunatic. Both Amir and Fannie were the perfect example of what the West should fear from Islamic extremists. They were in no way "desert folk" and certainly more tech-savvy than the tubby colonel, who viewed them as dimwitted. It was difficult for most Westerners to understand the attitudes about life held by people willing to give their own lives to further their cause. Amir clearly had other personal reasons for being so interested in Fannie, but it was also his culture.

Severov finally answered his commanding officer's question. "The guides have been helpful, but there is much I must tell you in person."

The colonel said, "That's fine, because we're going to move sooner than we planned. You should head back toward the border and double-check our route. Violence is subsiding in the West, and we'll need you to lead your tank platoons. How does that sound?"

Severov took a moment to look over his shoulder and see that Fannie had joined Amir near the front door of the hotel. "It sounds a lot safer than staying here."

It'd been a long day, and Vladimir Putin was happy to be back at his palace at Novo-Ogaryovo. He treasured the residence that had been built in the fifties and felt he used it most effectively. Not only was it his retreat from the stresses of his job, but it was his main office. Even though that was a contradiction in terms, he appreciated the time and effort it saved him of traveling into the main part of the city every day. He also enjoyed the grounds that were stocked with wildlife and the pool and workout areas that were never more than a few minutes' walk away.

He was surprised and not particularly pleased to be told that Yuri Simplov was waiting for him in his official office. Yuri was one of the few people who could ask for admittance in his absence and be allowed to wait. It was late and Putin was tired, and he would've preferred to hear any updates in the morning.

When they were alone in the office, Putin went to the comfortable chair behind the desk, making sure Yuri realized he still answered to Putin on everything. Putin said, "I really want to make sure you and I do not have more contact than usual during this critical period."

Simplov said, "But it's not unusual for us to talk four or five times a week."

"Yes, but many of those conversations are over the phone."

"I understand, but there is much to talk about," Simplov said.

"I just finished briefing Andre on the operation and trying to explain to him that the protests in the U.S. and Germany were unplanned and spontaneous," Putin said, "but now our agents are working to influence them. That is correct, no?"

"Our man in New York has taken advantage of an existing protest group and hired contractors to help incite them," Simplov said. "Germany is a different story. The German youth have been looking for a cause to protest and are anxious to convince the U.S. that Germany no longer needs them as a military force in the country. Their protests turned violent quickly without much prodding from us. But to be accurate, some of their protest groups were already controlled by our SVR agents."

Putin nodded and said, "Very good. It makes excellent television and focuses everyone's attention on an issue that doesn't even really exist. Sometimes fate smiles upon us." He knew the power of the media and how an intelligence agency could use it. Years earlier, he had directed Yuri to plant four bombs in apartments all across Russia, including Moscow. In September 1999, the blasts killed more than three hundred people and injured seventeen hundred. The country was outraged to learn that Chechen rebels were responsible. The administration had used it as an excuse to start the Second Chechen War by bombing Grozny, and Putin had used that success as a way to succeed Boris Yeltsin as president.

There had always been rumors that the FSB had been involved, and there was even an arrest of three FSB agents who were planting additional bombs. But the agency claimed it was a training exercise, and nothing was ever proven. The Duma rejected calls for an investigation, and all Putin had to do for that was make sure key members were appointed to vital positions of power. That included his friend Andre Maysak.

Putin looked across the desk at Yuri and said, "Where are we in our current operation? And start with the bad news first."

"We have lost the U.S. trader whose account we used to transfer the money. He knows nothing about us, but the FBI might be able to use him to find a connection to us. Initially, we hoped to eliminate him and make it look like a suicide. He has been much more resourceful than we expected. Still, our man in New York is determined to find him.

"You've already seen news reports that the Swiss bank was destroyed by a massive explosive device," Simplov said. "That was done by our allies. The blast killed the young man who introduced the algorithm into the stock exchanges. It also eliminated the original computer and will greatly slow down any investigation into the algorithm. If anyone is ever able to piece together what happened or who developed the program, it will be long after we have taken complete control of Estonia."

Putin nodded but refrained from giving any specific praise. This was the SVR's job, after all. The whole idea was for the agency to control situations like this, and he was not particularly happy there was a loose end like the missing trader.

Yuri said, "The terror attacks are drawing all the media attention, as well as the law enforcement and intelligence attention, in the Western countries. As we talked about earlier, the initial wave of attacks has run out of steam, and now the attacks are occurring with much less frequency. Some of these attacks were planned but had to be delayed for one reason or another. I think it is all working out to our advantage.

"The military is preparing to move and have conducted an in-depth reconnaissance of their route. We did make use of a talented Muslim to help there, but I'm assured the connection is secure. There appear to be no issues, and the Estonian defense force will provide little, if any, resistance. We feel that the sight of Russian tanks rolling across the border will be enough to cause them to surrender."

That was what Putin wanted to hear. Now he said, "So we can now focus on the military aspect of the operation. The Muslims have completed their assignments. We will see how long our truce lasts with them."

Simplov nodded his head. "I can have our contacts in ISIL eliminated, if you don't think we will ever have need of them again. We could even eliminate their contact whom we used during our recon of Estonia. I understand, however, she is French by birth and is gifted with languages. We might have more use for her later if you are comfortable with it."

Putin nodded his head. "We can always use good people. Leave the contact alone unless there is a problem."

"And the leaders in ISIL? We are technically fighting them in Syria."

Putin shook his head. "If this is successful, who knows what we will do in the future. There will always be rumors about who we do and do not work with. This throws some mystery into the mix. I just want to be clear, and this is important, the military phase can begin now, correct?"

Yuri smiled and said, "Without delay."

19

Fannie Legat tried to hide her disappointment when Anton Severov said he'd been recalled to his company. He told her while Amir was standing next to her and made no mention of their brief liaison. She hoped it meant something to him and she wasn't just another woman he had met during his career. Soldiers expected women to melt at their feet, but she had gotten the impression Anton Severov was different.

She appreciated how he had considered what the Russian invasion might mean to the people living in Estonia, as well as his professional demeanor as he made sketches and notes about their route. He was nothing at all like what she had expected. And she hoped he felt the same about her. Since she'd been sixteen, all Fannie had considered were the wrongs against Islam. Over and over her teachers and imams had told her essentially that everyone outside of Islam was a danger, but that Americans and Russians were an actual threat. She would often hear the older men talk about their time fighting the Russians in Afghanistan. That was where Osama bin Laden had learned many of his tactics and honed his rhetoric. The younger men talked about fighting the Americans in Afghanistan.

Partly due to the difference in decades, but also to a different philosophy, the Russians used brute force and tactics that drove all of the Afghanis away from them. Their tanks would level villages, and they would kill indiscriminately. No one was even sure why the Russians cared about Afghanistan. The popular political rhetoric was that the dying Soviet Union had to assert itself somewhere in the world, and Afghanistan was the best place to show off its military power.

The Americans were not met with as much resistance. Much of the country rallied to them in defiance of the Taliban. Also, the American tactics were considerably different. They avoided civilian casualties whenever possible and had such precision ordnance that they were able to take out military targets with very little collateral damage.

In the mosques and schools she attended, this distinction was never made. They talked about America as a breeding ground for a new generation of crusaders who saw Islam as standing between them and oil.

This experience with Major Severov had put a human face on the enemy. He'd even made her consider all the people who died in the bank building in Bern who had no knowledge of what was going on and were no immediate threat to Islam. Was this her conscience popping up?

The U.S. and Europe was another story. The French had kept her bottled up in a ghetto. The Americans treated all Middle Eastern people like petulant children or criminals. She abhorred their decadence and wastefulness, what Amir would call "sinfulness." She and Amir were what the West should fear. Intelligent and ruthless. Ruthless on a scale Westerners couldn't easily comprehend. Not only would she give her life for the cause, but she would sacrifice any of her comrades, too. As long as she hurt the West she would feel fulfilled.

She was sorry to see the town of Valga, on the Latvian border, disappear behind them as she headed north to the border with Russia. She had to talk the Russian major into sitting in the front seat, because he didn't like having Amir behind him, but he had agreed. Anton Severov mostly looked out the window but would occasionally glance over at her, and her heart felt like it would explode.

From the backseat, Amir said, "Perhaps once we get rid of you, we can straighten out Fannie and turn her back into a good Muslim."

Severov shifted quickly in his seat to look back at the little Iranian. "What's that supposed to mean?"

"It means it's none of your concern. You must plan to oppress these people in Estonia. You will not have time to worry what Fannie and I do once you are gone."

Fannie was about to say something, but she saw the look on Severov's face. She decided to see where this conversation would lead.

Grabbing sleep in short spurts had not helped Derek Walsh, and now, in the early morning hours, he sat on the edge of the bed staring at a TV, which was bolted to the wall, with the volume turned down low as he flipped between the different news channels.

Alena still slept soundly as he tried to piece together the events he was watching from around the world.

The BBC America channel focused on the meltdown of the London stock exchange, which had lost more than 16 percent in the last two days. They mentioned a faulty computer trading issue but acknowledged that the majority of that crash was panic selling by major funds. The newscasts showed protests turning violent in front of Parliament and even Buckingham Palace. English youth with shaved heads hurled bottles and rocks at police huddled behind shields.

The Russia Today "RT" channel seemed to cover the events in Germany, England, and the U.S. with a degree of glee not seen on other networks. He had barely even noticed the channel before, only seeing it in certain hotels. For the longest time he thought it was some kind of offshoot from MSNBC because they often talked about the same subjects with the same tone. It wasn't until recently he realized it was a news station owned by the Russian government. It covered American news in English, much like Al Jazeera America. In this case, economists Walsh had never heard of were talking about the inevitability of these crashes and the inability of Western nations to sustain any serious growth. Specifically, they talked about the American desire to dominate the world militarily, hampering its ability to advance economically.

Walsh shook his head and paused briefly on the Al Jazeera International channel, which surprisingly covered the events honestly. Its talking heads seemed disappointed that Islamic-based terrorism appeared to be on the rise again. They did not shy away from mentioning that the suicide bombers in Western Europe and the U.S. had mostly been identified as Middle Eastern nationals from Egypt, Saudi Arabia, and Yemen, and fighters who had been trained in Syria.

He listened for reports on death tolls in the U.S. Across the world there were people killed in attacks in Italy and France, a dozen more in London, twenty-two outside a military base in Germany. That made him worry about his friend Bill Shepherd.

One estimate was that over five hundred had been killed in Europe and more than two hundred in the U.S., with more than five times that seriously injured.

The biggest attack had been on a Swiss bank in Bern. More than seventy people were dead and dozens still missing in the massive debris. The investigation was still under way, but the size of the bomb indicated that it had been built into the structure of the building and had left a huge crater on one side and a shaky-looking column of offices along the rear. One report speculated that the bank was also the original site of the algorithm that was introduced into the financial markets. Even Walsh knew that couldn't be a coincidence.

Finally he settled on CNN, which interspersed inspirational messages from the president with news stories implying the worst had passed. It also had a panel discussion debating whether the presence of police officers had *incited* any of the protesters and caused more violence than it hindered. Walsh couldn't believe idiots that spouted that sort of bullshit. It was more popular and easier for CNN to carry that line than it was to look at the deeper issues and what would happen if the police were not in place. It reminded him of the protests in Missouri and how CNN jumped to conclusions about the use of force by a police officer, which were later definitively rebutted by forensic evidence. No one at CNN sounded eager to clear the police officer's name.

Walsh finally shut off the TV in frustration but felt no closer to sleep. He slipped back up onto the bed and tried to breathe deeply and clear his head. At least he knew Alena was safe. Now he had to keep her that way.

Major Bill Shepherd had used the several twenty-minute breaks during the inquiry board to run out and check on his men, who were either near the front gate or getting their gear ready for another night out on the line. The questioning had gone on much longer than he'd anticipated, but no one had thrown him any curve balls. Once he got a line on the German Ministry of Justice representative, he understood she was trying to create a narrative that relieved the Germans of responsibility more than she was trying to blame the U.S. military. Either way, it was just another day on duty. So he was happy.

He slipped back into his chair as the members of the board of inquiry finished up phone calls and got their notes in order. Shepherd expected the base commander to make some sort of final statement, but it was the FBI agent, Maria Alonso, who surprised him.

The sharply dressed and attractive young woman said, "From my training and experience in police work, it appears that the real failure here was in the civilian police's ability to control the crowd. I understand the need for the military to protect their base and personnel, but the civilian police should have that responsibility. I'd like to commend you, Major, on your decision to bring up marines, some of whom have had duty at embassies and understand the subtleties of security. Your actions undoubtedly kept the situation from getting out of control."

The German representative turned in her chair and said, "Are you saying it is my government's fault?"

The FBI agent remained calm. She even took a moment to flip her hair back over her shoulder. Then she said, "I'm not attempting to assign blame, merely complimenting the major on his actions."

The German ministry representative said, "And you say the situation didn't get out of control? There are more than twenty dead German civilians."

All of the military men at the table were smart enough to stay out of this fight. The FBI agent sharpened her gaze and said, "The people were killed by a terrorist. All of the preliminary forensics indicate it was a single person with a bomb strapped to their chest. Something civilian police would have been in a better position to deal with had there been more police outside who knew what to do. So in that regard, yes, it is the Germans' fault. I realize history has taught us that you will have a tough time accepting responsibility for something like that. But I can assure you, my report back to Washington will indicate that Major Shepherd and his men are heroes. My only hope is that action like that is not required again." She looked around the table, then stared at the German ministry representative again. "I assume the German government will provide adequate security from here on out. Is that correct?"

Shepherd had to hide a smile. The base commander was a little more obvious as he leaned back in his seat and said, "I think that just about wraps things up here."

Ten minutes later, as Major Shepherd was getting ready to leave the building and return to his unit, Agent Alonso stopped him in the hallway. He couldn't help but say, "Thank you for coming to my defense."

"No thanks are needed. You did a great job."

Shepherd thought she was flirting with him, but if he was wrong, it would be terribly embarrassing, so he just smiled and turned back toward the door. The FBI agent caught him by the arm with her hand and said, "There are a few things about it I'd like to discuss with you if you have time."

Shepherd turned and said, "I am at your disposal. I'm sure we can find an office to sit in close by."

The FBI agent said, "I was thinking more along the lines of dinner."

This time Shepherd couldn't hide his smile.

———

Walsh went over everything in his head. He wasn't used to considering people as suspects. So far, Charlie, the homeless vet, was the only person he could think of who would've talked, and that would explain how the Russians knew he was going to Alena's apartment. But he wasn't even sure that made sense. How would Charlie know where she lived or what her last name was? All Walsh had said was that she was a student at Columbia and lived near the campus.

Outside, the sun was just starting to rise. For most of his life, if he was awake at sunrise, it was for a positive reason. He was usually in a good mood. Either he had been out all night having a great time or he was so excited about something he got up early. He could remember growing up in New Jersey and getting up at dawn the first day after school was out just so he and his buddies could go exploring in some of the Pine Barrens. They often looked for the elusive "Jersey Devil," always without success. Even in the service he felt like he got the most work done early in the morning.

Today was different. He was dreading the day. He felt like things could only get worse. Even with this beautiful woman lying in the bed next to him, he was losing his hope. If this was a conspiracy, someone had been brilliant in its execution. There was almost no way he could explain how someone else had made the trades on Thomas Brothers' accounts. And the chaos that had followed had only muddied the waters and hindered any investigation.

He considered what would happen if he turned himself in to the FBI. He thought about Tonya Stratford and her background in banking. Would she be open-minded enough to listen to him? Finally he sighed and sat up in bed. He didn't want to wake Alena, so he carefully got dressed and decided to go out to find bagels and coffee.

He needed to get his shit together.

20

The streets were quiet at this time of the morning in Times Square on a normal day, but after two days of rioting and terror attacks, the place looked like Baghdad during an air raid. No one was on the street. Derek Walsh immediately found an open deli and grabbed a couple of bagels and some coffee. That was the extent of his original plan when he left the shabby hotel, but his mind kept going over the steps he could take to help himself out of this nightmare. The marines had drilled being self-sufficient and proactive into him. Even if it wasn't his nature, he knew now was the time to put that training to use. That was why, when he stumbled on an Internet café that had ten desktop computers with Web access for rent on an hourly basis, he didn't hesitate to step inside and slap down twenty dollars.

The clerk behind the counter was a pretty, twenty-year-old girl with some serious tattoos and more piercings than he could count on her left ear alone. She didn't care where he looked on the Internet or what he was doing. That was perfect.

There were five other people in the small business: a Finnish couple who were on vacation and trying to find an earlier flight home, a guy who looked like he might be homeless, and two young guys who looked like they'd been out all night partying. Whatever they'd rented a computer for, it certainly wasn't anything legal. Walsh might not have been a cop, but he wasn't an idiot, either.

He was surprised how fast the server was, and it only took him a moment to log into an account he still controlled that listed all of the financial advisers and people involved in banking based on their licenses. Tonya Stratford, the FBI agent, understood so much about trading that she had to have been involved in banking at some point in her life. So he took a shot and started looking through the series 7 and series 63 license holders over the last few years in New York. It didn't take long to find her and see that she also had a series 4 license. Apparently she was interested in supervising money managers as well as being one herself.

He took the information he found on her license and made a couple of simple checks through Google and a few other Web sites. He didn't understand how cops couldn't catch people immediately nowadays. He found that she lived in Flushing, had been divorced for two years, and received her bachelor's degree in finance from SUNY Stony Brook out on Long Island. He was impressed to see she later earned a master's degree from NYU and guessed that was while she was working. He found an article that mentioned her as an analyst at Lehman Brothers, and suddenly he had a clear picture of who he was up against.

He still didn't have the information he wanted the most. But checking on some sites that few people knew of, he found a credit application, and hidden at the bottom was a phone number. It was her personal cell.

Now the only question was if he really should talk to her.

Joseph Katazin woke with a start as pain shot through his cracked rib and welcomed him to the new day. He was alone in the king bed of the upstairs master bedroom of his Brooklyn home. He could hear his wife rummaging around in the kitchen downstairs. She hadn't spoken to him when he slipped inside during the middle of the night. He was sure it was because she thought he had a mistress somewhere. Another time, probably. He'd had several over the years, including a secretary at the import/export business that his wife made him fire. But she had no idea what he was up to right now.

He padded down the stairs, already dressed in Dockers and a loose shirt to hide the gun he intended to carry once he got in the car. She didn't even say good morning. Her first words were, "Can you be here for the new washer and dryer delivery this afternoon?"

"Not today."

"Why not?"

"Busy at work, my love." He ignored her rolling eyes and the heavy sighs. No matter what he did for the motherland, he still had a nagging wife just like everyone else. He decided to accept it and move on with his life. He was glad to hear that his daughter, Irina, had felt well enough to go to school, because he needed a few hours of uninterrupted time in his home office.

As if she were reading his mind his wife said, "Are you going to lock yourself in your room? What do you do up there? Troll for women on the Internet?"

Katazin thought about the Beretta in his car. It was a fleeting thought, but he realized it occurred to him more and more often. Aloud he said, "Why would I ever troll for another woman when I have a catch like you at home?"

He grabbed a banana and some coffee and stumbled into his office on the first floor, closing the door, but not locking it just in case his wife checked on him. He was dismayed to see all of the newscasts showing the streets quiet in Manhattan after the two days of protests and rioting. He'd already talked to his contact, who had no answers other than that many of the protesters were scared. Had the two prongs of his plan canceled each other out? Had terrorists kept the protesters out of the picture? That was the goal today: Stir up more protests.

It also could be the fact that Americans had such short attention spans. They were like little children. Only CNN had mastered the art of manipulating them. They knew what stories to pump and when to move on. Protests were the best video for them until there was a terror attack. In this case, the attack at Disneyland had drawn reporters like shit drew flies. Even Katazin thought that the attack had gone too far. How could the jihadists risk children's lives like that?

First, he would go meet with his contact who organized the protests, then he was on to real business: He would deal with Derek Walsh.

Mike Rosenberg worried he was paranoid. He checked for surveillance all the way from his house in Bethesda to his office in Langley. He felt nervous greeting the security guard at the gate whom he spoke to every day. He purposely left his cell phone at home. He decided he would call Derek Walsh when he got home. It was only an extra twenty or thirty minutes. And he had a lot to do before he could knock off for the day.

He made it to his office and was scurrying around, gathering information for his regular duties as well as looking at some of the reports about the money transferred from Thomas Brothers Financial to the bank in Bern, when his boss stuck her head in the door. A CIA lifer who had worked in the Far East, she wore middle age well and presented the ultimate professional demeanor.

"You're here early this morning," she said.

"I've got a lot going on today," he replied.

"Any idea what the protests are going to look like across the country? You think they'll pick up speed again or die out?"

Even though that was one of the issues he was supposed to be working on, the question caught him by surprise. He hesitated, then finally said, "Right now I'm looking at the money transfer that started the protests in New York."

"The one from Thomas Brothers?"

"Yes, ma'am." The military in him would never be completely gone.

"Why? We have people who specialize in that sort of thing."

He knew it was time to dive in. "Just a hunch. I'm good with making connections between events. It all ties together somehow. I just haven't figured it out yet."

"I need you on the protests." That was the end of the conversation. She turned and was headed toward her office before Rosenberg could appeal.

Now he really would be working off the grid. Great.

Anton Severov stood on a small, quaint bridge and looked out at the running stream the road passed over. It was late afternoon, and the sun made the water glisten like diamonds. All he was really doing was keeping his mind off of other things. He recognized that Fannie had been dragging the trip out as long as possible. They were still an hour from the border and had been driving most of the day. He appreciated the fact that she wasn't ready to let him go. He wished he had more time with her, too. Maybe after this operation was over they'd be able to see each other. If they weren't on the opposite sides of some kind of jihad.

He felt the beautiful French woman next to him, then looked up quickly to make sure her little Iranian friend, Amir, was nowhere around. He could see the dark-haired young man standing by the hatchback parked on the side of the road away from the bridge. It was one of the few moments they'd had alone all day.

Earlier, when Severov asked Fannie what kind of trouble Amir could cause if he told people they had slept together, she downplayed the issue. But it had stuck in his brain, and he was worried about her safety. Now he took her in his arms and gave her a kiss and held her at arm's length and said in a serious tone, "Really, what will happen if Amir opens his mouth about us?"

She paused, and that didn't ease his fears at all. Finally Fannie said, "It really depends on who he talks to. Some of the more enlightened men in our cause, let's say men educated in London, might understand and just have a stern discussion with me. Others, some of the old guard, will take it much more seriously. I could try to explain that I was using you, but they wouldn't believe me."

"Were you using me?" He almost melted when those wide dark eyes looked up at him and glistened with a tear. All he said was, "I already know the answer." Then after a moment longer he said, "So what do we do about Amir?"

Fannie shrugged her shoulders. "You're not talking about killing him, are you?"

"Would anyone miss him?"

"There would be a lot of questions."

"Maybe we can be more creative." He felt a pang of guilt talking so callously about a man who technically was helping in their preparations for war. Then he heard the little shit yell from the car, "Let's go. There is much to do."

Severov smiled, thinking, *Yes, there is.*

21

Vladimir Putin reclined on the balcony of his private residence. The leather-and-mahogany lounger was identical to one in his villa in the South of France. The unseasonably warm weather allowed him to enjoy his vast gardens and scintillating pools wearing only a sheer silk robe. It was not an image he broadcast to the media, but over the years he had grown used to his creature comforts. And he had earned them. As the leader of a resurgent Russia, he had a right to his lavish lifestyle.

Putin seldom drank, but since this was a special occasion, he treated himself to a snifter of Remy Martin Black Pearl Louis XIII cognac. There were fewer than eight hundred decanters of it in the world. That this single small bottle of cognac, aged for eighty-five years, cost more than his entire family had earned in the first twenty years of his life somehow made the taste even smoother.

In times such as these he sometimes thought about the multifamily apartment in Leningrad in which he'd grown up. His father rarely encouraged him to do anything to better himself, but his mother made him feel special. Along with the extra people in their small apartment was a small army of rats. One of his jobs was to keep the apartment clear of the vermin. He spent many hours chasing and killing them. One thing they had taught him was how ferocious they could be when trapped. It was a lesson he had learned well.

More importantly, he had learned not to work himself into a corner where he might be trapped.

If trapped, he'd learned to fight like a cornered rodent.

No quarter given.

His father had died when Putin was in his late thirties. He had seen his son rise through the ranks of the KGB and even witnessed the beginning of his political career. But he had no idea how far his son would go.

When he started in the KGB, Putin dreamed of being in a position of power in the agency. Promoted to colonel, he realized there was more he could do. As the deputy mayor of St. Petersburg, his hometown, he started to see the potential of political power and moved on to Moscow, working as deputy chief of the Presidential Property Management Department. Just two years later he was the head of the FSB—formerly the KGB—and found himself in a position to really make changes.

It was about this time in his life when he found himself trapped like one of the rats from his childhood. An overzealous Russian general prosecutor named Skuratov had started looking into then-President Yeltsin's inner circle. These were some of the people who had helped his rise. They could also be his downfall.

Putin had been able to remove Yury Skuratov after a video of him in a compromising position with two women in a hotel room appeared on national TV. Of course the video had nothing to do with the fact that Skuratov had initiated an extensive investigation with the French into money laundering by people close to Yeltsin, including the president's daughter.

Putin smiled when he thought about how he had manipulated those around Yeltsin. The old man was ailing, and when those closest to him looked for a possible successor, he made sure they knew all he had done for them. They had decided the FSB head's loyalty and quick action made Putin an excellent choice for prime minister—which would make him next in line for the presidency. Even if, by some miracle, Yeltsin lived out his term, the prime minister would have a huge advantage over anyone else in an election.

In August 1999, Putin slipped into the position. Even journalists approved of him at the time. One said, "He makes you feel as if he shares your opinions and has the same background as you." Clearly, growing up as a poor child in Leningrad before it became St. Petersburg was appealing to the masses.

And as for Yeltsin's oligarchs and top officials, he quickly cashiered those he deemed unreliable, replacing them with his own trusted cronies and KGB officials.

This was just another step in his country's evolution. He had done other things that people would have found contemptible. But there was always a purpose to them. Deploying members of the FSB to blow up the four apartment complexes in Buynaksk, Volgodonsk, and Moscow in 1999 was an example. They'd killed and injured over 1,300 people, but he'd managed to blame it all on the Chechens. Using the crime to rally the nation, he had simultaneously tightened his own grip on power. He'd also used the staged attacks as casus belli for a second war with Chechnya. Those bombings had galvanized the country against the rebels, and the Second Chechen War made him appear to be a strong leader.

Soon he was more than a strong leader: He was a dictator.

He smiled and poured himself another snifter of the Louis XIII.

Over the years many men and women had attempted to stop him. That they had the temerity to try never ceased to amaze him. After all, his ruthlessness was well established and notorious.

When Alexander Litvinenko, a former security officer, had tried to expose Putin's role in the apartment-complex bombings and other crimes, Putin quickly retaliated. Two of Litvinenko's fellow spies slipped polonium-210 into his tea at the Millenium Hotel in London, and Litvinenko spent weeks dying an unspeakably agonizing death.

Then there was the case of the investigative journalist, forty-eight-year-old Anna Politkovskaya. She had attempted to dig up dirt on Russian atrocities in the Second Chechen War and on Putin's murderous, dictatorial excesses—his dream of catapulting Russia "back into a Soviet abyss."

Well, it was a shame about Anna. She had arguably been the most impassioned and the most beautiful investigative reporter of her generation. Three bullets, and she wasn't impassioned or beautiful anymore. One tap to the head, two to the chest, and Anna was history.

Natalia Estemirova? A highly regarded human rights activist, she'd worked with Anna Politkovskaya on Russian atrocities in Chechnya. Three years after Anna was killed, Natalia took two rounds in the head. She wasn't a highly regarded activist anymore.

Paul Klebinov, the editor of Moscow's edition of *Forbes* magazine, had the impertinence to expose corruption among Putin's plutocratic supporters. He was shot to death in front of his office.

The thought of Klebinov's demise brought a small wintry smile to Putin's lips.

You can publish your exposés in hell now, Klebby old boy!

Stanislav Markelov and Anastasia Baburova? Stan, a top human rights attorney, had been Anna Politkovskaya's lawyer. He was was looking into the murder of a young Chechen by the Russian military.

He was also shot dead for his efforts.

Anastasia was killed when she ran up to help her friend.

So many journalists, so little time.

Today, it would be a ballsy reporter indeed who dared to criticize Putin or his friends.

It never ceased to amaze him what a few hundred killings and beatings could accomplish. Not only was the Russian media terminally cowed, but Putin was now going after history itself, the rewriting of Russia's past. He was achieving that by brute force as well. When the renowned human rights organization Memorial attempted to expose the atrocities of Stalinism, including the horrors of the Gulag—in the process, blackening the reputation of Putin's preeminent idol, Josef Stalin—Putin made short work of them. Turning the entire force of Russia's hopelessly corrupt legal system against Memorial, he now had that august operation on the brink of obliteration. They and their work would soon be flung down his own equivalent of the Stalinist "memory hole."

Nor did Russia's plutocratic elite—its ruling oligarchs—oppose Putin with impunity. Witness Mikhail Khodorkovsky. In 2003, he was "the Richest Man in Russia." After he complained personally to Putin about the Russian economy's pervasive corruption, however, Putin jailed Khodorkovsky and liquidated his assets, including Yukos Oil, the biggest oil firm in Russia. Yukos ended up as part of Rosneft, which was owned by one of Putin's friends.

The lesson was clear: Not even "the Richest Man in Russia" was safe from Putin's wrath.

Putin sipped his cognac and stretched. He remembered how U.S. business magnate William Browder had hired the Russian lawyer Sergei Magnitsky to investigate a massive fraud case involving Putin's government. His evidence implicated the Russian police, among others.

After his first full day on the job, Sergei was found beaten to death in police custody.

All investigations ceased.

Boris Berezovksy, a Russian tycoon in exile and an outspoken Putin critic, was found hanging in his ex-wife's shower in London.

Russian oligarch Alexander Perepilichny, after dying suddenly at forty-four years of age, was found to have been poisoned.

In 2006, Putin had even paved the way for such extrajudicial killings by passing laws allowing him to hunt down and kill his perceived enemies.

As much as he despised his chief American critic, Anne Applebaum of *The Washington Post,* he had to admit she had accurately summarized his career in four blistering sentences, calling it part of "the remarkable story of one group of unrepentant, single-minded, revanchist KGB officers who were horrified by the collapse of the Soviet Union and the prospect of their own loss of influence. In league with Russian organized crime, starting at the end of the 1980s, they successfully plotted a return to power. Assisted by the unscrupulous international offshore banking industry, they stole money that belonged to the Russian state, took it abroad for safety, reinvested it in Russia, and then, piece by piece, took over the state themselves. Once in charge, they brought back Soviet methods of political control—the only ones they knew—updated for the modern era."

Lucky for Applebaum she wasn't a Russian journalist.

He'd have made short work of her, too.

Still, one of the multitudinous advantages of a Putin-run press was that he could keep his private life private—especially his financial private life. With the Russian people suffering so much economic hardship, it would not do for them to learn how opulently he lived. That was one of the reasons he kept his sumptuous lifestyle a secret. For one of Russia's leaders to be known as one of the world's richest men would not be proper. Anyway, now, as he grew older, he realized there was more to life than just the accumulation of wealth. He couldn't even spend it all if he wanted to. Instead he wanted to think about the future and how he would be remembered. He was confident that once this operation in Estonia was over and his country emerged victorious, he would be remembered as modern Russia's greatest leader.

He took another sip of brandy and enjoyed the temperate weather.

Derek Walsh shuttled through the empty lobby of the run-down hotel. There was only one desk clerk on duty, and he wondered if the others had chosen not to come into work. The young woman behind the counter didn't even glance up at him as he bypassed the sketchy elevator and started up the three flights of stairs.

Alena was just stirring as he put down the now-cool coffee and the bagels. She got up and inched her way around the tight space into the claustrophobic bathroom. When she got out, still wearing the towel she had gone to bed in the night before, she looked beautiful. How did she do it? She started gathering her clothes and said, "What are we going to do first?"

"What do you mean?"

"I know you have to do something with the security plug from work. Do you need to get anything else from your apartment? We need to make sure we gather anything that could incriminate you."

"Incriminate me? I told you I didn't do anything wrong."

"In the part of the world I'm from, that never keeps anyone from being arrested. From what I've seen here in the U.S., it still won't keep you from going to jail. We need to be aggressive and gather any material related to your work or the money transfer." She took his face in her hands and said, "Let me help you. Use my debit card. Get the money you need. We can go on the run."

He liked her new proactive attitude. That was why he felt guilty when he said, "I'm not about to get you involved in this. You're going to have to wait here for me."

"Here, in this crappy hotel? Is this now my prison?"

"It's not exactly Guantanamo."

"It's not the W Hotel, either."

He didn't mean it to, but it came out as a whine when he said, "Please, just one day."

"You mean I can't even go to any classes?"

Walsh shook his head. "They might wait for you at Columbia. I still don't know how they found your apartment. But they know we're connected, and I can't risk your safety."

Now she looked at him with those big brown eyes and said, "What are you going to do?"

"Whatever I have to."

Bill Shepherd had sat in the simple officers' mess a thousand times, but tonight it felt entirely different. He was nervous. The normally busy dining room was nearly empty as everyone prepared for protests or rested from their sleepless nights. He sat in the far corner at a table for two with the delightful Maria Alonso sitting across from him. He didn't know if his nerves came from having a first dinner with a pretty woman or not wanting anyone else from the inquiry board to see him eating with the FBI agent.

It'd been a quiet meal so far, and they'd just chatted about their somewhat similar backgrounds. Her father had also been in the navy, and she spent time at bases on Puerto Rico, in San Diego, and in Virginia.

He liked the way her dark eyes met his and her hair would slip into her face occasionally. She had a very athletic build and soft, flawless skin.

He said, "I'm sorry we had to eat on base, but there's no telling what they might need me for, and I'm not sure it's safe off base."

"This is lovely. I don't mind at all."

There had been few protesters outside the gate. The story about someone from the U.S. military throwing a hand grenade into the crowd persisted in the German media. Even though there was no truth to it whatsoever, it had kept the protesters away. Shepherd would remember that for the future. Maybe a hand grenade once in a while wasn't a bad idea.

Maria said, "You really handled yourself well today at the inquiry. I couldn't believe they threw it together so quickly. From what I understand the representative from the German ministry insisted that it go forward."

"She didn't seem too happy when she left."

"She filed an official protest. She said that I was just siding with my country and that we had falsified forensic information."

"Will it have any effect?"

Maria shrugged. "Another German ministry official filed a complaint against a DEA agent who linked her son to a heroin-smuggling ring. Just to save the hassle, they sent the poor guy home. I doubt it'll get that far with this complaint."

They continued with their simple meal once the waiter recognized they just wanted to be left alone. Shepherd was picking at his steak when Maria surprised him.

She said, "Have you heard from your friend Derek Walsh?"

His head popped up involuntarily. Mike Rosenberg had filled him in on everything that had happened just a few hours ago.

The FBI agent asked, "How well do you know Walsh, anyway?"

"Come on, you know exactly how well I know him." He looked into that stunning face and added, "Is this an official interrogation?"

"I know the military uses back-channel communication all the time. The FBI agent working on this in New York, Tonya Stratford, was in the academy with me. We talk all the time. We're not idiots. We can look at someone's service record. I was just wondering if you had any ideas about him."

"I know he wouldn't do anything like what he's been accused of. One of our friends says it's a conspiracy and he can't trust the FBI. Is that possible? Do you guys ever go bad? Any past evidence of FBI criminal activity?"

She gave him a flat look, then said, "Sure, I guess. A couple of years ago one of our agents in El Paso, a guy named Eriksen, discovered a crooked supervisor. The agency hammered him. So it happens, but not very often, and Tonya is my friend. I think that's just an excuse for Walsh to keep running."

"And me to keep my mouth shut."

Shepherd was disappointed he had just realized what the whole point of this dinner was.

Derek Walsh felt a little uneasy leaving Alena at the hotel by herself. He'd sat and answered her questions, but ultimately he was the one who had to make some decisions. That was why he was heading in the general direction of Wall Street. He hadn't absolutely decided to go directly to Thomas Brothers Financial, but that was his inclination.

He strolled downtown on Columbus Avenue looking for exactly the right place to stop. He knew his next move precisely. He just needed the right spot to execute it. It would have been so simple if there were still public pay phones on every corner. But those days were long gone, and one call from his cell phone would render it more of a liability than an asset. Finally he found a subway entrance and was pleased to find two ancient pay phones stuck on the wall like an afterthought. The next question was if they worked.

As soon as he felt the lack of substance in the first phone's handset he knew it didn't work. The handle was just a plastic shell with no speaker or microphone in it. He didn't hesitate to grab the second handset, which felt more like a real phone, and was gratified to hear a dial tone. He dug in his pocket for two quarters, which the private carrier required on this phone. Then he dialed the number he'd found on the Internet for Tonya Stratford.

There were three rings, and he wondered if she would pick up on a number she didn't recognize. Finally he heard the connection and Agent Stratford's clear voice simply saying, "Hello."

He hesitated until he heard her say, "Hello" again. Then he blurted out, "This is Derek Walsh. Is there any chance we could talk without your partner beating me or you dragging me to jail?"

There was a long pause. He thought she'd ask how he got her number, but she surprised him. Agent Stratford said, "We have a little bit of leeway. There is currently not a warrant issued for you. But you've probably seen yourself on the news as a person of interest."

"If your interest is in arresting me, I may have a way to prove my innocence. You weren't listening to me when we talked about this before."

"And I won't listen to you over a phone, either. We have to meet in person. I promise you'll have a fair chance."

"There is some kind of bigger conspiracy working here. I keep running into Russian men with guns. One of them is the same man who mugged me last week. He's a middle-aged man with a scar on his face."

"Do you have a name?"

"No. But one of his associates is named Serge Blattkoff. And he was waiting outside my apartment."

"How did you get his name?"

"I happened to see his driver's license."

"How did you get away from him?"

"You'll know if you see him."

"When and where do you want to meet?"

Now Walsh took a moment and finally said, "I'll call you back when I have more information and I can think clearly. Until then, I'd appreciate it if I stayed off the news."

"No promises until we meet face-to-face. All I'm offering you is a fair chance to explain yourself."

Walsh hung up without saying anything else. He had no idea how hard or easy it was to trace a phone call. He immediately sprinted back up to the street and continued his walk toward Thomas Brothers Financial. He figured he'd be there sometime around noon.

Major Bill Shepherd took a moment to consider how this FBI agent had manipulated him into finding out information about his friend Derek Walsh. He didn't answer when she dropped the bombshell and made some comment about back-channel communication. Finally he said, "So this is an all-business dinner?"

"Enjoyable business, but business nonetheless." She had a smug smile that was not endearing in any way.

"I can honestly say I have not spoken to Derek in over a week."

"But you know he's in trouble and allegedly made a money transfer that is partially responsible for the protests and the financial markets collapse."

"A mutual friend told me about it."

"Who's your mutual friend?"

Shepherd realized how serious this was and didn't want to implicate Mike Rosenberg. He carefully wiped his mouth, folded the napkin, and stood up from the table. "As an officer in the United States Marine Corps, I pride myself on good manners. Good manners dictate that I excuse myself from dinner before I say something which would reflect badly on the Corps and me."

He turned and marched out of the dining room, happy he was able to get some distance before she started hitting him with more questions. But now he had to wonder how much of his life she had been investigating. Did she know there were several German women he kept company with?

Joseph Katazin was chilly and had thrown on a New York Giants windbreaker as he waited. He'd decided he needed to be more efficient and had told his contact to meet him at noon on Wall Street near the site of the most successful protests. Most of the protests had fizzled, but the terror attacks were still going on. It was only a matter of time before the

Staten Island Ferry and the subways were hit. Katazin wanted the protests fired up again as well.

He was on the edge of the courtyard of Thomas Brothers Financial and was disappointed to only see a dozen or so lackluster protesters holding signs and a couple even chatting with the police. That would not happen in Moscow after a display like the ones over the past two days. The police were a little less friendly.

Even the cops didn't expect much trouble. There were more on patrol than usual, but they didn't have their riot gear on, and there were no large groups of staged officers like there had been. Everyone had the sense that this had run its course, but if Katazin had his way, that wouldn't be the final chapter in this aspect of his operation.

The further the operation proceeded, the less contact he had with other areas, and now he was solely focused on what he could affect here in New York City. He could only assume the events in Europe were proceeding as planned and the Red Army was ready to move. He needed to give them more time and divert the U.S. government's attention a while longer. That was where his contact would come in—Lenny Tallett, a twitchy weasel of a man who talked too fast with a Bronx accent that made it hard for Katazin to understand. Just then he saw the thirty-year-old man coming toward him. As usual, he proudly displayed the tattoos stretching from his hands past the collar of his shirt and wore more than a dozen studs in each ear. A younger woman, perhaps even a teenager, hustled along behind him as he approached.

Katazin said, "Is this the crowd you expected?"

Lenny said, "It's about what I thought." His dark eyes darted around the area, focusing for a moment on a uniformed police officer across the street.

That made Katazin a little nervous, and he scanned the courtyard to make sure no one was close. There was one man on the far side of the courtyard walking up to a bench. No one else moved. Then Katazin focused his full attention on Lenny and said, "Who's your friend?"

"This is Alice. She's my girlfriend. She's also a witness in case you go nuts." He held up his hands in a defensive movement and said quickly,

"You have to admit you sounded a little unglued on the phone. I didn't know what would happen in person."

Katazin stared at the rail-thin young woman. She had a wide array of tattoos herself and light brown eyes that made her look like a deer eyeing a wolf. Her hair was frizzy and popped out at odd angles from under a wool hat with the Stand Up to Wall Street logo across the front.

Katazin decided he didn't have time for this and got right to the point. He looked at Lenny and said, "Are the protesters really just scared? Or are they lazy?"

Lenny shrugged and said, "Little bit of both. I worked with the people who showed up. But who shows up in the middle of the day during the week? Mostly unemployed and homeless people. They lost interest, and so has the media."

Katazin had noticed only one TV crew, stationed in a truck at the far end of the courtyard, and they weren't even filming at the moment.

He said, "What will it take to get the protests started again?"

Lenny smiled and said, "Money. Money to advertise on Facebook and other social media and to cover my time and talent."

Katazin recognized this wasn't an off-the-cuff answer. He had been waiting to spring this for some time. Finally Katazin asked, "How much?"

"Fifty grand."

The little anarchist-for-profit had answered much too quickly. This was part of a plot to extort money and nothing more. Katazin gave him a flat stare but didn't answer.

After twenty seconds of silence, Katazin said, "That sounds awfully steep."

"It's nothing compared to what the rich dude, what's his name?" He paused, then answered his own question. "George Soros. What he paid for the protesters in Ferguson, Missouri. He gave them millions to keep up the protests. And that turned out to be a fake issue. All I want is a measly fifty K."

In the ensuing silence Lenny blurted out, "It'll also keep me quiet."

"About what?"

"I don't know exactly, but there's a reason you want the protests. And I bet you don't want the cops to know. Let's call it fifty grand either way."

Anger flashed through Katazin as he calmly gripped the handle of the pistol he had in the pocket of his windbreaker. He looked around and realized too many people were close by, but it was awfully tempting. If only he had a knife on him this conversation would be over. He needed a few moments to think.

22

Vladimir Putin sat at his official desk in his office at the palace at Novo-Ogaryovo. He told his personal assistant he needed some quiet time to concentrate on several issues. His assistant, a former army captain, always did an excellent job understanding exactly what his boss was asking for. He was not easily bullied, either. If Putin asked for time alone, he got it. It didn't matter who came to his door or called demanding immediate access.

Right now he had difficulty concentrating on the daily, mundane demands of his job even if he was undistracted by visitors. All he wanted was information about the Estonian operation. He had always found it hard not to look ahead.

He was very pleased with the planning and work that had gone into this operation. It would cost almost nothing. Barely more than a military exercise. The distractions, financial and terrorist-wise, had not cost anything at all. And, from his perspective, had little risk.

He didn't care about the GDP of Estonia. It was strategically important for its location. It was one less border he would have to cross when Russia decided it wanted to regain even more territory.

As soon as they had control of the country, they would start to use the ports as a means to increase trade.

Putin blustered about NATO, and he did worry about them some. That was why they had gone to the trouble of causing the distractions to the West. There was no doubt the United States had a strong military; the question was the leadership's willingness to use it. Putin believed that by bringing terrorism to U.S. shores he would scare them into limiting their foreign commitments. Either way, he did not believe they were prepared to go to war over something as inconsequential as Estonia.

This was a political decision, and Putin knew his politics.

It was noon when Derek Walsh walked into the quiet courtyard of the three Wall Street buildings that included Thomas Brothers Financial, the tallest building to the east. Wearing a Buffalo Bills ball cap he'd found in the lobby of his hotel to cover his new hair. He sat on the first bench he came to and looked up at the building, almost forgetting what it felt like to work inside. Had he taken all of this for granted? He reached into the left front pocket of his pants and pulled out the Thomas Brothers security plug and started to think of ways he might slip into the building. After a moment, his stomach growled, and he reached for one of the pieces of classic pink bubble gum he'd grabbed from a dish at the hotel, knowing it would stem hunger in a pinch.

He looked around the courtyard and was amazed there was no one close to him. At the far end, closer to his old building, a man in a Giants windbreaker with his back to Walsh was having a serious conversation with a younger couple. To his left was the lone film crew from a local TV station, with no one manning the camera. CNN had gotten tired of the story with no real violence or connection to a missing plane.

The man talking to the young couple looked agitated, and it caught

Walsh's attention. He seemed familiar from behind, and Walsh waited a moment to see if he could get a look at the man's face. It distracted him from all of the problems he knew he'd face if he tried to enter the building, access Thomas Brothers' network, and retrieve the photographs on his security plug.

Someone plopped down next to him with a bag from a local sub shop. Walsh almost didn't turn away from the man talking to the young couple. Then he nodded to his new companion on the bench, and it took a moment for him to realize who it was. Holy shit.

At least Walsh had the satisfaction of seeing how shocked Ted Marshall was, too.

It was lunchtime at the CIA, and the cafeteria, which had several mainstream chain restaurants, was starting to fill up. Mike Rosenberg did not feel guilty in the least for having ignored his boss's order to get a handle on the protests that might start up across the country today. It had only taken a few minutes watching CNN and their moving story about the people killed from terror attacks to know that the country was in mourning and soon would switch to the next phase of grief, which would be anger. Only this time the anger would be focused not on Wall Street but on the people who launched the attacks. The streets were quiet in all of the major cities. It took him a while to find a newsfeed from a local New York station to see that the few people protesting in the same area as the last few days had no energy or enthusiasm.

He'd written a quick report on the matter but hadn't submitted it. It never paid to let someone know you could do your job much more efficiently and quickly than they thought. Jesus Christ, he was becoming a government employee. He had spent the remainder of the morning talking to several of the financial analysts who had uncovered all the information they could on the money transfer from Thomas Brothers Financial to the accounts in Bern, Switzerland.

Now, at his desk, he had a stack of records laid out in front of him.

Other analysts were looking at similar records, but everyone took a different path to find information. That was why it was rare that only one analyst examined something important. The bank had been very thorough in handing over information, obviously because it was a victim of a terror attack and everyone wanted to catch the people responsible. There were notes and phone numbers scribbled on the edges of photocopied sheets, and twice he needed the analyst in the next office to interpret scrawled notes written in German and French.

From what he could tell, a woman had opened all of the accounts that received money. All of the accounts were opened in the same branch of the bank in Bern. The woman used a name that had already led analysts to a dead end. As long as you provided something with your name on it, banks didn't really care how accurate your information was when they were doing business. It was only at times like this that they regretted not being more diligent.

Rosenberg felt there had to be another avenue. He looked through the records and jotted down a few notes of his own on a legal pad. He was missing something obvious. Then he noticed a phone number scribbled on the side of an application. It was in sloppy block handwriting that looked like a male's, but he needed to find out more.

He just wished he wasn't so worried about his friend Derek Walsh. There was no telling what Derek might do if he was pushed into a corner.

Rosenberg went to find an analyst to trace the phone number.

Joseph Katazin had slowly moved away from the protest area and into the courtyard with Lenny Tallett and his creepy-looking girlfriend walking along with him. The young man, who claimed to be an anarchist, had made it plain: He had moved on to extortionist. This was a headache Katazin did not need.

As they slowly walked, the younger man said, "You have no idea how hard it is to organize things like this. No one ever does what they're supposed to."

"Tell me about it."

"And then the trick is to get the crowds stirred up and fade from the front line so you don't get arrested. We used that trick at a couple of the presidential debates. The one in Miami worked especially well. Grabbed some of the hard-core anarchists out of Lake Worth and bussed them down to Miami and shit got real."

"But you can't do the same thing here for me today?"

"I can try, but it will cost you. So far I haven't seen any hint that you're willing to pay."

Katazin looked up and saw they were getting closer to the end of the courtyard. There were now two men sitting on a bench, and the TV camera was not far from them. He desperately wanted to teach this dog a lesson right here and now. Instead he tried to get hold of his emotions.

Derek Walsh looked up to make sure no one was close enough to hear anything he said to his former boss, Ted Marshall. The only people coming his way were the guy in the Giants windbreaker and the young couple he was talking to. But they were still too far away to hear anything. Walsh appreciated the stunned silence and the look of amazement on Marshall's face. Finally the older man stuttered, "Derek, what the hell are you doing here?"

"I guess I'm a little like a zombie in a movie. You come back to the place you know best."

"You need to get outta here before the cops grab you. There are FBI agents still in our office going through things. They've asked a lot of questions about you."

"Did anyone tell them where I live? Or who my girlfriend is?"

"I don't think anyone *knew* where you live. But every guy in the office knew you had a hot girlfriend. They just had no information about her. Barely anyone could even remember her name."

Walsh absorbed that information but still didn't know how the Russian figured out where she lived. He also felt encouraged at how open Marshall was talking to him and telling him about the FBI.

His former boss said, "You need to turn yourself in before something bad happens."

"What could be worse than what I'm going through now?"

Marshall was silent.

Walsh took a chance and said, "Listen, Ted, is there any way you could get me back into the office for five minutes?"

"What are you talking about? I'd end up in the cell next to you."

"Look, I have my security plug, and I activated an extra security protocol so that whoever made the trade would've had their photograph taken and stored on the plug. In order to get the photograph, I have to log back on to the network."

Now Marshall looked truly stunned.

Walsh had the plug in his left hand and thought about showing it to Marshall, maybe even asking him to access the network. That would solve the hassle of getting back inside, but something told him never to give the plug away. It was his only leverage. He was taking action. He was being a marine. And a marine wouldn't let something like the security plug out of his sight. Unless it was out of everyone's sight. It gave him an idea.

Just as he was about to say something else, Walsh looked up and realized that the man who was walking toward them with the young couple was the Russian guy who had already caused him so much heartache. Was he after the plug? How did he keep finding Walsh?

Without thinking, Walsh coughed, covering his mouth with his left hand. He spat his gum into his palm, then jammed the plug under the bench until it was stuck between the gum and a support. The security plug was firmly in place as Walsh turned his head in hopes that the Russian wouldn't notice him. His heart started to race, and his hand slipped toward the pistol in his belt. This was not the time to get into a gunfight. Nor would it help his status as a fugitive. He doubted it would convince Ted

Marshall to help him, either. He stole a glance and saw that the man was on the pathway that turned past the bench.

He found himself holding his breath.

Joseph Katazin just needed one empty street to stick a bullet into the side of the head of this moron. He wasn't crazy about having to kill the girl, too, but this was war, and the stakes were too high. He kept walking, drawing them along, hoping to find the right spot.

He also felt that Lenny Tallett was getting frustrated himself. The weaselly younger man said, "So are you going to pay, or what?"

Katazin looked forward for a moment to make sure no one was walking their way. He decided he was too close to the two men on the park bench and held up one finger, telling Tallett to wait. He was about to turn and look again at the two men on the bench when Tallett's girlfriend spoke up for the first time.

"I'm hungry. Can we talk about this over lunch? There's a pizza place on the next street." She had a Jersey accent.

Katazin turned and looked at the girl as they walked past the bench and toward the street. His car was parked two blocks over, and he kept praying for a quiet space to finish this business.

Katazin said, "I think we have an agreement. Follow me for just a couple blocks and I can come up with the cash." He could tell by the wide smile on Tallett's face that he had no idea what was about to happen.

23

Derek Walsh felt that he had made some inroads talking to Ted Marshall on the bench in the courtyard, but before he could close the deal and blatantly ask for entrance to the office, he was totally distracted by the approach of the Russian with a scar on his face. Marshall never looked up at the guy.

Walsh knew it was no coincidence the guy was in front of his building. He was starting to get a picture of a larger conspiracy. But at the moment the Russian was not looking around for him. He was here for some other reason. Perhaps it was to talk to the young couple he was walking with now.

All these ideas of conspiracy made Walsh think he had made the right decision running from the FBI. He doubted the federal government wanted to listen to stories about Russian conspiracies until he had more evidence. Tonya Stratford appeared to be coming around to a dialogue with him, but he'd feel better about the meeting if he already had the photograph from his security plug. He didn't think Agent Stratford's partner would give him much of a chance to talk.

Walsh was ready to take action when the Russian was at the closest point to the bench, but the man just kept walking with the young couple. They took the path directly out of the courtyard and into the street. Walsh turned to Marshall and quickly said, "Ted, you understand my situation and what I can do to clear myself. You know me, and you know I didn't do anything wrong. Think about that. I'll be in touch."

With that, Walsh sprang from the bench and started to follow the Russian guy down the street. He had no experience in surveillance and immediately realized how difficult it was. But he had questions that needed answers. Perhaps answers he could pass on to Tonya Stratford. Who the hell was this guy? What was his involvement? Walsh understood that some of the things he had said to Agent Stratford sounded crazy. He didn't want anyone to write him off as a lunatic.

The young couple stopped for a moment and bought something from a takeout window at a pizzeria. The Russian looked annoyed and hurried them along as the girl started to munch on a slice of pizza.

Walsh had no idea where this would lead or what information he might find, but this was a lucky break that he wasn't going to let slip through his fingers.

It was early evening when Anton Severov, Fannie, and Amir reached the Narva River, which were the natural border between Estonia and Russia. There was no one waiting to cross, and the border guards seemed less than interested in talking to anyone. He could see that on the Russian side of the river there were already a military vehicle and several soldiers waiting for him. They eased through the river crossing and stopped at the far side of the bridge. The Russian soldiers started to stir and get the vehicle ready to move. They were probably annoyed that it'd taken so long. Severov had told them he'd be at the border by six, and now it was after eight. But the idea of separating from Fannie was difficult for both of them.

The idea of having Fannie suffer any consequences for their night of passion was not only difficult, it was unbearable. That was why he had told Amir to walk with him.

Severov kissed Fannie good-bye and gave her a long, lingering hug. She whispered in his ear as he pulled away, "Promise to call me as soon as you're back on this side of the border." He nodded and turned to Amir, who appeared more anxious for Severov to leave than anything else. He walked toward the checkpoint and waved to the soldiers on the other side. The Russian soldiers must have spoken to the Estonian border guards, because they didn't even bother to come out of their comfortable checkpoint booth and waved Severov on.

This was working out better than he expected as he put his arm around Amir's shoulder and said, "You have been a great deal of help. I know we've had our differences, but I think you'll be happy with the results."

Amir swelled with pride, nodding his head as he walked along with the taller Russian officer.

Katazin turned the corner and saw his BMW up the street. There was no one in either direction, and if he turned the corner quickly, took action, and jumped in his car, he could handle this one problem in a matter of seconds.

His pulse increased, and he felt a thin line of sweat across his forehead. Outside of combat in the Russian military, he had never had to kill anyone. He had done some unpleasant things to find out information or enhance his reputation, but for the most part any real violence could be contracted out to men like Serge Blattkoff.

Tallett turned quickly, as if he had a sense of what might happen. Or maybe he just realized wandering the streets aimlessly was not going to gain him fifty thousand dollars. He said, "Do you have a stash house or something around here?"

Katazin said, "Something like that," as his hand slipped up to his front pocket. Once again he wished he had a knife, but two quick shots echoing through the buildings would be difficult to pinpoint. His alternate idea was to make it to his car where he had a Gerber hunting knife with a four-inch blade. He had found it helpful around the import/export business and kept it in the pocket of his driver's side door. It had never occurred to him to use it in this way.

Now Tallett was purposely slowing down and showing hesitation. "Where are we going?"

Katazin casually pointed at his BMW just half a block away and said, "I have your down payment in my car."

"How much of a down payment?"

He wanted to be realistic but also offer enough to entice the younger man to the BMW. After a moment of calculation, Katazin said, "Ten grand." Judging by the expression on Tallett's face, he had hit the figure right on the head. The younger man took his girlfriend's hand and continued to follow Katazin down the street.

Derek Walsh had no experience in police work other than watching *Law & Order* and reading Michael Connelly novels, but, like everyone else, he thought that made him competent to follow people and figure out what was going on. In this case he was right. He could clearly see something criminal was about to occur. Some sort of exchange. Just the way the Russian looked up and down the street and then headed toward a white BMW jammed into a space near a Korean grocery made it obvious.

Walsh knew he had to do something, but pulling his pistol and opening fire didn't seem like the right choice. Earlier, Agent Stratford had asked if Walsh knew this guy's name. Maybe he could take a step closer by paying attention and keeping his eyes open. He didn't know if the young couple were part of this conspiracy, but he was making mental notes on them as well.

The man was maybe thirty and wiry, with tattoos and piercings and close-cropped hair. The girl was much younger, probably not yet twenty, and also had some tattoos. She had dark red dyed hair and didn't seem to be part of the conversation as she finished the last bite of her slice of pizza.

Walsh was careful to stand on the corner and look into the window of a men's clothing store. It gave him a vantage point where he could not be seen easily by the Russian. It was a safe position, a strategic position, but something inside him said to move forward and take action. He felt the call and reached down to feel the grip of the Beretta tucked into his pants.

Severov wondered how this looked to the soldiers waiting for him at the vehicle. They had no idea or advance warning about Amir. All they saw was a Russian major hanging his arm across the shoulder of a little guy with dark hair. From a distance they could easily mistake Amir for a teenager.

As they walked, Severov said, "We're going to need several things if this operation is to be a success." He kept his voice serious and direct even though he had no idea what he was going to say. He just needed to keep Amir calm until they were across the border.

Amir looked up at him, obviously interested in dealing a blow against the Americans.

Severov continued, "We're going to need communications disrupted, and I think the best way to do that is to have you take out the cell phone towers about twenty miles from here on the main road. They are unguarded, and all you would need to do is cut a few wires." He didn't want the job to sound too difficult or dangerous. He was sure that, like most of the Islamic zealots, Amir would be happy to send someone else to their death but would be more cautious with his own life. His main reason for coming up with a crazy fake plan was to buy time as they walked closer and closer to the Russian soldiers.

Amir said, "I haven't heard anything about this before now."

"That must mean that they have a plan to take care of it. The other thing we could really use is your help as liaison with some of our Muslim soldiers. We tried to recruit evenly throughout Russia and the republics, and as a result we have a number of Muslim conscripts. It would help to have a man like you that understands what we're trying to accomplish talk to them."

Now Amir was clearly confused. "You mean after they cross the border? When Russia has taken Estonia?"

Now they were at the vehicle, and the three soldiers had snapped to attention. One was a driver, and the other two held Vityaz-SN submachine guns on straps across their chests. Severov felt this was a good position and knew the soldiers would follow his lead. He stopped and turned to face Amir.

"No, I mean that you need to come with me now to help in our camp before the operation begins. I was told you would do whatever I need you to, and this is currently my most pressing need. Please get in the vehicle."

Amir just stood there, stunned. Finally he was able to say, "You mean you are kidnapping me and taking me inside of Russia? I was never told to leave Europe."

"I was never told I'd have such a sniveling swine as a guide."

Amir turned, ready to sprint back toward the bridge.

Severov said to the two armed men in Russian, "Don't let that little ass leave. Throw him in the transport."

Amir struggled until one of the men struck him in the head with the butt of his small machine gun. Severov concealed a smile. He couldn't resist turning to look back toward the bridge and see Fannie's beautiful face. She knew exactly what was happening and why he was doing it.

Severov hoped she knew enough to get clear of the border and head back toward Poland as quickly as possible. A shooting war was about to start.

24

Derek Walsh watched the Russian as he paused near a parked BMW. There was no one else on the street near them, and if they were up to something criminal, now was the time to do it. The only thing that made Walsh wonder if this was some sort of criminal transaction was the young woman who was standing near the skinny tattooed man the Russian was talking to. She looked like she was totally out of place. She had no interest in what was going on. It made Walsh hesitate. He didn't want to put anyone else in danger unnecessarily.

But his whole life was unraveling, and this guy was the key to it. He had held him and Alena at gunpoint. Walsh could tell the cops everything that had happened. All he needed was an excuse to use his pistol as he approached the man. He knew he could put a couple of rounds into him before the man pulled his own gun, which Walsh was sure he had on him.

He stepped around the corner and onto the sidewalk. Now if the

Russian looked up he'd see Walsh. He started to walk forward, knowing that he would have to take action as soon as he was noticed.

Joseph Katazin kept Lenny Tallett's attention as he made a show of fishing for the key, then slowly inserting it in the door of his BMW. Right now his big choice was whether to use the pistol and drive away or open the door, act like he was reaching for a pack of money, but instead grab his knife and run it up into Tallett's throat. His only concern there was that the girl would be alert enough to run immediately. Then he'd have one more loose end. But it would be quieter to use the knife.

He opened the door and said to both of them, "Come closer, I got something you'll like in here."

That got the bored girl interested in leaning into the car, and Tallett just wanted his money. He moved closer to the car as well.

Katazin's heart rate increased as he decided to use the knife. He made one quick sweep with his eyes from one end of the street to the other. He noticed a man on the corner and paused. That wasn't what made him hesitate. It was the police cruiser pulling up slowly and stopping on the curb just behind the man.

Katazin said out loud, "Damn it."

Tallett looked up and saw the cops. He muttered, "Be cool, be cool."

Katazin was annoyed at the obvious instruction but realized the skinny street rat knew more about dealing with local cops than he did. He needed another plan and needed it quickly, so he slipped into the driver's seat of the car and said, "Meet me at South Ferry in two hours. I'll be on the dock. I'll have all of your cash then. It's not safe to give it to you now." He saw the barest of nods from Tallett, then pulled the door shut, started the car, and calmly pulled away from the curb, turning down an alley before he had to pass the police car.

Walsh heard the vehicle before he saw the reflection of the NYPD cruiser in the window of the shop he was in front of. He didn't want to draw attention to himself, so he kept walking toward the white BMW as he casually removed the baseball cap so anyone looking at him would think he was an older, balding man. Now that he had a gray stubble growing on his chin, the aging effect was more pronounced.

Almost immediately the Russian slipped into the car and pulled away from the curb, coming straight toward Walsh. At this point he didn't care if the man saw him or not. All he really needed was the license plate. It would almost be worth the risk to tell the cops to stop the car, but he doubted they would act fast enough or believe him, and then he'd be in custody with nothing.

After a few more steps the car came toward him, and he could hear the engine was badly out of tune. He barely noticed the young couple as they walked away from him on the opposite sidewalk. All he could think of was getting the license plate.

The BMW came closer, but from behind him he heard, "Excuse me, sir." It was the cop. Walsh didn't want to take his eyes off the BMW, but he didn't want to raise the cop's suspicions, either.

He slowly turned and noticed the BMW make a hard right down an alley. The opportunity was lost, and now he faced two of New York's finest. They weren't dressed in regular patrol clothes but appeared to be some kind of tactical team. They might have been dressed like that just because of the recent civil unrest, but Walsh was uneasy about it. The black fatigue pants and long-sleeve turtleneck T-shirts with NYPD logos made them look like combat troops.

Both of the cops were younger than Walsh and very fit. The officer addressing him was a black man with a shaved head. The driver, standing by the cruiser, had the pale, freckled face of a third-generation Irish cop. Squared away in tactically prepared positions, they appeared highly professional.

This could be trouble. He had to think fast.

Fannie Legat had an idea what was about to happen to Amir, but she was still shocked when she saw him turn to run back toward the bridge and one of the Russian soldiers struck him in the head with the butt of his machine gun. Then Anton Severov turned and raised his hands as he shrugged his shoulders with that goofy smile of his. He was protecting her the best way he knew how. In truth, it probably saved her the trouble of shooting the little Iranian before he could say anything to their superiors. Now she could blame the Russians, and there was really nothing her group could do about it. For the most part it seemed like they didn't trust Amir anyway because he was an Iranian. But the Iranians had wormed their way into a number of groups, either through financing or people with the right education, and none of them were particularly well liked in the radical circles. That might change once they got nuclear weapons, but for now they seemed to be more of a nuisance than anything else. Their efforts to control ISIS in Iraq had infuriated many, even though ISIS had made its own enemies within the radical world. Now, at least officially, Iran was at war with ISIS.

She waited until the Russian military transport had driven off to the east and out of sight. She didn't think Severov was cold-blooded enough to just murder Amir. He would find some job for him that would keep him safely stashed far into the Russian homeland, and maybe the crazy Iranian would find his way home one day.

It was time to focus on the operation once again. She started down the same highway headed south, only this time she intended to catch a flight from Tartu to Stuttgart and get back to business immediately. If the Russians did invade as she thought they would, anything she did to slow down the Americans would be helpful. Now her main target would have to be her marine major, Bill Shepherd. And she had the entire flight home to figure out exactly how she could use him.

Walsh knew not to do anything stupid or sudden, so he put on a smile and said calmly, "What can I do for you, officers?"

It was clear the passenger was going to do all the talking, as the driver stayed right next to the cruiser. Years of abuse and unnecessary officers' deaths had trained them not to get too close to people immediately.

The young man who was addressing Walsh had a very dark complexion, and his head was shiny in the midday sun. He said, "We were just wondering what you were doing on the street alone. We haven't seen many pedestrians the last few days in this area."

Walsh didn't know if it was a trick to get him to say something that would reveal his identity or if it was just a "stop-and-talk," as the cops liked to call it. He considered his options, and short of pulling his pistol and shooting fast, there were none. And no matter what he had done or how many years he could be facing in jail for something he didn't do, Walsh was not about to shoot police officers just doing their job. But he did decide that he wouldn't make it easy for them.

Walsh said, "Oh. I get it."

The cop gave him a quizzical look and said, "Get what?"

"In order to continue to do your stop-and-frisks, you have to get a certain number of white people in nice areas so the numbers even out. I don't agree with that, son." He liked throwing in the "son" to make himself seem older, even though he was probably only three or four years older than this guy.

"Not sure what you're talking about, sir."

That made Walsh wonder if the cop threw in the word "sir" to indicate to him that he was an old man. Either way, Walsh had this guy on the line. He said, "I'm talking about how you guys constantly ignore Mayor de Blasio and continue to do things like stop-and-frisk even though he said the practice would stop."

The cop near the car said, "And look where it's gotten us the last few days."

The black cop who had been talking to Walsh turned and gave his partner a sharp look that shut him up. He quickly turned his attention back to Walsh.

Walsh said, "I know you think he took the teeth out of enforcement and that he's cutting back on your authority, but picking on me when I'm not doing anything at all is not going to help."

The cop looked truly confused now and said, "All I said was, 'Excuse me, sir.' I don't know where the rest of this is coming from."

"It's coming from a citizen who believed the mayor when he said he'd stop making the city a police state. What's your probable cause for stopping me?"

"First of all, I don't need probable cause to stop you. Second of all, I am not stopping you, I was just going to talk to you."

"Am I under arrest or am I free to go?" Walsh had seen some attorney on TV say that was a phrase that forced cops to make a decision. Never give them a third choice.

The cop hesitated as he formed an answer. He was no idiot.

Walsh was ready with his next response when the cop turned as a radio call came over his handheld. The cops exchanged a quick look after a series of codes and an address not far from where they were standing.

Walsh recognized that the cop looked relieved they were getting a call.

The cop looked at him one more time and said, "Have a good day," and as he slid into the car, Walsh heard him mutter, "Dickwad."

25

Derek Walsh's encounter with the New York City police officers had emboldened him. They didn't recognize him, and he'd showed some balls. He needed to prove to himself he could get out of this, and for the first time he was starting to believe it. Now he sat in a diner off Spruce Street near Pace University's Manhattan campus. There were even a couple of cops at a booth not far from him, but his confidence made him feel like no one even noticed him. Perhaps his plea to Tonya Stratford really had kept his photo off the news.

He had his cell phone but was hesitant to use it. If he called a number and it was traced, they might be able to get a fix on his position by looking at which cell towers the phone hit. For now, no one even realized he had a phone.

He'd made one call to the hotel and had a short and somewhat unpleasant conversation with Alena. Her belief that she was imprisoned against her will had only grown since he'd left her earlier in the morning, but he convinced her that he'd be back by six o'clock and everything would be all right. She just had to be patient. It was a tough sell, but by the time he broke the connection he felt confident that she'd stay put and spend the day watching Jerry Springer and Steve Harvey.

Then Walsh decided to take one risk with this phone. He called the switchboard at Thomas Brothers Financial. He knew the system and realized it would be difficult to trace a call unless they were waiting for it. Something told him that Ted Marshall was sincere when he said he would help. He certainly was nervous enough in the courtyard to make Walsh believe he was scared. He got no benefit from Walsh being accused unfairly. Walsh was going to have to trust someone besides Mike Rosenberg.

When the operator answered, Walsh asked for Ted Marshall. His former boss picked up the phone on the first ring. Tension strained his voice when he said, "Hello."

Walsh said, "Ted, it's me."

"That's what I was afraid of. I've been a nervous wreck since I tried to eat my lunch on that bench. What do you want, Derek?"

"Just what we talked about, nothing more. Get me on the network and I'll get the photographs off my security plug." There was a long pause, and Walsh added, "Come on, Ted, you know I'm straight up. You can stay with me the entire time I'm on the computer."

"If you don't get the photos, will you turn yourself in?"

Walsh thought about it for a moment and said, "You can call the FBI while I'm in the office."

"That's the problem. There will already be FBI agents in the office. Usually they're totally focused on files and computers, but I will yell to them if you're not on the level."

"I swear I just need network access for my security plug. It will take like two minutes to see if I'm right. If not, I'm screwed anyway. Do you really imagine me as a fugitive for the rest of my life?"

Marshall sounded resolved as he said, "I guess not. It's just that this is such a huge risk. We've gotta make it looked like I just ran into you in the lobby. I'll need a little time. I've got some afternoon meetings, one of them with an FBI agent working in the office."

Walsh said, "I'm going to have to trust that you won't say anything. I really need to trust you."

"*Trust me!* I'm helping the guy who destroyed Western civilization."

Walsh had to chuckle at that and said, "Good point. What time?"

"Sometime around five would be good. Most of the FBI agents cut out between three and four."

"What if I were in the lobby at exactly four fifty?"

Marshall said, "I'll be sure to be in the lobby at exactly ten minutes to five. We're gonna have to make this fast."

Mike Rosenberg had gathered an impressive amount of information in a short time by maximizing the efforts of several analysts. That was one of the things he appreciated about the CIA: They worked together as a team. No one ever cared about personal credit or asked questions about what another analyst was working on. They truly followed the "need to know" doctrine, and Rosenberg felt a little guilty for abusing their trust. But he was doing it for noble reasons: to solve the riddle of this money transfer and, more importantly, to save his friend.

He had traced the scrawled phone number to a mobile phone issued in Germany. He tracked down the company, Vodafone, and found its law enforcement compliance office was located in Berlin. At this point he should have found a translator for the conversation he wanted to have with someone from that office. Instead, he decided to risk it and call himself, hoping to find someone who spoke English. This was not the sort of conversation he wanted someone to witness. He wasn't even sure what he was going to say. This stunt was not as an employee of the CIA. He had no legal authority; nor had he attempted to gain a subpoena and go through the Justice Department to have it legally served in Germany. By the time he had gotten through all that, Derek Walsh could be sitting in prison.

He dialed the ten-digit phone number that included the country code for Germany and waited as he heard the odd ringtone in his phone. A woman answered the phone speaking German. All Rosenberg caught was, "Vodafone and Schmidt." He recognized she was mentioning her company and her last name. For some reason this made him hesitate for a moment; then he said, "This is Mike Rosenberg from the United States. Do you speak English?"

There was a frustrated grunt on the other end of the phone, which made Rosenberg recognize the arrogance he had in calling and having no idea how to speak the native language. But the woman was a professional and managed an accented "One moment" in English before she put him on hold.

He intended to use a trick an FBI agent had shown him for getting maximum cooperation in a hurry without official paperwork. It was one of the things law enforcement occasionally had to do to protect citizens, no matter how underhanded or sneaky it seemed.

After more than a minute, another woman came on the phone. Part of this plan needed a female. Preferably a female with a family. He hated to be so manipulative but sometimes had to remind himself he worked for the CIA.

With almost no accent, the woman said in English, "My name is Barbara Gould. With whom am I speaking?"

The stern and direct tone caught him by surprise, but he managed to mumble, "My name is Mike Rosenberg, and I work for—" He paused for a moment. This could come back to bite him on the ass in a big way. Finally he decided to take the plunge and said, "The national police of the United States." He was hoping the German would assume every country had a national police force like Germany. It also would make it more difficult for anyone to figure out who called the company. They would probably assume it was the FBI, and interest in finding out more details would fade long before it was traced back to him. His only hope was that she would buy it and didn't understand there was no national police in the United States.

The woman said, "Yes, Mr. Rosenberg, how may I help you?"

Rosenberg smiled as he pulled the legal pad with his notes closer. Now he was getting things done.

Joseph Katazin waited on the platform of the Whitehall Street station. This time of day there was not a lot of traffic, and he thought he might get lucky and surprise Lenny Tallett as he got off the train. It was just a guess on Katazin's part, but an educated guess, that the little anarchist would take the train and get off at this station. Katazin had told him he knew a wooded area by the bus line under the Battery Park overpass. In fact, that was his fallback position. There was a surprisingly wooded area where he could do whatever he had to do and slip away. He doubted anyone would notice a body for at least a day. But he liked his plan to surprise the little creep. Then he'd take the N or R train uptown. No one would even know he was in the area.

At least now he was prepared. Not only did he have his pistol, but he had the knife he normally kept in the car. He also carried a vinyl satchel with some paperback books shoved in it to look like cash. He had scooped the latest Lee Child and Tess Gerritsen novels off his secretary's desk. He had novels by Brad Thor and Brad Meltzer in his own desk drawer. The four books together, along with some crumpled newspaper, made a credible bag of money. At least for as long as he would need it.

He planned to act quickly and quietly but was torn about what to do with Tallett's quirky girlfriend. He had no desire to kill her, but she could ID him, and there was no telling what secrets Tallett had already spilled to her. Once he was done with this problem, he could focus all of his attention on Walsh.

There were a few people at the far end of the platform waiting to go uptown. He could hear the train in the tunnel and knew it was about showtime. He was surprisingly nervous and felt a tremor in his hand. As a kid he never would've thought about spies being nervous. But he was realizing his lifelong dream, so he took a deep breath and made one more scan around the platforms.

To his right he noticed a young man for the first time. He was tall and slender with a scraggly beard and had a heavy coat wrapped tightly around him. His dark hair was cut short, and his eyes darted in every direction. Katazin tried not to pay much attention because he didn't want this guy being able to give a description to the cops later on.

The train rolled into the station, and Katazin immediately saw Tallett and his girlfriend through the window. The car was surprisingly crowded, and he hoped most the people would clear the station before Tallett noticed him.

There was a certain thrill to this kind of work, and the fact that he could surprise his target, blocks before he would expect it, was sweet.

26

Derek Walsh knew exactly what he needed to do. Sitting at a booth in the deli near Pace University, he'd scrawled several notes on napkins and was about to use the phone to gather more information. He'd already laid a twenty on the table to show the waitress he was going to take care of her for tying up the table, but business was slow, so it wouldn't be an issue.

Almost as a reflection of his mood, the weather was clearing, and the autumn sun cast a cheerful glow on the street outside. He noticed several young people walk by with backpacks and figured they were probably students at the private university. No one talked much about Pace in a city that boasted about Columbia, NYU, and Fordham.

The next call he made was a risk. He hoped this would all be over soon and he would have no need of the phone in the next few hours. One way or the other, this nightmare would be over.

He dialed Tonya Stratford's number, and she picked it up on the first ring.

He said, "This is Derek Walsh."

"That would've been my first guess. Where are you?"

"I'm still in the city, and I would like to meet you." He could tell there was a sense of relief on the other end of the phone.

Agent Stratford said, "That's good news. Tell me where you are and I'll come there right now."

"It's not quite that simple."

"It never is."

Walsh smiled at the slight humor she was finally starting to display. "I'll meet you in Times Square between five and six this evening. No tricks, no games, I should have everything I need, and I believe you when you say you'll give me a chance to explain."

"I try to deal honestly with everyone. I can't meet you alone. You've pulled too much shit."

"I understand. But I would prefer if you didn't use a SWAT team to knock me to the ground."

"I'll bring one or two other agents, all in plainclothes. But I don't want any funny business. Go right to the discount ticket booth, and we'll be there waiting."

"One more thing."

"I'm listening."

"You know my concerns about a conspiracy."

"Go on."

"I give you my word as a former marine officer and a gentleman that I will be in Times Square between five and six this afternoon. But I have no idea who to trust and how far this conspiracy reaches, so I'm asking you to keep it quiet and use the minimum amount of help you feel is necessary. Otherwise, there's no telling what will happen to me."

"Again, no promises. But I believe you when you say you'll meet me. And we will be in Times Square at five o'clock waiting for you."

"I'll see you then." That went as well as he could have expected. Now all he had to do was get the evidence and meet her. At least by setting up the meeting for five, he knew she wouldn't be at Thomas Brothers when he got there.

———

Since he was not using official CIA resources but relying on his own guile—and a ploy that the FBI used to get people to talk about different subjects by making it seem like they were investigating crimes against children—Rosenberg made it a point to chat with the woman for a moment and ask her first name. Even if this was rude to a German, it made him feel like he was making a personal connection. He called her Barbara several times, and she finally responded by calling him Mike. Then he got into the meat of his question.

He said, "Barbara, I have a very sensitive investigation involving a phone number that your company carries. We're trying to move quickly due to the nature of the investigation, and I was just wondering if I could get some basic information from you."

Her voice had softened considerably from her initial greeting, and now she said, "Of course, we now accept subpoenas directly from the United States via fax. It really doesn't take any longer than if we were dealing with the German police. I will even e-mail you the information back."

That didn't help Rosenberg at all. He started to move toward his original plan. "Here is the problem, Barbara, the investigation is extremely time sensitive, and we need to locate other victims as soon as possible. Most of them would probably be in Germany, or perhaps Switzerland."

Curiosity got the better of Barbara, and she asked, "Victims of what?"

Rosenberg knew he had her. "We have identified a serial pedophile who's using the phone to contact his victims. We desperately need the phone numbers he has called in the past thirty days or so just to make sure these kids are safe." He was surprised how guilty he felt lying like this.

The woman's sincerity didn't help him feel any better. There was a long pause, and Rosenberg looked up at the clock on his desk, watching the seconds tick by. Did the pause mean she was swayed by his request or that she was looking up the "United States National Police"?

Rosenberg had started considering an exit strategy when the woman said, "Oh my, I was just thinking about my two young children at home. Perhaps there is a way I can expedite the information."

"That would be very helpful and give us a chance to identify this man and perhaps have the German National Police pick him up as soon as possible." Rosenberg felt a little guilty lying to the woman, but justified it by thinking of his friend Derek Walsh.

There was a longer pause on the phone, and Rosenberg could hear the keyboard clicking. Then the woman said, "I can see that there has been a great number of calls in the past thirty days to a number of different countries."

Rosenberg was thinking, *Jackpot*!

The woman said, "I could e-mail these without the official stamp. They would not be able to be used in court, but once you send a subpoena we could send another copy."

"That would be perfect."

"I have to scan them, and it might take a little while."

"No problem, thank you."

Rosenberg smiled because he had a safe e-mail address that wouldn't be traced to the CIA.

He was in business.

For some reason Katazin kept an eye on the young man in the heavy coat as the train stopped and people started filing off. It was just something about him that didn't seem right. He switched his focus from looking for Tallett and his girlfriend to seeing what the guy in the coat did. The young man stepped toward the train but showed no interest in getting on. Then Katazin had a sinking feeling that he knew what was going on: This was one of the lone wolf jihadists who were supposed to hit the city over the next few days. Fate was a bitch, and luck wasn't with him today. Everyone had speculated that the jihadists would eventually hit the subway. They'd been trying for a couple of days already.

Just as Katazin formed that opinion, Lenny Tallett stepped off the train and practically ran right into him waiting on the platform. But

Katazin couldn't take his eyes off the young man in the dark, heavy jacket.

Tallett turned to Katazin and said, "What are you doing here? Were you on the same train as us?" When he didn't get any response, Tallett looked around the platform, then turned back to Katazin and said, "What's wrong? Do you want to just give me the bag here?" He scanned the platform again, then said, "Why are you staring at the guy in the coat?"

Before Katazin could answer, the man stepped into the train car where the most people were still lingering, glanced around quickly, reached into his coat pocket, and pulled out something that looked like the end of a jump rope. He shouted something and detonated the bomb wrapped around his chest. The flash was phenomenal. A second later Katazin felt the blast and a shard of glass etching a wound across his forehead. The blast knocked him off his feet, and he skidded across the platform floor until he crashed into a pillar. He barely caught sight of Tallett being thrown to his right and the girlfriend whizzing past him off the platform onto the tracks.

His ears were ringing so badly the wave of screams barely registered in his head. It reminded him of a mortar attack by the Mujahideen in Afghanistan, if the mortar had landed inside the tank with him. He tried to sit up as blood trickled from his ear. Now the smoke and smell of burned flesh was reaching him.

He twisted his body and slowly sat up and searched the platform around him until he found Tallett lying in a heap in the corner.

Tallett was moving. There were a dozen injured people on the platform and more dead inside the train, but somehow this asshole had survived.

Major Bill Shepherd finally laid his head on his pillow in his half of an officer's duplex he shared with an army lieutenant colonel on the base. Housing was based on several factors, but the main one was rank. In recent years, not as many officers brought their families to Germany, and that opened up the larger residences for bachelor officers. The small, neat duplex featured a bedroom, living room, and kitchen, which was plenty for Shepherd at this point in his life.

Between the inquiry and his impromptu interrogation by the lovely FBI agent, he ranked this as one of the worst noncombat days of his career. He didn't know what the implications for his advancement would be after the inquiry, and now, in the dark of his bedroom, he wondered if his connection to Derek Walsh would be a detriment as well.

If it had thrown his career off track, he didn't care. The marines stressed loyalty, and Derek Walsh had earned it. Anyone who knew him understood he had nothing to do with the allegations. But no one could deny the shock waves that had been sent across the world as a result of the illegal trade. It still felt manufactured to Shepherd. Why were so many people up in arms and prepared to turn violent about financial transactions? He felt like there was a larger plan in motion, and he had been quietly preparing his marines in case they had to act quickly.

There had been no protesters in front of the base this evening and, ironically, the first decent police presence since the trouble had started. Shepherd didn't think one was linked to the other. He suspected the police presence was a result of the inquiry and the Americans' complaints about support.

Just as he was about to nod off, his phone rang. It was his personal cell, which only a few people in the whole world ever called, and none of them about business. He reached over and recognized immediately that it was Fannie Legat. He didn't know if she had already come home, but for the first time in his life he would have to tell a woman he was too tired to meet her. Maybe thirty had hit him harder than he had expected.

He answered it with a pleasant "Hello" rather than his usual "Shepherd here."

Fannie's sweet voice said, "Hello to you, too."

He loved her French lilt.

She said, "I'm about to fly home now and was wondering if you wanted to meet for brunch. I have the whole day free if you are able to make it."

He made some quick calculations in his head and said, "I can make brunch about ten, and we'll have to see what happens from there." He couldn't keep the smile from spreading across his face as he stared up at the dark ceiling.

Fannie said, "The plane is at the gate. I can't wait to see you."

Shepherd needed a win like this to turn the whole day around. Now he had a reason to sleep soundly and get moving in the morning.

Hot damn!

He knew he needed his rest and shut off his cell phone. As soon as he rolled onto his side, he felt his consciousness slip away as he fell into a deep, well-earned sleep.

It took a full minute for Katazin to recover his senses and slowly start to stand. The cops would be here soon. He grabbed his knife and stumbled toward Tallett, who was still lying on the floor. All he had to do was stick the blade through the man's throat and there would be one less thing for him to worry about.

As Katazin approached Tallett, the younger man rolled to his knees, then got to his feet. He looked at Katazin for just a moment, then said, "Where's Alice?" He was suddenly in a panic as he scanned the platform. Without meaning to, Tallett moved away from Katazin to the edge of the platform, where he looked down at the body of his young girlfriend as she lay across all three rails of the N line. Her body sizzled from the electricity of the third rail like bacon in a frying pan. The stench reminded Katazin of Afghanistan. Burning flesh was burning flesh, whether it was in a remote mountain cave or the subways of New York.

Katazin walked up behind Tallett and put his arm on his shoulder as if comforting him, then plunged his knife all the way through the slim man's neck from right to left, hoping that it would look like a piece of shrapnel from the explosion had caused the damage. Tallett stood for a moment, not even turning his head to see what had happened, then crumpled on the platform and tumbled off onto the track.

In the spreading smoke and suffocating fumes, Katazin could hear a train in the tunnel coming to a stop early. There was no telling what chaos this would spread through the city. He'd better start heading uptown as soon as possible. He still had a lot to do.

27

Walsh felt like it had been a lifetime since he walked across this court-yard and into the Thomas Brothers Financial building. It was hard for him to believe it was only three days ago he had a normal life with a schedule. He was starting to understand how empty that life was and that it lacked a purpose. He decided he'd tackle one problem at a time.

He scanned the courtyard and thought it really didn't look much dif-ferent than it had at lunchtime. The same uninterested news crew sat on one side with no one working the camera, and a few lackadaisical protest-ers halfheartedly marched on the other side. It was nothing at all like the day the shit hit the fan. No one was calling for the end of life as he knew it or protesting the very idea that some businesses dealt with money.

Some of the activity had decreased because of fear. A few bombs set off across the country, especially at Disneyland, had sent a shock wave not seen since the September 11 attacks. Now Walsh was hearing about the bombing at the Whitehall subway station not far from Wall Street. Just a few sketchy reports and an increase in foot traffic coming from the Battery, but it didn't sound promising.

The situation developing around the country reminded Walsh of an experience in Afghanistan, one that had defined and troubled him for the past five years. Walsh had been trying to figure out how they were losing so many supplies during such a prolonged period of no combat operations. He knew that some of the local workers who came on the base would snatch what they could and sell it on the black market. He understood they were starving and that was what they needed to do to survive, but it was his duty to account for all of the supplies. More than once he had just handed money to would-be thieves and told them not to steal anything from the base. He knew it wouldn't have much impact, but his conscience had a hard time allowing desperate men and their families to starve.

One evening, he had been working outside the supply tent and had just realized he'd already missed dinner with his friends when he heard a commotion and some gunfire. He didn't immediately know if it was just a marine blowing off steam or trying to prove a point about what a good shot he was, or if it was something more serious. But as soon as he came around the corner of the tent he saw an Afghani man running with a U.S. military pack on his back. His first thought was that the shots were some kind of distraction so this man could steal from the supply tent. Shepherd wasn't going to allow that to happen on his watch.

The man was almost within arm's reach and didn't even notice Walsh. He acted on instinct and reached out quickly to grab the pack with his right hand and pull it as hard as he could. He twisted the thin man around, and the pack slipped off his back. Walsh was shocked by the weight of it. He wondered how such a slightly built man could've even stood up with it on his back. The pack pulled him to the ground as he raised his own rifle in case the man had any ideas about retrieving the pack and running away.

Then Walsh heard gunfire and the man fell. It was only then that he realized there were two other Afghans off to the side. They were both knocked down by gunfire as well.

Walsh saw his three friends, Mike Rosenberg, Ron Jackson, and Bill Shepherd, running toward him just as he realized the pack didn't contain supplies pilfered from his supply depot but held a bomb intended for the command bunker not far away. His next thought was whether the bomb was set on a timer or needed to be manually detonated. There was a white cord with a handle coming from inside the pack that lay limp on the ground. He realized at that moment that his stupid action had surprised the suicide bomber so completely he had yet to grab the detonation cord.

As his friends skidded to a halt on the dusty, dry ground, Walsh realized how foolish he'd been and started to back away from the bomb.

Jackson was already thinking ahead and looked up to make sure someone from EOD was coming toward them. Shepherd said, "Let's all back away from this right now."

All the marines on the base had been in combat, and none of them were stupid. A minute later there was a huge perimeter around the lone pack sitting in the middle of the base with three Afghan bodies lying nearby.

By the time everyone was done congratulating Walsh on his heroics, he couldn't bring himself to tell his friends the truth. He was so shaken he just kept quiet and nodded his appreciation.

One of the reasons he'd joined the marines was that he thought he could keep events like this from happening in his own country and terrorizing civilians who had no reason to ever see violence like that. Somewhere along the line his plan hadn't worked.

Sirens brought him back to the present, and he watched emergency vehicles race toward the lower end of Manhattan and felt like he should be doing something to help. That was why he missed the marines. Their mission was always designed to help someone, either help the army gain a foothold or help a population escape from oppression. He felt like he contributed when he was in the marines.

Now he felt almost useless as he considered only his own interests. He wanted to get inside the building, access the security plug through the Thomas Brothers network, and find out who the hell had wrecked his life. Then he could put this all behind him.

He was still dressed in the white shirt and dark slacks, and he had the pistol tucked in his belt. If Ted Marshall could be trusted, he would meet Walsh just inside the door and escort him up the elevators without having to go through any security checkpoint. With the subways closed it could be a little trickier reaching Times Square to meet Tonya Stratford by six o'clock, but he was confident he could make it if he had to.

He took a deep breath as he attempted to maintain a casual stride through the cement courtyard. No one appeared to pay any particular attention to him as he approached the cement stairs that led up to the wide glass doors. He could recall standing on the landing and leaning on the pillar during a break so he could call Alena while the other brokers and bankers furiously puffed on cigarettes. Now the landing was empty as he climbed the low stairs.

Just as he reached the landing he saw movement to his left behind the pillar. He turned, but all he saw was the barrel of a pistol pointed directly at his face. A man's voice with a slight Russian accent said, "Please don't do anything stupid, Mr. Walsh."

Mike Rosenberg had as many records as he could find regarding his friend Derek Walsh and the money transfer that had landed him in hot water spread over his desk. The original bank records had been destroyed in the explosion at the bank in Bern. Luckily someone had thought to scan most of the documents and upload them to the cloud, but it was slowing down the investigation. That was probably one of the intents of the bombing. People assumed in this high-tech world that everything was immediately digitized, but the fact was that businesses still generally wrote information on pieces of paper, then entered it into a computer. This appeared to be what the bank had done, and as a result, Rosenberg was left gaining information from poor scans.

Rosenberg also had the records from the cell phone number that was scribbled in the margin of one of the bank applications. There was an amazing number of calls, pages and pages of them, and the identify of the subscriber still had to be determined. Rosenberg didn't want to pull in other analysts on this project if he could avoid it. He checked his watch and saw that it was getting close to five. Since he had acquired this through unofficial means, he felt comfortable working on it from home. Nothing was stamped sensitive or secret, and he could easily take it out past the guards without raising any alarms.

He took one last look up at a television in the corner of his office as CNN aired another report from Disneyland, with the title underneath saying, "Loss of innocence." He had the volume down but assumed they had already created a theme song as well. All of this seemed tied together and linked to Derek Walsh somehow.

He didn't intend to get much sleep tonight.

It was the middle of the night, and Anton Severov had been unable to sleep. After getting Amir settled in a tent with several Chechen recruits, he'd tried to grab some sleep. The little Iranian was still furious and said to him as he left, "You are not the enemy of my enemy. You are just my enemy, and you will pay for this."

Severov gave him a hard look and said, "I could have just killed you."

"You'll wish you did."

"I already do. But make no mistake, my friend. This is not the U.S. Army. I can shoot you and no one will ever ask why. You are not even a Russian citizen. So I would watch my mouth and keep my attitude in check until we find the right time and place to let you go."

Amir just stared at him. His dark eyes hid any of the calculations he was making. At least Severov felt like he had taken Amir's attention away from Fannie, and she would be safe for the time being. He doubted that anyone would care about her personal habits once the military aspect of this operation was under way.

Again it was Amir's calm demeanor that made the threat so much scarier. But Severov had other things to worry about.

———

Derek Walsh sat quietly in the front seat of the white BMW he'd seen earlier. His hands rested in his lap as the Russian focused on the road but kept his right hand on the grip of a Beretta pistol very similar to Walsh's. His own pistol was now in the Russian's waistband.

The Russian had somehow managed to slip over the Brooklyn Bridge even with the increased traffic due to the subway bombing. He raced south through Brooklyn toward Brighton Beach, but he pulled off Ocean Parkway in the Midwood area and stopped in front of a six-story apartment complex that look like it was straight out of the seventies, with kids playing on the sidewalk and elderly people lounging around the front steps that led to a wide landing with several beat-up patio tables and chairs missing straps.

The Russian slipped the BMW into a spot across the street from the building and waited for Walsh to step out of the car, then walk around the hood and wait to be escorted inside. The Russian man said, "I assume you realize by now that I'll shoot you if you try anything funny." He let that sink in and then said, "You may not care about yourself, but think of the innocent bystanders and others that might be in the building."

The man nudged Walsh so that he would look up at the front door of the building. Then his heart stopped. The skinny Russian who had been outside his apartment, Serge Blattkoff, stood at the front door with Alena directly in front of him. He flashed the pistol in his right hand, then briefly put it to Alena's temple.

She stifled a scream and motioned for Walsh to come toward them into the building.

Things were not working out the way he'd planned.

28

Derek Walsh walked without resistance directly in front of the Russian. He knew the man had a gun in his back, but that didn't even concern him now. Alena's safety was foremost in his mind. He barely noticed the normal neighborhood activity going on around him as he climbed the stairs to the landing, entered the front door of the apartment building, and immediately turned right and slowly marched up the stairs. He thought about Alena, who had shown him tenderness and stood by him, even offering her own bank account in support. She had no business being sucked into whatever this was.

The second-story hallway was empty and had what looked like new carpet laid from one end to the other. It was cheap, thin industrial carpet, but at least someone was trying to keep the place up. The far end of the hallway turned gloomy, as none of the lights were on yet. It matched his mood. What could he do in this situation? Everything he'd worked for the last few days was for nothing. And now they had Alena. And he had nothing.

About halfway down the hallway a door opened, and the man shoved him toward the apartment. As soon as Walsh stepped inside he saw the smiling face of Serge Blattkoff. His left eye was still bruised and discolored. He looked like he was eager to exact some revenge.

Alena sat in a wide La-Z-Boy recliner with her hands stiffly gripping the arms. She sat perfectly straight with her legs directly in front of her as if she were preparing to model the chair in a photo shoot. Her brown eyes cut up to him, but she didn't say a word or move a muscle.

As soon as he was inside, Blattkoff shoved him onto a sofa, which faced out to a wide bay window. Alena was in his line of sight across the room. The questions in his head buzzed like a chainsaw. How had they found her? Why did they have her? But he knew not to ask any questions just yet.

The older man with a scar leaned on the arm of the sofa. He affected a casual attitude like a man at a beach club about to chat with a friend. Walsh noticed his eyes flick around the room to make sure his security measures were in place. Walsh had no doubt one of the men would easily shoot him if he tried to move, or worse, shoot Alena.

One floor lamp at the end of the sofa illuminated the whole room. He listened to the sounds of the apartment building but picked up nothing of interest other than someone with heavy footsteps walking on the apartment floor above them. He had already decided he wouldn't speak first.

Finally the Russian man said, "You're quite a resourceful young man. I have been very impressed with your ability to slip out of tight situations. But the only way you're going to get out of this is to give us what we want."

Walsh tried to stay calm and control his voice as he said, "And what do you want?"

"First, you can hand over the security plug from Thomas Brothers Financial."

That caught him by surprise, but he answered honestly. "I don't have it."

"Where is it?"

Now he lied. "The FBI took it when they arrested me."

The Russian smiled and let out an ominous chuckle. "I know you have the plug and activated the security feature that took a photograph of the trade. I will ask you once more in a pleasant tone: Where is the security plug?"

Walsh's first instinct told him that Ted Marshall was involved and had told them about the security plug. What would make a man sell out his company and his country like that? Walsh kept his eyes on the Russian as he thought about what to say.

Mike Rosenberg felt his stomach rumble from nerves the entire drive from Langley to his house in Maryland. Just the idea that he took something out of the main headquarters made him queasy. It didn't matter if the information came from an unofficial source based on his unofficial phone call or if it was the blueprints to an aircraft carrier; he had just broken half a dozen major rules at the CIA.

He walked in the door to his small house and slapped down the sheaf of papers that contained the phone numbers from Vodafone in Germany. He went immediately to the kitchen counter and grabbed his personal cell. He dialed Derek Walsh first but got no answer. His friend had not even set up a voicemail account yet.

He checked his watch and calculated how late it would be in Germany and decided he would risk bothering Bill Shepherd. He sure would love to talk to one of his friends.

He immediately spread the papers out on the kitchen counter and started looking at the phone numbers and determining what countries had been called. There was a mass of information in these pages, and he wanted to break the code and figure out exactly what some of the information meant. Then he had to figure out a way to explain it to his supervisor.

It was going to be a very long night.

Walsh looked around the room and saw nothing that would help him escape. There was the main door, a second door in the corner of the next room, and a narrow utility door that looked like it went from the kitchen to the end of the exterior hallway. At least his head was on straight enough to be thinking about escaping. This was a war, and that was what the marines had trained him for.

The older Russian with a scar on his face spoke Russian to Serge; then the younger man pulled Alena out of the La-Z-Boy as the older Russian jerked Walsh to his feet. They pushed them both into a spacious bathroom that had one tiny window. It wasn't big enough for either of them to fit through.

The Russian looked Walsh in the eye and said, "You make any noise or cause any trouble and I'll put a bullet in her pretty face." He pulled the door shut, and Walsh could tell someone was leaning against the outside. He didn't know why they had been moved, but he wasn't going to waste the opportunity.

He rushed to embrace Alena and said, "Are you okay?"

She just nodded her head, then laid her face against his chest as they both sat on the edge of the wide bathtub. She said, "Just give them what they want so they'll let us go."

"What if they don't let us go after they have what they want?"

"Then we're in no worse shape than we are now."

"Unless they kill us." He could see she was scared. Who wouldn't be? She was just a student and had no idea what men like this were capable of. He thought back to all the kindness she had shown him. Laughing at his corny jokes, giving him her debit card, trusting him with her heart. It hurt to think of her mixed up with him in something like this.

After a few seconds Alena said, "Where is the plug?"

"It's safe. I can get to it if I need it."

"I think you need it." Her tone had turned flat and cooler.

After a long silence Walsh said, "Do you know how they found you?" She shook her head.

"Did they take you anywhere else?"

"No."

Walsh tried to concentrate on the noises outside. He could hear people speaking, but it was mostly in Russian. He could barely hear any traffic sounds. The neighborhood wasn't particularly busy, and the apartment building was sturdy. Noise might not carry if he yelled.

Alena said, "Who is the old guy they keep talking about? The one that hit the guy who lives here."

"Charlie? He's just a friend of mine. A vet that's fallen on hard times. Why are they asking?"

Alena shrugged her shoulders. "They asked a lot of questions. Like if you talk to anyone on a regular basis, what you told the FBI. They wanted to know if you picked up on the fact that they were Russian. They asked everything. But mainly they want to know where the security plug is." She focused those big brown eyes on him and said, "Where is it?"

Walsh didn't want anyone to know that answer. Not even Alena. He just didn't answer as he started to consider what he might use as a weapon here in the bathroom. Perhaps if he struck one of them hard enough he could get the man's gun.

Then Alena stood up and stepped toward the door. Before he could ask what she was doing, she knocked on it hard. The door opened, and Serge Blattkoff peered in.

Alena spoke to him in Russian. Or was it some other Eastern European language? Whatever language it was, it wasn't Greek, and it made Walsh's stomach turn. He had been a fool.

The small plane Fannie Legat was riding in bumped along on its way to Stuttgart. She wouldn't have time to grab any sleep once she reached her home base but was pleased with herself for having so easily talked Major Shepherd into meeting her the following day. Now it was the middle of the night and she'd already found a small team to help her. It was a simple plan that would coincide nicely with the plans of the Red Army.

She intended to have a sizable bomb placed under whatever vehicle Major Shepherd drove to meet her. The café they were meeting at was close to his base, and he would be able to get back quickly. If all went as planned, they would still be at brunch when the news of the Russian incursion into Estonia reached him. She could picture him rushing back to his car and racing to the base. As soon as he reached the main entrance, another confederate would remotely detonate the bomb, causing all kinds of chaos and confusion.

It would also leave the marines, who Fannie understood to be the elite fighting force of the U.S. military, in disarray.

She could catch up on sleep sometime after that.

Mike Rosenberg could eliminate many of the numbers on the toll records he had taken from the office. It was a long shot, and the fact that the number was scrawled on the side of an application for a Swiss bank account in Bern might not have meant anything, but there were a bunch of calls to capitals all over Europe, as well as to cell phones that appeared to have come from Jordan and Syria. He did his best to eliminate the numbers he could find working through databases on the Internet. Some of the databases were well known and some much harder to find. Mostly all he could tell was if a number was a commercial number or not.

He also separated the numbers that had been called more than once and then grouped them by country. It appeared that whoever used the phone lived in Germany and made a number of calls in the Stuttgart area.

He swigged another gulp of coffee as he sat at his kitchen counter with CNN running on the TV in the living room. He had always thrived on doing several things at once. It was his job to stay up on current events, and at least he felt like he wasn't shirking his duties at the CIA while he worked on his own project.

It seemed that the lone wolf terror attacks had calmed down the protests across most of Europe and the United States. Even the Germans were saying that the protesters killed in front of the army base where his friend Bill Shepherd was stationed was the result of a suicide bomber.

They had identified the man as a disaffected French youth who lived in one of the "no go" areas that housed so many Muslims.

As always, Rosenberg perked up at any reports on the Russian economy. Every couple of years, people wanted to dismiss Russia as any sort of threat to the United States, and every couple of years, they were proven incorrect. With its economy in shambles and the price of oil still below profitability, Russia was becoming desperate to make itself relevant. More accurately, Vladimir Putin was becoming desperate to make Russia relevant, as well as to keep citizens supporting him.

The Russian military was still a potent threat, and one that no one with any brains underestimated. What Rosenberg was listening for was any information about the cyberattack that had hit Western Russia.

He paused for a moment as video of Russian tanks played on the screen, but there was no mention of any computer glitches.

At almost the same time, his eye caught a number on the sheet he was scanning. Something about the number seemed familiar and held his attention. Then he had an uneasy feeling as he reached for his own phone.

It only took a moment to confirm that whoever owned this phone in Germany and contacted so many people around the world, including Middle Easterners, also had called his friend Bill Shepherd.

29

Walsh waited a full minute before he stood from the edge of the bathtub and stumbled out of the bathroom, back into the living room of the apartment where he was being held. The Russian with the scar on his face, Serge Blattkoff, and Alena all sat casually on the couch together. It was clear to him that Alena had been the linchpin of this conspiracy from the beginning. He had these wild ideas that dozens of people were involved when, in fact, it looked like it was only his girlfriend.

The older Russian motioned him toward the La-Z-Boy on the other side of the room, where he gladly plopped, then worked the handle to elevate his feet. His legs felt weak, and the acid in his stomach wanted to burn a hole through his skin. The only bright side he saw was that he would probably be killed shortly and none of this would matter.

The man with the scar said, "My name is Joe. And like you, I am a soldier. I haven't enjoyed any of this."

Walsh said, "That makes two of us."

Joe said, "I can see how surprised you are. That's the whole idea. You're a smart guy, you were in the marines. You have to know this sort of game goes on all the time."

"What game?" The exhaustion now was in his voice.

"Spying and connected operations."

He focused on Alena and said, "From the beginning?"

At least she looked guilty. And she couldn't speak. It was Joe who said, "You brought this on yourself. You showed a weakness for women when you were in the marines in Germany. A man who has a thing for blond girls is an easy target."

"My girlfriend in Germany was a spy, too?"

Now Joe chuckled. "I'm afraid you're giving yourself a little too much importance. No, she was just some drug-addled beauty. But we decided if she could cause that much trouble for you we could arrange for one of our exchange students to bump into you." He ran his hand through Alena's hair, then patted her on her shoulder.

It made Walsh shudder, and Alena pulled away from the older man's touch.

Joe said, "The day we made the transfer of money to Switzerland, we had two protesters stop you outside your office to grab your security plug."

Walsh remembered the encounter and how he reacted aggressively. He had inadvertently thwarted their first plan.

"When that didn't work, we had to use dear Alena to slip the plug out of your pocket before you went to dinner. While you were away a couple of hours, many of the world's most despicable terrorists were having their coffers replenished with money from accounts held at Thomas Brothers Financial. The accounts were carefully chosen. They were long-term accounts not often utilized or audited. I'm sure your country's FBI has figured that out by now."

Walsh said, "So you picked Thomas Brothers because of me?"

"Not entirely, but you were a pleasant and easily accessible surprise. In fact, you were the perfect dupe. We just had no idea we'd be able to use you so effectively. Now it's simply a matter of tying up some loose ends."

"So that's all I am? A loose end."

"No, Mr. Walsh, you're much more than a loose end. You see, everyone else is a contract employee, doing this for money. I'm the only one with other motives. I have to live with the results of our activities long after we are done. You are more than a loose end; you have also been a major pain in the ass. That's why I'm not going to waste any more time with you. Tell me where the security plug is or my friend Serge is going to snip off your fingers and then your penis. All in a matter of a few minutes." He paused as Serge held up a heavy pair of shears that looked like some kind of surgical tool.

Joe added, "Is that really what you want?"

All Walsh could do was think, *No, I don't want that at all.*

Mike Rosenberg was in a panic. But like any good marine, he got over it quickly and took action. The first thing he did was grab his personal cell phone and immediately press the contact for Bill Shepherd. He had no idea why his friend's phone number was on a potential terrorist's list of calls, but the two of them could figure it out. He just needed to reach him.

The call went immediately to voicemail and Rosenberg knew that meant the phone was turned off. He looked up and saw that it was nearly seven o'clock his time, which meant it was one o'clock in the morning in Germany. He didn't know if Shepherd was trying to catch up on his sleep after some exhausting days or if he was in danger. In fact, Rosenberg had no idea what any of it meant.

He tried to call Derek Walsh again. The phone rang, but he got no answer.

He swallowed the panic and started to figure out a plan.

Walsh tried not to cringe when Serge stood up with the pair of heavy shears in his hand. He closed the extended footrest on the La-Z-Boy and shifted his weight so he could at least jump up. Joe shook his head as he raised the pistol and aimed it at Walsh's groin.

Joe said, "No one will bother with a single pistol shot in this neighborhood. Russians tend to mind their own business. All that will happen is you will be on the ground in pain with a bullet lodged in your testicles and Serge will be cutting off your fingers. You can avoid all that by simply telling me where your security plug is."

Walsh's mind raced, and he decided that if he told them it would at least buy him a few more minutes to figure out what to do. But before he could say anything they heard running footsteps in the hall and a young voice shouting something in Russian. Walsh could tell by the way the two men looked at each other it was some sort of an alert.

Joe put his finger to his lips, telling Walsh to stay silent. Alena sprang up and ran to the doorway. Serge set the terrifying shears on a table next to the sofa and pulled his own pistol. Walsh recognized it as an Eastern European model he had occasionally seen NATO forces carrying. He thought it was a CZ of some kind.

Walsh stood up. He was taller than either of these men by a couple of inches. He tried to give Alena the stink eye, but she was listening to orders in Russian. He saw the older man, Joe, rummage through a drawer and then pull out something that looked like a paperweight. He handed it to Alena.

Walsh was so shocked he said, "Is that a grenade?"

Joe said, "A last resort, I can assure you. Now you go in the back room with Serge."

The lean young man reached across and grabbed Walsh by the right arm and pulled him along, then shoved him through the door first. They passed the bathroom, then entered a rear bedroom. Once he was past the doorway and near the windows, Walsh turned back to face the angry young Russian who a few moments ago was prepared to amputate parts of his body. As soon as Walsh turned around he noticed his Beretta and cell phone sitting on the pillow of the bed.

As if reading Walsh's mind, Serge said, "Don't think about it. I shoot you if you step any closer. Just keep quiet for few minutes."

He reinforced his statement by raising his pistol and aiming it at Walsh's head. Walsh raised both of his hands to signify he meant to keep calm. He was extremely curious what the warning from the hallway was. He glanced out the window and saw no unusual activity. He didn't hear anything coming from the hallway.

He looked at Serge and said, "What's the problem?"

Serge said, "Strangers in the building. Maybe police looking for you. No one knows about us."

Walsh thought, *I do.*

Someone had run through the hallways and warned everyone that there were strangers on the block. Most people assumed that meant some form of police. Joseph Katazin had to assume the worst and started making plans in his head for how to escape. He thought about walking out right this second but couldn't leave Derek Walsh. When it came down to it he'd sacrifice Serge in a moment, and even Alena if he had to, but he needed to make sure Walsh hadn't talked to other people, and he needed to know where the security plug was. If he could get the plug, it would keep his contact a secret and delay the FBI investigation into everything that went on at Thomas Brothers. That was a contact Katazin would like to keep safe and operative for the future. Also, it would keep the FBI from tracking the theft back to him.

He stepped across the room and looked out the window. No matter how subtle law enforcement agents tried to be, they could never mix perfectly in a neighborhood like this. Everyone here spoke Russian. Everyone. They took care of themselves and each other. There might be violent family feuds going on between them, but if the police intervened everyone turned against them. It was very similar to the mentality that Russia had taken advantage of in the Muslims. Aside from a positive relationship with Iran and Syria, Russia wasn't particularly well liked in the Middle East. But now they were using the anger built up for generations to bring the Western world to a virtual standstill.

He couldn't abandon his operation so casually. There was enough drug dealing and meth making going on in the apartment building and several of the surrounding duplexes that the police could be going anywhere.

Then Katazin heard a foot shuffle in the hallway. His military training allowed him to keep calm and focus on the sound. He looked over at Alena and motioned for her to pull the pin on the grenade, then hold it firmly. She cocked her head. He made a motion again, and she nodded. Then she pulled the pin on the grenade and gripped it tightly in her left hand.

Katazin pointed to a spot in the middle of the room and told her to wait. He backed away toward the kitchen, noticing the window over the back counter. He stepped into the kitchen itself, keeping the gun hidden from view. There was a knock on the front door. A woman's voice said, "Mr. Blattkoff, are you home?"

As he was considering what his next move might be, Katazin heard a simple ringtone from the back bedroom. He wondered if it could be heard in the hallway as well. He turned his pistol toward the front door and decided this might be a good time to squeeze off a few rounds, then slip out the window in the kitchen. In all likelihood whoever was behind the door would blame Serge.

He looked over at Alena standing terrified in the middle of the room, holding a U.S. military surplus Mk II fragmentation grenade. She was the only one who knew details about his activities.

That left him with some uncomfortable options.

Walsh watched as Serge pulled the wooden door to the bedroom closed. It didn't fit the frame perfectly and left a gap where Walsh could see into the other room. He'd tried to get a picture of the apartment in his head. He had no idea what he was about to do, but he had to do something. He lowered his hands as he eased slightly closer to Serge. The young Russian was distracted by something going on in the other room and was looking out the crack in the door.

If the cops were about to enter, he couldn't let Alena toss a live grenade at them. He just needed an opening. Then he heard a knock. At almost the same moment, Walsh's phone on the bed began to ring.

It distracted Serge just enough for Walsh to plunge his whole body at him, hitting him so hard that his Eastern European pistol flew straight into the air and he crashed through the door onto the floor with Walsh on top of him.

Walsh scrambled back into the bedroom and snatched his pistol off the pillow as Serge regained his senses, found his gun on the floor near him, and swung it toward Walsh. Instinctively Walsh raised his own gun and fired twice.

That was when things got hazy.

Katazin was still looking at Alena when he heard the two gunshots from the rear of the apartment. His initial thought was that Serge had just shot Derek Walsh. Before he could process it, the back door burst into splinters and three men wearing black fatigues rushed into the apartment shouting, "FBI, nobody move."

Katazin knew he had to act quickly.

Walsh held the gun steady as he watched Serge look at him in shock when both bullets struck him in the sternum. He thought about bursting into the living room and then considered the grenade that Alena was holding and the fact that the older Russian with a scar would've been alerted that Walsh had his pistol.

His decision was made for him when there was a tremendous crash from the far end of the apartment and he heard someone shout, "FBI, nobody move."

Walsh wasted no time twisting and racing through the bedroom, then ducking behind the bed, out of sight. He didn't want to risk hurting an

FBI agent or vice versa. He could just catch a glimpse of men in black fatigues racing in a straight line toward the living room. He kept low and crept up the edge of the bed to snatch his phone off the pillow and tuck it in his front pocket.

He listened to the commotion in the front room.

This was the worst position Katazin could have found himself in. The FBI agents in black fatigues raised their small MP-5 machine guns and froze at the sight of Alena standing in the middle of the room with her hands raised. Katazin didn't know if they realized she was holding a grenade in her left hand.

He swallowed once, took aim, then put a single 9 mm bullet into the back of the girl's head. She crumpled to the ground as if she'd fainted, and he could hear the grenade clearly strike the wooden floor. The FBI agents standing at the door didn't react instantly.

Katazin ducked behind the kitchen counter and slid next to the dishwasher as he heard the deafening blast of the grenade, then felt the flash of heat throughout the apartment.

He didn't even take a look at the carnage he had just caused. Katazin sprang to his feet, turned, and burst through the tiny utility door. The blast and ensuing chaos had created a brief opportunity to slip outside into the crowd of locals milling about, trying to see what was happening.

Katazin hurried down the street to his BMW without anyone questioning him. He now felt like he owed Derek Walsh on a personal level for all the trouble and stress he had caused. The former marine had done his best to screw up Katazin's plans, and he was sick of it.

30

Derek Walsh had experienced grenade blasts in training and once in real-life combat. The concussion of the explosion tended to travel along the path of least resistance. Doorways were a particularly bad place to stand. But having a solid wall and a bed between him and the blast made it nothing more than a very, very loud noise. The floor shook, and he could see the flash and felt the rush of heat, but he was not injured or even particularly dazed.

But he did recognize that the blast might have killed FBI agents and, more likely, the woman he thought was his girlfriend. Now smoke started to drift through the apartment, and he could smell something burning. He looked over his shoulder at the window he planned to jump through in just a second. It was his hope there was a fire escape, but he was prepared to make a leap to the ground rather than stay and face whoever was left after the grenade blast.

Walsh stood from behind the bed, careful to keep the gun pointed at the ground. As soon as he stood, he saw that one of the FBI agents had been blown through the outer room and into the bedroom and lay moaning on the ground. His ballistic helmet was twisted at an odd angle, and his body sprawled on the hard wooden floor.

Walsh turned and looked at the window but knew he couldn't leave yet. He stuck the gun in his waistband and bounded to the wounded man. He focused on the man because he knew he didn't want to see what had happened to Alena in the other room. His combat first aid training came right back to him, and he removed the man's helmet and saw that he was about the same age as Walsh, with hair longer than the typical military recruit's. On the left side of his neck a piece of shrapnel or perhaps the frame of the door had left a four-inch gaping wound; blood was pooling on the ground beneath his head.

Walsh looked around for an instant, then grabbed the pillow off the bed and slipped off the cover. He folded it three times and then put direct pressure on the man's neck. It was then that he looked up and noticed two others lying on the ground in the other room. They both seemed semi-conscious and were moaning, but they were both moving slightly as well. That was a good sign.

Walsh called out to them, "Hang on, fellas. Help is coming." In fact, he had no idea who was coming. The Russian with the scar could step around the corner and start shooting at any moment. He blocked it all out of his mind while he concentrated on this man's injuries.

The FBI agent tried to speak, but Walsh told him to keep quiet and still. He could feel the man's heartbeat. It was starting to fade, and that caused Walsh to panic a little. Then he heard voices in the main room. First, it was a man's deep voice that said, "Holy shit." Then a woman's voice called out, "Doug?" Then the woman said to someone, "Check the kitchen. Our guys are in the other room."

Walsh could hear a commotion and footsteps as he continued to put pressure on the young FBI agent's wound. Then a head popped around the corner from the main room. Walsh glanced up and immediately recognized Tonya Stratford.

She said, "What the—"

Walsh barked an order. "Get over here. I need help, quick." The FBI agent rushed toward him as someone else came through the door to help the other two injured men. Walsh edged to the side and said, "I need you to hold this tight to his throat. Is someone calling for fire rescue?"

As she moved to get into position to hold the blood-soaked pillowcase to the wound, Agent Stratford said, "We called. Paramedics should be here in a few minutes."

Now Walsh changed position and loosened the man's ballistic vest carrier to check for other wounds. He lifted the man's shirt and found one gash in his abdomen that wasn't serious. The stress of the event was starting to catch up to him, and the adrenaline was dumping from his system. He said, "How'd you find me?"

Agent Stratford concentrated on stopping the bleeding but said, "I had surveillance on the apartment after you gave me Blattkoff's name. When you didn't show at Times Square, I got a call you were seen being escorted in here, and we made a quick plan."

Just then another head popped around the corner, surveying the injured man. Then he noticed Walsh and said, "Jesus Christ, I can't believe the shit you cause, smart guy."

Walsh looked up to see agent Stratford's partner, Frank Martin, raise his service pistol and aim it at him. The guy apparently still held a grudge for Walsh giving him the slip on Wall Street.

Fannie was exhausted by the time she made it to her apartment in Stuttgart. It was the middle of the night, and the streets were absolutely silent. But she had been on the phone constantly since she'd landed, and there were already three men waiting for her when she arrived. These were trusted men who'd helped her with several major projects and never looked down on her for being a woman.

Almost as soon as she walked in the door and got settled at her kitchen table with the others, one of the men said, "Where's Amir?"

"Helping the Russians."

"When will he be back?"

"Later. You know how the Iranians are. They want to make sure they back every possible player in a conflict so they always look like they're winning. We see it in Syria. We even see it with the Islamic State. They don't want to be left out completely. So Amir will help the Russians until it's time to not help the Russians anymore." That seemed to satisfy everyone. She looked across at a middle-aged, heavyset bald man. "Were you able to put together what I asked for?"

The man bobbed his head and said, "I have a very powerful C-4 package that will fit under virtually any vehicle with magnets. The combination of the explosive and the fuel in the car will cause the blast radius to spread thirty meters in every direction." The man was so excited he looked like he was talking about his children doing well in school. "The blast will break windows up to five hundred meters away. The Americans on the base will think a nuclear weapon went off."

"And you won't have a problem being in position to see when he enters the gate with the vehicle?"

"I have already scouted it. It won't be a problem with a cell phone detonator already attached to the device. Just give me a little notice so I'm not hanging out too long in front of the base."

Fannie had to smile thinking about the carnage the blast would cause and the confusion it would sow among the American ranks. She hoped she was able to pull it off before they had word that the Russians were crossing the border into Estonia. It could delay action for several hours at the base.

Thinking about all of this made her worried about Anton Severov. He'd be facing the Americans in a few hours, a day at most. This was the confrontation that the world had been waiting to see for the past sixty years.

Walsh froze at the sight of the pistol pointed at him and instinctively raised his hands. When he stood, he stepped away from the FBI agent with the gun and past Tonya Stratford, who was still tending to the wounded man.

Agent Stratford said, "Hold on, Frank, he was helping our wounded."

"He's a fugitive. I've never lost a prisoner, and this asshole is not going to be the first."

Walsh was going to answer but saw the rage in the man's face.

The burly FBI man said, "I'm done having him make fools of us."

Walsh didn't wait to see where this was going. He continued to back away with his hands up, then threw himself into the window and felt the glass and wooden frame break away behind him. He tumbled out of the window wondering how far he would fall, then realized he had landed on a fire escape. The landing jarred his head and clanged in his ears. He didn't even wait for his head to clear as he rolled and found the elevated ladder, which dropped immediately to the ground with him at the end. The jolting stop knocked him onto a small patch of grass, but he wasted no time springing to his feet and racing toward the sidewalk. He heard a shot from the window but didn't turn around. As he sprinted down the sidewalk, he saw two Chevy Impalas parked at odd angles in the street. He knew who the cars belonged to. He slipped out his pistol and put a bullet in the front passenger tire of each car.

He made a hard right turn and found himself once again running for his life.

31

Derek Walsh cut across two streets and saw a brightly lit gas station and a woman standing next to a VW sedan at the pump. The driver's door was open, so Walsh bolted directly into the car, turned the key in the ignition, and sped away without a second thought. He was just under the street light when he heard shouting in Russian and then the rear window of the sedan shattered. He looked over his shoulder to see that the middle-aged woman in a long overcoat had a revolver in her hand and was firing at him. *What was up with these Russians?* He never planned to come to Brooklyn again.

He continued north and skipped the Brooklyn Bridge, instead turning onto the island of Manhattan by way of the Williamsburg Bridge. He turned north a few blocks and then left the car, with the key still in the ignition, near Houston Street. It was too late to go by Thomas Brothers. At least with the revelations about Alena, he now believed Ted Marshall was on the level and could be useful. There was no telling what the FBI thought of him right now. It seemed like Tonya Stratford was on the verge of believing him, but her partner was on the verge of shooting him.

He needed to figure out where to go. Then he had an idea.

Walsh had spent more than an hour sitting on a bench in a park off Houston Street. Only a few people had cut across the park in the time he'd been sitting alone, and that suited him just fine. He was still in shock but starting to accept the fact that he'd been used. He'd been used in the worst possible way. He'd been used against his own government. He felt violated. None of these feelings bothered him, because they kept his mind off Alena. Walsh couldn't accept that she didn't have feelings for him. It might have been an assignment, but it morphed into something else. Luckily she would never be able to refute that. He'd already heard on the news that two people had died in a police raid in Brooklyn. He hoped that meant all three of the wounded FBI agents would survive.

Something else that had struck him in the past few hours was the fact that he had been sitting on the sidelines while something like this was cooking. In the marines he felt like he had a purpose. In the financial world he just felt like a tool. He needed a purpose. All marines needed a purpose.

He no longer just wanted to clear his name. It wasn't about him anymore. It was about stopping this plot and its ultimate goal. He was ready to turn himself in, but maybe he could help the FBI. He felt that Tonya Stratford might be realizing that about now. He had purposely kept his phone turned off in case they had some way to track him he wasn't aware of. He also wasn't ready to take any calls.

Finally, when he'd had enough time in the park to clear his head, he started walking toward Bleecker Street. It didn't take long until he saw several men huddled in front of a doorway. It was the shelter Charlie had taken him to for his one night of decent rest.

Before he even reached the door one of the men turned, and he could see it was his friend. The former Army Ranger waved and said, "I've been worried about you."

"You and me both, brother."

Anton Severov had barely shut his eyes when he heard shouts and a commotion not far from his cot. He bounced up immediately and saw that flames were rising into the night sky a couple of hundred yards from his position. He slipped on his boots and tunic and, fastening buttons as he went, jogged toward the commotion.

As he approached, several officers were running the same direction he was, while many of the enlisted men were moving away from the flames. He could see three trucks were clearly on fire, and there was a group of about thirty men in front of the trucks chanting something.

Severov recognized a sergeant watching the spectacle and said, "What the hell is going on?"

"It's the Chechen recruits, sir. Something has them all stirred up. They just keep chanting, 'God is great.'"

"Has anyone tried to disperse them?"

"No one is sure how much force we can use."

Severov snatched the AK-47 from the man, stepped forward, and fired a burst into the air. That caught everyone's attention and spurred several other officers to action. Someone struck one of the Chechens with the butt of a gun and knocked him to the ground. Others started shouting for all of the men to sit down and put their hands on their heads. That opened the way for others to move forward and use fire extinguishers on the burning trucks.

It was some kind of demonstration, or possibly a revolt. Severov realized that if it had gone on longer it might've sucked in more of the Chechen recruits and could have ignited into something more serious.

It took a little time for Severov to find Amir. He was looking for his former guide to see if he had anything to do with the revolt. If he established that Amir instigated it, Severov wouldn't have any issues with shooting the Iranian punk.

He found Amir sitting with the group of young Chechen recruits, with one of the men translating from English to the others. Amir was holding an impromptu class on Islam and the future. Severov held back and listened to see if the man said anything that would incriminate him.

Amir said, "This is a wonderful opportunity to embarrass the Great

Satan. Americans are greedy and don't follow the tenets of Islam. Most of them have no faith at all and have been left wandering by their leaders. You have a chance to find glory for our cause."

Severov listened as a translator repeated everything in Chechen, with a slight Chantish accent. He recognized him as a sergeant who worked in the motor pool. Many of the Chechens were reduced to more menial jobs. That might change after tonight.

Amir looked over to Severov and smiled. He knew there was nothing the Russian major would do in front of an audience of Chechen truck drivers. He couldn't hide his satisfaction at seeing flames behind the major's profile.

Severov knew he'd have to deal with this terrorist sooner rather than later.

Mike Rosenberg prided himself on keeping his cool. As a G-2 in the marines he frequently went out on missions with the platoons who were receiving his intelligence. He even managed to get permission for Derek Walsh to come on a couple of the missions, although most of them were relatively quiet.

His toughest combat assignment was in Afghanistan when the small unit on patrol that he was attached to came under attack and was forced into a defensive position between two mountains. They never knew the exact number of enemy combatants facing them, but from the rate of fire Rosenberg had estimated that somewhere between 120 and 150 fighters had converged on the spot after the first few hours of the fight.

Their radio operator had been killed in the initial assault, and it took an enterprising Apache pilot to start searching for them off the usual trails. In the hours that they were pinned down by enemy fire, Rosenberg kept his cool and returned fire when he had a clear target and generally tried to keep his head on straight. The Apache pilot managed to scatter some of the closest fighters and call in an air strike, which to this day was etched in Rosenberg's memory like a still photograph.

The four F-15s roared across the valley and dropped a mixture of ordnance that was so explosive it sucked the air out of his lungs for a moment. The few trees and exposed boulders were vaporized instantly.

He stepped out from behind cover and looked out over a barren valley, knowing no one had survived the air strike. But he was never scared.

At this moment, he had to admit he was in a panic. He had just found one of his best friend's phone number on the toll records of a suspected terrorist. He had gone through dozens of potential explanations, and none of them panned out in his brain. His next thought was that if *he* found these records, someone else would be onto them very soon as well. He doubted the FBI would waste much time in tracking down Bill Shepherd, and Rosenberg's fear was that they wouldn't give him a chance to explain. Exactly like what had happened with Derek Walsh. It was this mistrust of the premier federal law enforcement agency that had Rosenberg incapacitated with fear. He had nowhere to turn.

He checked the toll records again and saw that Shepherd had called the number and the number had called Shepherd at least nine times in the past month. This wasn't just a wrong number.

He looked up at the clock. Now it was nearly nine o'clock, which made it about three in Germany. He didn't know if he could wait much longer.

32

Derek Walsh sat at a long table and finished off his third turkey sandwich while Charlie parked himself across the table like a guard dog, keeping the other residents from getting too close while he ate. The shelter was just five large rooms that used to be a grocery store. The first room was a welcome center that allowed visitors a respite from the cold or heat of New York and offered water and snacks all day. The second room was for overnight visitors and had six picnic tables that would hold a total of thirty-six residents. The third and fourth rooms were male dorms with a single cot for each resident, and the last room was for female residents and held up to eight women. Showers and bathrooms were attached to each dorm. The place was clean and ran smoothly.

A TV in the corner of the room played a local New York newscast, which was covering the explosion that had killed two people in Brooklyn. Right now all anyone knew was that the FBI had entered an apartment and the result was two dead people and the evacuation of the building while they searched for hidden explosives. Of course everyone assumed it was some sort of terrorism investigation. The most persistent speculation was that it was tied to the terror bombing of the Whitehall subway station that killed nine people. The city was in an uproar.

Walsh looked up at the screen and recognized the street he had run down to escape. Every person the TV station interviewed on the street had a Russian accent, and every one of them had some comment about Muslims moving into the neighborhood being why things like this happened.

It was true that blood was thicker than water, and every ethnic group tended to protect its own and blame someone else. The Russians used this to great effect, making their organized crime apparatuses extraordinarily difficult for the police to infiltrate. Walsh had read a number of articles about how the Russians had not integrated into society as much as other groups, and one of the theories about why was that it was difficult to tell a Russian from an American just walking down the street. They didn't face the pressure of other ethnic groups to conform.

Walsh's personal experience told him it might have something to do with their ruthlessness as well.

Charlie said, "I won't ask you any questions about what happened, but by the way you keep watching the TV, I'm guessing that explosion had something to do with you."

"I should have it all cleared up by tomorrow."

"That's what you said two days ago."

"That seems like a lifetime."

Charlie chuckled and said, "I hope you at least learned something from all this. That's the only reason God puts us through all these tests."

Walsh thought about the older man's comment as he glanced around the room at the other homeless people. He had learned quite a bit. He would never complain about a job or apartment again. He no longer regretted that he had not seen much combat in the marines. Half the men in the room were veterans. It wasn't like half the U.S. population was veterans, especially here in New York, where they had one of the lowest rates of military recruitment in the country. These were issues he had never considered before. Combat had greatly affected these men and the way they dealt with other people. It was as if an entire generation of heroes had failed to assimilate back into society. Walsh had no idea how to fix the problem. But he would no longer ignore it.

Charlie said, "You look like shit."

"In this case, looks are *not* deceiving."

"You think a good night's sleep will help? Me and some of the boys can stand watch if it would make you feel better."

For the first time since any of this had happened, Walsh felt safe. He could trust his brothers in the military to look after him. Tomorrow he'd call Mike Rosenberg and explain everything that had happened. Maybe by then Rosenberg would have made some progress on his end.

Anton Severov paced back and forth as tanks fell into position. A young lieutenant, who wore his hair slightly too long and had an urban accent from Moscow, jogged up to Severov and saluted.

Severov didn't have the energy to ask any questions; he just looked at the younger man.

The younger man said, "Our jump-off time has been delayed, Major. The colonel would like you to meet him in his command tent in forty-five minutes."

Severov looked up at the sky as the rising sun illuminated the light clouds. Their plan was to be across the border before dawn. Now he wondered if they'd get across before lunch. In fact, he still wondered if it was a good idea to even try this.

Finally Severov nodded his head in dismissal of the young man. He walked down the line of three T-90s with their engines idling and their crews making last-minute adjustments. He was truly torn. He had spent the last decade wanting to engage NATO in a major tank battle. He envied the Israelis who got a chance to kick some ass every couple of years when someone in the Middle East had a memory lapse and forgot what it was like to go up against a professional army. On the other hand, Severov's recent trip through Estonia reminded him of the collateral damage that would occur once the shooting started. The idea of smashing ancient villages to gain a tactical advantage on NATO troops didn't appeal to him.

He also thought of Fannie Legat. If they didn't cross the border, he'd have a very difficult time seeing her again. At least as long as he held Amir on this side of the border, there was one less thing that threatened her.

A sergeant sitting on top of one tank called out to him. "We're all ready to go, Major. Any idea what time they'll take us off the leash?"

Severov stepped closer and shouted over the sound of the idling tank. "I wouldn't get my hopes up for an early departure, Anatoly. My bet is this wolfhound stays on the leash for a while longer." He looked up and down the line of tanks and the trucks assigned to him, then back at the burly sergeant. "Grab six good men with rifles and keep patrolling this line of tanks on both sides until we're ready to go. Can you do that?"

The sergeant hopped down onto the ground and faced the taller officer. "Are you still worried about the Chechens, Major?"

"I worry about everything. That's my job."

It was almost midnight in Brooklyn as Joseph Katazin sat on the closed seat of the toilet in his upstairs bathroom, assessing his injuries. Surprisingly, considering there had been gunfire and a grenade blast, the only thing that really bothered him was his ankle. Then he twisted quickly and realized his ribs still hurt as well. This was not how he pictured his later years as a deep-cover spy in the United States. What happened to his idea of sipping fine whisky with a cultured contact who told him about the inner workings of the Pentagon? But this was real life and these were real injuries. And they hurt.

He wrapped an Ace bandage tightly around his ankle and swallowed four aspirin. As he sat and looked over the vanity to see the cuts on his forehead and across his nose in the mirror, his wife pulled the door opened slowly. The action made him jump.

She had a heavy bathrobe pulled tight around her ample body. "What are you doing at this hour?"

"I took a tumble at the office and hurt my ankle." He was shocked to see a look of concern on his wife's face as she opened the door all the way and stepped in to inspect his first aid. As she leaned over and looked at the bandage he said, "It's nothing, really."

She switched her attention to his head and touched one of the fresh abrasions. "Did you fall off the loading dock?"

"Yes, I wasn't paying attention and stepped off backwards. My ribs are a little sore, too."

His wife reached into the medicine cabinet, pulled out a bottle of peroxide and poured some onto a cotton ball, and started to dab the cuts.

A few seconds later his daughter appeared in the doorway like an apparition. Fear spread across her face as she said, "What happened? Daddy, are you all right?"

He held out his arms, and she ran over to him. He looked into her sleepy eyes and said, "Just a little accident. I'm fine." He brushed the hair out of her face and felt her forehead to make sure her fever had not returned.

The girl said, "Did you hear about the explosion?"

"On the way to Brighton Beach? Yes, I heard."

His wife said, "The news said it might be terrorists living in an apartment, but those Russians would never let Muslims move into one of their buildings."

"Not everyone is as closed-minded about new neighbors as you think. It sounds like a reasonable explanation to me."

His wife moved the bloody towel that he had been using earlier, and instantly he remembered why he had set it on the counter. She stepped back and said, "Why do you have a gun in here?"

Could this night get any more frustrating?

Severov was surprised to see two command vehicles parked outside the colonel's tent. He took a moment to straighten his uniform before he stepped up to the guard at the front and identified himself. The guard was not from any of his units and snapped to attention as if he were at a tourist spot in Moscow showing off for the European visitors.

Severov stepped past the man and immediately came to attention when he saw the commanding general standing next to his portly colonel.

The colonel turned, smiled, and said, "At ease, Anton." Once Severov relaxed his stance, the colonel said, "The general was just commenting on what an excellent job you did scouting the route."

"Thank you, sir." He still stared straight ahead instead of engaging the superior officers.

Now the general stepped toward him. He was about the same age as the colonel but clearly did not have the same tendencies toward overindulging in food and drink. He was an athletic man with broad shoulders in his midfifties. His short hair was graying at the temples, and he had the look of a combat veteran. His uniform was neat and boots well polished.

The general said, "We're still going into Estonia, Major. We're just doing it a little later than we thought. Right now we expect our jump-off point to be about 1100 hours local time."

Severov made no comment, although apparently his expression changed slightly, because the general said, "You may speak freely, Major. You don't like our idea?"

Severov turned toward the battle-hardened general and said, "Sir, with respect, why would we wait? The longer we stage, the greater the chance of someone noticing us."

"We're not concerned by that, Comrade Major. The best NATO can do is try to turn some of our Chechen recruits against us."

Severov decided not to mention his contribution to the angry Muslim recruits in the ranks. He did say, "The little revolt has made the men jumpy and suspicious."

Now the general stepped close to him and said, "Have you ever met Vladimir Putin?"

"No, sir."

"I worked with him several different times. He is a great leader for our country and arrived on the scene at exactly the right moment. He is not a man I'm about to tell that the Russian military cannot handle unruly Muslims, then roll into a virtually defenseless country and take it over before NATO can mount a counterattack."

"So we go?"

"It's taking longer to stage, but it will happen. You can count on being in Estonia by noon and at the far border by sometime tomorrow. If the route is as easy as you said in your report, we will have no problem rolling our tanks at high speed. I doubt the little notice they have of us gathering on this side of the border gave anyone time to plant land mines or IEDs."

The general stepped over and put his hand on Severov's shoulder. "This military operation is part of a much more ambitious plan, Major. All the news you've been reading from the West about financial crisis and terror attacks is accurate. These were planned and directed by Russian operatives working closely with jihadists. The idea was to distract the U.S. and Europe while we make another land grab. We need a forward operating base in Europe, and Estonia fits in nicely with our plans. It also has an excellent infrastructure for telecommunications. All of this will help us as we regain our status in the world."

Severov had already figured all this out. He blurted, "Is the extra land and infrastructure worth a war?"

The general chuckled. "Who would fight for Estonia? Latvia? No, I think NATO will put up some token resistance and then roll over. It will be just like the West's complaints about Crimea. Americans pay little attention to Eastern Europe. We'll roll south with little problem." The general took a seat on a field stool near a desk.

Severov remained silent and waited to hear his orders in this grand scheme. Finally the colonel said, "Anton, on top of commanding your tank platoons, we want you to take charge of this potential Muslim uprising within the ranks. We need them focused on the welfare of Mother Russia, not Allah."

Severov said, "Why take them at all?"

"We'll need them for construction and manual labor. They are vital for now."

Severov nodded.

The colonel said, "Perhaps it would be a good exercise if you pulled one or two of them from the ranks and made them examples. Perhaps just a quick firing squad or maybe a summary execution in place so that everyone can see their bodies as we leave. Do you think you could handle that?"

Severov was about to object when he thought of the perfect person to use as an example. Instead he said, "I am a soldier. I will follow orders."

The colonel chuckled, slapped him on the back, and said, "Good man, good man."

Katazin froze in place sitting on the closed toilet seat as his wife stared at the pistol that had been hidden under the towel on the bathroom counter. His daughter appeared to be stunned as well. His eyes went from the pistol to his wife, then to his daughter.

Katazin cleared his throat and said, "It's simply for protection."

His wife said, "For an import/export business that doesn't deal in cash transactions?"

"Who are you? Michael Bloomberg? I can carry a gun."

"But why would you?" She looked at her daughter and said, "You. Get back to bed right now."

Katazin's daughter knew a storm was brewing and not to talk back to her mother when she used a tone like that. She turned and scurried out of the bathroom and down the hallway to her own room.

Now his wife's attention was back on him. "You had something to do with that explosion down in Midwood. Didn't you?"

"Really, sweetheart, I don't see how you come up with ideas like that. It's really no big deal."

His wife started backing out of the bathroom. She didn't say anything, which was unlike her and was the worst thing she could do. She could make one phone call to the authorities and he could be in real trouble.

She even threatened the security of the operation that was just now about to pay dividends. He couldn't let that happen.

Katazin thought how easy it would be to walk her down to the car, pump a couple of bullets into her, and dump her body into the East River. But it was just a fantasy. He had considered it before.

When she turned and hustled into the bedroom, and appeared to be looking for her phone, the thought went from fantasy to serious consideration. He scooped up the Beretta and stuck it in his waistband, pulling his white undershirt over the grip of the pistol. He stood up slowly, testing the tightly wrapped ankle. It felt better than he'd thought it would, but now his ribs hurt from the way he'd slouched while working on the ankle.

When he stepped into the bedroom, his wife was slipping her phone into the pocket of the thick bathrobe. She slowly walked out of the bedroom saying, "I'm going to check on Irina."

Katazin watched her step through the door and realized he had made tougher decisions already tonight.

When Derek Walsh awoke on the cot in the homeless shelter, he lay still for a moment while his eyes adjusted to the light. He saw the outline of two men, one on each end of his cot. A streetlight shone in through the one window in the room, casting an eerie shadow of the men onto the floor.

Walsh quietly reached under the cot to feel the handle of the Beretta he had wedged between some slats. He didn't need it. He knew the two men were there to protect him. Charlie and the other five veterans were taking turns on watch to make sure no one surprised Walsh while he was sleeping. He had no doubt of the men's integrity or honor. At least while they were sober. He understood the military fraternity and how seriously these men were taking their duty.

When this was over, Walsh recognized he had a duty he had been avoiding. He would find ways to help men like this all over the city. But first he was going to uncover the conspiracy, and for that he would need to contact Agent Tonya Stratford. As long as her partner didn't kill him first, he felt he had a real shot at convincing her to help.

33

Major Bill Shepherd lay on the bed in his quarters on base, watching the sun spill into the room. He had purposely left the curtains open so that his body might get back on some sort of schedule regulated by sunrise and darkness. It was the first night he had gotten more than a few hours' sleep in four days. His rested body, along with the anticipation of seeing Fannie at a restaurant not far from the base, put him in an excellent mood. Unless some emergency came up, he was free until at least two o'clock in the afternoon. Anything could happen in that length of time.

He was a little bit of a player, even though he prided himself on being honest with all the women he dated. Shepherd was also cautious. He didn't want to be taken for a sap like Derek Walsh, who had fallen for a local girl who had somehow gotten hold of his official credit card and bought TVs and stereos for everyone she knew. Poor Derek was horrified and humiliated. Shepherd felt for his friend but wanted to learn from his example. He was vigilant with the women he met. He never kept anything other than his ID, one credit card, and some cash with him when they went out on the weekends. The clubs in Stuttgart liked the young

American soldiers, who never hesitated to spend all of their pay on alcohol for the local women and beer for themselves.

He had to admit he was intrigued by Fannie's good looks and demeanor. She was more mature than most of the women he dated even if she was the same age. So far, he had not made a move, but maybe the time would be right after brunch today.

He took his time getting out of bed and cleaning up. He wore new fatigues that were crisp and had sharp lines. Per a suggestion by the CO, he would carry an issued M-9 Beretta pistol. He intended to tuck it in his waistband with his fatigue shirt hanging over it. He didn't like drawing attention to the fact that he was armed unless he was on a specific detail and wore a pistol in a holster on a web belt.

He walked by his office just to check in and let his aide know he was going off base. As he stepped in he looked at the startlingly young sergeant and said, "Anything cooking, Chip?"

"Not really, Major. All the reports of protests have died down across Germany. They're leaving a twenty-four-hour police presence in front of the base for three more days. And no one is in sick bay with any illnesses or injuries."

"Outstanding."

The young redheaded man picked up one piece of paper and said, "NATO is monitoring some activity in Western Russia near Estonia. They believe it has to do with Russian military exercises. Satellites haven't been able to bring up any new information, so they intend to do a fly-by in the next hour or so to get a closer look. Doesn't sound like something we should worry about."

"Chip, today is too beautiful to worry about anything. I need you to call up a car for me. And I'll be off the base until after lunch."

"Do you want a driver with the car, sir?"

"Not today. I think I can manage a Humvee on my own for a few hours." His mood seemed to be contagious; the young sergeant gave him a big grin and said, "Consider it done, Major Shepherd."

Fannie Legat had everything in position. She intended to sit at a table inside the small café. That would give cover to the men who were going to plant the bomb under the major's vehicle. They made it sound like it would only take a moment and was not a problem, but Fannie's experience told her that it was best to plan for delays and problems rather than hope they didn't occur.

She carried a Walther PPK .380 pistol in her purse. That was her fall-back position. If she was forced to shoot the major in the restaurant, that would be the end of her cover here in Germany. Her next stop would be somewhere in the Middle East where she would blend into the background. At least she was confident she would have a position of power within her own group. She had proven her worth time and again. Even if the bomb plot was a complete success, it was time for her to move on. No one had her real name or could identify her easily. She would slip out of Germany.

She had watched the early morning news to see if there was anything happening on the Estonian border. So far all was quiet, and she wondered when the invasion might come. Fannie was worried about Anton Severov. Like all soldiers, he tended to downplay the danger, but she knew that if NATO took action there would be a real fight and Estonia would be turned into a battleground.

Right now she had to focus on what she could do to help in the struggle. Maybe taking out a small cog in the American war machine would pay big dividends later.

Joseph Katazin pretended that he was asleep as he felt his wife rustle in the bed next to him. He knew she had to be upset and possibly scared of her own husband. It was probably a good idea, because now he was looking at her as a liability rather than a mere nuisance attached to his long-term assignment here in the United States. He tried to plan out the scenarios. If he said nothing, he risked her going to the police and identifying him. If he waited, she might keep quiet, but if he stepped out of line in the future or she caught him with another mistress, he couldn't be sure she would keep her mouth shut. And if he shot her and then dumped her in the river, he had to face his daughter and tell her what had happened. Or tell her a convincing lie. It wasn't his wife or her life that concerned him. It was how it would affect his daughter.

He had already called for someone to replace Serge. They were sending a young man he had worked with before who called himself Jerry. The steroid freak was tall and imposing, and his real name was Yuri or something similar from the old country. He was not nearly as clever or diligent as Serge, but he would probably work out for the day. Once everything was finished, Katazin would have no more use for the young man. He would pay his employers and hopefully never have to deal with him again.

All he really needed him to do was help him handle Derek Walsh's body. And maybe his wife's, too.

In the busy camp by the Estonian border, Major Anton Severov had not yet acted on his idea of using Amir as an example. The idea of shooting an unarmed man did not appeal to him, no matter how obnoxious that man was. Severov was surprised when he saw the general walk toward him half an hour after their meeting. He was still close to the command tent, going over some basic instructions with his captains and lieutenants as trucks and command vehicles puttered by, all finding their place in the line. The skies were clear, and it would be only a matter of time before the activity was noticed by a NATO satellite. The younger men all snapped to attention at the sight of the athletic-looking general. He returned a professional salute and said quietly to the major, "Do you have a few minutes?"

Severov didn't hesitate to dismiss the men; they had plenty of work to do anyway. He wondered what the general needed from a lowly major. The older man said, "Walk with me while I inspect the troops." Severov fell in beside the general and matched his quick stride.

Severov had not realized how much rank meant until he walked with a general through a busy army preparing for war. As if by magic, vehicles stopped and people stepped out of their way. It was almost as if there were no obstructions at all.

The general finally said, "Do you think it's a good idea to execute a few recruits as an example?"

Severov hesitated.

"Speak freely, Major. I don't have time for indecision."

"No sir, I don't. I think it will hurt overall morale. Especially among the Muslims."

"Then disregard the order. You have enough to do."

Severov couldn't believe how relieved he was.

As they walked along, the general said, "Give me your honest assessment, Major. How much trouble will we have crossing the border?"

Severov hesitated, knowing the Red Army's practice of never giving an honest assessment to someone who doesn't want to hear it. But he felt this general was truly interested. Finally he said, "We'll have no problem crossing the border or even advancing through some of Estonia. The problems will come when we meet resistance. That's when we'll see how serious NATO is. I also don't like my men looking over their shoulders at other soldiers and wondering if they will be caught in some kind of revolt."

The general nodded as they walked, then said, "You make good, practical points, Major. I respect that. But I also think I have a better idea of what Comrade Putin expects from our friends in NATO. They have lost their teeth. The true strength of NATO lies in the United States. The United States currently has a president who will not risk significant political capital or military power on a country as inconsequential as Estonia. He won't even admit that terrorism is a threat to his way of life."

Severov appreciated the lesson in politics even if he already understood all of that.

The general continued. "Even when he was vice mayor of St. Petersburg, Putin was considering the bigger picture. He learned what it was like to not only govern but to administer government programs. Make no mistake, Russia is in a bind right now. We have no real products other than oil, and this Saudi effort to cripple the American fracking industry has had the side effect of crushing us. Soon we will see shortages of food and other basic goods, and people won't be as enthusiastic about the government or its leaders."

"So this is a military action born of desperation?"

"All good military actions are based on desperation."

It was well before dawn, and the street was deserted as Derek Walsh slipped out of the homeless shelter, still wearing the same white shirt and blue pants he had taken from his apartment. They were noticeably wrinkled, and the shirt had several different bloodstains from God knows what over the past couple of days. He tried to be quiet when he left. Charlie was on guard duty and insisted on coming with him as a bodyguard. Walsh didn't mind the company.

He had a plan, but even in his head it sounded crazy. The first part of it required finding a vehicle. He headed down to Houston Street and was shocked to see the Volkswagen sedan he had taken from Brooklyn the night before. Even with the rear window knocked out, no one had bothered it during the night. He realized it might be on police watch lists, but it couldn't be that important if no one had noticed it parked right on the side of the street in lower Manhattan. Besides, he had no money for a cab to take him where he wanted to go.

Charlie started asking questions, but Walsh turned around and said, "You can come with me, but you have to keep quiet for a while. I need to think."

That seemed to satisfy the older veteran, who willingly climbed in the car and got ready to go. He didn't even ask where the car came from, how Walsh knew it was there, or why the rear window was knocked out. He just sat in the front seat and waited as Walsh cranked the car and pulled away from the curb slowly. He didn't want to draw any attention to them.

It wasn't until he was northbound on the FDR that Charlie started to show more interest. When he finally made his turn Charlie said, "Why are we going through the Queens–Midtown Tunnel? Where are we headed?"

"Flushing."

"To watch some tennis?"

"To talk to an FBI agent."

"That doesn't sound like a good idea."

"It's the only one I have left."

34

Even by Mike Rosenberg's standards of getting up early, this was ridiculous. It was still the middle of the night, and the house he was living in felt unnaturally quiet. At least in apartments and barracks you often heard the neighbors. Here in suburban Maryland it was like a graveyard. He was trying to call Bill Shepherd to find out why his number was on the toll records of a suspected terrorist. During the night he wondered if his friend even had an idea who he was calling. Maybe it was a front business. Maybe it was just a mistake. God, let it be an honest mistake.

The number continued to go directly to voicemail, and he finally left a message, hoping Shepherd would call him back as soon as he turned on the phone. The frustration was eating him alive. This was not only personal; there was the very real element of duty involved in it as well. This was ultimately CIA business, and even if he was going to have trouble explaining it to his bosses, he couldn't let it slip through the cracks. His main hope was to call his friend first, at least to find out what exactly was going on.

Rosenberg hoped he'd get hold of Shepherd before he walked back through the doors of the CIA. Ethically he didn't think he could sit at his desk and ignore information like this. That was the culture of the agency and one of the reasons he joined the CIA instead of one of the other federal agencies. Despite what the public might have thought or understood from media reports about the use of torture or other negative facts, considering what they had to battle on a daily basis, the workers were incredibly dedicated and ethical. It started from the top and worked its way all the way through the agency.

He tried Derek Walsh's number one more time but got no answer there, either. He was almost starting to think his phone was the problem. He decided to keep dialing Shepherd's number until the major picked it up.

Fannie Legat arrived early at the café just to make sure everyone understood their role and their position. She was starting to get concerned that there had been no news of Russian military movement into Estonia. That didn't change her resolve now. No matter what, this would cause a serious crimp in military activity around the base near Stuttgart. She nodded to her associates, sitting in a nondescript Swedish sedan at the far end of the street so they could see anyone who came or went.

Fannie had picked her table with the utmost care for strategic value. She could see the front of the restaurant and even the street, but the major would be stuck looking only at her. That was why she wore a ridiculously low-cut top to show off her assets and let her hair hang down around her shoulders. It was not particularly modest, but it was effective, and she justified it by the ultimate goal.

There were two more men who would take up a position closer to the base and should be able to see when the major drove back through the main gate. Just as with her bomb at the bank in Bern, a simple cell phone call would detonate plastic explosive and cause a tremendous blast when added to the vehicle's fuel. She had already determined that a blast at the front gate to the base would be devastating. Ideally she would time it so it was coordinated with the first Russian movements, but that didn't look like it would work out.

She was done with her work in Germany anyway and would now be able to convince her superiors she should fight like other members of the jihad. The one thing that tugged at her guilt was the major himself. Although he was an American and represented much of what she found distasteful in the world, he had been courteous and decent to her at every turn. She suspected that was his nature more than just an act. Occasionally she thought about the people who died in furtherance of their cause. Sometimes, when she was alone, she would even consider the ramifications of a single death, such as how parents might be affected back in the United States. Usually those thoughts didn't coincide with the death of a person in the military. She understood that was because it was easy to look at a soldier as a number or an impediment, as opposed to a real, living breathing person.

The time she had spent with Major Shepherd, in an effort to gain any possible intelligence, had taught her that he wasn't quite the devil most Americans were made out to be. And she had to admit that his death would be unfortunate and cause her some guilt.

But that was what happened in war.

Major Bill Shepherd was behind the wheel of the Humvee. It wasn't stripped down for field use, but it was by no means a luxury vehicle, either. It was tough and had its uses, but he wondered why on earth anyone would buy a Humvee for a family car back in the United States.

He checked his watch and saw that it was about quarter to eleven. He needed to get a move on. On his way out the main gate he stopped and looked to make sure everyone was in position and doing their job. Even though the army personnel maintained routine security and operated the main gate, he liked to see everyone doing their job. As he slowed to speak to the sergeant at the gate he looked down the street and noticed two groups of bored German police leaning against cars about fifty yards apart well outside the gate. He hoped they stayed bored.

The main entrance and exit to the base was as secure as anything in the area. Metal barricades, which could pop up on a moment's notice, could keep suicide bombers and heavy vehicles from reaching the security checkpoint. The armed soldiers at the gate could have their M-4 rifles up and spraying a vehicle in a matter of seconds. The security sweeps by soldiers and vehicles covered the entire perimeter of the base and reinforced the main gate on a regular basis. Shepherd didn't see any weakness in the defense.

He looked from the driver's window down to the young sergeant and said, "Anything unusual today?"

"No, sir. Everything appears to be quiet. You and your marines were a big help the other night."

"That's what we're here for. If there are no beaches to storm, we can sure as shit put down a riot." He glanced into the twenty-foot-wide, air-conditioned security hut and said, "We seem to have a full house today."

"We're training another shift, so there'll be sixteen of us on until 1500. Then they'll go back to eight."

Shepherd approved of the young sergeant's tone and attitude. This would be valuable training. He looked down and said, "I'm off for a nice meal and will see you before 1500."

"Have a beer for me, Major."

Shepherd laughed and said, "I'm on duty, and it's too early for beer. I'll have a Bloody Mary for you."

This was going to be a spectacular day.

Derek Walsh sat quietly as he watched the front door of Tonya Stratford's tiny brownstone in Brooklyn. The sun had not yet come up, and the street was still asleep. There was not a single light on in any of the houses in the neighborhood. This was the kind of place he would've liked to live and used to think he'd be able to on his salary from Thomas

Brothers. He had done some research during his limited computer time yesterday and discovered that federal agents made decent money. If she was a GS-13, getting an extra 25 percent as callout pay and a subsidy for living in an expensive city like New York, Agent Stratford was making over $130,000 a year. Not exactly the view most people had of police work.

Walsh was thankful Charlie had dozed off almost as soon as he had parked the VW. He was surprised how the missing rear window caused almost no distraction once he was used to the extra noise of the wind. After he was done here, he'd abandon the car. One way or the other, he wouldn't need it again. He just hoped that there were no industrious cops in the area who would check every parked car. He was purposely in a dark spot between two streetlights and ducked low in the seat.

The problem was that now he had time to consider everything that had happened and process the fact that not only was his girlfriend dead, she wasn't really ever his girlfriend. He just couldn't wrap his head around the fact that she could fake her feelings for him for so long and in so many situations. On the other hand, as he considered their relationship, he really hadn't spent as much time with her as he thought. There'd been several long stretches when she said she returned to Greece, and they rarely had more than one date a week when she was in town. But that didn't change the fact that his feelings for her were real, and that was why he was in total shock as he realized he would never hold her in his arms again.

He had seen the effects of grenades in Afghanistan. He was glad that he hadn't stepped into the living room to see what this one had done to her. He was also glad he he'd been able to help the wounded FBI agent. The guy was in bad shape, and Walsh didn't think he would've made it if someone hadn't given him attention immediately. Not that anyone at the FBI would appreciate it. Walsh felt good about it anyway.

He was trying to keep his spirits up as he considered what his life would be like without Alena in it. Even if he was able to make all the charges against him disappear today, what did he have to look forward to? Lonely evenings in his tiny apartment by himself? Working eighty hours a week at a job that didn't help anyone?

He could use this experience. He needed to find something with meaning. As these thoughts boiled in his head, something caught his eye. A light in the upstairs bathroom of Tonya Stratford's house popped on.

He wasn't the only one who couldn't sleep.

Bill Shepherd was running a few minutes late, but he didn't like to push a Humvee too hard on the highway. German drivers tended to be safe, if a little fast in their driving habits. The road was not crowded as he decided to hit the gas harder. It was just now eleven o'clock, and all he could think about was Fannie's smiling face when he walked through the doors of the café.

He pulled off the highway and realized the café was only a mile up the road where several main highways came together. It was the start of the urban sprawl of Stuttgart. The area catered to many of the young servicemen and focused more on nightclubs than on pleasant cafés.

Shepherd's phone rang in the cargo pocket of his fatigues. He had to shift at an odd angle to reach it because of the pistol he had in his waistband. It was not a regulation way to carry the M-9, but it was more surreptitious, and the Germans weren't crazy about seeing guns in public.

He stole a quick glance at the phone and saw it was his friend Mike Rosenberg. He didn't hesitate to answer. "Mike, what time is it over there?"

"Five."

"Mike, this is a bad connection. Is everything okay?" He listened but caught only a few words. Something about phones. He hoped the interference might clear up, but after a few seconds he ended the phone call. He was getting close to the café and would try to reach Mike after brunch.

He pulled onto a side street and saw several parking spots open directly in front of the café. Everything was working out perfectly for him today.

———

Anton Severov, sitting in the commander's seat of his tank, in line with his unit, ready to cross the border, glanced at his watch for the fifth time in the last hour. The Narva River was up ahead, just out of sight. Beyond that was Estonia. Who would have guessed anyone would consider conquering the small republic an actual military feat. They still were not rolling, and it was practically midday. The sun was bright but not brutal. The cooler autumn temperature relieved the worry of heatstroke. He wondered if they would feed the troops lunch before they moved. He had waited for word and even called the colonel himself. He could tell by the portly man's curt manner that he was under a lot of stress. They all were. They were potentially starting World War III. But he was told to stand by and be ready to move. That was it. And that was what he had to tell the captains and lieutenants and sergeants who all showed their anxiety by asking him repeatedly when he thought they were going to move.

A few minutes after noon he heard several rifle shots ahead of him. Then the sign to go came over the radio. It was happening. He couldn't deny the fact that he was excited. Soldiers were when they were about to do something like this. He still had serious concerns about the operation itself, but the idea that he could face an American or German tank on an open field was exhilarating. All of the tanks started to crank up their engines at once and rolled as if they were one giant caterpillar. It was only half a mile to the Narva River, and after a couple of minutes he saw that the route was completely open and the scout vehicles were rolling across the bridge without opposition. By the time his tank got to the bridge he was standing tall in the cupola, taking in the full view of the river, bridge, and town before him. To his left, several Russian soldiers held a group of Estonian border guards at gunpoint. Severov noticed one border guard was lying on the ground in a pool of his own blood and a second sat on the ground leaning against a post and holding a bullet wound in his shoulder. The others apparently had enough sense to surrender immediately.

Severov sincerely hoped the rest of Estonia had that much common sense. He doubted NATO did.

Mike Rosenberg sat alone in his rental house and frantically hit redial, trying to reach Bill Shepherd. He didn't know how much his friend had heard from the first call, and now all he got was a carrier signal saying the call did not go through. He looked at his clock and couldn't believe it had only been one minute since he had gotten through to his friend. He dialed the phone again and again. On the fourth try he wanted to slam his phone onto the floor. Instead, he screamed out in anger and knew he sounded like a wild animal that had been wounded. He wondered if all of Western Maryland could hear his frustration.

He took a moment, sucked in a deep breath, and dialed the phone again. He needed to get through to his friend before he went to work.

35

Yuri Simplov rushed into Putin's office in the palace at Novo-Ogaryovo. The former KGB man was as excited as Putin had ever seen him. He wore a sport coat over casual clothes, and his hair was not in its normal perfect position. He looked like a child about to open a gift.

For his part, Putin stayed in his seat behind his great desk and remained placid, waiting for his old friend to say what was energizing him. When Simplov realized Putin wasn't going to ask, he simply said, "It has begun. I mean the military aspect of the operation. We have crossed the Narva River and are moving swiftly through Narva. The supplies for the long-term occupation of the country are starting to move on a combination of passenger and freight lines. One of the largest convoy trains will be moving south with our troops shortly."

Putin still kept silent as he stared over his desk at Simplov. Finally he said in a very quiet tone, "Any issues?"

Now Simplov stepped over to a chair and slid into it.

"Yes?" Putin said, beginning to grow impatient.

Finally Simplov said, "One French reporter was poking around about the intrusion into the financial markets in New York and London. She spoke to a tech person who said the algorithm was quite sophisticated, and he speculated it had originated in Russia. She was trying to uncover more information, so I ordered her eliminated."

"Where?"

"Paris."

"Can you have it done quietly?"

"It's already done. A simple car crash. She was forced into a tree at high speed. Our people verify that she and her teenaged daughter were dead at the scene. I can show you a photo if you'd like."

Putin held up his hand to stop Simplov from shoving his phone in Putin's face. "That won't be necessary. I've seen your work before. I trust it was handled correctly." That made Putin consider everything he had heard up to this point. He said, "What about the American trader in New York? Have we caught up with him yet?"

"Our man in New York is looking for him. He has been told to go to ground once the military action is in full swing. If he hasn't found the trader by then, we'll have to take the risk that the trader won't speed up the FBI investigation. We believe that our agent in New York must escape before the FBI has any leads on him."

"Good thinking. Now the ball is in NATO's court."

"This is what you wanted, no?"

Putin nodded his head slowly as he considered how history would judge this entire operation. He said, "I did. I still do. I don't think I'm wrong. NATO won't move militarily. I believe that at worst, we're looking at sanctions from the UN and perhaps something more from the U.S. But we will survive either."

Simplov said, "The Estonian border guards surrendered after a couple of shots were fired. I'm told the Estonian citizens are just watching the convoys like it's a giant parade. There have been no real media reports on it as of yet, but I know that will come in the next hour."

Putin waved his hand and said, "Downplay everything. From calling it a minor incursion to confirming the very small military force we have used. You know what I want."

Yuri stood up, sensing that their conversation was over and knowing he had much to do. He turned and headed for the door.

As he was about to leave, Putin called out, "Yuri." He waited for his friend to turn and look at him. "Good work."

Major Bill Shepherd pulled down the side street and saw the café facing out with a wide courtyard in front of it. He'd eaten at the place a couple of times in the past, but not often enough to worry about an old girlfriend wandering in or one of the waitresses recognizing him. This was the outskirts of Stuttgart. More accurately, it was the edge of the urban sprawl, and the upscale area attracted all types of people. He knew his younger marines liked to hit a couple of the clubs in the area on Friday and Saturday nights. They felt safe, and he had heard good things about how they were treated by the locals. Like all military men, he worried the attitude could change. There seemed to be a growing sentiment that the U.S. military should pull back from many of its bases. No one would be happier about closing bases in Germany than the Russians. They tended to learn from history, whereas the U.S. allowed history to fade from memory.

Shepherd had sat in a number of meetings where the comparison between Hitler and Putin almost slapped him in the face. Historians would point out the differences and say Putin was much more like Stalin, but to Bill Shepherd he was acting like Hitler as far as his interest in expanding influence and grabbing land. Shepherd was disappointed there were still no real efforts to contain the Russian leader. He'd scooped up Crimea with hardly a comment from the West, and his puppets were moving Ukraine closer to total chaos. Shepherd had seen other studies that showed the Baltic States were at great risk as well. But for now he was satisfied that his marines were doing their job at the base in Germany and he had earned this morning off to spend with the lovely Fannie Legat.

There was almost no traffic as he easily maneuvered the big Humvee down the street. He was a little surprised Mike Rosenberg hadn't called him back. He checked his phone and saw there were no calls and decided to catch up to his friend after brunch with Fannie.

There were two spaces open directly in front of the café, so he pulled the Humvee to the curb. He took a moment to look through all the windows in every direction. It was a very quiet day. Two men were on the sidewalk up the street, but other than that, the only face he noticed was Fannie's. She gave him a beautiful smile when he looked through the main window of the café.

He opened the door and stood in the street, taking a moment to straighten his uniform and cover the bulge of his M9 tucked inside his belt. It was nonregulation way to carry a sidearm, but he liked keeping everything out of sight off the base. Most Europeans were crazy about gun control and freaked out seeing even military personnel carrying any firearm. He looked down at his phone for a moment, considering, then placed it on the seat. He didn't want anything to distract him from Fannie.

Mike Rosenberg had not felt this kind of anxiety since he was in combat with the marines. The fact that he was just pacing in his own house made that seem even more ridiculous. He desperately wanted to reach his friend. He was about to give up and make a call from a landline inside the CIA headquarters in Langley. He was going to have to tell them what he'd found anyway, but he had hoped to give his friend a heads-up first.

He took one more shot at it. This time he didn't hit redial but entered the number digit by digit and was surprised to hear a ring over the line. Had he really gotten through again? His heart was pounding in his chest, and he desperately hoped his friend would have a reasonable explanation for why his number was on a suspected terrorist's phone records.

After three rings he started to get nervous that Shepherd wasn't going to pick up. The fourth ring made him think he was about to get voice-mail.

The fifth ring put him into a depression.

Derek Walsh noticed several lights on downstairs in Tonya Stratford's brownstone. It was about a quarter after five, and he didn't think she left for work this early; however, after everything that had happened, maybe she had a plan like he did. He was impressed with her work ethic and hoped she had enough compassion to hear him out, but as he stood there Walsh suddenly tried to think of a coherent way to express what had happened.

He didn't want to come across like a nut, but he knew the entire con-spiracy theory did sound a little far-fetched. His hope was that she'd found something in her investigation about the Russians. It would be easy to just surrender now, but he could be of use. His country might actually need him. That trumped all of the two years he'd worked at Thomas Brothers. In that time he had made little money and not contributed to society in the least. Standing in front of a stranger's front door was more important than all of the trades he had ever made. That was a sad commentary that he didn't want to dwell on.

He thought he heard some movement inside and suddenly wished he had time to call Mike Rosenberg. Maybe he had tied something together as well. No matter what happened, he didn't want to throw his friend under the bus for communicating with him while half the world wanted to hang him.

He glanced over his shoulder to make sure Charlie was still comfort-able as he slept in the car. He couldn't really see anything in the dark, then noticed headlights coming from the opposite end of the street. There was no way not to look suspicious standing out on the sidewalk without anyone else on the street. The car moved slowly, and suddenly Walsh wondered if it was a police vehicle. He took the only chance he saw and climbed the three steps to the landing in front of Tonya Stratford's front door and made it look like he was locking it.

There was a lot that could go wrong with this plan.

Joseph Katazin came awake with a start. He didn't know why his heart was pounding, but he was wide awake and it was not yet sunrise. He sensed that it was close to dawn, but it wasn't until he twisted in the bed and saw his digital clock that he knew it was after five. He settled back into the bed and felt the different twinges of pain from all the injuries he had suffered. The one he'd have to deal with the most was his ankle, because he intended to do a little walking today. He would walk until he found Derek Walsh and put a bullet in his head.

There was not much more he could do on the operation other than tie up the loose ends and delay the inevitable FBI investigation into what happened. He didn't think anyone would ever be able to tie the protesters to his plot, and his luck with the suicide bomber in the subway would cover his killing of Lenny Tallett. Then his mind settled on another potential loose end: his wife. She still lay in the bed next to him, rigid as a board. He doubted she had slept the whole night, but she was probably too scared to try to leave. He was frustrated because she was not something he should have to worry about while the biggest operation of his career was under way. Realistically, she was a potential threat, and he had to make a decision about what he intended to do.

He eased out of bed and slowly put some weight on his ankle. It wasn't as bad as he'd thought it would be. He shuffled to his closet and pulled on some clothes. He knew his wife was faking being asleep now, because she was always up before him. It was a point of pride with her that she make him coffee.

Katazin gingerly came down the stairs and flopped onto his couch to turn on the TV. He recognized his superiors had purposely left him in the dark about many elements of the operation, even though it was entirely his idea. It made sense that he would not be aware of the exact military action that would be taken. He had to believe the Red Army would move soon; he didn't want to consider the possibility that he'd gone to all this trouble and moved all that money just to fund a few minor terrorist attacks that wouldn't add up to a thousand deaths across the world. He knew the small and uncoordinated attacks were minuscule, but their cumulative effect was obviously incredible. Many of the Western countries were frozen with fear over what could happen next. Katazin hated to admit it, but it was also a little embarrassing that Russia couldn't fund the attacks and distractions and had to resort to theft. They were lucky Katazin had turned that into another plus by motivating the protesters and diverting resources to their silliness.

He realized how excited he was as he searched for CNN. He felt like a child watching a parade. What would happen? As soon as he found the channel he realized there were no blazing banners of "breaking news" and no theme songs dedicated to the ongoing coverage they reserved for major events. It was the news as usual. Celebrities, sports, more celebrities. What was it with Americans and celebrities? Then there was the daily story of some weird crime that happened in Florida. A man beat another man to death with an alligator. Typical. But there was nothing, not one word, about world-shattering events in Eastern Europe.

That put him in a dark mood.

As he turned to climb back up the stairs, he thought once again about his wife as a potential threat.

Bill Shepherd parked in front of the café and had already shut the door to the Humvee when he heard his phone ring on the seat. He hesitated, torn between rushing to see Fannie and concerned that there might be a problem that Rosenberg needed to talk to him about.

After a moment he turned the handle, yanked open the door, and reached in, wondering if he could answer the phone before it went to voicemail. He swiped his finger across the screen and said, "Mike, can you read me?"

On the other side of the line in a clear voice he heard his friend Mike Rosenberg say, "Shep, I read you."

Shepherd looked up and saw that Fannie had stepped toward the door, so he held the phone tight to his ear as he locked the Humvee once more and slowly started strolling to the front of the café. He said into the phone, "Everything all right?"

"No, I need to ask you something straight up on our personal phones. No official communication."

"Sure, go ahead." He slowed his stride as he waited to hear what his friend had to say that warranted such a grim tone.

Rosenberg said, "I have the toll records for a phone that belongs to a suspected terrorist."

"I'm listening."

"And your personal phone number is on them. It looks like you called the number several times, including Tuesday night, a couple of times Wednesday, and once yesterday morning. I got the records after that. If I go back during the month, it looks like you started contacting the phone about a week ago." He gave Shepherd the number, digit by digit.

Now Shepherd froze in his tracks as he thought about the limited number of personal calls he made. The only person he had called with that frequency the past two weeks besides his family, Derek Walsh, and Rosenberg was Fannie. He didn't need to hear all the digits to the phone number to confirm his fear. Quickly he said, "Do you have any identification for the terrorist? Male or female?"

"I believe it's a female that opened a bank account in Bern. She has calls all over Europe as well as to other suspected terrorists."

Shepherd noticed Fannie stepping out of the doorway of the restaurant and took a quick glance around the courtyard. The two men who were down the street on the sidewalk were now closer. One carried a heavy satchel, which looked more like a duffel bag. Both men had dark hair and scraggly beards. This was no time to be politically correct, so he decided to jump to a conclusion based on their appearance. He could explain his mistake later if he had to.

Shepherd spoke quickly into the phone, saying, "Mike, in case anything happens to me, the number I was calling belongs to a white female who claims to be from France and is using the name Fannie Legat. I was just trying to get to know her and never told her anything of importance. I met her one morning over coffee, and I'm about to walk into a café where she is waiting for me."

"Walk away."

"That's a good idea."

Shepherd saw that the two men were now staring directly at him and Fannie had stepped into the courtyard and was reaching into her purse. He said into the phone, "Too late now. Remember what I told you."

36

Derek Walsh waited by Tonya Stratford's front door as the car slowly drove past. He didn't want to be obvious but felt like crowding against the wall away from the street. It didn't look like a police car, and no one showed any interest in him. Suddenly he realized he was directly in front of the door so he jumped off the landing. He took a moment to reposition himself and was careful not to be too close to the front door if it opened unexpectedly. It was never a good idea to startle someone carrying a gun. He had left Charlie snoring soundly in the front seat of the VW when he made his way toward the front door of Tonya Stratford's residence. He had no idea if she lived alone or had a boyfriend or maybe even her parents living with her. The Internet tended not to give that kind of information.

He was a little chilly in his simple white shirt with the sun just starting to throw light over the top of some buildings to the east. He was nervous, but this had to be done. He'd left his pistol under the front seat of the VW so there would be no mistake about what he was trying to do. He didn't want to get shot now because of information he needed to get to someone about what these crazy Russians were up to. He should've realized it was a more sophisticated plan than just someone trying to rip off Thomas Brothers. His only leverage was the security plug, and no one was going to use it but him. He wasn't going to tell anyone where he had hidden it and wouldn't let it out of his sight once he had it in his possession.

Just as Walsh was starting to wonder how long he'd wait, he heard some movement inside the brownstone by the front door and noticed the lights upstairs were now turned off. Almost a minute later the knob of the front door turned and the door swung outward onto the low landing.

Now he wasn't sure what he should say or when he should say it. Agent Stratford's back was turned to him as she secured the door, so he just cleared his throat and said, "Good morning, Agent Stratford." He tried to keep his voice level and calm.

It didn't work as well as he had hoped.

Standing in the courtyard in front of the café, Bill Shepherd slipped the phone into the cargo pocket of his fatigues and realized quickly this was no mistake; he was in the real shit now. He slowly started to walk backward toward the Humvee as Fannie sped up to catch him, still trying to make it look like she was waiting for a rendezvous. Her right hand was inside her purse.

He turned his head quickly and saw that the two men on the sidewalk were now almost in front of his vehicle and the man with a duffel bag was setting it on the ground. This was a tough position between two threats, and he didn't even have his weapon in his hand yet. He quickly calculated the rounds in his pistol. One in the chamber, and he'd counted fourteen in the magazine when he checked it, securing it in his waistband. But who was the bigger threat? Two unknown men near cover, or a woman who probably had her hand wrapped around a pistol at that moment?

He tried to be casual as he let his arms drop to his side and his left hand grasped the bottom of his fatigue blouse. He was going to move quickly once he lifted the blouse and reached for the pistol. He glanced around for his own cover. The only chance he had was to dive for some heavy potted plants, and even that didn't give him much protection.

One of the men on the street shouted something in German. He thought the man was yelling to him, then realized it was a question directed at Fannie.

Definitely not a good sign.

Fannie Legat realized something was wrong once the major started walking toward her on the concrete path that weaved between buildings from the street. He was on the phone and getting information that made him hesitate. Some instinct told her she couldn't wait. He wasn't going to meet her. He looked splendid in his military uniform. That would make this easier. He was even dressed as her enemy. And if he was getting information about her, she needed to stop him before he could use it. She hated the fact that she might waste an opportunity to really hurt the U.S. military.

She stepped out of the café waving to him, hoping he would overcome whatever concern he had, but instead she saw him slip the phone into the lower pants pocket of his uniform, then turn and see her associates as they approached his vehicle. Both of the men were German-born Muslims who had been part of their movement since their teens. One of the men carried the plastic explosive that was to be placed under the vehicle.

She could see the hesitation in the major's face as he looked back and forth between her and the man. Then he started to lift his shirt, and she realized he was carrying a gun.

Typical American.

As soon as Walsh cleared his throat and said, "Good morning," he was shocked at how quickly Agent Stratford moved. She jumped away from the locked door and fell into a crouch behind the low landing. Somehow she had pulled a pistol and had it pointed directly at Walsh's head.

Her first words were a harsh whisper. "How in God's name did you find me?"

"The Internet. You'd be shocked at what you can learn on a few simple sites."

She kept her position. "Just when I was starting to think you were slick, you do something this stupid. Are you crazy? After what happened last night the entire Bureau is focused on finding you."

"Is that why you're getting an early start?" He realized he had inadvertently raised his hands.

Tonya Stratford slowly rose to her feet with her gun still pointed at him. She scanned the area quickly, then focused entirely on him again. "Are you alone?"

"I have a harmless old man asleep in the car. He has nothing to do with any of this other than being concerned about my safety." He noticed her eyes track across the street, then down to where the VW was parked. He was impressed with her powers of observation.

"Turn around and place your hands against the building."

He didn't argue. Once his hands touched the building he felt her kick his feet back farther so he was completely off balance. She quickly used one hand to pat down his body on both sides. Then she said, "Stand up and turn around."

She took a couple of steps away from him and let the pistol drop to her side. "Lower your goddamn hands. You look like the victim of a street robbery."

"At least you realize I'm a victim. I didn't move that money. Those crazy Russians kidnapped me last night. If you can get me into Thomas Brothers for ten minutes I can prove to you I'm innocent, and at the same time we'll discover who transferred the money."

"There are still FBI agents over at that office working. I couldn't get you through the front door without someone raising the alarm, even if I did believe you. Why don't you give me the plug and I'll get it to a computer."

"This is no offense to you personally, but I've been through too much the past few days to let anyone else handle the security plug."

She nodded slowly and said, "I can see your point."

"C'mon, Agent Stratford, let's cut the shit. You *do* believe me. I could tell last night. I could tell when I called you. You know there's something fishy going on here, and I can point you in the right direction. If all else fails you'll still have me in custody at Thomas Brothers."

"I have you in custody now."

Before Walsh could answer, he heard a rough voice say, "No you don't. Drop the pistol."

He looked up and Charlie was standing there, pointing a pistol at the FBI agent. All he could do was cry out, "Charlie, no."

Shepherd never panicked as he pulled the semiautomatic pistol from the leather inside-the-pants holster. Instructors at Officer Candidates School at Quantico would have fainted if they saw him carry an official sidearm in such an unorthodox and unauthorized holster. Today it did the trick perfectly. He pulled the pistol and moved quickly to dive behind the cover of the heavy potted plants to the side.

The first bullet came from the street and flew wide of his position. Fannie hadn't started firing at him yet. Somehow, in the odd void of time in which firefights take place, he was able to think about how he wouldn't want to shoot a woman he had feelings for. Even if she had never reciprocated them.

Then a smaller-caliber bullet struck the cement near his head. That was Fannie. She had retreated to the edge of an outdoor stairway and had heavy concrete protecting her. He thought she was firing a .380. Not that the smaller caliber wouldn't kill him if she found her target, but for right now he was focusing on the man with a 9 mm who was standing in front of his Humvee and apparently didn't think anyone would shoot back. That was a guy who had never been in combat.

Shepherd risked popping out from behind the heavy planter, aimed his pistol, and fired three times. The man had already started to fall to the ground as Shepherd ducked back behind the planter. Now he turned his attention back to the stairs where Fannie was hidden. He couldn't see her and tried to figure out if she had changed positions. The last thing he wanted was her popping up out of nowhere with a pistol in her hand.

In the big scheme of combat, this was not particularly challenging to a marine who had fought in Afghanistan and Iraq. He had been part of the battle for Fallujah and seen what street-to-street fighting could be like. Having a couple of middle-class Europeans haphazardly shooting at him didn't concern him as much as what was in the satchel one of the men in the street was carrying. It could be anything. His imagination took hold and he decided he had to leave this secure position and stop the remaining man in the street from causing some serious casualties in a civilian neighborhood.

Shepherd peeked out from behind the planter and couldn't see Fannie anywhere. He turned his head, scanned around the Humvee, and saw the man near the back of the vehicle. Shepherd sucked in a lungful of air, then didn't hesitate once he decided to move. He sprang up from behind the planter and rushed the vehicle with his pistol up in front of him. He couldn't risk glancing behind to make sure Fannie wasn't about to shoot him in the back.

He was about halfway to the Humvee when he heard the first shot from behind him.

Fannie had been shocked at the quick and decisive action from the U.S. Marine major. It reminded her of all the propaganda she had ever seen or read about the U.S. Marines being the finest fighting force in the world. Maybe it was true. She also wondered how he became suspicious. It appeared that someone had called him with information, because he'd been walking to meet her and then slowed. His facial expressions gave away everything she needed to know. Now she wasn't sure what would happen. Her grand plan of destroying the front gate of the base was ruined. Her only hope for *the cause* was that the death of an officer near the base would sow seeds of concern among the troops. Perhaps they could use the bomb in some other way.

She had sought cover in the cement walls of an outdoor stairway. She fired one round to the area of the courtyard where the major had jumped. There were heavy planters filled with soil and growing a variety of plants and bushes. When she peeked around the corner ten seconds later, she saw the major pop out from behind one of the planters and fire three times toward the street. She didn't know if he hit anything, but he clearly was uninjured and still capable of defending himself.

For a brief moment, Fannie considered cutting her losses and fleeing. She was much too valuable to the organization to waste her skills, skills no one else possessed, by being killed or captured trying to kill a single U.S. military officer. Then she got hold of herself. She would never be able to face misogynists in her group who already thought women were weak. She could blow up a hundred banks and they would never give her credit for being cold and tough. If she ran now she would never hear the end of it. Besides, she had gone into this part of the operation without any authorization or acknowledgment from her superiors. They thought she and Amir were still acting as guides for Anton Severov. The Russian major was another reason she wanted to hurt the Americans. She would do any-thing to protect him. Fate was cruel and mischievous.

She peeked around the cement stairwell again just as the major moved from his position and ran toward the big, ugly military vehicle. She jumped out and started running behind him, still ten meters away. In front of the big vehicle she could see the body of one of her men crumpled on the ground. Why would the major risk himself like this?

Fannie fired once on the run and watched as a bullet flew wildly to the left. She thought it hit the vehicle, but she wasn't certain. The major didn't even look over his shoulder. He was focused on the other man, who was now emerging from the side of the truck with the satchel around his side and a small Italian machine gun up and ready to fire.

Her man was distracted when he saw Fannie running behind his target. It was clear he wasn't confident all of the bullets would go just where he aimed. She watched as the major dove for cover behind a low, decorative brick wall. Fannie kept running toward him, knowing she would have an opportunity to shoot at him unobstructed as he sought cover from the machine gun. Just as she was about to reach the angle from which she could fire at him behind the low wall, Fannie saw the major sit up and shoot four times at the man with the machine gun and the satchel on a strap around his shoulder.

Almost immediately she realized the bullets could detonate the home-made explosives in the satchel. Before she could stop and line up a shot on the major, who was behind the wall again, a flash in the street blinded her; then she heard the explosion at almost the same time the shock wave carried the intense heat across her face and body. Her blouse began to melt across her arms, and she felt her long hair sizzle. Then the blast itself knocked her off her feet.

Even in her dazed condition as she tried to scramble for whatever cover she could find, she realized the second blast was the fuel tank from the military vehicle going up. It was even more powerful than the first explosion.

The heat, sound, and force of the detonation sucked the air out of her lungs as she clung to the wooden bench she'd crawled behind. She wondered if this was what hell would feel like.

37

Walsh froze as he stared at Charlie holding the gun on the FBI agent. There were too many ways this could turn to tragedy. Despite his appearance, Charlie was a combat veteran who knew his way around guns and had already proven he could act under stress. He had overpowered Serge Blattkoff. Walsh didn't want to think what he could do now that he had a pistol in his hand.

For her part, Tonya Stratford remained calm, even though she had not dropped the pistol from her hand. He didn't want either one of these people hurt. He had seen enough bloodshed in the last twenty-four hours.

Walsh held up both hands, trying to avoid panic while telling Charlie this was not what he wanted to happen. "Just calm down, Charlie. She and I were talking. She's going to help me."

Charlie shifted his bloodshot eyes to the FBI agent and mumbled, "Is that true?"

She nodded her head slowly.

Charlie looked back to Walsh, who reinforced it by lowering his hands. He started to breathe a sigh of relief as Charlie lowered the gun, but he kept his eyes on Agent Stratford, who didn't know Charlie the way he did. Suddenly the idea of the older veteran being shot by a federal agent terrified him. Walsh took a quick step and stood in front of Charlie, then reached down and plucked the gun from his hand. He immediately turned and handed it to Agent Stratford, butt first.

Walsh looked Agent Stratford in the eyes and saw the decision-making process running through her head. He knew that if someone pointed a gun at a federal agent, that person generally went to jail on some charge. Then Agent Stratford took the gun and let out a frustrated sigh. Walsh relaxed because he knew even an experienced FBI agent would have a difficult time arresting a homeless man who'd served his country in combat.

Now the question was how she felt about *his* status as a former military man and if she believed his story.

Joseph Katazin quietly got dressed, careful not to give his wife an excuse to leave the bed. He had considered the information she'd figured out a thousand different ways and recognized that to follow operational security he would have to eliminate her. He kept thinking of the practical aspects of disposing of her body. Now that he was faced with the need to do it, he had to consider the consequences. It was no longer a game where he was liberated from a tyrant; now he was wondering if his loyalty to Russia could make him murder a woman he had lived with for fifteen years. The mother of his daughter. A woman who, while suspicious and nagging, had done nothing to deserve something like this.

He glanced over at the bed and realized she remained stiff because she was thinking the exact same thing. He didn't believe she had figured out his actual plans and position in the Russian government, but she knew he was involved in some dangerous shit. The stereotype of the Russian mobster wasn't completely wrong. Like the Italians when they first moved to the United States and had the cover of a foreign language as well as a tight-knit community, the Russians had found profit in illegal activity. The law enforcement officials of the United States had a difficult time infiltrating the Russian mob. It was easy to think anyone with an accent was involved in criminal activity. Why should Katazin's wife be any different?

Once he was dressed and had pulled on his most comfortable shoes around a swollen foot and sore ankle, Katazin retrieved his Beretta from the dresser drawer. He held it in his right hand as he stared down at the lump under the covers of his bed. He could hear a slight whimper and realized his wife knew exactly what was happening.

This was not how he thought he'd feel. This was not the cold calculated decision he believed he could make. But she could destroy everything he worked for and send the police on a trail that could derail years of work. He was even surprised when he felt a tear well up in his left eye and run down his cheek along the tiny crater of his scar.

Just outside the border town of Narva, Estonia, Anton Severov had the driver pull off to the side of the narrow thoroughfare so he could sit in the top of the cupola and watch the vehicles move smoothly along the road. It was hard to believe he was acting like a tourist here just a few days ago and was now part of a giant convoy of combat and supply vehicles.

He had just seen the start of a train with three locomotives pulling a line of cars that carried everything from ammunition to tanks. Earlier he had seen a train of tankers filled with fuel. Each stretched as far as he could see. Kilometers.

It was incredible. No one had seen movement like that since World War II. He was in one of five lines of tanks and troops moving south. Each force contained more than forty tanks and a hundred support vehicles and personnel carriers. Someone had confidence that they could stop any large-scale NATO air strikes.

The ground shook with the movement of the vehicles, and it filled him with awe. This was what he had dreamed about since his first days in the army. The minor skirmishes with the Muslim rebels were not a proper place for heavy armor and tanks. This was a mission that called for skilled tank commanders. He just wished he had more confidence in the overall plan.

The general had shown unusual trust by telling him what was going on and the purposes of the operation. Any idiot could figure out Russia was looking for more land and President Putin was ambitious, but the idea of gaining a foothold in Europe made sense if NATO didn't object too strenuously. He was just a soldier and followed orders. It was rare to get a glimpse inside the command staff's thinking. Somehow it made him feel more enthusiastic about the operation.

The residents of Narva were gathering on the sidewalks to watch the parade that passed by without a word. Overhead, four scout helicopters were fanning out ahead of the column. The plan for any operation like this was to get as many of the ground forces across the border as possible before putting too many aircraft above them. The theory was that radar would have a much more difficult time picking up low-flying helicopters than supersonic jets. The U.S. satellite reconnaissance would show the movement of troops, but the Russian high command was counting on the delay in the satellite and then the warning to NATO. The theory was that a quick crossing over the undefended Narva River would allow a strong foothold in Estonia should NATO and the U.S. react more aggressively than anyone anticipated.

Severov was satisfied that everything was secure and was feeling good about his job scouting Estonia. He had been so worried about the events of the night before that he hadn't thought about Fannie much as they prepared to depart. He would call her this evening when they were a hundred and fifty miles inside Estonia. He liked the idea of someone worrying about what could happen to him.

Just as he was thinking about the beautiful French Muslim, a truck carrying troops rumbled along the road slowly, and his eye caught the scowling face of one man at the very rear of the truck, sitting on the hard wooden bench.

It was Amir.

The scene outside the café was gruesome. Blood was splashed along the concrete, windows broken by gunfire. Scorch marks from the blast radiated out in all directions as the police held onlookers at a safe distance. The Germans were not used to scenes like this on their streets, at least not since the 1940s. The firefight had been quick and brutal, but Major Bill Shepherd was unharmed and relieved to see that there were no casualties among bystanders. The German police had responded with astounding speed and efficiency and immediately realized that the two men Shepherd had killed by his vehicle were on a watch list for terrorists. One of the men was difficult to identify because the large, homemade C-4 device in his satchel had not only destroyed the Humvee but had scattered the terrorist over a blast radius of about forty feet.

Now officials from the base as well as Shepherd's commanding officer were on the scene, and they were arguing about the need to question the major right now. Shepherd had overheard one of the police officers telling his commanding officer in English that it looked like the terrorist had detonated the device in the satchel himself, which made sense, but somehow was not as satisfying as Shepherd's idea of combat.

No one had found any sign of Fannie Legat. Shepherd told them where he had last seen her and the direction she was running when the bomb detonated. She was much closer to it than he was and had no cover. That led to the theory that she had been killed and some of the body parts spread across the road were hers.

At this point, Shepherd didn't care. There would be some questions about his connection to her, but the fact that he had never gotten intimate with her and she had tried to kill him should reassure everyone that he was not part of some complex conspiracy.

More and more personnel arrived to clean up the scene and find out what was going on. Then he saw all the U.S. military officers on their phones at the same time. That was never a good sign.

His CO turned and walked directly to him, pushing past a German police investigator who wanted to talk to Shepherd.

The marine colonel said, "Are you doing all right, Major?"

Shepherd nodded his head and stood up to show that he wasn't even shaky after the event.

The colonel said, "Good, because the balloon just went up. Russians have crossed the Estonian border in force, and we need all hands on deck. We'll square it with the locals. But you need to come back with me and get your units ready to move. I want you out in the field directing your platoons of marines as we try to stop those sons of bitches before they can annex the whole country."

Shepherd couldn't help but wonder if this attack and the Russian incursion were somehow connected.

In his bedroom, Joseph Katazin kept his hand on the butt of the Beretta 9 mm sitting in his waistband. He knew his wife was wide awake even though the room was still quite dark. He said in a low, calm voice, "It's time to get up, dear. I need you to give me a ride to the office." Once he had her out of the house he could figure out what had to be done.

The figure on the bed stirred slowly, then pushed the blanket off. She sat on the edge of the bed and looked over her shoulder. It was something Katazin had never seen. She was scared.

He waited patiently while she got dressed. After a few minutes she paused at the bathroom door and said, "I have to wake up Irina."

"Why?"

"We can't just leave her alone at home. She's only a little girl."

"It won't take that long. You can be back here before she wakes up."

The look his wife gave him told Katazin everything he needed to know. She knew she was not coming back to the house. Like any good mother, all she was worried about was her child. She was willing to leave the house without resistance just to make sure her daughter was safe. That struck a chord with Katazin. He still saw no other alternative.

Just as he reached for the knob of the bedroom door, there was a light tap on it from the hallway. He moved his right hand from the pistol and opened the door. His daughter stood in the hallway, the long T-shirt that she always slept in hanging to her knees.

She stepped right past him and walked to her mother, saying, "Mama, my throat hurts again. Will you make me feel better?"

Katazin's wife stammered as she searched for the right phrase. She clutched the girl in her arms as if she were saying good-bye.

It was at that moment that Joseph Katazin realized he would have to take the risk and let his wife live. There was no telling what was going to happen after today anyway; at least this way there would be someone to take care of his daughter. Even though he knew he would never be able to see either of them again.

He eased down on his right knee and held out his arms, motioning for his daughter to come give him a hug. She squeezed him tight, and he realized how much he was giving up for patriotism. He whispered in her ear, "Mama will take care of you. I have to go to work early today." He held on to her for a few seconds more, and as he released the hug he said, "Remember that Papa loves you."

38

Less than two hours after Bill Shepherd had been forced into a firefight with a woman he thought was a flirt and her terrorist partners, he was preparing to board a Black Hawk helicopter to be transported to Estonia along with six platoons of marines. They were formulating their combat plans now, but everyone agreed that they couldn't fight the Russians in Estonia if they were sitting on their asses in Germany.

The briefing in a hangar on the base's tarmac was businesslike and efficient. A tall, lanky general stood next to a giant screen showing satellite photos of Estonia, then maps. The general even accepted notes as he was speaking. Shepherd knew he was getting intelligence from the CIA, information from live satellite feeds, intelligence from the Defense Department, and comments from his senior staff, all while holding the attention of the forty-two officers in the briefing. The general said, "The bottom line is simple: We're in a shooting war. I don't know how serious or for how long, but our orders are to work with the limited Estonian defense force and intercept the Russian force and buy time for more assets to arrive."

From the crowd of officers someone said, "Sounds like they don't want another Crimea."

Someone else said, "Or Hitler."

That brought some knowing nods from the group. Most good military officers had studied history and knew that if people didn't change it, history tended to repeat itself.

The general was in no mood for a peanut gallery. Shepherd hung on his every word.

"Right now we know the Russians are moving at least five separate divisions south from the border. Each one has thirty to fifty tanks, antiaircraft support, troops, and supplies. It's a massive effort. In addition, several trains are under way with follow-on supplies and additional artillery and tanks. If we allow them to get dug in along the southern border, we'll have a hell of a time knocking them back."

He looked around for questions. The room was silent. The general continued. "We are loading tanks for a fast move through Poland by rail. We also have fast-moving armor on its way. Air cover is moving into position as well. We are currently evaluating the Russian antiaircraft assets and planes in the area. In short, they caught us completely flat-footed."

He started to hand out specific assignments. Armor officers were to focus on moving their tanks and supply vehicles into position; the infantry would support them and set up forward operating bases in southern Lithuania. It looked like the U.S. was going to cede a lot of the country to the Russians before any fighting. At least they intended to fight.

Finally the general turned toward Shepherd and the other eleven marine officers sitting near the front. "You marines are going to deploy ASAP and meet up with some of the Estonian troops you trained with over the past six months. You are to disrupt the Russian supply chain and make them think twice about advancing. I don't care if you slow them with shoulder-fired missiles or mines, or by destroying roads and bridges, your main objective is to buy us time. Is that understood?"

As one, without meaning to, all the marine officers shouted, "Sir, yes, sir."

It gave Shepherd chills and made him proud at the same time.

After the briefing, as he was racing to where his platoons were gathering, the colonel caught up with him.

"You straight on this, Major?"

"Yes, sir."

"You will be with your units at the tip of the spear. Probably before we have much support for you. Pick your spots and do what you can to slow them down. We intend to drop you and your Estonian partners near a rail line we believe they will use to move supplies. There's no telling what the president and Congress will decide to do, and I don't want a truckload of marine casualties if we're just giving away the whole country anyway. Be smart. Hit and move. No stand-up fights. Is that clear?"

"As crystal, sir."

Now, getting ready to fly to a war zone, Shepherd was trying to understand all the factors that typically went into a fluid battle situation. The reports were still sketchy, but it was clear that Russian armor and a long supply convoy had crossed the Narva River and were moving out along the highway system in Estonia. This was one of numerous training scenarios they had considered over the past couple of years. They had war-gamed what would happen if Russia invaded Belarus, Estonia, and a number of other NATO allies. Now that this had happened, the problem of transporting artillery and tanks to the front line became much more than academic. Train lines had always been a key to moving armor a long distance, but this fight could be reached by moving some of the tanks at top speed through Poland and into Estonia. That would take time, and it would be up to his marines and airpower to slow down the invasion.

Shepherd's commanding officer, a very fit colonel who had served in both Iraq wars, jumped into the Black Hawk and sat on the bench next to him. Their headphones connected to each other and allowed them to speak in a reasonable tone over the growing noise of the rotors and equipment being moved across the tarmac.

Shepherd said, "Colonel, I have to tell someone that I wonder if my incident with the Frenchwoman and the terrorists is somehow related to this Russian move into Estonia."

The colonel, who had always been somewhat informal, looked at him and said, "No shit."

Shepherd had to smile and added, "I just thought someone should consider it. It sounds like you already have."

"Not just me. I was just reading an intelligence report linking all of the lone wolf terror attacks, as well as some of the financial market problems, to some sort of scheme to distract the West as Russia gobbled up Estonia. I think the intel boys are a little embarrassed they didn't pick up on this sooner."

Shepherd considered this and wished he could call Mike Rosenberg back. He had texted him that he was safe and thanked him for the warning, but they hadn't been able to speak because things happened so quickly.

This mission would be his chance to make up for his poor judgment with Fannie Legat. But it was also his chance to be what he had trained for most of his adult life: a U.S. Marine in combat.

Anton Severov bounced in the main hatch of the tank as it moved along the edge of the road. He continued to stare at Amir just so the Iranian didn't think he was getting away with anything. Then the column came to a halt, and commanders were called to a briefing being held under the awning of a closed souvenir shop on the edge of the road. Severov hopped off the tank and trotted along, hoping the column didn't stay stationary for long. It seemed like he was the only one nervous about a counteroffensive by NATO.

He slowed before he reached the giant awning, which provided shade to the entire group. They were roughly twenty-five officers facing the general and four of his junior staff. Severov noticed the nod the general gave him as he stepped into the shade of the awning, brushing some dust off the breast of his tunic.

Three vehicles parked next to the building told Severov everything he needed to know. Two Kurganets-25 fighting vehicles, modified for command and control with extra radio and satellite capabilities, had to belong to the general. But it was the vehicle next to the armored personnel carriers that caught his attention. He noticed other tank commanders staring at it as well. It was a T-14 Armata tank with a 125 mm main gun and the sleek design of a modern mechanized predator. It took Severov's breath away for a moment. Why weren't they using these as main combat vehicles? Why was the only one he had seen in the field assigned to protect a general? These were questions he intended to ask later.

The general stepped up and addressed the crowd, taking everyone's attention away from the remarkable tank.

"Gentlemen, we have made significant progress. All of you worked very hard and overcame tremendous obstacles to make this happen. I can assure you this meeting is not wasted time. While we are stopped, your men are being fed and as many vehicles as possible are being fueled. I just wanted to give you an overall view of the operation and what to expect going forward." One of the aides moved a map of Estonia closer to the general. The general pointed with his left index finger at their approximate location. "It's true that we got a late start, but we are already this far into the country and have met no resistance, with our supplies coming across the river and following behind the main column and by rail. We have scouts out ahead of us, and now more fighters are being launched to give us excellent air cover. There are a few reports of Black Hawk helicopters landing, but we have no information about what that means. The official NATO response has been a few nuisance air attacks with their forward-based F-16s.

"From the beginning, the idea was to follow our Crimea strategy and enter the country with as little fanfare as possible. With the West occupied by minor terror attacks and a financial crisis, it seems unlikely that they will put up much of a fight for a country with such strong former ties with Russia. We can justify anything we do by the number of Russian speakers living in the country. Our goal is to reach the far border. At that point it will be decided if we go further or fortify our position."

The general stepped away from the map and tried to adopt a casual pose as he addressed the majors and colonels assembled in front of him.

"This is a golden time for Russia as we finally start to expand our influence again. Estonia offers us a strategic foothold back into Eastern Europe as well as a remarkable infrastructure and resource for technology. We must be careful not to cause collateral damage and incite the population against us. We hope to control the country like any other republic. We want them to be proud to be part of the new Russian Empire. That's one of the reasons we're not rolling across their fields and destroying their farms. We have men ahead of us diverting traffic, keeping the road open, and we hope to complete our mission without causing much damage. That being said, if we do meet resistance from NATO or even partisans, we will take all action necessary to eliminate the threat. Is that clearly understood?"

Severov answered with the rest of them with a loud "Yes, sir."

As Joseph Katazin drove toward the Wall Street area in his BMW, he didn't know where Derek Walsh was at the moment, but he knew where he'd be some time this morning. He had been chasing the former marine when there were other things he should've been doing, but eliminating Walsh solved a lot of potential problems. It would remove a link to him and slow down the FBI investigation. It would also protect the asset he had used to help on this operation. Those were both vital. He also had a personal stake in dealing with Walsh. The man had outwitted him and forced him to kill the lovely Alena. He had to pay.

Katazin picked up his new employee, Jerry, and after a few minutes of futile conversation with the muscular dullard he decided the man was expendable if it should come to that later in the day. The steroid freak sat silently in the passenger seat, occasionally perking up at the sight of an attractive woman on the sidewalk.

Jerry was in his early thirties and stood just over six feet with broad shoulders and a tattoo that skittered up from below the collar of his shirt. He wore a heavy plaid shirt as protection against the cooling temperatures and as a way to hide the Ruger 9 mm he had stuffed in his belt. No doubt the muscle-head would come in handy if things turned sour later in the day. At least he wasn't currently having to help Katazin dispose of his wife's body. The farther Katazin got from the house the better he felt about his decision. He had grabbed a small duffel bag and filled it with the important things from around his house, including some cash and photos, several of his daughter and one of the family at Christmas. It wouldn't be safe to go back there after today.

He stopped at a coffee shop near his office and left Jerry in the front seat of the car. He didn't need company today, especially from a big lump like Jerry. As he sat at the counter, composing his order for coffee and doughnuts, he glanced up at the TV and saw a special report on CNN. The closed captioning told him everything he needed to know as he saw file footage of Russian tanks. Russia had crossed the border in force and was now invading Estonia. It was unclear what NATO would do, but at least it told him his plan had worked well enough for the military to move forward with its part of the operation. He felt a warm wave wash through him and realized it was a combination of pride and patriotism. Things would never be the same. At least for him. Now he was about to work on an entirely new life.

Perhaps a Russian life.

Severov considered the briefing he had just received and decided he needed to keep track of every detail possible as the column moved closer to potential combat. He had the driver pull their T-90 directly behind the truck where Amir sat among thirty other men. They were essentially all Muslim conscripts, as well as a man suspected of being a homosexual whom they rounded up out of convenience instead of suspicion of being part of the demonstration. All of the men looked sullen, and most of them probably realized things were not going to go well for them whether they were involved in any revolt or not.

Severov had often considered how the accused were treated in the Russian military. Especially the Muslims. It was no wonder there were regular uprisings in some of the largely Muslim republics. They were considered criminals who must prove their loyalty instead of loyal citizens who must be proved to have participated in criminal activity. No one in authority seemed to care about the distinction, and the truckload of men in front of him told Severov that things were only going to get worse.

Before he could consider the serious implications of his line of thought, Severov heard the sound of jet engines in front of him. He scrambled to lift the binoculars hanging around his neck and get a look at what was making the roar in the sky. He hoped it was just Russian jets they had brought up as support. The giant fireball that filled the lenses of his binoculars confirmed his worst fear as he tracked the dot in the sky and could just make out U.S. markings on the wings. One of their forward attack F-16s had just devastated the road in front of them. God knew how many men perished in the swirling inferno that was already fading back to just a small fire in the road.

The action had stirred the men in the truck in front of Severov. Some leaned out to try to get a view while others started to pray. Severov understood the reasoning behind both courses of action. Unfortunately, if the Americans decided to work their way down the line, neither praying nor having a good view would save your life.

Someone in the Russian high command had misjudged what the U.S. and NATO would do in response to the invasion. The question now was, would this be enough to stop the Russian juggernaut? Severov was prepared for combat and even to give his life for Mother Russia if necessary. He wondered how many other men traveling with him felt the same way. This attack would give the commanders pause and slow everything down.

Exactly what the Americans wanted to happen.

It'd taken some fast talking, but Derek Walsh had convinced Tonya Stratford to let Charlie walk away from the front of her brownstone. Walsh gave him twenty dollars to find his way back to Manhattan and grab something to eat. Then he had turned his attention to convincing the FBI agent she had to get him into Thomas Brothers Financial.

She turned her dark eyes toward him and said, "This goes against everything my partners and I have been discussing for the past few days. You need to be in custody, not dragging me into your own investigation."

"You know I might be onto something or you wouldn't even be considering it. Just twenty minutes in the office. I've explained what I want and why I have to do it myself. I trust you enough to have surrendered. Show me a little consideration. This conspiracy could be big. I want to help."

"What if it turns out that there's nothing to your story at all?"

"Then you charge me. I'm not sure with what charges, but I'll accept them."

Agent Stratford said, "I have an indictment we've been working on. Right off the top of my head we'd hit you with fraud by wire and then the good old standard, U.S. Code 18.656—theft and embezzlement. You see, it's always better to make an arrest first, then add on charges. We're considering some kind of treason charge if it turns out you knowingly helped enemies of the country. I don't know any of the statute codes on that because I've never investigated a case of treason. My partner, Frank, would add on a dozen more charges if he got the chance."

Walsh held up his hands and said, "Just check out what I'm saying and we might save you a lot of trouble. If I'm wrong, you lose nothing and I go to jail. Considering how much work someone put into this scheme, I'll be happy to not be dead." He kept a steady gaze on her.

"You haven't told me where the security plug is."

"You haven't told me you're going to go along with my plan yet."

"Smooth. And after what happened with the Russians, I can understand your concerns. But I need some assurances I will get some return on my risk."

"What assurances would you like?"

"You get one chance to pull up the photos from your security plug. After that, if it doesn't work, you cooperate fully with me."

"I thought I *was* cooperating fully."

"We'll get in there about eight thirty, before the bulk of the other FBI agents show up but not too early to raise suspicions."

"I like this plan. It's the first plan I've liked since this all started."

"You better hope it works out."

Walsh knew the FBI agent had no idea how much he hoped it would work out.

39

Sitting on the cupola of his tank, staring to the horizon, Anton Severov realized there was no secrecy left and the Russian military presence in Estonia was now worldwide news. That fact was reinforced by several squadrons of Russian-made MiG fighters roaring ahead of them to clear out any NATO air threat. The earlier strike had taken out four tanks and two supply trucks. When they rolled the burning remains of the vehicles off the road, Severov caught the unmistakable stench of burned flesh. There were three bodies near the truck, but no other human remains were obvious. He could tell by the demeanor of the men in the truck ahead of him that it had a severe effect on morale. He could fight toe-to-toe with tanks, but they were woefully unprepared to handle air strikes without the assistance of the Russian air force.

Severov still viewed the field from the top of his tank, confident that the NATO forces had not put snipers in the field yet. It also gave him a chance to keep an eye on Amir, who was still sitting in the rear of the truck directly in front of him. He leaned on the Kord heavy machine gun, making sure the belt-fed 12.7 mm ammo was seated properly in the receiver. If something did happen, he could bring the Russian-made gun on target in a matter of seconds.

Far in the distance ahead of them, he saw flashes in the sky and real-ized it meant the Russian jets were engaging NATO jets in air-to-air combat. This was quickly escalating more than any of his comrades had thought it would.

Was Estonia really worth another war?

Major Bill Shepherd checked his watch and then the gear strapped to his back and sides. It was midafternoon when the Black Hawks set down outside Mustvee, Estonia, on the banks of Lake Peipus. Shepherd looked over the tiny town of fewer than two thousand residents, who were not prepared to see U.S. Marines spreading out near the highway that passed through it. He hoped the quaint town would be spared any damage, but experience told him that wouldn't be the case. Reports had the bulk of the Russian force on this highway, with the lake on their left.

His force of about eighty marines had taken on twenty-two Estonian soldiers, who carried shoulder-fired rocket launchers and some C-4. They split into ten groups, each armed with a variety of portable weapons designed to slow down the tanks. Without a screening force of infantry in front of them, the tanks were vulnerable to small arms and rocket fire. Despite what he'd been told by the colonel, Shepherd decided to go with one of the teams. He didn't want to say he missed the opening shots of World War III. He also felt the younger men would benefit from the pres-ence of a senior, battle-tested officer. At least that's what he intended to tell his superiors if anyone got their panties in a bunch that he was out here.

Behind them, Shepherd heard the engines of an F-16 as it struck at another target. He figured the F-16 was part of a small detachment in Estonia meant as a deterrent to a Russian incursion. Apparently the Russians didn't believe the U.S. would use force to protect the small country. Shepherd couldn't blame them. Even as he heard the jets attack-ing and his team prepared to fire a rocket-propelled grenade, he was sur-

prised the U.S. leaders had committed to action so quickly. Perhaps they realized that if a few soldiers were killed immediately by Russian arms, the public sentiment would swing dramatically in favor of fighting for Estonia. That was not an idea most Americans considered. Some people understood that it was the right thing to do to try to straighten out some of the regimes in the Middle East and that a side benefit included a flow of oil. But the idea of defending a small country like Estonia—with no natural resources that the West needed—would confuse the average American.

Derek Walsh tried not to fidget as he stood in the lobby of Thomas Brothers Financial. It had only taken a moment to retrieve his security plug from under the bench in the courtyard. Agent Stratford shuddered when she realized he had used chewed-up gum to hold the plug in place.

It was almost eight thirty in the morning, and the building was starting to get busy. Tonya Stratford stood right next to him with her FBI badge on a chain around her neck. He wasn't sure if she was advertising that he was in her custody even if he wasn't in handcuffs or if she didn't want anyone to bother them. Either way he stood there and noticed the suspicious look from the security guards who last week had greeted him warmly every time he walked through the doors. Now they regarded him as a thief and possible traitor. Everyone in the building knew the story by now. He had been on the news as a "person of interest." That was as good as being convicted in most people's minds.

Whatever happened with the investigation, he knew he didn't want to come back here. Not only did the unwelcome feeling push him toward the door, but now he knew he needed to contribute. Once he realized he was a small cog in a big plan and someone was trying to undermine the U.S. government, he felt that old spirit well up inside of him. He had to fight back.

They slipped onto an elevator and jumped off at the 31st floor. Agent Stratford, who had one hand wrapped around his right arm, said, "You wait here for a minute. I'll run through the office to make sure none of

our people are there. If they are, we're going to avoid them long enough for you to stick in the security plug and pull off the photos you want. We'll decide our next move after that."

Walsh just nodded his head. It was a good plan and what he'd wanted to do all along. He watched as she pushed through the double glass doors that led to his former offices. He could picture Ted Marshall or Cheryl Kravitz already in the office and directing their small army of traders. They would be back up to speed by now as long as the entire financial community hadn't lost faith in the company.

He stepped over to the giant window that looked over the courtyard and along the street. There were still a few signs of damage from the protests. A statue at the end of the courtyard lay on the ground. Some of the low hedges had been trampled and not replaced. For the most part the city had done a decent job cleaning up the broken glass and all the trash the protesters had discarded. It wasn't quite on the scale of the mess the Occupy Wall Street people had made, even though the protest had been more violent. The sheer amount of garbage the Occupy people had produced was mind-boggling. This was just annoying.

He noticed more policemen, several of them wearing body armor and MP-5 submachine guns strapped around their chests. The city was still tense after the bombing of the subway in lower Manhattan and several other attacks. The few news reports he had caught were speculating that the explosion and shootout in Brooklyn where the Russians had kept him captive were part of the terror plot.

Unable to stand still, he reached into his pockets, then absently cracked his knuckles. He wanted to get this over quickly.

Then he heard a male's raspy voice say, "Hello, smart guy, remember me?" As he turned around, strong hands clasped around his upper arms and shoved him to the floor. The violent action stunned him, but as his head cleared he realized he was looking straight up into the face of Tonya Stratford's angry partner, Frank Martin.

Joseph Katazin took a moment to lean against the park bench at the far end of the courtyard in front of Thomas Brothers Financial. His ankle throbbed, his ribs were still sore, he had a headache, and now his back was starting to cramp up. This was not how he envisioned his career as a spy. He needed some sleep, two Advil, and a decent meal.

The one thing that sustained him was the success of the operation. The Russian military was on the move, and he had helped buy time and distract the U.S. as well as its NATO partners. His meeting with his contact had been short but did wonders for his morale.

His new assistant, Jerry, made it clear he didn't like any show of weakness, but he kept his mouth shut. Lucky for him, because in his current mood, Katazin wanted to shoot him. They were both armed with handguns, and that should be all they needed. His biggest concern was that Walsh could now recognize him. Before, he was just a vague face; now he had spent time with the marine, and he doubted he would be overlooked.

Katazin turned and said, "Let's wait closer to the door."

Jerry spoke English with a thicker accent. "What if he doesn't show?"

"Then you still get paid and you might have a job working with me over the weekend. Is that so bad?"

Jerry held up both of his hands and said, "Just asking."

"But we can't fool around. If we see this guy, we need to cap him and get moving quickly. Understood?"

Jerry nodded.

They slowly made their way along the outer edge of the courtyard until they were almost in front of the entrance. He would be able to see anyone coming from quite a distance away, and just in case Walsh was moving quicker than he thought, he would easily catch anyone coming outside from this exit.

40

Derek Walsh felt the barrel of the gun in his ribs as the older FBI agent shoved him into an empty elevator. Just as the doors were closing Walsh said, "You don't understand. I'm here with your partner. I'm working with you guys now."

The red-faced man said, "You're not working with *me*. You caused me too much shit to skate on any of this."

Walsh was a little confused and kept expecting Agent Stratford to stop this. He also wondered why the FBI agent hadn't handcuffed him. He said, "Can you just call Agent Stratford?"

"I'll call her after you're secure in lockup. We need an arrest on this whether she knows it or not. I am doing her a favor. By the time you work your way through the system, you'll understand how much trouble you're in. And I know the guys in the city holding cell will treat you right. That's why I'm taking you there instead of the federal corrections holding facility downtown."

Walsh was trying to think what he could do. He realized if he punched this man, even Tonya Stratford wouldn't be able to help him. It felt like the elevator was closing in around him as he became short of breath and started to sweat. This guy was completely out of his head.

The FBI agent said, "Did you think it was cute having those protesters rough me up the other day? Or how you were able to walk away from a scene that involved three FBI agents being wounded? I don't know who you think you are, but you're about to have a reality check."

The elevator opened, and the FBI agent shoved him out into the lobby. As they made their way to the doors that exited into the courtyard, Walsh considered the chances of this guy shooting him if he ran. If he couldn't outrun this tub of lard, maybe he didn't deserve his freedom. He took in a couple of deep breaths just before they got to the door and planned how he would sprint ahead and get his distance right from the beginning. He would head to the end of the courtyard and turn down the same street where he had followed the Russian.

Walsh glanced over his shoulder just as he reached the front door. The FBI agent was still only two feet behind him. That might be all the lead he needed.

Joseph Katazin stood a few feet from the stairs leading to the entrance to Thomas Brothers Financial. Jerry, standing next to him, might as well have been one of the decorative pillars in front of the door. But maybe he could attract enough attention that no one would notice Katazin. He was still formulating a plan about what to do if they saw Walsh coming up the courtyard. Right now his easiest option was just to shoot the former marine and be done with it. He didn't waste any time explaining this to Jerry. Anyone who didn't want to wear a coat on a cool day like this because he wanted to show off his biceps wasn't smart enough to understand the intricacies of international espionage.

Katazin turned toward the front entrance and was stunned to see the door open and Walsh standing there with another man. The second man was short and pudgy and clearly over fifty. He looked like he might be some sort of law enforcement officer. Katazin didn't understand the situation, but he knew that it was a rare opportunity. He didn't want Walsh to see his face, so he turned quickly, looking directly at Jerry, and said in Russian, "The younger man in the white shirt. He's our target. Shoot him and meet me back at my car." Katazin waited until recognition swept across Jerry's face. He was confident the big moron would do his job, and at this point Katazin didn't care if he shot the other man, too, as long as Walsh was killed. Katazin wanted to escape, so he abandoned his own desire for elaborate revenge.

He stepped away and cut through some low bushes to reach the sidewalk before the shooting started. He watched as Jerry carefully reached under his loose shirt to pull a pistol. Katazin intended to be on his way across the street by the time he had the gun on target.

He felt a certain measure of satisfaction knowing this end of the investigation would be over. He just hoped Walsh hadn't had time to explain everything he knew to the cops. After Walsh, there was only one other person he needed to deal with, a person in this same building. He knew he was sacrificing Jerry to get this done, but it didn't bother him. At least not nearly as much as shooting Alena in the head to make her drop the grenade. That was a real decision. That would haunt him. No one would miss a steroid freak like Jerry. He'd pay a small fine to the organized crime family that allowed Katazin to rent their man, but that would be the end of it.

It was what came after that concerned Katazin. He would be on the run unless he could utilize some of the measures he had put in place years ago to hide effectively within the borders of the United States.

Or he could always take a trip back home.

Moving through the great glass door to the courtyard, Derek Walsh was about to spring to freedom away from this angry FBI agent who clearly had his own agenda. Even if he was handcuffed, he'd be able to outrun this moron. With his hands free, his sprint would put him out of reach within a matter of seconds.

He scanned the courtyard and saw that it was nearly empty. He wouldn't have to do any complicated weaving to make a break for the far end and then into the maze of streets that would offer him sanctuary. There were two men right near the door off to the side, but as they reached the top of the stairs, one of the men turned and hurried off toward the street. The other man, a muscle-head who stood at least six foot one, turned and assessed them with dark eyes. Something about the man's demeanor and interest in them caught Walsh's attention, and he kept his focus on him.

Just as they were about to step down onto the first stair, Walsh realized the man was reaching for a pistol and saw a flash of blue metal come out from under his loose short-sleeved flannel shirt. Without hesitation, Walsh stepped to the side, grabbed Martin by the arm, and pulled him along with him over the side of the landing so they would have the cement staircase as cover. He only had time to shout, "Gun."

Walsh heard the FBI agent mumble a protest as he was jerked off his feet. They sailed the four feet through the air, and somehow Martin ended up underneath Walsh as they hit the bushes and grass of the ornamental area. The FBI agent acted like an air bag, taking the brunt of the fall plus the added weight of Walsh on top of him. His breath rushed out in a loud "Ummph."

Just as he rolled off the FBI agent, Walsh heard the first shot and saw it ping off the edge of the landing. He knew there would be more bullets coming his way and the man would run to the edge of the stairway in a moment. He looked down and realized Frank Martin was out of the fight for at least another minute, so he reached to his side and felt for the gun that was in his right hand before they fell. It was loose on the ground, wedged against the FBI agent's ribs. Walsh picked up the Glock model 17 and fired a round before he even stood up. He just wanted to scare the man away if he could. When he peeked over the edge of the stairs he saw the man still standing with his pistol up. Walsh fired two quick rounds and ducked as the muscle-head returned fire.

Now Martin was catching his breath and struggling to his feet. He motioned for Walsh to hand him the pistol. His attitude toward

Walsh had clearly changed drastically since Walsh had kept him from being shot.

Walsh couldn't help but peek over the top of the stairs as the FBI agent did the same with the pistol up in front of him. The muscle-head had backed away from them and still had the gun in his hand. Martin popped off two quick rounds, which made the man turn and dart toward the street. The muscle-head fired one round wildly, which struck the front door of the building, causing an odd crack that almost looked like a professional cut down the middle of the door. The FBI agent returned another round.

This round went wide right and struck the windshield of a car coming down the street. It was a gray Dodge Charger and was traveling on the fast side. It swerved for an instant, the driver obviously distracted as the windshield spidered into a thousand cracks. The driver righted the car just as the muscle-head stepped into the street. The sound of the impact was sickening as bones snapped and tires squealed. The muscle-head flew into the air and landed in a lifeless heap on the opposite sidewalk.

The FBI agent calmly looked at Walsh and said, "I didn't expect that at all."

41

It had been nearly an hour since Walsh had witnessed the muscle-head assassin run down by a car in the street. They had tried to give the man aid, but he was dead by the time Walsh had reached him. The FBI agent checked for any sign of life, but the impact from the car had been devastating, leaving the man's neck twisted at an odd angle and his left arm splintered in several places.

After the events of last few days, this one seemed relatively tame by comparison. It had taken a while to straighten out the scene, and quickly Walsh understood why Tonya Stratford's partner had his job. He was calm, cool, and collected at every moment and explained exactly what was going on. He answered questions from his supervisors, then immediately came upstairs to join Agent Stratford and Walsh. He clearly appreciated Walsh's efforts to keep him from being shot.

Now Walsh sat on a padded bench near his old desk while Cheryl Kravitz, his immediate supervisor, argued with Tonya Stratford about allowing anyone access to the network until she had cleared it with both their IT and legal departments.

Cheryl said, "Can't we hold off on doing this for a little bit? I mean, you just killed a guy out front."

Frank Martin leaned forward and said, "Technically the car killed him, but this smart guy saved my ass, so you're gonna shut the hell up and run along. We have work to do." He patted Walsh on the shoulder.

Walsh suddenly realized how entertaining the FBI agent was when his anger wasn't directed at him. His attitude was sort of like the marines: Americans loved them; everyone else wanted to avoid them. That was a handy reputation to have. It was effective, too, as Cheryl turned on her heel and marched away to confer with Ted Marshall, who was busy in his office.

Agent Stratford motioned Walsh over to his old computer. She handed him the plug as he sat down. He couldn't help but take a deep, cleansing breath. He cut his eyes up to Agent Stratford and then her partner. This was it.

He explained the process as he inserted the security plug in the USB port. "Once the plug is inserted, I enter the trading program, enter my password, and this screen comes up." He waited as the two FBI agents examined the trading screen. "Now I would enter the number of the account the money is coming from and the routing number for the bank and account the money is going to. It's not particularly complicated or difficult."

He searched for the program on the security plug and brought up the tools screen. "This is where I can access every overseas trade I've made in the past year." He gave them a minute to examine the new screen that listed hundreds of transactions. "As you can see, there is a tiny icon for a photograph next to each transaction. If you look at my last four transactions, they're the ones in question." He pointed to the screen to show the top four transactions.

This was it. Showtime. He took another breath, and a very clear photo popped up on the screen. He did it with the remaining three transactions, and a similar photo appeared.

Walsh mumbled, "Oh my God."

The older FBI agent said, "That explains a lot."

Agent Stratford glanced around the office and said, "We have to move."

———

As Shepherd and his men started assessing the column in front of them, Shepherd heard something in the distance. He held up a hand that stopped everyone in place. He turned to the Estonian lieutenant and said, "Do you hear that to our left?"

The young lieutenant turned his attention from the tanks on their right and scanned the horizon on the rolling hills to their left.

Shepherd said, "That's a train." A minute later, a slow-moving locomotive appeared in the distance. Instantly Shepherd realized the train, carrying supplies and reserve tanks, was more vital than the column they had been watching. Trains were one of the reasons they had been dropped here. He couldn't pass it up. He kept most of the men in place as he grabbed the Estonian lieutenant, two of the men who were best with explosives, and an Estonian private, who was weighted down with packs containing C-4 and two spools of det cord.

Shepherd scurried away from his men toward his left, with the others following him quickly.

The Estonian lieutenant said, "Major, I don't understand. We can knock out two or three of those tanks quickly."

Now Shepherd was running, looking for the train tracks. "Or we can take a risk, knock out these tracks, disrupt heavy supplies, and really throw a monkey wrench into the Russians' plans."

The Estonian cocked his head and said, "What's a monkey wrench?"

Inside Thomas Brothers, Walsh stared at the photograph on the screen. It was Ted Marshall. The look on his face said he had no idea he was being filmed. It was clear that the two FBI agents immediately understood what had happened. Walsh turned his head toward the glass office where his boss usually sat, and had been working just a few minutes earlier.

It was empty.

Panic rose in his throat. Ted was the key to the whole conspiracy. He could explain what had happened and expose the people funding a terrorist group. Now he was gone.

As soon as she realized their new suspect had vanished, Agent Stratford immediately grabbed her phone and started calling in help. Her partner called out to other agents in the office, and everyone started to scramble. Obviously they now believed Walsh's story, because no one even bothered to watch him as all the agents bolted out of the office to catch Ted Marshall.

Walsh wanted to see what was happening. He *needed* to see it. Were they watching the courtyard? The front door? Technically it was the front door, but no one used it. He had to tell someone where to search. Now, for the first time in three days, when he needed an FBI agent, he couldn't find one.

Anton Severov commanded the eight tanks, fourteen personnel carriers, and seventeen trucks in this section of the column. Although it was only about a fourth of the column and less than a fiftieth of the total expeditionary force, he felt the pressure and responsibility of command. He had hundreds of men in his command if you included the ground troops riding in the carriers. It was terrifying. Especially now as he was learning of the NATO strike.

He listened to the radio chatter and heard the stutter of gunfire behind the terrified report that tanks on the parallel road were taking fire. He felt as if he were the only one who had expected resistance as he scanned the grassy hills surrounding him, trying to spot any danger. A helicopter zipped overhead, but it was headed to a specific location and not looking for NATO soldiers waiting to attack the column. The fact that jets had engaged them earlier, and there had been reports of Black Hawk helicopters and an attack on a column of tanks on a parallel road, led him to believe that NATO was planning some sort of major counterattack here. Men could only be on edge for so long; then they started to lose that alertness that can save a soldier. They needed to either engage a threat or take a break.

Severov had command of the center of the convoy with nine T-90 tanks, six ancient T-84s, two Pantsir S-1 self-propelled portable anti-aircraft guns that would be used during encampments, and the associated support vehicles, including transport trucks. The truckload of Chechens, including Amir, was directly in front of him less than thirty meters away. Every time he looked in their direction, Amir was smirking at him as if he knew something no one else did. Quickly Severov scanned the horizon again. His gunner was reclined in his seat trying to stay as comfortable as possible until the action started. They had slowed the convoy to a maddening thirty kilometers an hour. He didn't know the reason, but more aircraft had gone ahead of them, and he wondered if there were dogfights over the interior of Estonia.

Then he saw it. The first streak of a shoulder-fired rocket-propelled missile off in the distance. It erupted from the tall grass with a flash that caught his eye. He couldn't identify the type right away, but it streaked forward and struck a tanker truck half a mile in front of him, causing a tremendous explosion. Almost before he could react he saw more trails of rockets coming from the low hills toward the convoy. He immediately dropped into the turret and slammed the hatch shut. He yelled to his men to prepare for battle as he leaned forward to look through the commander's viewfinder. The viewfinder was set directly in front of him, and just as he adjusted the sight to the truck holding the Muslim recruits, he saw it enveloped in an orange ball of flame.

Severov could feel the heat inside the tank as the driver immediately took evasive action. The tank careened off to one side as Severov swung the viewfinder to see what had happened to the truck. And Amir. The flames lifted into the air and dissipated as the shell of the truck fused with the ground. No one moved. In fact, Severov thought it looked like no people had even been sitting in the rear of the truck.

Now he was in a real war.

42

Derek Walsh decided he needed to help find Ted Marshall. He had unraveled too much of this mystery not to be included in something like this. Plus, he felt his knowledge of the building would give him an advantage over the FBI agents searching for his boss. As soon as Walsh burst into the lobby from the forward stairwell he saw most of the FBI agents already outside in the courtyard fanning out. It was a logical move if that was the only door you had ever used to enter or exit the building. Walsh knew some secrets. He started to check the hallways leading out to the street away from the courtyard. In an adjacent lobby, Walsh looked to his left and was not terribly surprised to see Ted Marshall hustling for the front door with no one paying any attention. He must've hidden in a bathroom long enough for everyone to pile out the courtyard door. It was slick and clever and about to backfire.

Walsh took three quick steps to get going, and by the time Marshall turned around, Walsh was heading toward him like a guided missile, using the full force of his body and shoulders to drive Marshall into a column, then knock him onto the ground, where the finance manager wheezed, trying to get air back into his lungs.

That was as satisfying as anything Walsh had done in the past year. He resisted the urge to kick the man in the head while he was lying on the hard marble floor. Then Walsh heard someone behind him.

"Nice work, smart guy." It was Frank Martin, and he casually strolled across the lobby, the only one who'd noticed anything unusual. He barely broke stride as he scooped up the shaken Ted Marshall and motioned for Walsh to follow him. They made it into the lower front stairwell that no one ever used. He unceremoniously dumped Marshall on the first step and stood over him like an interrogator looking at a spy during World War II.

The FBI agent said, "You have until the count of five to start talking or your life goes down the toilet so quickly you'll feel like a turd."

Marshall hesitated for a moment.

The FBI agent said, "One," in a flat voice.

Panic highlighted Marshall's voice as he said, "Hold on. I need a second to gather my thoughts."

"Two."

Walsh was beginning to really like this guy. Now that they were buddies his shtick was entertaining.

Marshall started to weep and rubbed his eyes.

The FBI agent just said, "Three." Then, without much space, "Four." He added, "If it helps you, we know all about the Russians." He turned his head and winked at Walsh.

It was a bluff. They didn't know shit about the Russians. This guy was good, and Walsh was impressed.

The FBI agent said, "Maybe I'll just toss you outside and let the protesters know who you are and what you did."

Finally Marshall said, "Okay, okay, I did it. I made the trade. But it wasn't my idea."

Now the FBI agent's tone changed. "Whose idea was it?"

He sniffled, then wiped his nose on his sleeve. "It was Katazin's."

Walsh was about to ask, *"Who?"* when the FBI agent held up his hand to stop him. He wanted to maintain the illusion that they already knew all of this.

Marshall continued. "He made me. He blackmailed me. I had no choice. He used the girl, Alena. He had photos."

That hit Walsh hard, but he kept quiet.

The FBI agent said, "You made some money, too, didn't you?"

It took a moment, but he nodded his head. "They paid huge fees for transactions before the ones to Bern, and I got some into one of my own accounts. The night we made the trades on Derek's account they knew exactly which accounts to hit. We didn't think anyone would notice for a while."

Walsh put in, "That's why they wanted me dead. To make it look like I did it, then committed suicide."

Marshall's expression told him he was right.

Walsh felt ill again.

Anton Severov screamed at the driver to pull the T-90 off the road and into a gully that would offer some protection from rockets. He barked the commands as he tried to find a target from his commander's station. The smoke from the burning truck and other vehicles that had been struck blocked his view, so he threw open the hatch to get a better view outside the cupola. He raised his head cautiously and peered through the binoculars, surveying the wide open fields in front of him. The stench of burning flesh stuck to the inside of his nostrils. His eyes watered from the smoke.

The tank swerved hard and came to an abrupt stop, trying to use the little protection the gully provided. Severov noted that most of his tanks were doing similar things. He hoped the tanks ahead of him knew what was going on. There was no telling how many soldiers were hidden in the grass. Why hadn't the scouts reported anything? This was exactly what they did not want to happen. Their entire military plan counted on tactical surprise.

His earlier ideas of gaining glory on the battlefield by fighting the best army in the world had dissipated as soon as he looked over at the incinerated truck. There was no glory for the men who smoldered in the back of the destroyed vehicle.

All Severov could think was that there wasn't supposed to be any resistance this soon. The general had told him there wouldn't be any resistance at all! He feared that this battle could resonate across the globe. His opening actions might dictate the course of the war. That was a lot for a tank commander to consider as he searched for a target.

He saw a flash of something metallic in the distance around the low bushes that intertwined with the grass. He gave the position to the gunner and felt the turret start to move.

Severov knew he was too late. The trail of the rocket allowed him to track it easily as it rose above the tall grass and homed in on his T-90. He lost a visual as the rocket got closer, but knew when it hit by the intense heat and noise.

But the pain only lasted an instant.

Frank Martin looked around the enclosed stairwell and barked at Derek Walsh, "Go find Tonya. I'll wait here with this shithead." Walsh nodded and turned to find Agent Stratford.

The FBI agent and Marshall stayed put, with Marshall seated on the second stair and the agent standing over him. Walsh paused, sensing something in Marshall's mood. The financial manager was past the nervous phase but seemed to be considering something. Walsh was going to say something as Marshall sprang with surprising speed, driving his head into the shocked FBI agent's chin and knocking him back onto the hard cement floor by the stairs, where he slid into Walsh. Martin and Walsh got tangled, and Walsh lost his balance, falling next to the FBI man.

Marshall wasted no time and took the opportunity, turning and bursting through the door into the lobby. It took a moment for Walsh and Martin to untangle from each other and stand up to give chase.

As soon as they entered the lobby, Walsh realized Marshall had a plan. The lobby was empty, and no one even looked up in their direction.

The FBI agent scanned the room frantically, looking for where the money manager had fled. He let out a string of obscenities, which *did* draw the attention of the security guard. When the man looked their way, Martin yelled, "Did you see anyone just run through here?"

The older black man just shook his head.

The FBI agent screamed out another obscenity.

Walsh said, "You guys aren't very good at keeping people in custody, are you?"

Martin gave him an angry look, but he was used to it by now.

So far, Joseph Katazin's day had not been anything like he had expected. At the moment he was wondering if he should just flee the area without trying to tie up any loose ends. Jerry was dead, and there was still quite a crowd around the crime scene. Certainly he had tipped his hand, and Walsh would not be unaware next time. The whole series of incidents had soured his stomach and exacerbated his headache.

He sat in the driver's seat of his BMW across the street from the back of the Thomas Brothers Financial building. Or it could have been the front. Everyone seemed to come and go through the courtyard. His stomach growled as he considered his options and daydreamed about putting a bullet into Derek Walsh's groin. That would be sweet.

Common sense took hold, and he decided to pull away from the area and move on to his new life. Then fate intervened. He couldn't believe his luck when across the street he saw the door from the lobby to Thomas Brothers blast open and his former associate Ted Marshall stumble into the street in a complete daze. Marshall looked up and across the street as if he wanted to cross. This appeared so easy it could be a trap.

Katazin decided he needed to take his shot.

43

Katazin couldn't believe how easy this was. One thing he had learned was that you must take advantage of luck. Fate had thrown a loose end in front of him, and he decided to take what he could. He gunned the engine of the BMW, pulling away from the curb with the screech of his tires. Marshall was oblivious as he stumbled across the street. Katazin didn't even have to steer into him. A smile crept over his face as the car made violent and direct contact with the money manager's body. Marshall was lifted into the air and bounced off the passenger side of the roof, landing on the ground in a heap.

Katazin casually glanced into the rearview mirror to see the lifeless body lying in the middle of the road. He wouldn't be giving any information to the FBI. One less loose end to worry about.

He kept his foot on the gas as he accelerated away from Thomas Brothers Financial. A few blocks later he slowed the car to a reasonable speed and decided he would head on to Philadelphia, where there was a safe house, and await his next instructions. He'd ditch the car once he was away from the city and find something in Jersey he could use. The contacts in Philadelphia would provide him with another car and the proper paperwork he'd need to blend in as just another immigrant to the sprawling U.S.

Maybe he would even get to see his daughter again one day. Maybe he would even run into Derek Walsh.

Katazin turned up the radio as he listened to the somber voice of the U.S. newscaster giving as much detail as he knew about the first U.S. engagement with Russian troops in Estonia.

He knew he had done all he could as a patriot.

In Estonia, Bill Shepherd and his men had reached the railroad tracks. Shepherd looked at his man with engineering experience and said, "What's the best way to knock the train off the tracks?"

The young sergeant said, "You mean the train coming this way right now? I don't know that we can. It's only a minute away."

"How do we do it?" Shepherd had no time to waste.

The sergeant said, "I guess if we placed the C-4 under the tracks and blew them just as the train arrived, we could at least derail a car or two. Any break in the line could have catastrophic effects as the train rolls forward."

"I like the plan and the chances. Let's go."

They had no shovels or equipment. Their mission was to hit and run and stay as safe as possible. But Shepherd realized what an opportunity this was. He reached down with his bare hands and started to pull away the rocks and sod next to the track. His example encouraged the others, and suddenly all of the men were digging frantically with their hands.

Now Shepherd could feel the vibration in the track as the train got closer. His fingers started to bleed from digging into the ground with his bare hands.

The sergeant prepared a charge of C-4 as Shepherd yelled to the others, "Take cover back over the hill. Do it now." He stayed with the man as he set the charge, and then they both dropped back quickly. They were using ancient Estonian det cord to trigger the C-4 and had to unspool it as they backed away.

Shepherd knew the train engineer had seen them and was already trying to slow the momentum of the train. He could see how long the train stretched into the distance and that it carried everything on a mixture of flatbeds and boxcars.

They ran out of cord a hundred feet from the tracks. Shepherd turned to the sergeant and said, "Join the other men. Hand me the detonator." He took the simple electronic device and made sure the sergeant was secure behind the hill. When the train was directly in front of him, on top of the charges they had set, Shepherd pushed the button on the detonator.

He prayed that there was enough explosive to cause at least some damage. Suddenly he saw the flash and heard a tremendous crack roll across the ground. The explosion wasn't enough to lift the train off the ground, but it wobbled. And as it wobbled farther down the track, the wobble became more pronounced. Then the engine jumped the tracks and tipped over on its side, sliding in the endless field of grass.

Shepherd couldn't believe their good fortune. Then he realized the cars behind the engine were starting to pop off the track as well. He looked down the line of cars and realized momentum was still carrying them forward and he was in their path.

He turned and started to run over the hill, feeling the ground shudder under the weight and force of the derailing train. One of the boxcars was now skidding across the dirt directly toward him. He leapt as hard as he could off the top of a low hill, then covered his head with his hands as he hit the ground.

He could see the shadow of the boxcar block out the sun as it came to a stop on the edge of the hill directly above him.

They had done a lot more than just slow down the train.

Walsh and the FBI agent had figured out the only place Marshall could have gone was through the front door squirreled away in the corner of the lobby. As soon as they found themselves outside, Walsh heard the sound of an accelerating vehicle, but his eyes were drawn to the body in the middle of the road.

Both men rushed to the still figure of Ted Marshall. His right leg was twisted behind him at a sickening angle from the hip. His forehead was split open, and clear fluid was leaking onto the ground.

Martin searched for a pulse in his neck but quickly determined the man was dead. Then he turned and looked at Walsh and said, "I guess this is the day where car accidents really help me out."

Walsh understood exactly what the FBI agent was talking about.

He had a feeling his ordeal was finally over.

44

Bill Shepherd entered the fortified old farmhouse that stood behind the front line that had been established from Tartu to Parnu in the western area of Estonia and held firm for the past two weeks. Inside the farmhouse, the main room was used as a briefing hall, and the smaller bedrooms off to the side had been turned into offices. The U.S. government had paid the owners a fortune in rent. The alternative was to stay in a building that could be on the front lines of the major shooting war between Russia and NATO.

Shepherd stood in the back, as he did almost every day, and let the more senior officers each take one of the twenty chairs lined up in front of a giant, 60-inch screen that showed everything from snippets of war footage and news coverage to detailed maps of different areas. The first few days of these briefings had been tense, with officers itching to get back out to their units, thinking there would be Russians to kill. But the political posturing between all the countries involved had stalled any immediate violence, and now, almost two weeks after the first shots were fired, there was not much more than a few skirmishes here and there, with no NATO casualties in more than four days.

Today, a stubby army general had flown in from Washington to give them a quick overview and fill in the gaps on what led to the current stalemate. Shepherd appreciated that the command staff wanted to keep them all informed and shut down as many rumors as possible. But where the military was involved and soldiers could communicate, there would always be rumors.

The general covered their deployment, saying, "It's our opinion that the destruction of a supply train on the first day and NATO air power surprised the Russians and that shock slowed them to a complete stand-still on the second day. There's still no official truce, but they have not been building their forces the way we would expect if they intend to push on." Then he looked directly at Shepherd, who was standing next to his commanding officer. The general said, "The marine units that deployed before army armor got into position on the very first day did a great job on the front line. Everything the Russians had was focused on air defense. The units of marines, working with Estonia Defense Force members, armed with their Man-PADS and other easily maneuverable portable weapons, did wonders. They may even have given us a blueprint for any future conflict. They knocked out a train carrying vital supplies, and that forced the Russians to reconsider their plans."

Shepherd tried to suppress a smile, but every marine in the room was grinning from ear to ear.

The general continued. "We believe the rash of terror attacks around the world was somehow connected to this military operation. I know you guys are able to see the news once or twice a day, but the lone wolf terror attacks are continuing, especially in England, France, and Germany. The U.S. has experienced some attacks, but nothing like in the days leading up to the military operation."

The general paused and glanced around the room to see if anyone had any specific questions. Then he addressed the crowd more casually. "Back home all the public cares about is your safety. The U.S. cares about its troops, not Eastern Europe or the independent nations that make it up.

But we, as students of history, like all good soldiers should be, know that Russia is on a similar path to that of Germany pre–World War II. Our politicians may not be smart enough to see where this could lead, but we are ready to stop them here.

"Today, more tanks are joining us from Germany and France. The Red Army's reinforcements feel more like they're posturing. We keep asking the question, why would they fight over Estonia? Someone pointed out they probably asked the same question as they were coming over the border. But we will maintain our status quo." A map of Estonia appeared on the giant screen as the general said, "We are stopped on this line a little more than halfway down the country. The northern half of the country has suffered little damage and we would like to keep it that way. Some idiot politician from Northern Estonia has declared independence and claims that Russia is their protector. This is startlingly similar to what happened in Crimea. Now that Russia knows we're willing to expend military power, maybe they'll think twice before venturing into another Eastern European country. But who knows with that knucklehead Putin in charge."

Shepherd chuckled along with everyone else and decided he liked this general even if he was from the Pentagon. The briefing went on for almost an hour as the general took questions from every corner of the room no matter the rank. The general talked about what he thought led the Russians to this military action. He said he thought it was primarily an economic move as the ruble tumbled in value and Russia's only decent nonalcoholic export, oil, was selling at such a low level. They had to do something, and this seemed simple at the time.

Shepherd found his mind starting to drift as he thought about how wild the last few weeks had been. He'd spent little time considering how Fannie Legat had used him and tried to kill him. His success on the battlefield in the initial days of the war had also defused any concerns the marines had about him associating with someone like Fannie. There was one interview where he explained exactly what had happened, and that was it. He was just a lonely marine far from home who was attracted to a pretty Frenchwoman. He had no idea about her connections or even that she was Muslim.

No one had found any trace of her, but an investigation had named her as the chief suspect in the bombing of the bank in Bern, Switzerland. It was hard to believe a woman he spent time with was capable of killing so many people and hiding it so well.

Mike Rosenberg had saved his ass. When they had spoken two nights ago Rosenberg told him that their friend Derek Walsh was free and clear of any suspicion in the financial crimes. He even hinted that the crimes Walsh had been accused of were connected to this military operation as well. Fate was a weird and cruel force, but it still couldn't overcome friendship and the U.S. Marines.

Fannie Legat sat alone in the quiet room of the clinic she had been cooped up in since the day of the explosion. It was an hour north of Stuttgart and run by a doctor who was sympathetic to their cause and often treated people in her network who'd been wounded. While not a plastic surgeon, he had clearly saved her life and done his best to ameliorate the damage she suffered when the bomb went off near the café where she was meeting the American major.

It had been more than two weeks, and a steady diet of painkillers had kept her from going insane from the burns on her shoulder and face. A sturdy cement bench had deflected some of the blast, and she'd had just enough energy to stumble from the area into her vehicle on the far side of the café. By the time she had arrived at the clinic the smell of burned flesh and the melted synthetic fibers of her floral-patterned dress had faded to a miasma of nauseating aromas. The doctor had assured her it was a psychological effect, but that was all she smelled now.

She stood up from the chair on unsteady legs and shuffled toward the mirror on the medicine cabinet in the small bathroom next door. Every day, about this time, when her bandages were off for several hours, she came to stare at herself in the mirror. The left side of her face was essentially intact. When she turned in profile she looked like her old self. Even her manicured eyebrow showed no signs of her trauma. But the right side was a map of agony. Starting near her ear and moving across her cheek to her mouth and around her eye, the ravaged skin looked like something from a prehistoric reptile. The hair on the right side of her head had been singed and shaved away. No eyebrow would ever grow on that side of her face again.

She felt no sorrow or pity for herself. This was a risk she was willing to take. Her only regret was that she had not been as successful as she wanted.

She had heard nothing about her Russian major, Anton Severov. Nor had she any news about Amir. Not much information was coming from the Russians, but they were still trying to use her group of affiliated Muslims to attack the U.S. indirectly. Now, more than ever before, she was in favor of that.

Soon, when she was strong enough to leave the clinic, she could make the U.S. pay for what happened to her, as well as what they had done to her people.

Putin sat at his desk, reading every report and update on the situation in Estonia he could get his hands on. The NATO response had not been massive, but it had been enough to stop the Russian invasion. At least temporarily. He had made the decision a little more than a day after they had crossed the border, after a U.S. Special Forces unit had managed to derail a train with a huge amount of supplies on it, to hold in place and see what developed.

At the time, Russia still controlled the skies with a canopy of SAM missiles and a huge array of aircraft constantly in the air. There had been some early dogfights with some American planes, which had been stationed in Estonia, but even those had been pulled back. It was the early engagements with U.S. Special Forces that made Putin understand he needed to stop the advance. The U.S. was committing more resources than he had anticipated.

Going against his original plan, which involved simply moving the small force back into Russia, Putin attempted to split his forces and protect the northern part of the country. His troops had taken control of the capital, Tallinn, very quickly and then gotten a politician from the area to declare himself the new president and claim that he had invited Russia in to help save the ethnic Russian minority, which was being oppressed. No one in the world believed it, but it was important to get the message out.

That left some very messy questions, and even Andre had not been able to get full support from the Politburo. Instead, they been asking who had planned the operation and if there was any truth to the rumors that Russia had conspired with Islamic terrorists to launch attacks. Putin felt his power threatened and needed a scapegoat; that was why he had called this meeting.

As he got up from his desk and walked down the hallway toward the main conference room, several security personnel he had alerted followed him into the room. These included three extra FSB agents who had been briefed on what was about to happen.

Several key members of the government were present in the enormous conference room, including Andre Maysak and Yuri Simplov. They all sat around a long table with a spot open in the middle where Putin always sat. Two of the more influential ministers sat immediately to his left and right. Andre was among them. Yuri Simplov always stood behind the representatives for the intelligence community. He liked to keep a low profile, and Putin didn't want any attention drawn to him at meetings like this.

Most of the people in the room wore business suits, although there were several in military uniforms. The fact that the majority of the people in the room were over forty indicated that this was a senior group, which carried real power in Russia.

As with many of the things Putin did, there was a certain dramatic and theatrical aspect to this gathering. He made sure there were at least two people in the room who would blab everything that happened to the right media people. It was typically well planned and well thought out.

The room was more crowded than he had anticipated, with several secretary-level administrators, as well as a number of simple politicians. It was a little raucous and loud at first until Putin gained control by speaking up from his seat near the giant window that looked out over the gardens.

Once he had everyone's attention, Putin started slowly. "As you know, we were pushed into a corner and sent a small military force into Estonia in an effort to save a number of ethnic Russians who had come under increasing threat from certain elements inside Estonia. Some of their own politicians asked for the action.

"Our forces moved through the city of Narva and further south with no bloodshed. It was not until a sneak attack by NATO military units that there were any casualties from the operation. From the beginning that was the goal of the operation. A simple, bloodless rescue and support of certain elements of the Estonian government which were being repressed."

Putin took a natural pause and looked around the room to see if there was any dissent or questions from the assembled group. He noticed the Russian general prosecutor taking notes as he'd hoped she would.

"In an effort to avoid serious casualties on either side, our military has held its position in a line along the middle of Estonia. As we anticipated, the Estonian people rallied to us, and those in the northern part of the country have asked us to stay for security reasons. We currently have a team in The Hague negotiating with NATO about how Estonia will be administered. We are prepared to do whatever is necessary to protect the people of Estonia and the ethnic Russians living inside the country."

Putin stopped and gave everyone a chance to absorb this information, because the real meaning of the meeting was about to become clear. This entire meeting and the subsequent media coverage of it was designed for one real purpose. Putin wanted to make sure no blame was assigned to him if some aspects of the operation in Estonia were discovered. He had a short statement prepared, which would cover these main points and also explain why he was going to take the actions he had set in motion.

"It has come to my attention that several aspects of this limited rescue operation were subverted by people in our intelligence community. They utilized intelligence sources and conducted operations not authorized by me or my administration. While the rumors about these operations are greatly overblown, I cannot tolerate any actions that violate civilized behavior."

Putin knew he had to act quickly now because he saw Yuri Simplov shift in his seat. The deputy director of the SVR had to know what was coming and who was about to be blamed.

Putin said, "That is why I am dismayed to announce the arrest of several members of the SVR." He nodded his head in the prearranged signal as the three FSB agents moved in behind Simplov and secured him just as he was leaping to his feet.

There was the expected commotion as Simplov struggled momentarily until one of the FSB agents whispered in his ear.

Putin realized the man had just told Simplov that they were holding his wife and three children in custody and all four would be charged with treason, even his nine-year-old daughter, if he didn't comply immediately.

Putin was confident this threat would keep his former friend quiet until the quick investigation led to his execution.

The crowd watched silently as Simplov was led away by the FSB. There were no brutal tactics, nothing that would indicate the man's life was essentially over. This could not have gone better from Putin's perspective. Tomorrow all anyone would talk about was how Putin had to arrest his longtime friend, and people would believe something was actually being done about the rumors that Russia had collaborated with Muslims in the string of terror attacks that had occurred across the globe recently.

Only Putin and Andre Maysak knew the truth. Andre had counseled Putin that now that their alliance with the Muslims was finished, they could expect their own wave of terror attacks.

Russia had survived attacks from extremists in the past, and it would do so in the future. For now, Putin was satisfied he was secure in power and had taken the first step toward regaining control of Eastern Europe.

He was not unhappy with the way the operation was proceeding, but he realized there was much more to do to secure his legacy.

Derek Walsh sat on the edge of a small pier near South Ferry. He looked out over the East River and took a deep breath of the cooling autumn air. It had been two weeks since he'd emerged from a cloud of suspicion. He had seen so much and experienced such trauma during the time he was hunted by the FBI and the Russians that the last two weeks had seemed like a dream.

Thomas Brothers Financial was closed, but they had acknowledged he was a victim in the fraud that had funded terrorism. After all the effort the news media had put into the story, now they only focused on the conflict in Estonia, and he had barely been mentioned on TV again.

The FBI, mainly through Tonya Stratford, had been surprisingly forthcoming and kept him updated on the investigation that was still ongoing. They had linked a number of incidents together, including the bombing of a bank in Switzerland and some of the lone wolf attacks across the U.S. Some of the attacks were simply copycats, but others had been coordinated. There was a general belief that it was a smoke screen to allow the Russian military to invade Estonia.

He had watched the news more in the last two weeks than he had in the years he had been out of the Marine Corps. Once the balloon went up and he knew he had friends on the front line, he was desperate to hear anything he could about the fighting in Estonia. He'd also noticed, at least here in the United States, that the general public had refocused its attention and this nonsense of U.S. citizens fighting for ISIS was finally being taken seriously.

Walsh had spent a week in Philadelphia with his mom and younger sister and felt like his priorities were straight for the first time since he left the marines. He would never go back to Wall Street.

The day before, he had visited his friend Charlie, who was living in a halfway house designed to help older vets in Yonkers and attending

AA meetings on a daily basis. With a decent diet and no drinking, the former Army Ranger looked ten years younger.

Walsh appreciated the breeze blowing off the river, but when he turned his head he saw who he had been waiting for. His friend Mike Rosenberg walked toward him. Walsh had never considered himself a hugger, but he embraced his friend. This guy had really gone out on a limb for him and more than anyone else was responsible for uncovering the conspiracy.

They had talked on the phone every day since the bad dream had ended. Walsh had even worked up the nerve to tell him that when he grabbed the suicide bomber in Afghanistan he thought it was just a thief and the pack was full of supplies.

Rosenberg laughed and said, "You really thought I hadn't figured that out years ago? C'mon, Tubby, give me some credit." Talking to Mike or Bill Shepherd was like wearing a comfortable old shirt. It always felt right.

Now all he had to do was restart his entire civilian life. After what he had been through that would seem easy.